Wrong Town

A Mark Landry Novel

By
Randall H. Miller

This is a work of fiction. The names, characters, businesses, places, events, and incidents contained in this book are either the products of the author's imagination or used in a fictitious manner. Any resemblance to actual persons, living or dead, or actual events is purely coincidental.

Acknowledgements

I would like to thank Maggy and Michael for their endless patience. I love you both very much. I would also like to thank Eric Curtis, John Irving (not that one), Colonel Don Paquin (U.S. Army), Lieutenant Colonel John Palo (U.S. Army, Retired), Robert Hennessey, Michael McCarthy, Brian T. Witkowski, Steve Tarani, the Sig Sauer Academy, Rob Pincus, Steven Branca, Mary Beth Autry, Todd Bennett, Michael McLain, Richard C. Miller, Chris Halleron, and many others who were kind enough to contribute to the creation of this story in some way.

"And those who were seen dancing were thought to be insane by those who could not hear the music." – Unknown

One

"Pick one," said the black-robed imam after opening the door to the packed gymnasium-turned-prison. "They are all virgins."

The sound of Amir's combat boots against the hardwood floor announced his arrival and sent chills through the building.

Submission came easier to the older women, but the younger girls grew more frantic each time a warrior entered—and with good reason, as they were more likely to be chosen.

Amir took his time and examined a dozen different candidates like cattle before deciding on a young girl with chestnut eyes, long black hair, and nascent curves.

"She has no experience, so she may need to be encouraged to please you," he was advised.

Amir's encouragement came in the form of strangulation as he writhed on top of her, tightening his grip the more she resisted. Jealous warriors would later erupt in laughter as he joked about the moment when the flicker of light in her eyes went dark.

After bathing her filth from his body, he stood before the bathroom mirror and began the lengthy process of shaving his thick, long beard as he had been instructed.

Three years.

Three long years of fierce, righteous combat not seen since the Prophet and his companions had fought for the same sacred soil. And Amir's ferocity in battle and fearlessness under fire had not gone unnoticed. When other foreign recruits had hesitated, he had charged forward to kill the enemy and ceremoniously executed the cowards in his ranks afterwards. To him, displaying the slightest hint of disloyalty or fear, on or off the battlefield, was simply unforgivable. Yet he had no real authority—only the power of his presence.

His reward was ceaseless praise and respect from everyone who fought alongside him. "You should star in the execution videos, Amir! We can only imagine the prayers your actions would inspire, and how many hits you would get," they would say.

Hits. This war is not about hits.

"I am here to serve at the will of Allah. Whatever best serves him and the Caliphate, I will do out of honor and love," he had said modestly around the fire. Deep down, he had known that being passed over for video production was a blessing and further evidence that God's plan for him had yet to unfold.

Anyone who appeared in official videos instantly became a global reality star and therefore less useful outside of Islamic State–controlled territory. Facial recognition. Gait recognition. Thermal fingerprints. Spectral and chemical imaging. Their fates were forever tied to the soil underfoot. Several who had enjoyed folk-hero status for their video performances were then publicly executed for the sins of arrogance and pride. Amir silently questioned such charges.

Are they arrogant and prideful? Or simply giving their brother warriors the inspirational leadership they crave?

Regardless, his anonymity outside the Caliphate meant that he was still eligible for the holiest of missions. The ones that required fierce close-quarter combat experience, a keen intellect, unshakable faith, and a Western passport.

The most righteous battles are fought in the West—the Dar al-Harb—where heroes become legends.

If martyrs are the crown jewels of the faith, the warriors who strike directly at the heart of Satan are the sparkling emeralds. When the State's chief spiritual guide had tapped him on the shoulder, he felt as though the hand of God had reached down from heaven and touched him. He had been chosen.

Amir tossed his tattered black uniform onto the floor next to the girl's corpse and put on Western clothes. He brushed back his blond hair and rubbed his hands against his smooth face. Slinging the backpack over his shoulder, he looked into the mirror one last time and smiled wickedly. The transformation was shocking. He was reassuming an identity he had renounced long ago.

Two

Despite driving through the night from northern Virginia to Boston, Mark Landry was not the least bit sleepy. There was simply too much to think about during the seven-hour trip. He had been back in the U.S. for just six days after two solid years abroad and hadn't had much time to readjust to the sights, sounds, and pace. The drive had given him that much-needed opportunity as he made his way north with the radio off.

As his dark blue Ford Explorer emerged from the I-93 tunnel that runs under the city, the sun started to rise beyond the Bunker Hill Monument to his right. He squinted and reached for his sunglasses. Soon Boston began to shrink in his rear-view mirror as he drew closer to home.

Home. Whatever that means.

Mark had been home only a handful of times since graduating from high school more than twenty years ago. And when he did visit, he was usually in and out within a few days and rarely touched base with the few friends he still had there. He could have stayed longer but instead chose to get back to work. There were places to go, things to do, and bad people to track and occasionally kill.

Thirty miles north of Boston, he turned off the exit ramp onto the last stretch of road toward his hometown. He thought back to his one and only meeting with his high school guidance counselor, about a month before graduation.

"Come on in, Matt, I mean Mark," she said. "I thought I had met with everyone under my supervision, but I just noticed your name on my list so I sent for you immediately. Are you new to the school system? When did you arrive in town?"

"Kindergarten."

She forced a nervous laugh, not sure if he was serious. "And what do you think you'd like to do after graduation? You've got decent grades so you have lots of options."

"I leave for Army basic training next week."

"Oh, the U.S. Army?"

"No, the Salvation Army," he said somewhat sarcastically, but with a smile that showed enough respect to soften the barb. "Yes, the U.S. Army. I'm hoping to do four years while I figure out what I want to be when I grow up."

Before he had finished speaking, she had already dropped her head, checked his name off her list, and called in the next student. When she finally looked up from the stacks of paper on her, Mark had already slipped out and dissolved into a crowd of students in the hall. A month later he reported for duty at Fort Benning, Georgia. There were no tearful goodbyes. In fact, there were very few goodbyes at all.

The toughest part of training for Mark had been the sweltering heat. The rest was relatively easy. Do what you're told and don't complain. He made a few buddies in his squad but said very little to anyone else. About half of the fifty men in the platoon were reservists who would be going home after infantry school anyway. Most of the remainder would immediately join active duty units across the country. Four of them, including Mark, had enlisted with the Ranger option and would immediately report to U.S. Army Ranger School, headquartered right there at Fort Benning. Two ended up quitting in the first few days, and the third fractured his leg fast-roping from a Black Hawk helicopter and was medically dropped. Mark was the only one of the four to graduate and earn his Ranger tab. He was immediately assigned to 3rd Battalion, 75th Ranger Regiment, where he would serve with distinction for the next twelve years.

Mark turned right after entering the town limits and decided to drive around a bit to get reacquainted with the scenery and see how much things had changed. The cemetery could wait.

Some of the businesses had changed, and there were more buildings than he remembered. There also seemed to be more foot traffic around town on sidewalks that looked new—or maybe he had just never noticed them before. Traffic was heavier and drivers shared the clean streets with joggers and cyclists. He passed a gas station and noticed a police cruiser tucked back against the side of the building. He glanced at the small airport on the other side of the street, and his thoughts returned to his perhaps soon-to-be-over career in special operations. The tiny runway reminded him of his first taste of combat in Afghanistan just a few weeks after the September 11 attacks.

Upon reaching Afghanistan, the 3rd Ranger Battalion, along with elements from the various Special Mission Units (SMUs—Delta, SEALs, Special Forces, etc.) and CIA paramilitary forces, first spent weeks gathering intelligence on al-Qaeda and Taliban forces. Lightning-fast nighttime raids on active terrorist training camps and enemy positions followed. Mark soon lost count of how many doors they'd kicked in and how many terrorists they either snatched from their beds or killed before they even knew they'd been found.

After a year of missions in Afghanistan, he had returned to Fort Benning for one month before redeploying to Iraq to join the hunt for Saddam Hussein and his deranged sons, Uday and Qusay. As one of only a few Rangers handpicked to join "Task Force 20," Mark exchanged direct fire with Uday and likely fired one of the bullets that killed him. Four months later, as part of a similar task force, he was within arm's length of Saddam as the dictator emerged from his infamous "spider hole" near his hometown of Tikrit, although official credit was given to the 4th Infantry Division. As the conventional soldiers basked in the glory, the operators simply moved on to the next target.

Mark's last mission as a Ranger—although he didn't know it at the time—was to hunt down and kill the leader of al-Qaeda in Iraq, Abu Musab al-Zarqawi. After over a month of surveillance activity, Mark helped laser-guide a pair of five-hundred-pound bombs through the roof of an al-Qaeda safe house as Zarqawi arrived for a secret meeting. Moments afterwards, he arrived at the site in time to peer into the terrorist's eyes as special ops medics tried in vain to stabilize him. Zarqawi's dead body was a welcome sight to everyone; he had personally beheaded American civilian hostages and terrorized Iraqi civilians with impunity. But the image that stayed with Mark was that of the mangled bodies of a woman and young child who were also killed in the attack. He never learned who they were or how they ended up in the safe house. The image haunted him for several days, until he was distracted by a most unexpected conversation.

Mark and the rest of the Task Force had been enjoying a well-deserved few days off at their secret base in the desert, still close enough to the war's center of gravity that they could assemble and deploy to "hot spots" if needed, but far enough away to avoid the throngs of crusading journalists whose antics constantly put troops at risk, as well as the never-ending parade of politicians and celebrities whose visits to the country caused security nightmares for everyone.

Mark had just finished eating lunch in the task force chow hall and was on his way out when a man he'd never seen before called him over to his table and asked him to sit down. The man opened the conversation with a question.

"How'd you like to get out of this sandbox and work somewhere else for a while, maybe permanently?"

Mark examined the gray-haired man as he continued eating and guessed that he was in his late fifties. The man wore casual navy blue slacks, desert boots, a pressed short-sleeved white button-down shirt, and a tan vest with a slight bulge over his left breast that betrayed his sidearm. He wore a titanium watch on his left wrist. A satellite phone sat on the table next to his tray. Wearing just a black t-shirt, black shorts, and flip-flops, Mark felt underdressed for a moment but didn't show it.

"Can I bother you for a few more details?" Mark asked matter-of-factly after a few seconds. The man answered without looking up.

"What else would you like to know, Mark?"

He knows my name. I wonder what else he knows.

"Well, how about we start with who's asking. You obviously know—"

"My name is Dunbar," he blurted while extending his hand. "And you're right. I obviously know a lot about you already or we wouldn't be talking, and I wouldn't have just made you the offer I did."

"And about that offer, Mr. Dunbar. What exactly does it entail besides getting out of the sandbox?"

The man motioned for Mark to sit across from him. "It's just Dunbar. I'm offering you a chance to shed that uniform and a lot of the bullshit and restrictions that go with it. You'd be working on an entirely different battlefield with a carefully chosen handful of the country's best operators … assuming you make it through my qual course," he added casually. "That's my standard pitch, which I have given very few times. If you accept and make it, you'll never see another regular army unit or task force ever again. That's all I can tell you for now." Then he awkwardly switched to Spanish and asked for the salt.

Unimpressed with the clumsy change of language, Mark reached with his left hand, without taking his eyes off Dunbar, and put the salt on the table next to his satellite phone.

Dunbar smiled. "*Gracias.*"

Mark nodded his head and looked around the chow hall. Nobody had been watching their conversation—or if anyone was, they were hiding their interest very well. He turned back to Dunbar.

6

"Would I be familiar with any of the work your unit has done? Any missions I might know of?"

Dunbar put down his knife and fork, sat up straight, and stared intensely into Mark's eyes, speaking very slowly. "No. There is absolutely nothing we've done that you or anyone else would be even vaguely familiar with. That's the way it has always been. And that is the way it will always be. If you're looking for glory or think you may want to get an easy book deal some day, then go join a fucking SEAL team. If you want to make history, follow me. Do you understand what I'm saying, Landry?"

The intensity of Dunbar's eyes distracted Mark enough that he didn't even notice that the older gentleman had switched to German. He merely nodded and responded, "*Ja, Ich versteche.*" *Yes, I understand.*

"Good," Dunbar continued in English. He then removed a piece of paper from the inside of his vest and slid it across the table. "Here are the financial particulars of the job compared to what you're making now. It's not the main reason why anyone joins the Family, but it certainly doesn't hurt. If you accept my invitation, you'll learn more as you need to know it."

Mark looked down at the paper. The next words he heard came out of his own mouth, and yet he was surprised to hear them. It was as if someone else had said the words and he was hearing them for the first time along with Dunbar. "I'm in."

"That's the kind of decisiveness I'm looking for," Dunbar said in a low whisper, but loud enough for Mark to hear. "The process starts right now. See the tall gentleman in the blue shirt waiting patiently on the other side of the chow hall?"

Mark turned his head sideways until he could see the man in his peripheral vision. Then he turned back to Dunbar and nodded ever so slightly.

"I see him."

"His name is Doc. Go talk to him. Maybe we'll talk later—maybe not," Dunbar said as he wiped his mouth with a napkin, picked up his tray and satellite phone, and walked away in the opposite direction.

What followed would be the most intense six hours of Mark's life that didn't involve gunfire, sex, or booze.

Three

Doc started by asking Mark about his earliest memories, leaving no stone unturned right up to the moment when they met in the chow hall. Then he whizzed back and forth over the timeline and hammered him with rapid-fire questions that Mark was sure he already knew the answers to. After that, he varied the pace of questioning and asked the same questions in slightly different ways, so as to evaluate Mark's honesty as well as his demeanor, mental stamina, and patience. He occasionally threw in embarrassing, deeply personal questions. Just keeping up with the barrage of interrogation was an exercise in intellectual gymnastics, but Mark had been around enough to know that eventually his actual answers would be less important than his ability to take the heat. He also knew that the ordeal would eventually end, and that he would never hear the specifics of how well or poorly he performed. He would just get a yes or a no.

"Stay right here. I'll be back," Doc said in a soft voice. He opened the door, walked down the hall, and entered another room on the opposite side of the hall. Dunbar was there, with his satellite phone to his ear and his eyes on two laptop computers sitting on the table in front of him. Doc could not see what he was doing but waited patiently for him to finish his call and look up.

"Talk to me. Abridged version please," said Dunbar.

"He's all set. No surprises. Raised by a single adoptive mother, Agnes Landry from Watertown, New York. Parents unknown. They never turned up and he never looked for them. Uneventful childhood and upbringing. Much more sociable and charming than I expected from someone with so few friends growing up. Not a single high school teacher could remember having him in class, and it was next to impossible to find anyone in his hometown with more than a fuzzy recollection of him. Good grades but not great. Naturally flies under the radar. No picture in his high school yearbook. He is listed as "camera shy" which means he didn't care to be included. Growing up, he spent nights and weekends training in the basement of a Catholic church—they called it the dungeon—with a priest friend of his adoptive mother, Father Peck."

Dunbar raised his eyebrows.

"No, nothing like that. The priest taught him wrestling, judo, and some other mixed martial arts. Rough as hell but not abusive. Never played any team sports. When he wasn't busy training in the dungeon, he was volunteering with Agnes at various churches, charities, orphanages, soup kitchens, etc., mostly in Lawrence, Massachusetts, where there's a largely Latino population. That's where he learned Spanish. Never had much time to be a kid."

"Sounds like he was raised by Mother Teresa."

"Not really. Agnes was a nun at one time early in her life, left it behind when she adopted him, and never explained why but never stopped acting like one. A career German teacher in a Catholic school. She also taught him German at home. He has near native fluency in Spanish and German. Physically, he is in excellent shape. No disqualifying preconditions. Social drinker with no detectable bad habits. He's 5'10", about 195, and I think he has a high tolerance for pain."

"What gives you that impression?"

"Downplayed battlefield injuries he's received over the past few years. Stuff some troops would get Purple Hearts for. Spent the better part of ten years getting knocked around by the priest in the dungeon. He's tough but not sadistic. I like him. Gets a bit jolted by collateral damage, but that won't be an issue in his new line of business, assuming he makes it. I have no concerns and I think he has an excellent chance of making it through qual. Green light."

Without another word, Dunbar stood up and made his way down the hall to the room where a man was waiting patiently to hear about an opportunity that had not existed when he awoke that morning. When he threw open the door, a startled Mark Landry instinctively leapt to his feet.

"Pack your shit, Son. You're leaving the sandbox today."

From that day forward a small group of unknown—and largely unknowable—men and women had become his surrogate family. Now, eight years later, Mark was turning slowly into his hometown's cemetery to say goodbye to the only other family he had ever known.

Four

Dunbar was the founder and head of the Tactical Training Unit (TTU), which was sometimes alternatively referred to as the Battle Training Unit (BTU) or the Intelligence Focus Group (IFG), and occasionally as the Battle Administration Detachment (BAD). The name changed frequently and without notice in order to avoid unnecessary oversight from the bean counters, congressional committees in D.C., crusading journalists, or foreign spies. Dunbar and his band of operators, uninterested in keeping up with the name changes, simply referred to themselves as "the Family." As an unwritten rule, the few outsiders familiar with the organization knew to stick with whatever its official name was at the time. "The Family" was for Family members only.

Besides Dunbar, Doc was the most influential and high-profile member of the organization. He was the first person all new Family members spoke with at length, and debriefing with Doc was mandatory after every mission, whether or not any shots had been fired. He knew everything there was to know about each operator and was equally concerned with mission accomplishment and their personal welfare. In short, he made sure nobody was wound too tight for living. If they were, he'd talk them off the ledge and help them get their heads on straight. It was Doc who first broke the news about Agnes Landry's death to Mark.

He had delivered the message a week earlier on a small U.S. Navy vessel somewhere in the Mediterranean. Mark had just completed a search-and-destroy mission in eastern Ukraine with his frequent mission partner Billy, a boisterous good ol' boy from Oklahoma City. Over the previous three years, they had successfully completed similar missions across Europe without detection or incident, and this one had been no different. It didn't hurt that their target, a Russian arms dealer on the verge of selling chemical weapons to al-Qaeda terrorists, was also an arrogant—and ultimately predictable—drunken idiot. Mark had shot him in the head twice with a suppressed Bulgarian Makarov 9mm as he soaked in a local prostitute's tub. Mark and Billy were out of the country before the body was even discovered.

After debriefing the operations folks on the details of the mission, Doc asked Mark if he could have a private word with him in the next conference room after he wrapped up. Mark spent a few minutes in small talk with Billy, who was about to take leave to spend some time with family in Oklahoma. They parted with a hug, and Mark pulled him tight.

"Don't go cheating on me."

"Later, man. I'm catching a ride off this thing in thirty minutes. Don't call me unless World War Three breaks out," replied Billy.

Mark smiled back and nodded. "Go, before I cry," he added sarcastically.

Mark was heading to his quarters for some much-needed sleep when he remembered that Doc wanted to speak with him about something. He knocked twice on Doc's door as he entered and plopped down in the nearest seat.

"What's up?"

"There's something I need to tell you, Mark."

Doc's change in tone and demeanor from the briefing room got Mark's attention immediately. Since he had no family besides Agnes Landry, who was well into her eighties and very frail the last time he saw her, he assumed it must have something to do with her.

"Agnes?" he asked.

"I'm sorry. She passed away just over a week ago in her home. We briefly considered pulling you from the field, but—"

"No, that's fine. She never would have wanted that." Mark bowed his head, exhaled deeply, and paused for a few seconds before asking.

"How?"

"She fell, Mark. She fell down the stairs. I spoke to the local authorities myself and the autopsy report suggests she died instantly. She didn't suffer. I'm sorry, Mark. We all are. We know how much she meant to you," said Doc before stepping out of the room.

Mark said nothing as he stood up and walked to the small porthole that passed for a window. He just stared into the darkness and grudgingly accepted the fact that the only person who ever loved him, the only person willing to take him in and care for him and raise him, was now with the God she lived to serve. He closed his eyes and compartmentalized the grief with the help of several deep breaths. There would be time to grieve later.

When Doc returned, Mark was back in the chair flipping through his own personnel file, which had been left out on the desk. Doc snatched the file out of his hands and playfully smacked him on the top of his head with it. "Just because it has your name on it doesn't make it yours."

Mark shrugged his shoulders and looked away as Doc continued.

"It's time for some career counseling, Mark." The change in tone was a not-so-subtle hint that they were getting back to business. Mark sat up a little straighter and remade eye contact.

"You're still a young man but you've already got your twenty years. If you wanted, you could retire today and ride off into the sunset. Between your pension and all the money you've socked away over the years, you could have a pretty comfortable retirement. Or you could get a job in the private sector, barely work, and still probably make yourself a small fortune." Doc paused and waited for a reaction.

Mark ignored the comment about his personal finances. Obviously, the Family kept tabs on its people. That would include how much money he had and where he kept it. He paused briefly to search for the right words. They never came, so he decided to just cut to the chase.

"Are you trying to get rid of me, Doc?"

"Not in the least. You have a home with us as long as you'd like. Operations, training, admin—you name it." Seeing Mark wince as he mentioned training and admin, he pointed to the thick file sitting on the desk in front of him. "I'm just saying, with a record like yours, you can pretty much call your shots and pick your spots."

Mark's reaction to the compliments was to look away and fidget in his seat. Doc grabbed the file, opened it on his lap, and thumbed through it slowly, even though he knew most of it by heart.

"Stellar evaluations covering eight years in the Family. Almost no time off unless I forced you to take it. Great peer reviews from team missions. Multiple one-man missions. Awards, decorations, no disciplinary or security issues. A model operator."

Mark interrupted. "The same can be said about every other Family member."

"Normally that would be true," Doc replied. "But your file contains something that no other member in the history of the Family has ever had in their file."

Mark thought hard for a few seconds, furled his brow, and looked at Doc sideways. "What's that?"

Doc removed a single sheet of thick, heavy paper from the folder. He held it in front of his face with two fingers and peered at Mark over the top of it. Mark maintained eye contact for a second before dropping his eyes to the lavish seal that adorned the top of the page: the official seal of the President of the United States.

"Berlin," said Doc.

Mark had not seen the letter since the day it was delivered. It contained numerous typed paragraphs praising his courageous service, followed by several sentences elegantly written in the Commander-in-Chief's own hand. Mark nodded and Doc dropped the paper back into the file.

"You are on leave as of right now. Take as much time off as you want or need, but don't even think of coming back to work for at least a month. The rest of the Family has everything covered. Hell, take a few months if you want it. You've earned it."

Mark returned to his quarters on the bottom deck of the ship without making eye contact with anyone he passed on the way. He had much to think about, but the first order of business would be to go home and pay his final respects to Agnes Landry. He was asleep as soon as his head hit the pillow.

Five

When he finished his prayer, Mark opened his eyes just in time to notice a police cruiser approaching out of the corner of his right eye. He ignored it and kissed his hand before bending down and placing it gently atop Agnes Landry's tombstone. After a few solemn seconds he whispered aloud.

"Goodbye, Agnes. Thank you. I love you."

He let go of the stone and stood up straight. As he did, he heard the soft sound of footsteps approaching from behind. He didn't turn around until he heard the voice.

"You okay?"

"Yeah," he said as he slowly turned to face the speaker.

Five feet away stood a female police officer with deep brown eyes, dark brown skin, full lips, dark black hair pulled back into a tight ponytail, hands on her hips, and a half-smile on her face that could melt a glacier. Mark looked her in the eyes and half-smiled back. Then he pointed with his chin to the mobile camera that was pinned to the center of her pressed uniform, between her badge and nameplate.

"Is that thing on?"

"No."

"Prove it."

Officer Luci Alvarez's smooth face broke into a wide grin and then a beaming ear-to-ear smile straight out of a toothpaste commercial. She stepped forward, clasped both of Mark's hands in hers, and kissed him softly on the side of his clean-shaven face. With interwoven fingers, they firmly embraced and kissed each other's cheeks several times before backing off like two kids at a church dance, afraid of being observed by a chaperone.

"I was wondering when you were going to show up," she said first.

"Don't say that. I got here as soon as I could."

"I know that," she said as she slapped his shoulder. "I'm just saying it's good to see you."

"I wish I could have been here sooner. And I'm sorry I didn't let you know when I was coming."

"Spare me. I had low expectations to begin with. Two calls in two years—actually, one call and one drunken voicemail from God knows where. Physically showing up is a huge improvement."

He pondered the drunken voicemail for a second.

Serbia? No, couldn't have been. Chechnya? Maybe Vienna or somewhere in Romania? Wherever it was, it had to have been before Berlin. Whatever. Doesn't matter.

"How'd you know I was in town?"

"You passed my cruiser next to the gas station across the street from the airport. Didn't you see me sitting there, or have you forgotten about all that 'situational awareness' you used to always preach about?" she said, exaggerating the military term for effect.

"I just assumed whoever was in the cruiser was sleeping or playing with their smartphone. A band of gypsies carrying kidnapped children could have pranced by that cruiser and I doubt anyone would have noticed," he deadpanned.

"Yeah, well, I noticed a suspicious looking middle-aged white male with Virginia plates and followed you here."

"Since when is thirty-nine considered middle-aged?" he asked, feigning insult as best he could but knowing she could read him like a book.

"Since now," she said.

A gravelly voice broke in, talking through the tiny speaker attached to the front of her right shoulder.

"Control to 307."

Luci held up a finger with one hand, tilted her head toward her shoulder, and reached with the other hand to push the talk button on the side of the radio.

"307," she answered.

"Proceed to 39 Main Street and speak with the owner about some new graffiti on the side of the building. Sounds like it's more of the same. Investigate and file a report, please."

"Received," she answered.

She turned her attention back to Mark, who spoke before she could.

"What time are you off? Stop by the house later if you want. I'll be there."

"8 p.m., but who knows these days. Depends on a few things. I'll try."

"Just stop by. I'm much more fun than chasing teens with spray paint," he offered sarcastically.

"Very funny. Goodbye for now. Glad you're home," she said as she grabbed him firmly around the bicep and squeezed. "Maybe you'll see me later. Maybe you won't."

15

He watched her walk away briskly and didn't take his eyes off her cruiser until it disappeared over the far hill of the cemetery. Then he turned to the tombstone one last time.

"Thanks for her too, Agnes."

Six

Agnes Landry had been a woman of many skills, but the ability to sit still was not one of them. She had taught German at Saint Patrick's Middle School in southern New Hampshire for over fifty years and put in just as much time, for no pay, with a long list of charities and nonprofits, mostly in Lawrence, Massachusetts, where she had had many friends—most of them nuns.

She opted not to drag Mark north with her every day to attend Saint Patrick's. Instead, for reasons she never explained, she enrolled him in the local public school system. In exchange, he had to spend his weekends washing dishes, serving food, and helping people less fortunate than he. He was rather ambivalent toward this work until he reached his mid-teens and started taking an interest in girls. That was when he and Luci Alvarez met for the first time.

He hadn't been crazy about attending the annual summer youth dance at Saint Lucia's in Lawrence but figured it couldn't be any worse than scrubbing pots and pans, delivering meals to the sick and elderly, or performing basic handyman chores for people he'd never met and would probably never see again. But he actually liked the outfit Agnes had bought for him to wear for the occasion: tan khakis, white oxford cloth button-down shirt, navy blue blazer, and bright red tie. He topped off the outfit with a pair of docksiders that had seen better days. When he emerged from his bedroom and shuffled down the stairs, Agnes sent him right back up to put on socks and a belt.

She kept talking, calling toward the ceiling as he complied. "These kids are much more formal than the kids in your school, Mark. I've seen what some of those kids wear in public. Most of them wouldn't even be let into Saint Lucia's tonight. They may be wealthier, but the kids you'll meet tonight have better manners and a sense of the occasion that'll be good for you to experience."

She turned around to find Mark already back downstairs and ready for inspection. She looked him up and down, smiled, kissed him on the forehead, and winked at him. "Who knows, some of it may even rub off on you."

Thirty minutes later Mark—the only person wearing casual khakis and a sport coat—was drowning in a sea of brightly colored formal gowns and dark, double-breasted suits. He and Agnes both surveyed the dapper crowd and then looked at each other.

"At least you're wearing a belt and socks," she said before walking over to join the other chaperones.

Mark spent the next hour trying in vain not to look self-conscious. He found that task impossible while standing still, so he started taking slow laps around the cafeteria, acting as if he knew where he was going and occasionally smiling at the girls.

Besides Agnes and a few other chaperones, he was the only white kid in the room. Still worse, it was mid-July and there was no air conditioning. Even though none of the other dancegoers was displaying a bead of sweat, Mark's shirt was soon soaked and his hair visibly wet from perspiration.

The last straw came when a group of dancers passed by and Mark was almost floored by the cloud of perfume and cologne that traveled with them. He made a break for the bathroom, where he removed his coat and splashed cold water on his face. Then he occupied the stall closest to the window so he could cool off, breathe, and collect his thoughts.

Scrubbing pots and pans and serving food to old people wouldn't be so bad right now.

Once he had caught his breath and enough of his sweat had evaporated, Mark put his jacket back on and walked out of the bathroom, directly into a group of boys who had obviously been waiting for him.

"You lost?" asked one of the bigger boys.

"No."

"You got a problem?" asked the smallest one in the group.

Mark said nothing but looked at him as one would look at an annoying mosquito, then attempted to walk around the group and back to the dance. Several arms pushed him back.

"Look, I don't want any trouble, guys. I'm actually on my way out."

They all started talking at the same time in response, and Mark couldn't follow a single word. He attempted to walk around the group another time but was again pushed back as they fanned out to block the hallway. This time a different kid, not as big as the first but with a huge head, stepped forward and tried to grab Mark by the collars of his new sport coat.

Mark slapped his hands down, which incited a roar from the other boys, and simultaneously shuffled backwards down the hall to draw the kid away from the immediate support of his buddies.

"I don't want any trouble," said Mark two or three times before Big Head lunged at him and gave him no choice. Mark stepped to his left while bringing his right hand up to simultaneously parry the clumsy strike and trap the other boy's hand in a painful wristlock. Slamming him up against the wall would have immediately drawn the rest of the group into the fight; instead he cinched the wrist as hard as he could without breaking it and pulled him in close enough for a very brief conversation. His Spanish surprised the other kid.

"I don't want to hurt you or any of your friends, but I will if you don't cut the shit right now." He squeezed the wrist even harder and pointed at the other boys with his free hand. "I'm going to let you go now. Tell your friends to back off and don't think for a second I can't get you right back in this position whenever I want. Got it?"

"*Sí, sí.* Just let me go, man, we were just kidding! Nobody was gonna hurt you, man! We were just playing."

Mark knew this was complete bullshit. These kids were no gangbangers, but they certainly wouldn't have let up if Mark had cowered and begged for mercy. No, they would have doubled-downed and enjoyed their momentary position of power over what they assumed was some rich white kid from out of town looking to invade their territory. He resisted the urge to break the wrist and let go.

Big Head grabbed his nearly broken wrist with his good hand and winced. Mark looked up in time to see the other boys part like the Red Sea, their eyes following Luci Alvarez as she entered the fray with the grace, confidence, and presence of a queen. She wore her straight black hair down to her shoulders. Bright red lipstick. Perfect teeth. A strapless dark blue dress hugged her curves until just above the knee, and she had the smoothest bronze legs Mark had ever seen. She topped it off with a pair of high heels so high that most white girls her age, or any age for that matter, could never manage them. Yet she made it look easy as she walked slowly, heel to toe, one foot in front of the other as if walking on a tightrope, fully aware that all eyes were focused on her.

Seven

"There you are!" she said to Mark as she grabbed his hand. "He's with me, Cacón," she said coldly to the other boy, who was still trying to determine if his wrist was broken. Then she looked Mark in the eyes and winked. "Follow me. "

Once again the crowd parted as Luci moved slowly and confidently down the hall with a smile on her face, holding Mark's hand behind her, pressed against the small of her back as she walked. He simply followed, eyes straight ahead, resisting the urge to steal glances at her body. "I'm with her," he casually said to the crowd as they passed by.

"Let's go to the lounge so we can talk. There are a bunch of chaperones in there so nobody will bother us," she said over her shoulder once they had cleared the crowd.

"What did you call that guy? Cacón?" Mark asked.

"Yeah, why?

"Just wondering," he answered.

"It means big head."

When they entered the lounge, Luci let go of Mark's hand and pointed to two chairs in the corner. "Grab those, I'll get drinks."

She returned with two plastic cups filled with ice cubes and red fruit punch.

"Thank you," said Mark politely.

"No problem. I'm Luci. What's your name, where are you from, and how the heck did you end up here?" she asked bluntly.

Mark explained his relationship to Agnes Landry and was unsurprised when Luci said "*Sí, Doña Landry!* Everyone knows her."

Talking to Luci came easy to Mark. She was warm, confident, and sharp as a tack. And she was the most gorgeous girl who had ever paid attention to him.

"So, back in the hallway earlier. Why did you help—"

"Why did I help you?" she interrupted.

"No, them. I was doing just fine. Why did you help them?" he replied with a wide confident smile that took her by surprise. He no longer seemed like some random gringo in distress. He was confident but not arrogant, and for Luci his quiet confidence was a welcome change from the boys she was used to interacting with. It showed that he had nothing to prove. Her eyes widened for a split second, her body language loosened up, and she subconsciously leaned in just a little bit closer.

"Let's just say I know what it's like to be the only different person in the room," she said with a softness and vulnerability he had not yet witnessed. "I don't expect you to notice, but I'm the only *colombiana* here tonight, and my family is one of the few Colombian families in a city full of Puerto Ricans and Dominicans."

Mark switched to Spanish.

"*I figured something like that. I noticed almost immediately. You carry yourself a bit different. Not better or worse—just different. And when I saw the way those guys parted for you, I knew that somebody different, somebody special, was coming through the crowd.*"

Luci's eyes and mouth popped open, but she made no sound until she had covered her face with her hands and bowed her head. Then she let loose with a laugh so loud it turned the heads of everyone in the room. She smiled warmly with half-closed eyes. "How long were you going to wait before you let me know you speak Spanish? Until I said something stupid in front of you? Or about you? You're full of surprises!"

They sat together and talked the rest of the night, exchanged phone numbers, and never once noticed the empty punch bowl or dwindling crowd. When Luci's friend tapped her on the shoulder to say that it was time to go, they stood up and she kissed Mark on the cheek. He watched as she reluctantly walked away. Agnes had watched the exchange from her chaperone's perch and put her hand on Mark's shoulder as she approached from behind.

"Let's go home, Romeo."

Eight

"You are supposed to be changing a flat tire. Why are you smiling?" asked the tall, bearded instructor. "Do Americans smile when they change tires? No. They grimace and complain about each and every little inconvenience that life throws at them. If you are to blend in, you must do the same."

The warriors listened and continued changing the tire with appropriately pissed-off American looks on their faces while waiting for the targets. When the car approached and slowed to a halt to offer assistance, both men simulated attacking the driver and family with pistols and knives.

"Very good, the bloodier the better! Replace the Mercedes-Benz hood ornament with the father's head in front of the children if you can! Enjoy it! Drink it in and give all praise to God!" he preached to his eager pupils.

Amir joined the chorus of war cries and felt his adrenaline rush as he imagined himself hacking away at the man's wife and children with his own knife.

How much longer must I wait for the glory I have earned?

"Two weeks," the imam had said. "Two weeks of very special training for our most special martyrs. Then you will depart for the Dar al-Harb and fulfill your destinies."

Amir had bristled at the words. More training. More time.

Be patient. God has chosen you.

He had breezed through the training thus far and easily outperformed all the other chosen martyrs.

"Now simulate the mission again, but this time only using your left hand," the instructor had said to Amir with a smile as he pointed to the two-story structure on the other side of the fence.

Child's play.

The former athlete vaulted over the fence, rapidly crossed the twenty yards or so between the fence and house, and scaled the corner bricks until he was high enough to disappear into a second-story window. This time the warrior playing the father of the family was awake, with a gun in one hand and a flashlight in the other.

"Who is there? Get out of my house right now! The police are on the way," he managed to say before having his throat slit from behind. Amir decided to save his bullets for the police and slaughtered the children in their beds with the knife—all with his right arm tied tightly to his side.

Single targets. Multiple targets. Stationary targets. Moving targets. Intensive close-quarters battle training. Pistols. Rifles. Knives. Hand to hand. Two weeks without knowing the details of his holy mission. Two weeks to sharpen every skill and plan for every conceivable contingency. Two weeks of torturous waiting … now complete.

The spiritual council awaited him on the other side of the door. He breathed deeply, checked his appearance one last time, and knocked twice.

Nine

Agnes Landry's house—now Mark's—was a small colonial that sat directly at the end of a downhill cul-de-sac exactly four miles from the town center. The main floor had a kitchen with a small diner-like booth built into the corner, its straight-backed seats slightly more comfortable than church pews. There was also a family room that Agnes had called the "parlor" and a tiny half-bathroom. Next to the bathroom was another room just big enough to hold her desk, a few filing cabinets, and a rocking chair. Upstairs were two bedrooms of equal size and one full bath. Due to constant water seeping through the fieldstone foundation, the unfinished basement had been used only to store a handful of metal folding chairs that Agnes would lug upstairs when her guests outnumbered the seats available. There was no garage. Acres of protected forest abutted the back of the house.

Mark turned on to Chestnut Lane and started the final descent to the house. He breathed deeply and let gravity do its work as he coasted past the few other homes that shared the wide street. As a child he remembered running to the top of the hill and letting all types of balls—even a bowling ball once—roll freely and find their own way down the hill. No matter where he released them, they would always funnel into his narrow driveway before ending up in the woods behind the house.

Over the years, those woods had been the resting place of countless neighborhood balls, bikes, skates, toys, and (during one slippery winter) a poorly parked car that had slid all the way down from the first house at the top of the street and straight through the Landrys' driveway before nearly shattering on impact with a cluster of deep-rooted walnut trees. "See that? It's a good thing we don't have a garage," Agnes had said as she handed Mark a shovel and sent him out to clean off her snow-covered Buick.

Mark climbed the wooden stairs that led to the side door and opened it with the key he had pinched between his thumb and pointer finger. He carried nothing else. His bags could wait until later.

Ten

When Officer Luci Alvarez arrived at 39 Main Street and parked her cruiser, an impatient forty-six-year-old Lee Carter was waiting at the side of the building with a gallon of white paint and a roller. Once Luci finished taking pictures and filling out her report, he would quickly paint over the graffiti and hope that none of his daytime drinking customers leaned against the wall before it dried.

Carter was the third-generation owner of the Witch Hunt, a pub opened by his grandfather, whose love of local history was surpassed only by his love of whiskey and a captive audience for his stories. The pub's name was a nod to the infamous 1692 Salem Witch Trials, to which the town had sent more than its fair share of accused. He was talking on his cell phone while pacing and waving his arms when Luci arrived.

Lucy depressed the talk button on her radio and spoke clearly.

"307 to control."

"Control's on," answered the same gravelly voice from before.

"I'll be out at 39 Main."

"Received."

Lucy emerged from the cruiser with her camera in hand and waved at Mr. Carter before moving around and opening the trunk to retrieve a tape measure, latex gloves, evidence bags, and a few other things she knew she wouldn't need. She had answered identical calls nearly a dozen times over the past few months, and this was her third or fourth visit to the Witch Hunt. She paused for a moment to take a deep breath before closing the trunk and walking calmly yet purposefully toward the agitated pub owner.

Luci Alvarez, age thirty-eight, was born in Bogotá, Colombia, to struggling parents who sent her to live with her grandparents in Lawrence, Massachusetts when she was three. Life was not easy for one of the few Colombian families in what had already been a predominantly Puerto Rican and Dominican city for decades. Actually, life wasn't easy for any Latino family in Lawrence, but it was particularly difficult for Luci's, because their roots were no more stable than the broken sidewalks on which she walked to school.

Carlos Alvarez, a custodian and handyman, and his wife Carmen, a cleaning lady at the district courthouse, worked their fingers to the bone and pinched pennies in order to provide their granddaughter with every opportunity they could afford. Unfortunately, that was not very much. But what they had lacked in financial means they easily made up for in love, attention, and encouragement. As a result, Luci stayed out of trouble when many of the other girls in the neighborhood did not, and her academic performance earned her a full tuition scholarship to Boston University, where she eventually graduated summa cum laude with a B.S. in psychology while working a side job.

After graduation, which neither of her actual parents attended or acknowledged, she had worked at various counseling jobs before acing the civil service exam and joining the Lawrence Police Department. But a corrupt city government and a depressed local economy that generated ever lower municipal tax revenues eventually threatened to kill her hopes of a long career policing the streets and helping young people make good decisions. With her stellar resume and skills, she searched for open positions on police forces in surrounding towns. When an opportunity in Mark and Agnes's hometown presented itself, she quickly traded uniforms before she could get furloughed. Now here she was, a highly educated, naturalized American citizen dedicated to public service, about to be judged solely on her ethnicity by a man who had obtained his only job by inheritance.

"I thought you said you were going to do something about this?" Mr. Carter said after abruptly finishing his conversation and stuffing his cell phone into the front pocket of his faded jeans.

Luci looked up at the fresh graffiti for a moment before turning his way and speaking. "Good morning, Mr. Carter," she replied.

"Good morning," he replied, annoyed by the pleasantries. "Seriously, when are you going to do something about those people?"

"I'm not sure which people you're referring to, Mr. Carter."

He rolled his eyes. "For the love of God, they're practically signing their names all over town. Why can't you just go down to where they all live, find the ones responsible, and take care of this before it escalates? It seems to me it wouldn't be that hard," he added with a heavy dose of condescension.

"We're doing our best, Mr. Carter. I can promise you that," she answered cheerfully. "Let's see what we have today." Luci raised the camera to her eyes, backed up until all the graffiti fit within the frame, and snapped several photos. Then she lowered the camera and spent a few moments looking at the wall and soaking it all in, as if studying a piece of modern art at a museum instead of fresh graffiti on Main Street. She stepped forward and ran her hand along the wall.

The same paint. Does that mean anything? Is it coincidence? Did different people paint these? Or is it all from the same person or group of people? If it is the same person or group, are they deliberately making them bigger to increase the impact? What's the goal here? Marking territory? A warning? Or could it just be some kind of hoax or prank? Each piece of graffiti has the crown and letters, but no other message.

Then she turned her attention back to Mr. Carter.

"Any idea what time it happened, Mr. Carter?" she asked.

"I closed up and left at about 2:45 a.m. Must have been after that."

"Have you considered adding an outdoor camera to your security system?"

"No, I haven't," he said angrily. "I'll fight crime on the inside of my business, Officer Alvarez. You guys are supposed to have the outside covered, right? My taxes already help fund the police department. You want me to buy your equipment too? Besides, you and I both know those people are vandalizers and would just rip it down."

Luci continued listening and smiled, using every shred of self-discipline she could muster to keep her thoughts to herself.

Vandalizers? You must mean vandals. English is my second language and I know that. And cameras don't discriminate. A camera right here would catch the comings and goings of all the Witch Hunt's customers—and you too. What time people come and go. Who they come and go with. A camera here might boost security, but it could also be bad for business. I'm sure you have already considered that.

"I'll file a report and recommend the late shift increase its presence here during those early morning hours. I'll also ask around to see if anyone saw or heard anything between 2:45 a.m. and sunrise. If I learn anything, I'll let you know. I'd ask you to do the same."

"In other words, I shouldn't count on you ever actually finding out who did this," he asked, eyes quickly darting right and left before he continued. "You know something—I'm not racist, so don't take this the wrong way, but some folks in town think you may be protecting these people. Not because you necessarily agree with them, but maybe because you're afraid of them or something. I don't know," he said, his voice trailing off at the end as if he realized his remarks were baseless but still felt obliged to finish.

Luci was unfazed. "Thank you for sharing that, Mr. Carter. I don't waste a lot of time worrying about what other people think. I can't control that. I just focus on the things I can control, like doing my job. I'll be in touch. I hope your day gets better from here." She smiled and walked back toward her cruiser.

He shook his head from side to side.

Why didn't you keep your big trap shut, Carter? Dammit.

"You too, Luci. Thanks," he called out as she was walking away.

Lucy started her cruiser and grabbed her radio.

"307 to Control. I'll be clear from 39 Main."

"Received."

As she drove away from the Witch Hunt, she could see Lee Carter starting to paint over the graffiti in her rear-view mirror.

Something tells me he's going to need a lot more paint before this is over.

Eleven

Frank Tagala held the blinds of the window open with one hand and his binoculars up to his eyes with the other. After Agnes Landry's son—or stepson, or adopted son, or whatever he was—had carried his last load of bags into the house next door, he lowered the binoculars and let the blinds snap shut. Frank was pretty sure he spotted at least one rifle case mixed in with the other suitcases and backpacks. But he also recalled that the kid was some kind of soldier, so he wasn't very concerned. He had other things on his mind anyway. He turned around and made his way across the darkened family room and back into the kitchen.

He made one last review of his notes before collecting the multi-colored folders and random photographs scattered across the kitchen table and dropping them into a wide, hard-shell briefcase. He snapped the combination lock closed, placed the case in the cupboard under the kitchen sink, and tethered the reinforced handle to the pipes with a steel bicycle lock. Finally, he closed the door and secured the cupboard with a very old child safety lock.

Ten minutes later Frank emerged from his bedroom wearing a pair of black dress slacks, black Italian loafers, and a black polo shirt beneath a black sport coat. A stainless steel watch hung loosely around his left wrist, and he wore a matching stainless steel wedding band although he had not seen or spoken with his wife or daughter in years.

He patted his front pockets to make sure his keys and wallet were where they should be. Then he removed the .40 caliber Glock 27 pistol from the holster concealed deep behind his right hip. He pointed the muzzle of the gun at the floor with his right hand and used his left to slowly pull back the slide until he could peer through the ejection port and see the shiny nickel casing of a 155-grain hollow point bullet in the chamber. Then he rode the slide all the way forward and gave the rear sights a firm bump with the palm of his hand to make sure the gun was in battery. Satisfied, he returned the Glock to its holster. He had already verified that the two thirteen-round backup magazines attached to his left hip were full, and the snub-nosed Smith and Wesson .38 Special revolver strapped to the inside of his left leg just below the calf didn't need checking, so he stared at the bottle on the kitchen counter instead.

Frank's mind weighed the pros and cons of having another drink before such an important and dangerous meeting, but his body had already made its decision. He sat back and watched as his left hand retrieved a chilled glass from the freezer and his right hand grabbed the large bottle of cheap vodka on the counter. He filled the glass to the brim and stood still for a moment. After a preliminary deep breath he lifted the glass to his lips and drained its entire contents down his throat and into his empty stomach. He contemplated another drink, but instead set the glass and bottle down on the counter and headed outside to his car.

At six feet three, Frank still had a commanding presence and impressive agility, but his once athletic build was starting to deteriorate. He looked gaunt and unhealthy. The dark bags of flesh under his eyes distracted from the elegance of his thick gray hair. He was fifty-six, but he appeared ten or more years older than that.

Frank started the car and checked his watch. It was 6 p.m. He should arrive in Boston by 6:45, in plenty of time for his secret 8:00 meeting on the water.

Francis Tagala's grandparents, Virgilio and Angelica, knew only a few words of English when they arrived in the U.S. from Italy and settled in Boston's North End. The decision to emigrate had not been easy, but the newlyweds felt that it was God's plan for them to make the journey. They arrived with just one suitcase and a little under $300 between them. But what they lacked in wealth, they more than made up for in work ethic and optimism.

Within six months of their arrival, Angelica was pregnant with the first of their four children. She and Virgilio did whatever it took to give their children the best opportunities they could. Their kids, deeply grateful for the parents' dedication, passed up opportunities to branch out and opted instead to stay in the North End, working alongside mother and father. But that instinctive obligation to stick around lasted only one generation. It changed with the first grandchild, Frank Tagala.

Like his father and grandfather, Frank spent much of his youth lifting boxes, stocking shelves, and busing tables. But he also dreamed of a different life and knew there were bigger and better opportunities out there than working his ass off in the North End for the rest of his life. Although he got in a lot of fights as a kid, he was also the first in his family to finish high school. After graduation he struggled for several years in a community college before eventually transferring to a four-year state school as a commuter student. It took him three more years to complete the last two years of study.

His entire family attended his graduation and cheered wildly as he walked across the stage with a bachelor's degree in criminal justice, although nobody knew what the hell he could do with it. But the celebration and accolades had barely ended when Frank's father, Virgilio Jr., dropped dead of a massive heart attack at age forty-four. Frank put his dreams on hold and rallied around his mother with the rest of the family. He suffered silently in tedious jobs for almost ten years before his mother took him aside one day in tears.

"Go, Francis. Go do whatever God calls you to do. Virgilio's parents and my parents all came here so our families could have better lives. But we're all so stubborn and focused on work, we're letting it all fly by. Life is so short, Francis, so short. Please go soon or you never will. And always put your trust in God," she cried.

Her blessing was all he had needed. Two months later he accepted a position with the U.S. Border Patrol. It wasn't his first choice, but he would have taken almost any job in federal law enforcement just to get his foot in the door. He worked hard and bit his tongue during a two-year stint at different posts along the Mexican border that nearly drove him insane. He then leapt at an opportunity to transfer to the Bureau of Alcohol, Tobacco, and Firearms.

Academically, Frank struggled greatly in Special Agent training for the ATF. In his view, there was too much talking and not enough doing. But he gutted his way through the seemingly endless hours of lectures and reading and made up for his lackluster grades by excelling in all other aspects of the program. He thrived in weapons training and had an intuitive understanding of tactics. His instructors gave him the nickname "Gladiator" for his fighting skills and stamina. But what impressed his superiors the most was his ability to build rapport with just about everyone he met. Frank was tough as nails, but he also had a magnetic, disarming personality. Even though he graduated nowhere near the top of his class, he was still invited to choose his first field assignment. After listening to his instructors' counsel and asking God for guidance, he decided on the Boston Field Office. Frank was going home.

He hit the ground running and quickly made a name for himself in Boston as a dependable partner with natural street smarts. He volunteered for the toughest assignments and led the way in dangerous maneuvers without ever losing his cool. He worked undercover and developed a network of informants across the city that bewildered his superiors. Got a problem with the Irish criminals in the South End? Talk to Frank. Need information on Latino gang leaders? Talk to Frank. Wondering who was responsible for last night's drive-by shooting? Ask Frank. If he doesn't know already, he will soon.

Frank's intuition and reliability were showcased early in his career, on a Saturday afternoon in Boston's Chinatown district. He and his partner had been working undercover on an arms deal with some Asian gang members when Frank sensed that they had walked into an ambush. When one of the gang members pulled a large revolver, Frank drew his pistol and dropped him along with two other would-be assailants before they could access the rifles they had hidden under their long trench coats. The other three opened fire from across the street and a fierce exchange followed. Two of the assailants were killed; the third got away after putting two 9mm rounds into the midsection of Frank's partner. Thanks to Frank's crucial first aid, the injured officer survived, although the physical and psychological impact of the incident caused him to retire.

Frank was commended for his performance under fire, and the incident became a case study for agents across the country. ATF instructors started seeking his counsel, and he was often asked to visit other field offices to talk about the incident and about crisis response strategies. The director knew him by name and his place in bureau history seemed solidified. That was the first half of his career. The second half was much different.

Like all organizations, over time the bureau began to change. The senior agents and deputy directors who knew Frank by name left, replaced by a younger crop of leaders who, as Frank later reported to the retired brass, "had absolutely no fucking idea how the real world worked." As a consequence, the rulebooks got thicker and the wide discretion that agents once enjoyed gave way to bureaucratic checklists and pussyfooting. These so-called leaders seemed much more concerned with protecting their own rear ends than the bureau's actual mission.

What exactly is our mission?

After the September 11 attacks, the Bureau of Alcohol, Tobacco, and Firearms tacked the word "Explosives" onto the end of its name; the addition made sense, but the agency's responsibility for alcohol and tobacco regulation was shared with other federal institutions. The identity crisis was intensified by tremendous overlap and territory disputes with the Drug Enforcement Agency, the Federal Bureau of Investigation, the U.S. Marshals, the Department of Homeland Security, and U.S. Customs and Border Protection, as well as local and state police.

To make matters still worse, the new generation of leaders to whom this bureaucratic redundancy all seemed normal could barely contain their disdain for the old-school agents like Frank, viewing them as loose cannons who needed to be closely managed. Frank was accustomed to getting evaluated solely on the results of his labor; now the neatness of his reports and strict adherence to regulations took precedence, and every action was questioned and second-guessed.

Frank handled the cultural shift grudgingly but adequately until his actions in the Chinatown shootout came into question. In a series of training memos, the firefight was dissected and picked apart by several agents who didn't even have driver's licenses when the episode occurred. The younger agents questioned Frank's reflexive actions and posited that perhaps the fight could have been deescalated or avoided. Frank contemplated answering the revisionist history with memos of his own, but a colleague talked him out of it. "Don't bother, Frank. You'll just come off looking defensive and it'll start a feeding frenzy with these assholes. The people who matter know you did the right thing. That's enough. Let it go," the colleague said.

So Frank decided to be the bigger person and ignore the Monday-morning quarterbacking. But six months later the most vociferous of his critics, an Ivy Leaguer named Ashton Brown, became the new Director of the Boston Field Office, Frank's direct boss. Frank briefly considered requesting a transfer, but his stubborn Italian upbringing and sense of personal pride overrode the impulse. *Why should I leave? This is MY home. Screw him.*

He thought back to his mother's advice about always trusting in God and decided to stick it out. Besides, he had only a few years left until retirement.

Ashton Brown made Frank's life uncomfortable from his first day as the bureau's youngest field office director. He ranted and raved at every available opportunity about how the bureau needed to undergo a fundamental transformation if it was to meet the demands of the twenty-first century and how they couldn't afford to teach old dogs new tricks. Brown listened to no one and typically ended meetings with provocative, morale-killing expressions like "Get on board or get out." The environment had become toxic to all but a few agents who silently agreed with Brown while trying to play both sides of the fence. The rest of the staff criticized Brown behind his back. Frank tried to act prudently, but eventually his impatience and dissatisfaction began to get the better of him.

When Brown intimated his support for a failed bureau operation known as Operation Fast and Furious, Frank almost lost his mind. During that operation, ATF agents allowed illegal firearms to fall into the hands of criminals with known connections to Mexican drug cartels. They intended to track the weapons but ended up losing track of them, and one of them was later used to kill a U.S. Border Patrol agent assigned to a checkpoint that Frank had guarded years earlier. As Brown explained the story and the rest of the agents sat silently, Frank dropped his forehead onto the conference table with a loud thud.

"Is there a problem, Tagala?" asked Brown.

He answered without raising his head from the table. "Yeah. Our mission is to take guns away from bad guys. Our mission is not to give guns to bad guys. There was a time when this very simple concept was well understood."

"Well, the world is a lot more complex these days, Tagala. Maybe too complex for someone as simple as you."

Frank raised his head and forced a smile. "It makes no sense to me, but I barely graduated from a state school. I guess you need an Ivy League degree to understand why facilitating the transfer of guns to narco-terrorists is a good idea."

All but a few managed to stifle their chuckles, but the humor was quickly replaced with semi-horror when Brown doubled-down.

"The only problem with the operation was a lack of proper planning and field leadership. And while the concept may seem like a bad idea to the creatively bankrupt, it's an excellent example of thinking outside of the box. We need more bold operations like Fast and Furious, not less."

Frank left the office shortly thereafter and spent the rest of the day at a bar in the North End. When he woke up the next day at noon, alone in his bed at home, he had no recollection of when or how he had gotten there. When he finally stumbled downstairs, he found his furious wife with one hand on her hip and pointing out the window with her other hand at his car, which was parked in the middle of the front yard.

Frank had always drunk his fair share of alcohol, but what agent didn't? The job is highly stressful and involves frequent life-and-death decisions. Surely the agents were entitled to a few drinks.

While Frank had had a few rough patches over the years when he fell into binge drinking, he had always been able to snap out of it before jeopardizing his job and family life. But that delicate balance collapsed under the emotional pressure of Brown's directorship. Special Agent Frank Tagala had climbed into a bottle, and several years later he had still not come out.

Now, almost twenty years into his career and just a few months from retirement, Frank was on his way to Boston to negotiate an illegal purchase of automatic weapons from a Russian arms dealer. He reached down and touched the rosary wrapped around the stick shift and recalled his mother's words.

Trust in God, Francis. Always trust in God.

The arms deal was to be Frank's last hurrah, after which he would ride out his final months at the bureau and quietly retire. But God had other plans.

Twelve

Mark was crashed on the sofa in the family room when he heard two chirps from his encrypted smart phone, indicating a secure text message. He opened his eyes, cursed himself for leaving the phone on the kitchen counter, and considered blowing it off, but then forced himself to get up and check the message.

All his bags were still stacked in the kitchen. He unzipped his backpack, removed his laptop, and set it down on the table in the corner before retrieving his phone from the counter. He scanned his thumb and entered the twelve-digit security code that opened up the phone for general use. The secure text message appeared immediately.

SENDER: Doc
MESSAGE: Hope you made it home safely. Condolences again. Take your time. No rush to get back to work.

Mark exhaled and started tapping away at the screen with his thumbs.

REPLY: Sure you're not trying to get rid of me? All good here. Talk soon.

He opened the doors and spent several minutes staring into the empty refrigerator. He breathed deeply and looked around the kitchen and into the sparsely furnished family room. Agnes had never made much money and had a set routine for every payday. First, she would pay the bills and put a little something in her rainy day fund. Whatever was left she would share with people who needed it. The result was a perfectly adequate, but somewhat austere existence.

The house was completely quiet, without a single sound beyond his own breathing. This was the only home he had ever lived in, and now that it was his, he wasn't sure if he even wanted it. Homes are like relationships; they require stable partners, people to nurture and care for them. Mark's life thus far had not been conducive to homes or relationships. He had had a few girlfriends over the years but never allowed himself to get too serious, because he always knew that he would eventually have to leave—and that he would be unable to explain where he was going, what he was doing, or when or if he would ever return.

Maybe it's time to settle down and start a new chapter.

Mark's partner Billy had been married for fifteen years, ten of which he had spent working with Dunbar and the Family. He seemed happy and always eager to get home and hug his wife and daughter, whereas Mark merely treaded water until the next assignment. Mark was happy in a way too, but he usually kept himself busy so he wouldn't have to reflect much on his own personal life. Now, in the silence of Agnes's house—his house—he was starting to realize just how alone he was.

Maybe it is time.

Thirteen

Luci stared at the split monitors atop her desk in the back of the police station. She had already uploaded the new graffiti photos and wanted to compare them to the previous photos she had taken from different locations. Eleven separate graffiti incidents had occurred by now. As she looked over the pictures from the other incidents, one thing was obvious: the graffiti was getting bigger, as if someone was raising his or her voice to be heard.

The first piece of graffiti, painted on the side of the high school gymnasium, was only about three feet by three feet. Since then, the size had grown steadily. The drawing painted on the wall of the Witch Hunt the night before was a bright gold, five-pointed crown approximately six feet high and eight feet wide. The crown was outlined in black with the letters ALKQN painted in bright red underneath.

Luci typed "Latin Kings graffiti" into Google and scrolled through the images. The first examples that popped up were very similar to the graffiti that had been appearing around town—a golden crown with ALKQN below it. She clicked on websites and skimmed the information, most of which she had already known for years.

> The Almighty Latin King and Queen Nation, known as the Latin Kings for short, was founded in Chicago during the 1940s. Originally a primarily Puerto Rican organization, the contemporary Latin Kings now represent a wide range of Latino ethnicities. With chapters in dozens of countries, the highly organized Latin Kings rank as one of the largest Hispanic street gangs in the world.

Luci knew the rest of the story by heart. The ALKQN started as a Latino pride organization and mutual support network but had morphed over the years into a street gang with connections to illicit drug trafficking, racketeering, illegal guns, and inter-gang violence. The story wasn't quite that simple, but Luci rarely wasted her time trying to explain the nuances to non-Hispanics. Contrary to popular belief, the ALKQN did not speak with one voice. Some groups of Kings and Queens denounced all forms of crime and violence but remained members out of ethnic loyalty and a sense of belonging. Many current and former members reported anti-

Hispanic racism as the driving force behind their decisions to join. The group was not perfect, they argued, but it offered protection from other gangs and unconditional support in a country where anti-Hispanic rhetoric had been rising steadily for decades.

For six months now, Luci had been the department's community policing liaison to the only low-income housing project in town as well as the high school crisis officer. She had yet to identify any Latin King members or spot their notorious black and gold colors anywhere, and flying under the radar was not their style. But there were thousands of Kings and Queens in Massachusetts, including nearby Lawrence. Maybe they saw an opportunity in the growing rift between white and Latino residents and were trying to exploit it in order to gain a foothold in town. At this point, all Luci had was pictures of graffiti; everything else was speculation.

She thought back to her sociology and group dynamics coursework at Boston University. "Nationalism is a deeply psychological and complicated thing," she said out loud.

"What's that, Luci? What's complicated?" asked a gravelly voice coming from behind her.

Luci spun her chair around to face the shift commander on duty, a muscular forty-five-year-old sergeant named Doug Cromwell. "Nothing, Sarge. Just thinking out loud."

Cromwell held a cup of coffee in one hand and rubbed the back of his clean-shaven head with the other. The muscles in his forearm and bicep bulged as he moved his hand back and forth. "More of the same graffiti, eh? What do you make of it?"

"Honestly, nothing yet. All we have is graffiti and it doesn't tell us much," she answered.

"Okay. Let me know if you need anything from me. Graffiti by itself is easy. You just paint over it and move on. It's the other stuff that concerns me, but so far we haven't had any of it. If that changes, you let me know immediately, all right?"

"You'll be the first to know, Sarge."

Luci returned to her screens and took one last look at the photos before closing the files and shutting down her workstation. She looked at her watch and smiled. It was 8:15 p.m. She had time to go home and shower before visiting Mark.

Fourteen

Mark was on his second beer and his third episode of *Magnum P.I.* when he heard a car pull into the driveway and pieces of light spilled through the blinds.

Luci? Probably. Hopefully.

He got up from the couch and walked to the side window. There was no need to verify that the 9mm was on his body. It was there. It was always there.

Luci emerged from her car wearing a Boston Red Sox t-shirt, jeans, and four-inch heels. Her hair was down. Bright red lipstick.

How the hell does she walk in those things?

Mark twisted the doorknob, pulled the side door open a few inches, and drained the rest of his beer as he walked back into the kitchen to grab another one. Luci gave the door two quick knocks as she pushed it open and entered the house.

"*Policía*," she joked.

About to toss his bottle cap into the narrow trash can across the kitchen, Mark paused and turned his attention to Luci.

"In that case, you're gonna need a warrant and perhaps some backup."

Without looking, he tossed the bottle cap and missed the can by a good three feet.

"Beer?"

"One and done. I'm driving and I have an important meeting in the morning."

"Glass?"

"Please."

Mark grabbed a chilled glass from the freezer, filled it with beer, and placed it on the counter in front of her.

"Thanks."

"Cheers," he said while holding his bottle out in front of him.

She lifted the glass and looked into Mark's eyes as they toasted. "Cheers." Then she put the lipstick-stained glass back on the counter.

Mark took a seat in the corner booth and stretched his legs out on the bench. Luci stood leaning against the kitchen counter.

"What's new? You look fantastic."

"You sound surprised."

"A little. I figured fighting crime all these years would take its toll," he said.

No response. She took another small sip of her beer, looking at the glass first to ensure that she put her lips in the same place as before.

"You okay?" she asked after a few seconds of silence.

"Yeah, I'm okay. About as good as can be expected. I wish I could have been here, but that's the price you pay sometimes. I always knew that. Agnes always knew that. Now I just need to figure some things out."

She wasn't listening. As he was talking, he followed her eyes across the family room to the staircase. After a few seconds he understood why she was distracted.

"You were here, weren't you?"

Luci bowed her head and nodded slightly.

"Yeah. I was standing by dispatch when one of her friends called. She hadn't shown up for something and they couldn't get in touch with her. They were worried. I came out to check on her."

Mark looked away, rested his beer bottle on his bottom lip, and let gravity fill his mouth with a healthy sip before returning his attention to Luci.

"I'm glad it was you, and I know it must not have been easy. Thank you."

She pointed at his bags, still strewn about the kitchen floor.

"I'm not going to ask if you have a license for whatever's in the rifle case."

"Good, because I'm pretty sure I don't. Never ask questions you don't want the answers to, Officer Alvarez," he said with a smile. "It's a safe town anyway thanks to crime fighters like you. If history is any indication—"

She cut him off with a raised hand and grabbed her glass with the other before slowly and gracefully making her way toward the booth. Mark recognized the subtle expression on her face, shut his mouth, and braced for what he knew was coming. Her heels made a soft clicking sound as she glided across the hardwood floor. She didn't speak until she was seated across the table from Mark.

"Every time you say something stupid or sarcastic about cops, I like you a little bit less," she began. Mark knew better than to interrupt when she was annoyed.

"I'm proud of what I do and I'm proud to work with just about everyone in my department. We do good things. So you can drop the snarky 'crime fighting' comments. Got it?"

"I'm sorry. I didn't mean it like that," he said, raising both hands, palms out.

"What exactly are you sorry for?" she asked with squinted eyes.

"What do you mean?"

"You said you were sorry. For what?"

Mark was momentarily confused with the question before it registered.

Ah, I get it. She wants me to say it out loud. A confession. It's a cop thing. Ask the right questions and the suspect will hang himself with his own words.

He took a deep breath and looked directly into her eyes.

"Luci, I'm sorry for being a dick."

Eyes locked on his, she slowly took a tiny sip of her beer before replying.

"Very good, Mark. You appear to be trainable. There may be hope for you yet. By the way, when you mentioned history, that reminded me that I bumped into Andy today. I told him you were in town. Didn't think you'd mind."

"Andy? That's fine. He's probably the only other person I'd like to see while I'm here."

"And how long will that be?"

"No idea. At least a month. Maybe forever."

This was a first. Mark had never mentioned or entertained the possibility of coming home and staying home. She made a mental note of his comment but gave no reaction.

"What's Andy up to?" Mark asked.

"Still teaching social studies at the high school, and I think he's department chair now. Assistant football coach and local history expert. Every Thursday he gives a quick spiel on town history to a packed house at the Witch Hunt. I've never attended, but I hear it's a hoot."

"I imagine so. He always could tell a story."

They filled the next half hour with small talk about the town and Luci's relatively new position as community policing liaison to the growing Latino population. Whenever the topic turned to Mark's career, she knew to keep her questions vague and not to expect much from his answers. They listened closely to each other and tried to ignore the eight-hundred-pound gorilla that was always in the room—their on-and-off relationship over the years. Luci finally looked at her watch and stood up.

"It's late for me. I need to get some sleep."

Mark rose and followed her out the side door to her car. She paused for a moment before opening the door, getting in, and rolling down the window. No hug, no kiss.

"Listen, I did a full inventory of the house after Agnes died. In the top drawer of the desk in her office is a small box with your name on it. There's a note inside. I have no idea what it says, and I made sure nobody else does either."

"Okay. Thank you."

"And if you want to see Andy, he'll be at the Witch Hunt tomorrow night doing his thing."

"Want to go with me?"

"Sure, why not? As long as you promise to behave," she said after a pause that lasted a second too long for Mark's liking.

"Good. Pick me up at eight sharp then," he said before turning and heading back into the house.

"Why the hell do I have to pick you up? Why can't you pick me up?" she asked, clearly annoyed.

He stopped walking and turned back to face the car with a wide grin.

"It's just better that way. I'm pretty sure I don't have a driver's license either."

Luci smiled and shook her head as she backed out of the driveway. The smile was gone by the time she reached the top of the hill.

Mark Landry. Back in town, but for how long? Don't do it, Luci. Don't fall for him all over again. You'll only get hurt when he leaves. And make no mistake—Mark Landry always leaves.

Fifteen

Mark stood motionless in the kitchen for a few minutes with an unopened beer in one hand and a bottle opener in the other. Then he dropped the opener back into its drawer, returned the beer to the refrigerator, and began pacing slowly around the kitchen and family room.

Don't do it, Mark. Just don't do it. At least think things through. Take your time. Be smart. Think of her. You may leave and then you'll be the asshole … again.

He stopped at the bottom of the stairs and recalled his last night in town before shipping off to basic training twenty years earlier. Agnes sat on the bottom step in her light blue terrycloth bathrobe and watched Mark pace the family room.

"What's on your mind, Mark? Why all the pacing? It can't just be boot camp. My guess is you're less worried about what happens at Fort Benning than what happens here after you've left."

"Yeah, I am worried. I'm worried about you—that I'm leaving you to live alone. And I wonder about Luci. I worry she'll find someone better and forget about me and there'll be nothing I can do about it."

"Don't worry about me. I'm never really alone. But you're right about that last part. You can't control those things. You just have to do the right things and pray for the best."

"But do you think I'll ever find anyone as special as Luci?"

"You're asking yourself the wrong question, Mark. That's what you ask yourself when you're shopping for a new car. True love doesn't work that way. When you're truly in love, you don't sit around wondering if there's a better deal out there somewhere. You can't even consider being with anyone else. You'll know when you've found the right person. Maybe it's Luci, maybe not. Time will tell."

"Have you ever been truly in love?"

Agnes stood up, tightened the robe around her waist, and stuffed her hands into its front pockets. She took a deep breath and smiled.

"Treat Luci right. Always be honest with her and respect her enough to give her the space to make her own decisions. Be patient. You're young, Mark. If it is meant to be, things will work out. These things can take time."

"Yeah, but how much time?"

She began slowly climbing the stairs and continued to speak over her shoulder.

"Who knows? Life always has more questions than answers, Mark. It could take twenty minutes. It might take twenty years."

Twenty years. And here I am in the same exact spot.

Sixteen

As Mark slowly cracked the door to Agnes's office, light from the kitchen splashed against the far wall and illuminated the one and only crucifix in the house.

"There's no need to wear your faith on your sleeve, let alone every wall of the house," Agnes once said to Mark on the way home from visiting a friend whose home looked like a shrine at the Vatican.

He felt for the switch against the inside wall and flipped the lights on. The room was bare and his footsteps made no sound as he drifted across the thin area rug that covered all but a few inches of the small room. He pulled the top drawer open with both hands and discovered a small wooden box that had seen better days. A thin rubber band held a small piece of light blue paper in place. Written on the paper in black ink was Mark's name.

What's this, Agnes? Is this a goodbye? A parting gift perhaps? The number for the plumber?

As he contemplated the contents of the box, soft knocking at the side door intruded on his thoughts. He closed the drawer, flipped off the office lights, peered around the corner in the direction of the noise, and paused. He had heard no car but could see that the sensor light had kicked on. The knocker had approached the house on foot and was not deterred by the light. Through the blinds, he could see the figure of a person. Mark took comfort as the meek knocking continued. Bad guys—at least the kind he was used to dealing with—didn't tend to stand in the spotlight and announce their arrival.

"Who is it?"

A muffled voice answered, but he could not make out the words.

"Who?" he repeated.

"It's Kenny."

Kenny? Kenny who?

"From next door, Mark," the voice continued, making Mark wonder if he had been thinking out loud.

Kenny Harrington. Does he still live next door?

He opened the door wide and smiled at the tiny figure in front of him.

"Hi, Kenny."

Although they were the same age, Kenny's stature and demeanor had always made him seem younger by comparison. Neither of those things had changed; he was still barely five feet tall, and his slumped shoulders and bowed head made him seem even shorter.

"Hi, Mark," he whispered. "Sorry to bother you."

"You're not bothering me, Kenny. Come on in. Want a beer?"

Kenny stood straighter and raised his head at the unexpected invitation. A faint smile occupied his face, and Mark saw a brief flicker in his eyes before he redirected his gaze to his feet and slouched again.

"No, thanks. I can't stay. If father notices he's alone, it'll scare him."

Mark maintained his smile but squinted slightly.

"Father has dementia. Mother died three years ago so it's just us now."

Mark searched for the right words but knew he'd never find them. Instead he offered the typical anodyne response.

"I'm sorry to hear that, Kenny. Let me know if I can ever help."

Kenny nodded his head and awkwardly shifted his focus left and right, then resumed speaking.

"Father and I were sorry to hear about Agnes. She was a big help to us these past few months. Always checking on us and bringing home-cooked meals when she could. We're sorry she's gone."

Mark smiled and nodded politely.

"Me too, Kenny. Me too. What can I do for you?" he replied politely but in a tone that indicated it was time to move on from the topic of dead matriarchs.

"I don't know how long you'll be home, but if you need Internet you can connect to my Wi-Fi. Agnes never had Internet here for some reason."

"Okay, thanks. I appreciate that."

Kenny continued after several seconds of awkward silence.

"The network is called *theshire*, all one word. And the password is *Bilbo*, with a capital B."

The Shire. Bilbo. Right. Seventh-grade English. Tolkien.

"Okay, that should be easy to remember," Mark said with a chuckle.

47

"Do you remember that class? Reading that book? Mr. Marcell?"

"Of course I do, Kenny. It's still one of my favorites too," Mark said unconvincingly.

"Yeah, he died last year too."

Jesus, you're full of great news tonight, Kenny.

Mark couldn't think of anything to say, so he stood silently, hoping that Kenny would wrap things up on his own.

"Was that Luci who just left?" Kenny continued.

"Yup, that was her," Mark answered, glancing at his watch.

"Okay, well, tell her I said hi … she was always nice," Kenny said. He turned and firmly grabbed the handrail with his right hand, carefully lowering his left foot to the next step down. After lowering his right foot, he paused briefly before carefully stepping off again with his left foot. He repeated the same set of motions until both feet reached the safety of the driveway.

Mark watched him walk to the end of the driveway and turn right toward his house before calling out to him, "Kenny, feel free to cut across the lawn next time. No big deal, man."

Seventeen

Thirty miles south, ATF agent Frank Tagala was getting slammed against the hood of an unmarked police car while three cops struggled to get handcuffs on him. This was the fun part for Frank, because it meant he was no longer in grave danger. But he was still in character and needed to make things look authentic.

The arms deal had gone down as planned. Within seconds of the exchange, a flood of federal agents and Boston policemen covered by rooftop snipers had taken control of the area and everyone in it. As Frank struggled, he screamed across the hood at the three Russian mobsters he had spent the past six months setting up.

"You fucking stupid pieces of Russian shit! You set me up. You're all dead men. You fucked with the wrong guinea!"

He tried to kick, punch, bite, and smack the three young officers as they scuffled. Their explicit instructions were to meet force with force, but they had not expected such resistance from another lawman, and Frank showed no signs of letting up. Frustrated and scared, the youngest of the three stepped back, drew his Taser, and lit Frank up like a Christmas tree. The other two stood wide-eyed as Frank howled.

"Motherrrr Fuckerrrr! Fuck, fuck, fuck! Ahhhhhhhhhhh!"

After he collapsed to the ground, they had him cuffed and in the back of the cruiser in less than fifteen seconds. With their lights flashing and sirens screaming, they headed away from the harbor toward the debriefing area. Behind the car's heavily tinted windows, Frank caught his breath and spoke first.

"Jesus Christ, kid! I said it had to be convincing, but you deserve an Oscar. Shit, that fucking hurt."

"I'm sorry, sir. I don't know what happened. I panicked," offered the rookie cop sitting next to him in the back seat, his nervous fingers fumbling to unlock the handcuffs that held Frank's wrists tightly behind his back.

Both men swung back and forth in unison as the cruiser banked left and right, weaving its way through Boston's narrow streets at high speed. Frank breathed deeply and rubbed his wrists to get his circulation going again. The cop in the passenger seat, a veteran sergeant, rotated to face the rear of the vehicle.

"Seriously, what the fuck were you thinking back there, Tortellini?"

Frank jumped in before he could answer.

"Tortellini?"

"It's Tarentini, Sir. And I accept full responsibility. I know I fucked up."

Frank laughed out loud.

"Relax, Tarentini. It hurt like a son of a bitch, but you three would have never got cuffs on me unless I gave up. And that would have been a dead giveaway. Russians are assholes but they aren't stupid. You improvised. A warning would have been nice, but everyone's safe now and it's over. Let's not relive it."

Frank looked at the sergeant, who took his cue to drop the issue.

"It's over now. And at least you were smart enough not to use your gun," Frank joked as he punched Officer Tarentini in the shoulder.

Two more months. Two more months of this shit and I'm done.

Eighteen

Everyone stood and gave Frank a round of applause when he entered the four-bay garage that had served as his field mission support center. Rows of monitors and other electronic equipment filled long tables set against the back wall. Technical support personnel had already made backups of the video and audio as supervisors watched over their shoulders and drank coffee.

Everything had been done by the book, and a strict chain of custody virtually eliminated the risk that the charges would be tossed out on a technicality. Frank's last hurrah had been as clean a job as anyone could ask for. No injuries. Bad guys in custody. Fewer guns on the street—in this case, twenty Russian-made AK-47s and a dozen Sig Sauer M400s off the street. AKs are a dime a dozen, but the fully automatic capable Sigs were a very rare find. Representatives of the U.S. Attorney's Boston office witnessed the entire operation. A slam dunk by any measure.

Frank smiled and nodded in the direction of the applause as he walked toward the restroom. His bag sat on a table next to the door. Once inside, he locked the door and hung his coat on a rusty hook that clung to the wall by a single screw. He dropped the bag on the counter next to the sink, washed his hands, and splashed cold water on his face for several minutes, taking long, deep breaths with his eyes closed. Unzipping the bag, he grabbed a towel and dried his face and hands. Then he reached back into his bag, fishing around while avoiding his reflection in the small cloudy mirror that hung over the sink.

He squeezed three plastic nips of vodka into his mouth and buried the empty containers in the trash can. Then he quickly brushed his teeth and gargled with mouthwash. Minutes later he emerged from the bathroom with his hair slicked back and clean clothes on, just as the vehicle carrying the guns he had purchased was arriving. Frank started for the vehicle but saw his boss, Ashton Brown, making a beeline for the three cops who had cuffed him.

This can't be good.

He changed directions and arrived just in time to hear Brown's opening statement directed at the rookie, Tarentini.

"What the hell is wrong with you? Do you think you can go around tasing federal agents—or anyone else for that matter—just because you feel like it? I want your name and badge number, right now."

The sergeant stepped forward to speak but Brown held up a hand and cut him off.

"Save it, sergeant. I didn't ask for your input."

Brown got within inches from Tarentini's face and continued.

"You're all done. If I have anything to say about it, you'll have a hard time getting a job as a mall cop. That would have been excessive force by any standard. What the hell is your problem? Why the hell did you decide to use your Taser when you *knew* you were dealing with an undercover agent? I want an answer!"

"Because I told him to," said Frank as he approached Brown from behind. "Good job, kid. You did the right thing. I just wish I didn't have to tell you so many times. 'Tase me' is a pretty straight forward command, right?"

Frank smiled and shook hands with all three cops. Brown craned his neck and looked at him sideways.

"You mean to tell me that you told this officer to tase you?"

"Yeah. It was my fault anyway. I got carried away resisting and we had to make it look good. No time to wait. If they didn't escalate their use of force quickly, the Russians might have known something was up. Mission accomplished. That was great work, guys. Thanks."

Brown shook his head from side to side and folded his arms.

"You expect me to believe that, Frank? If that's the case, the audio should have picked it up. It didn't. So maybe you're lying to protect this guy."

"Technology fails all the time. Believe me, if he tased me on his own we'd be having a different conversation right now. These guys were on the ball and saved the sting. Good work, guys."

Frank looked at the sergeant, who knew that was his cue.

"I heard you, Frank. Sorry you had to say it a few times, but it took me by surprise. Thankfully, Tarentini took the initiative and got it done. Good save, kid."

Brown turned his back, took several steps away from the group, and bowed his head with his hands on his hips. Frank winked at the cops like the class clown playing a prank behind the teacher's back, promptly dropping the smile when Brown turned back toward the group.

"Get out of here. All of you. Just go."

The three cops didn't need to be told twice. They headed for the exit while Frank started walking toward the evidence truck.

"Where are you going, Frank? I just said you were all set. Go home."

"Just want to take a look at the hardware again."

"Not necessary. You've already seen it. Now your job is done. Let everyone else do theirs. Go home, Frank."

Frank wanted to argue the point but was distracted by thoughts of the vodka bottles and chilled glasses in his refrigerator at home. He decided to leave before he could push Brown too far or say something he might regret.

Just go home.

"Whatever you say, Boss."

In a few weeks this asshole won't be my problem anymore.

Nineteen

The alarm on Mark's phone started to chirp and vibrate at 4:45 a.m.

Not today.

He picked up the phone, killed the alarm, and set it back down on the night table, next to the loaded Sig Sauer P226 9mm that was rarely beyond arm's reach. Then he rolled over and immediately fell back asleep.

His eyes didn't open again until just before 7 a.m., when the room started to get warm. Sitting on the edge of the bed, he checked his phone for messages, although he knew that Doc and the Family would leave him alone as long as he was on leave. It also meant he would be out of the loop—something he was not accustomed to.

He opened the window and surveyed the backyard and forest that abutted the property—his property. It was mid-May. The grass was green but urgently needed to be cut. Agnes's multi-colored flowerbeds were in full bloom, and the edge of the forest was a dense wall of browns and greens.

After splashing cold water on his face and brushing his teeth, Mark turned and gazed into the full-length mirror, wearing only a pair of dark blue boxer shorts.

Twenty years and still in one piece. You are one lucky bastard. Take it and move on, or go back to work and keep pressing your luck? That is the question.

He lowered his gaze and settled his eyes on the thin purple scar that ran across his abdomen. The Family's surgeons had stitched him up as best they could, but Mark thought it still looked like a medieval C-section. Not to mention a constant reminder of darker times.

Berlin. Thanks again for the souvenir, Brother.

After opening the windows to air out the house, he plopped down on the sofa with a bowl of cereal and turned on the news. A drop-dead gorgeous blond woman with piercing blue eyes spoke into the camera from a studio plastered with patriotic themes.

Red, white, blue, and blonde.

"A gunman opened fire at a church picnic in a suburb of Minneapolis yesterday and detonated an explosive device as a group of brave parishioners attempted to overpower him. Fifteen people are dead and dozens of others injured. This is the third such attack on American soil in as many weeks. Is this the new normal? Is the president doing enough to keep Americans safe? We'll have an all-star panel ..."

Mark turned off the TV and finished eating his cereal in the kitchen booth. His phone whistled like a catcall from a construction worker, indicating a text message from Luci. He smiled, picked up his phone, and looked at the screen.

SENDER: Luci
MESSAGE: Google the "valley insider" if bored ... c u @ 8.
REPLY: Will do ... see you then.

Twenty minutes later, Mark was sprinting up the hill in shorts, running shoes, and a t-shirt loose enough to mask the 9mm strapped tightly to the small of his back. When he reached the top of the hill, he slowed to a trot, turned around, and let gravity do most of the work on the way back down to the house. On the tenth ascent he kept going, turned right at the end of the street, and headed toward downtown.

Twenty

Approximately one hundred miles north in New Hampshire, John McDonough popped two of his wife's anxiety pills into his mouth and chased them down with a glass of cold water. He closed his eyes and slowly rolled his head from side to side to loosen the muscles in his neck. Then he rolled his shoulders from front to rear a dozen times before moving on to his breathing exercises.

Inhale through the nose—one, two, three, four. Hold it—one, two, three, four. Exhale through the mouth—one, two, three, four. Inhale through the nose—one, two, three, four. Hold it—one, two, three, four. Exhale through the mouth—one, two, three, four. Inhale through the nose ...

His heart rate began to settle and his muscles slowly relaxed.

That's it. Just breathe. You are okay. Everyone is okay. Nothing is happening. It's all in your head. Just breathe and relax. Inhale through the nose—one, two, three, four. Hold it—one, two, three, four. Exhale through the mouth—one, two, three, four ...

Three quick knocks at the locked bathroom door shattered his focus.

"Honey, are you okay in there? I'm running out for my checkup so I'll see you later, okay?"

Linda. It's Linda. It's only Linda. Calm down. Inhale through the nose ...

McDonough bowed his head and his lightheadedness quickly turned to confused terror and tunnel vision. He reached blindly for the sink with his left hand to steady himself, staring at the Smith and Wesson M&P 9mm gripped tightly in his right hand, the barrel pointed at the thin wooden door. He did not remember having drawn the gun from its holster.

Breathe deeply, then answer. Breathe deeply, then answer. Breathe deeply, then answer.

She waited for a response with one palm flat against the door and the other pressed gently against her swollen belly. He put the gun back in its holster and supported himself on the sink with both hands.

"Yeah, I'm fine. Just catching up on some reading, Baby. I'm good."

"Okay. I'll see you tonight. Be safe out there, okay?"

"Yeah, okay. You too. Let me know how everything went. Sorry I can't go."

"Ok, I'll text you as soon as I'm out."

56

McDonough waited in the bathroom as Linda waddled her way down to the garage. She struggled with both hands to get the seat belt around her waist and adjusted the seat as best she could. When she started the car, the baby kicked hard.

"Okay, buddy. Calm down. Momma's ready to get this over with too. You'll be out soon enough. Work with me, little man."

As Linda pulled out of the garage, McDonough inched his way from the upstairs bathroom to the kitchen. Every few steps he paused and stood motionless while his mind raced, stretching a thirty-second walk into several long minutes. From the kitchen, he gazed out the sliding glass door at his soon-to-be-finished deck. Once it was completed, he would immediately move on to another major project. Anything was better than talking.

One day I'm gonna run out of shit to build.

McDonough made one last check of his uniform in the full-length mirror he had installed next to the front door. Then he pulled down the visor on his cap with one hand while measuring two fingers from the bridge of his nose with the other. Standing up straight, he pulled his shoulders back, forced a smile, and walked proudly and confidently to the patrol car parked in the driveway.

Twenty-one

Mark slapped the side of his mailbox as he completed his run and slowed to a brisk walk. The box popped open, revealing a thick stack of mail. With hands on hips, he walked around the cul-de-sac to cool down. It was hotter than he had imagined. The sweat-soaked t-shirt clung to his body. He made a mental note to add a runner's belt and water bottle next time to help him conceal his handgun.

After cooling down and stretching in the front yard, Mark started for the house, then remembered the mail. As he walked back toward the mailbox, out of the corner of his eye he noticed Kenny and his father walking slowly out their front door. They paused and then cautiously descended the front stairs, one step at a time, as Kenny coached and encouraged his father.

"Okay, Father. Left foot first … good. Now bring your right foot alongside your left … good. Now step off with your left foot just like me … good …"

Kenny helped his father lower his body into a lawn chair and sat down beside him. Mark waved as he walked across the lawn in their direction.

"Good morning," he said cheerfully.

Kenny waved back but said nothing. His father sat motionless, head down, staring at the grass. Kenny awkwardly shook Mark's extended hand without looking at him.

"Great day to sit outside, eh? Good morning, Mr. Harrington."

No response.

"Father's not very talkative today. Okay, Mark?" Kenny offered defensively.

"Understood. No worries, Kenny. How are you guys doing today?"

Kenny looked at him with an expression that said "*How the hell does it look like we're doing?*" Mr. Harrington sat motionless in long pants, a tucked-in button-down shirt, and a black ball cap. He could not have dressed himself.

Mark smiled and looked closer at the cap. Embroidered at the top, in thick block letters, were the words "Vietnam Veteran." In the center sat the red, white, and blue logo of the 82nd Airborne Division. If the word *Vietnam* had been missing, he could easily have been mistaken for a World War II veteran. Mr. Harrington's days of walking were numbered. Soon Kenny would be assisting him from room to room and from chair to chair.

Scattered on the cap were about half a dozen small pins. Mark's attention was drawn to the miniature Distinguished Service Cross and Ranger tab.

"Okay. Well, you gentlemen have a good day. I'll be around if you need me for anything."

Kenny nodded. Mark bent down, rested his hand on the old man's knee, and looked deep into his vacant eyes. "Rangers lead the way, Mr. Harrington," he said.

To Kenny's surprise, his father raised his head slightly and grunted. The old man breathed heavily and struggled to speak, his eyes focused on Mark's.

"Yes ... Rangers ... yes," he said, managing a faint smile.

Mark smiled back, but the flicker in Mr. Harrington's eyes lasted only a moment before going out like the pilot light on a gas stove. The blank expression returned and he lowered his eyes to the grass.

Mark stood up and turned his attention to Kenny, who looked as if he was fighting off a panic attack, his eyes focused on the top of the street. A police cruiser was rolling down the hill.

Luci?

He squinted through the sun and sweat to see who was driving, but all he could see was a man's expressionless face, the eyes masked by an oversized pair of dark-framed sunglasses. The officer stared in their direction as he made a slow, wide U-turn in the cul-de-sac.

"Do they come down here much?" asked Mark.

"Almost never," Kenny whispered. "Not without a reason."

The driver finished the turn and continued staring at the three men as the cruiser rolled slower and slower. When the car was nearly at a full stop, the officer acknowledged the three men with a slight raise of his chin before turning away and accelerating back up the hill.

Twenty-two

Amir had flown directly from Istanbul to Montreal. He smiled cheerfully at the other travelers as he waited patiently in the queue for Canadian citizens. The immigration officer who examined his documents had asked few questions but studied his demeanor closely.

"Three years is a long time. What were you doing in Turkey?"

"I started out teaching English but ended up helping to run a shelter for child refugees," he said, looking her square in the eyes.

"Did you travel anywhere else while you were abroad?"

"No. I was in Istanbul the whole time."

"Which shelter?" she asked.

"Pardon me?"

"Which shelter did you help run?"

"Saint Lucia's, not the one by the Blue Mosque, the one closer to the spice bazaar," he answered.

"Where did you teach English?"

"All over the city. I taught new hires for the Ministry of Tourism," Amir replied.

"Sounds like a fun job. Why did you switch?"

"We saw a lot of refugees on their way to Europe. Many of them were orphans. I wanted to help. So I did."

"Welcome home," she replied with a smile.

Within thirty minutes, Amir had retrieved his suitcase, cleared customs, and was on the street hailing a cab.

"Take me to the sleaziest place you know," he said with a smile to the Pakistani cab driver.

"Sorry, my friend. I take people where they want to go. Not where I think they want to go."

Amir stuffed one hundred American dollars through the slit in the glass. "Take me to the sleaziest place you know," he repeated.

The driver nodded.

Amir recalled what the head of the religious council had told him during his final holy meeting on the Syrian side of the Turkish border: "You may enter the country without incident but still be watched by the Canadian authorities. For two days you must look and act like a young infidel. Indulge like an infidel, but stay vigilant. Such behavior is not a sin, for you are not a Muslim when you commit those acts. Everything you do is in the service of God and therefore pure. But you must ensure that you have not been followed."

Two days later, he was sitting in the corner of a Saint Catherine's Street coffee shop with the worst hangover of his life. The two previous nights were a blurry montage of hookers and booze in his cheap motel. He was reminded of his wild, empty college days before Islam entered his life, and he felt sickened. He glanced at his watch. It was 10:30 on the nose.

Where is my facilitator?

At 10:45, an unremarkable man in his mid-thirties entered the shop.

Hello, brother. Is that you? Why have you kept me waiting so long?

The man approached the table and placed his hand on the back of a chair. "Is this seat taken, my friend? My feet are tired from the journey," he said.

"No," answered Amir. "I was saving it for someone but it doesn't look like she is coming. Please, sit down."

Meaningless chitchat ensued until the tables near them cleared out.

"Listen closely because I am only going to say this once. You are truly a blessed man. Your ultimate destination is Satan's capital city, Washington, D.C."

The words were balm to Amir's impatience.

Yes! I will strike at the birthplace of Satan!

"When do I depart?" he asked.

"Soon. Very soon. You know, warriors are usually tasked with a single mission. But you are tasked with two. The council must think very highly of you to bestow such an honor."

"Two? D.C. and then what?"

"No. You have it backwards. Later, I will show you the specific location of your next meeting, where you will learn more. For now I will tell you that your first mission is to quickly train local martyrs and send them to their glorious deaths. You will simply plan the missions and put them in motion. You will not participate. You are much too valuable to risk losing. And the glory you will bring to Allah in Washington will light up the skies!"

The facilitator registered Amir's elation with the news and decided to float an additional benefit. "You know, I met just this morning with another martyr for your mission, and she is as beautiful and pure as the morning dew. Perhaps she will be waiting for you in paradise, eh? Always ready to fulfill your every need."

Amir cut him off quickly.

"My own needs are irrelevant. I am here in the service of God, not to think of my own interests. What more do you have to share?" he asked.

"Wait ten minutes and meet me across the street in the blue BMW parked next to the subway. From there we will travel directly to your vehicle. The clothes and belongings in your hotel are no longer necessary. Everything you need is in the rental car. Leave this place in ten minutes and do not deviate from my instructions. Soon you will know everything that's expected of you."

The facilitator rose, pushed his chair in, and slowly exited into the crowded street.

Whatever mission I am given, I will deliver times ten and earn my place in history. Insha'Allah.

Twenty-three

Luci entered the playground, closed the chain link fence behind her, and smiled at the chorus of greetings.

"Luci! Luci's here!"

Half a dozen kids almost bowled her over as they gathered around, all vying for her attention.

"*Hola, amiguitos,*" she said before a round of hugs, kisses, and high-fives.

On the other side of the playground, a mother quietly extinguished her cigarette and stomped the butt into the sand with a sandaled foot. A young man casually drained the remaining contents from a can covered by a paper bag and tossed it into the garbage barrel. Several teenage girls left without saying a word.

Luci surveyed the scene, smiled widely, and gave a casual all-inclusive wave to the remaining adults. Most waved or nodded back; several simply looked away with blank expressions. Walking slowly into the middle of the playground with a gaggle of children in tow, she laughed and continued scanning the area.

Where are you, Julia?

As each kid received their precious moment of Luci's attention, the group of children dwindled to just two: a little girl who hadn't said a word or let go of Luci's hand since she arrived, and a little boy attached to her leg like a Koala bear. He held on tight and giggled as Luci limped slowly around the park.

An old woman spoke softly from her perch on a graffiti-filled bench as the trio passed by.

"*Ella no está aqua, mija.*" She's not here.

Luci stopped, looked down, and rubbed the little boy's head.

"*Dónde?*" *Where?* she asked the woman without looking at her.

"*No sé, posiblemente cerca del andén del tren con los otros niños.*" I don't know, maybe down by the train tracks with the other kids.

Luci reached down, scooped up the little boy, and repositioned him on her hip.

Gracias, Doña.

Twenty-four

Mark finished drying off and tossed the towel into the hamper in the corner of his room. He put on shorts and a t-shirt, retrieved his 9mm from the nightstand, and returned it to his waistband before sitting down comfortably in an old upholstered armchair positioned in the corner of the room.

With his back straight, feet flat on the floor, and hands resting gently on the armrests, Mark slowly inhaled through his nose until his lungs reached full capacity. Exhaling completely through his mouth, he closed his eyes and allowed his mind to drift. With each successive breath, his heart rate decelerated and the world around him started to dissolve ...

"Stop thinking about your thoughts."

"How do you not think about your thoughts? They're thoughts—that's what they do," Mark replied sarcastically.

"The key to meditation is to not struggle with your thoughts, Mark. Don't try to fight them, just acknowledge them as they float in and out of your consciousness and continue to breathe deeply," said Father Peck as he opened a small window, allowing the dense winter air to spill into the church "dungeon."

Mark sat upright atop a soft pillow in the middle of the concrete floor. Sweat from the preceding two-hour workout ran down his head in all directions.

"Fine. But I've been trying this for a few weeks and can't say it's doing much for me. I'm good for two or three minutes, tops. After that I start to get bored and frustrated. Can we do something else, please? What are we anyway? Are we Buddhists now or something?"

"No, we're just humans. And God has given this important gift to all of us, not just Buddhists. Close your eyes again, breathe, and let go completely."

Mark rolled his eyes before clenching them shut. Father Peck stood directly behind his student and continued coaching.

"Breathe in deeply and hold it for a moment. Don't force anything— just fill your lungs with air, then slowly let them deflate on their own. When you exhale through your mouth, expel all your inner angst, anxiety"—the priest paused to nudge his student between the shoulder blades with his knee—"and your sarcasm with it."

Mark suppressed a smile. Father Peck spoke softly as he paced back and forth with his head down and his hands clasped comfortably behind his back.

"Breathe in and fill your lungs. Feel your chest gently expand. When you're ready, exhale through your mouth and let go. Feel the floor underneath you dissolve as you lose touch with your physical body. Imagine you are floating on your back in an infinite sea of tranquility. A warm light shines from above. No

fears. No worries—only peace and tranquility. You are surrounded by the love of your creator. Tell your muscles to relax and let go. And breathe ..."

As his body started to relax, the tension in Mark's face slowly began to erode and the soreness from his training soon dissipated.

"Thoughts will appear. They may be happy, sad, angry, or scary. Simply acknowledge them, but do not struggle with or judge them. Just let them swim by like colorful tropical fish as you float effortlessly and bask in the warm glow of God's unconditional love. And breathe ..."

When Mark opened his eyes, Father Peck was seated on the floor directly in front of him with his back against the wall and a stopwatch in his hand.

"Much better. How do you feel?"

"Pretty good, actually. Different. How long was that?"

"Forty-two minutes, Mark. Forty-two minutes."

The silence was broken by the soft sound of wind chimes coming from the smartphone in Mark's lap, indicating that his forty-two minutes of meditation had ended. He opened his eyes and rolled his neck from side to side for several seconds before slapping the armrests with his hands and pulling himself to his feet.

Time to get unpacked.

Twenty-five

When things started to get loud and the boys became unruly, Julia looked at her two best friends and raised her eyebrows.

Want to leave?

They knew from experience that it was better to simply depart than to announce their intentions; doing so would just invite unwanted attention and the inevitable "oh, you're too good to hang out with us" bullshit from the loudmouths in the crowd. So they slipped away quietly and followed the narrow, well-trodden footpath up the hill toward the main road. From there, it was only a five- to ten-minute walk back to the projects.

When they crested the hill and emerged from the woods, they waited several minutes for a break in the heavy traffic so they could cross the street. A voice from behind them called Julia's name. She turned and saw Officer Luci Alvarez standing in the door of a small family-owned diner with a cup of coffee in her hand. She shook her head and muttered under her breath.

Man, what the fuck?

"Guys, I'll catch up to you. I just remembered I gotta get some stuff for my grandmother at the pharmacy. Don't wait. I'm in no rush to get home anyway."

Her friends shrugged their shoulders and continued on while Julia turned around and made her way to the diner.

"Didn't I tell you snitches get stitches around here?" she said as she slipped past Luci in the narrow doorway without making eye contact. Once inside, she took a seat, arms folded tightly, at a two-person table in the far corner, next to the rear exit.

Luci rolled her eyes at the comment.

This isn't exactly the inner city, Julia.

She took a slow sip of her coffee and remained in the doorway for a moment. Then she walked back to Julia's table.

"Are you hungry?" she asked.

"Honestly, are you trying to ruin my reputation or something?"

"Looks like you already got that covered if you're hanging out down there. I asked if you were hungry. I'm starving," Luci said, examining the menu.

"No."

Luci slowly ran her index finger down the numbered items on the menu, stopping her bright red nail whenever an item caught her eye.

"It all sounds good to me right now."

"Do I have to sit here all day watching you decide what to eat? I have a life, you know."

"Nope," answered Luci as she slid the menu to the end of the table and held up four fingers to the owner behind the counter in the kitchen.

"Number four?" he confirmed.

Luci nodded.

"So, what's new? How's everything going?" she asked.

"Everything's fine. Can I go now?"

Luci cocked her head to the side and smiled.

"Seriously? You can talk that way to me if you want, Julia. But I don't think I've ever been anything but courteous to you. If I'm wrong, I apologize. A girl deserves to be treated with respect, right?"

Julia averted her gaze for a moment before unfolding her arms and pressing her palms against the seat cushion at her sides.

"No, you haven't. Don't take it personally. I've been bitchy to everyone lately."

"How come?"

"No idea."

"How are things at home?"

"Home is fine. School sucks. Typical teenager stuff. Nothing to worry about and nothing I care to talk about. Again, don't take it personally."

Luci took the last sip of her coffee and smiled as an elderly waitress immediately appeared and refilled her cup.

"Okay. And I'm only going to say it once so don't freak out on me, but you're seventeen, soon to be eighteen. If you end up in the wrong place at the wrong time again, don't expect any leniency."

"From who? You?"

"Cops, prosecutors, the people in black robes—the system has little empathy and I don't have any favors left to cash in. I'll always be here for you if you need me, but you're basically an adult now. Act accordingly."

The waitress reappeared and gently placed Luci's sandwich and fries on the table in front of her. Julia reached across the table and snatched one of the fries.

67

"School's almost out—any summer plans? You'll be a senior when you go back. How cool is that? Have you given any thought to what you might do after graduation? College, maybe?"

"I waited this long to get out of school—going right back in is the last thing on my mind. Besides, I can't afford to even apply most places, and in case you haven't noticed, my family doesn't have the money to send me to BU."

Luci took a bite of her sandwich and held a napkin over her mouth as she chewed. Over Julia's shoulder, she saw a cruiser slowly drive by but didn't pick up the driver or car number. She sipped from a plastic water bottle before replying, punctuating her words with a more serious tone.

"Neither could my family. But I knew that at an early age, so I worked my ass off and got a scholarship. That's probably not an option for you right now, but there are other ways to make things happen."

"Like what?"

"Go to community college and work your ass off. Get good grades and keep applying for scholarships. Get a job and start saving money. I'll help you where I can, but these are decisions only you can make. It won't be easy. Hell, even with a full ride I still had to work to cover my bills. Life was anything but easy during those four years."

Julia stole another fry and craned her neck to survey the empty diner.

"It's just us," Luci said reassuringly.

"You're so beautiful, everything you do is glamorous. The way you're eating that nasty-ass sandwich is glamorous."

They both laughed and Julia took another nervous look around the diner as Luci continued.

"You know, when I was in college, guys asked me out all the time but I always said no. Had to."

"Why?"

"Partly because I was always busy either studying or working. But mostly, I was embarrassed and didn't want anyone to know that while they were out having fun, I was usually mopping floors and cleaning other people's toilets."

Julia put both palms on the table and leaned forward.

"*You* cleaned toilets? You? Not buying it—not with those nails. Besides, I'd rather be homeless than scrub other people's toilets."

Luci extended her arms, spread her fingers, and smiled at her hands.

"You're right about that. I didn't have these nails back then."

Julia sat back, folded her arms again, and cocked her head to one side.

"So what's your excuse now? How come you don't have tons of boyfriends?"

"How do you know I don't?"

"It's a small town. I'd know."

"Then I guess you already have your answer," Luci said with a smile.

Her cell phone vibrated loudly on the table next to her plate. She picked it up and checked the message.

SENDER: Sergeant Cromwell
MESSAGE: Return to station to take walk-in stolen property report

She waved at the waitress and mimicked signing the palm of her hand with an invisible pen. The waitress promptly placed the bill face down on the table as Luci wrapped up her conversation with Julia.

"We both have to go. But listen, Julia. Life has dealt you some bad cards, but that doesn't mean you have to fold your hand. Just play the cards you've been dealt as best you can."

Luci reached into her front pockets, produced a small box and a plain white envelope, and set both of them on the table. She tapped her hand first on the box and then on the envelope.

"This is for you and this is for your grandmother."

"What's is it?"

"Just a little gift from me to you, and some money so your grandmother can pay the phone bill and get the service reconnected. It's been out for a month. I'm not spying on you. I cosigned for the account, so they send me notices as well. Now get out of here—I have a reputation to protect too, you know."

Julia nodded, stuffed both items into her pockets, and started walking toward the front door. Halfway across the diner, she glanced out the window, noticed a cruiser parked across the street, and froze. She strained her eyes but could not clearly see the driver.

Creep alert.

She sighed deeply, turned around, and quickly left the diner through the rear exit.

Luci watched her leave, then flipped her check over. It said the amount due was zero. She put ten dollars on the table anyway and walked toward the kitchen to thank the owner.

Sergeant Cromwell watched from his cruiser across the street. He checked the time on his watch and made a mental note before putting the car in drive and heading toward the projects.

Twenty-six

When Julia arrived home, her grandmother was in the kitchen cooking enough rice, beans, and chicken to feed an army. She kissed her gently on the cheek and set the envelope on the counter.

"*Te lo manda Luci, Abuela.*" *Luci sent you this.*

She climbed the stairs to the second-floor bathroom and locked the door behind her. Then she pulled the small box from her pocket and opened it, finding a handwritten note and a tiny black pouch.

Julia,
You need the space to become your own person so I won't be checking in on you as much. If you need me, I will always be here for you. Until then, I've asked this little guy to watch over you. —Luci

Julia opened the drawstring on the pouch, held it upside down, and shook it gently until a silver necklace with a guardian angel charm slid into the palm of her hand. She grasped the clasp with two fingers, dangled the gift in front of her eyes, and smiled. Then came the tears.

Thank you, Luci.

Twenty-seven

Ghassan muted the television in the corner of the small dining room while shaking his head and muttering something under his breath in Arabic. Balancing the red tray in front of him, he wobbled his large, seventy-two-year-old frame over to the booth in front of the window. The tray pitched back and forth as he walked, but miraculously the drinks did not spill.

After placing the tray on the table and wiping his sweaty forehead with a dirty handkerchief, he squeezed himself into the booth across from Officer John McDonough.

"How long have I lived here, John?" he asked in good but heavily accented English.

McDonough grabbed his chicken shawarma and drink from the tray.

"A long time. As long as I can remember."

"That's right! A long time, right? Since long before this violence became so commonplace," he said, pointing angrily at the television.

McDonough finished chewing and took a long, slow sip of fruit punch.

"What happened now?" he asked.

"Same shit. Yesterday I was sweeping in front of the restaurant and a car full of teenagers drove by me chanting "USA! USA! USA!" I've been an American citizen longer than they been alive. But they are just stupid kids. Their parents worry me more."

Ghassan pulled the remote control out of his apron and clicked off the TV. "How many people live in this town? Four thousand? Five thousand?"

"About that."

"When Aaeesha—Jesus bless her soul—and I came here from Beirut, it was half that. We came to get away from wars and live in peace. Live free or die, right? And I opened this place—the great Baba Ghassan's! Best shawarma in all New Hampshire."

McDonough smiled and nodded as he continued to chew.

"But over last few years, people have started treating me different. They stop talking when I enter stores and constantly ask me what I think about terrorists and Islam and all kinds of stupid shit that has nothing to do with me. When I tell them I've been a Christian my whole life, I can see in their eyes that they don't believe me. None of them know anyone who was ever killed by terrorists, but I lost many friends and family to these pigs in my life. And it kills me that I have to answer for them."

Ghassan paused, turned his head toward the kitchen, and shouted loudly and unexpectedly.

"Yasir! Yasir! Come out here!"

McDonough, startled, dropped his thick plastic cup, spilling his remaining fruit punch onto the dark wooden table. When the puddle reached the edge, blood-red droplets fell in slow motion before bursting one at a time against the white tiled floor. He sat frozen, eyes fixed on the spill, until the sound of Ghassan's voice brought him back to the present.

"And bring a towel!"

"Shit, I'm sorry, Ghassan," he said, trying to shake off the fog.

"No problem. I need to keep this kid busy anyway."

The kitchen door swung open, and a thin male in his early twenties entered the dining room, wearing a Yankees cap cocked to one side. The cord from his headphones ran underneath his t-shirt to the iPhone in his front pocket. A small piece of paper towel dangled from one hand as the other danced to the hip-hop playing loudly in his ears.

Ghassan shouted louder this time.

"I said bring a towel, not a tissue! A towel, Yasir! How can you clean this mess with that?" he said, pointing at the spill with both hands.

Yasir nodded, spun around to the beat of the music, and kicked open the swinging door to the kitchen.

"And stop kicking my door!"

McDonough oscillated his gaze between the kitchen and Ghassan but said nothing.

"Don't be deceived by appearances, John. He is even dumber than he looks."

Yasir quickly reappeared with two white kitchen towels, headphones now wrapped around his neck. He spread the first towel out over the table, let the second drop to the floor, and used his foot to wipe up the mess. McDonough stared at the table as a small red spot appeared in center of the towel and quickly spread. He redirected his attention out the window to his cruiser in the parking lot.

"This is Yasir, my cousin's grandchild. He is staying with me for a while."

"Good to meet you," said McDonough with a nod.

"Whassup?" answered Yasir with a raise of his chin.

Ghassan stifled the urge to burst out angrily again and spoke instead in a slow, deliberate tone.

"Whassup? Is that how a man speaks to another man? Can you not see he is an authority figure? Not to mention older than you, a Marine Corps veteran, and soon to be blessed by God with a son of his own. Yasir, if you want to be taken seriously in this country, you have to be a serious man."

"Sorry, Ammu. It's nice to meet you, sir," Yasir said with a smile as he extended his hand to McDonough.

"Same here."

Ghassan waited for Yasir to finish cleaning the mess and return to the kitchen before speaking.

"He is dumb as a bag of falafel, but I try not to be too hard on him because he's been through a lot. His father moved their family—all Christians—from Lebanon to Syria for a job just before the fighting started. Almost a year ago, Yasir went to the capital to do errands for his father. By the time he returned, the whole neighborhood was blown to shit by explosions and fighting. Most of his family was dead and his two little sisters, whom he practically raised, had been taken as prisoners. So he walked over fifty miles to the Lebanese border. He's stupid, but it's not his fault. He just needs direction and a purpose, anything besides the hip-hop that now tortures me day and night."

They were both chuckling at that last phrase as the radio on McDonough's belt came to life.

"Station to Officer McDonough."

"McDonough," he answered.

"Can you please swing by the cemetery and speak to the caretakers about some headstones that were vandalized?"

"Roger, en route."

He sprung to his feet and reached for his wallet.

"Go, it's on me, John. Headstones? Jesus, help us. Is nothing sacred these days?" said Ghassan as he wiggled his way out of the booth.

McDonough peeled a ten-dollar bill from his money clip, slapped it on the table, and spoke over his shoulder on the way out the door.

"Thanks, Ghassan. Have a good one."

As the officer reached for the cruiser's door handle, he caught a glimpse of his reflection in the window and froze again. The front of his heavily starched white uniform shirt was splattered with dark red stains. He breathed deeply through his nose and reassured himself as he slowly opened the door and slid behind the wheel.

Deep breath and exhale. Deep breath and exhale. It's not blood. It's not blood. It's not blood.

McDonough put the cruiser in drive and pulled away from the diner while adjusting the rear-view mirror. As he turned left onto Main Street and headed toward the cemetery, he caught a brief glimpse of Ghassan and Yasir standing expressionless, side by side, staring at him out the front window of Baba Ghassan's.

It's not blood, John. It's. Not. Blood. And this is not Fallujah.

Twenty-eight

Andy O'Rourke was at the tail end of his story when Mark and Luci quietly entered the Witch Hunt. He stood on the raised hearth of the fireplace, surrounded by a sea of eager townspeople who hung on his every word in complete silence. Early in his presentation there had been one distraction, the grumbling of an old ice machine in the corner of the bar, but after seeing a few annoying glances, Lee Carter, the bar owner, silenced it by stepping on its cord with one foot and kicking the electrical socket with the other.

A waitress waved to Luci from the far end of the bar.

"Follow me," Luci told Mark.

Mark obeyed the instruction and stayed close behind Luci as they weaved their way in and out of the silent multitude of men and women standing shoulder to shoulder. The waitress pointed to a small table in the corner of the bar. Luci mouthed *thank you*. Then she held up two fingers with one hand and brought the thumb of her other hand up to her lips, indicating that she wanted two beers. The waitress acknowledged the order with a wink and a nod.

Mark sat with his back to the wall and scanned the room. He leaned across the table and whispered to Luci, "Is it always like this here?"

"Only when he's on stage."

Andy moved slowly from one end of the fieldstone hearth to the other as he played to the room, his words charming the crowd. Luci and Mark did not notice the waitress as she quietly set two beers on the table without taking her eyes off the show. Andy's voice intensified as he built to the climax. He paused methodically after each line to let his words float through the air and melt into the crowd.

"The naked man lay flat on his back, covered by a wooden plank that left only his head exposed ... the crowd heckled and shamed him as their demands for a confession grew louder and louder ... town officials stacked the largest stones and boulders they could find on top of the wooden plank ... his face turned red as a tomato and you could hear his bones start to crack ... witnesses say his eyes looked like they were going to pop right out of their sockets ... his tongue was squeezed right out of his mouth and oozed down the side of his face ... the sheriff used his cane to tuck it back in ... and just as it seemed that the old man was about to release his final breath and cross over to the afterlife, he mustered every ounce of his remaining energy and tried to speak … the interrogator silenced the jeering townspeople and knelt next to the accused … he put his ear against the dying man's mouth and strained to hear what he could only imagine would be a full confession … an admission that he had indeed willingly entered into an evil pact with the Prince of Darkness himself … he struggled for oxygen … then he opened his mouth and offered only two simple words for his executioners … 'More weight!' "

The crowd burst with laughter at the punch line. Andy slowly bent down, picked up his empty glass, and raised it high above his head.

"And on that note—more beer, barkeep!"

He leapt from the hearth and disappeared into the crowd. The laughter faded into applause and the rapping of knuckles on the tables and bar.

Mark turned his attention back to Luci.

"He should run for mayor."

"He'd win."

The audience dissipated as people took their seats and spread out around the bar. A third of the crowd left immediately. Lee Carter stood by the door and grinned at them as they exited.

"Good night. Thanks for coming. Come again. Thank you, great to see you all."

It wouldn't kill you to buy a drink and eat some wings.

Twenty-nine

"So what happened? Why did you guys break up?" asked Luci, slowly draining the last sip of her beer.

"I don't think I would characterize it as a breakup. It was probably over before it even started. As always, I had to travel for work. When I was gone, she had more shoes under her bed than a Holiday Inn."

Luci struggled unsuccessfully not to laugh and quickly brought a napkin to her mouth to keep the beer from escaping. Mark smiled widely.

"It's funny now. At the time, not so much."

"I still can't believe you dated a stripper."

"Luci, please—*exotic dancer*. And she claimed to be retired. Anyway, now that I've thoroughly embarrassed myself by sharing my awful judgment, what's your story? How come you're still single?"

Luci finished wiping her mouth and looked at the lipstick-stained napkin.

"I've had some dates over the years and maybe one or two guys I would call boyfriends, but no one who ever had any real potential."

"How come?"

"Who knows, Mark? And I don't lose any sleep over it. Maybe it's the same as with you—the job gets in the way. I don't want to date another cop because I don't want my whole life to be about the job. And civilians can't seem to ever get past it. Being a cop is a big part of me, but not all of me. Get it?"

"More than you can imagine."

Luci's expression turned sour and she rolled her eyes.

"Luuuci! You have some 'splaining to do!" said an approaching voice.

Mark turned to see a man in his mid-thirties with a beer glass in one hand and dragging a chair behind him with the other. On top of his wavy brown hair sat a pair of dark-framed, oversized sunglasses. Two days of scruff covered his handsome face, and his untucked blue oxford cloth shirt was mostly unbuttoned, revealing a white tank top underneath. He put his glass on the table, spun the chair around with one hand, and sat down uninvited. Then he leaned back and clasped his hands behind his thick head of hair.

"Lee tells me there's been more graffiti," he said matter-of-factly.

"What do you want, Charlie? Can't you see we were having a discussion?" she said with a nod in Mark's direction.

"I'm just asking a question, Luci. Most of us know you'll eventually figure it out and save the day. Others say putting you in that position was a mistake because of your background. But rest assured, the people who matter know that's not true and you have our support."

"My background? What that's supposed to mean?"

"Your ethnicity, whatever. Those people don't matter anyway. Just forget it. I still have some influence down there, so let me know if I can help. There's some benefit to being an outsider to the community you police. You know, not being so familiar. But I'm sure you're doing a great job. Besides, it ain't exactly Queens down there, right?"

Mark watched as Luci's breath quickened and her chest started to rise and fall visibly. This guy was pushing her buttons, but she shrugged it off as quickly as it came on and forced a smile.

"And I thank you for that. It's nice to know you've got my back," she replied with a hint of sarcasm so slight Mark knew it must have been for his benefit.

The man turned his attention to Mark, who was scanning the crowd.

"Who's your friend?"

"Mark this is Charlie Worth. Charlie, Mark Landry."

Mark slowly turned his head and the two men locked eyes. Charlie offered his hand.

"Good to meet you, Mark. You on the job?"

"On the job? You mean am I a cop? No. No. Civilian. I'll leave the dangerous stuff to the professionals," he answered, politely shaking Charlie's extended hand.

"Yeah, I know what you mean. I spent five years in Queens before transferring to this country club. Suffice it to say I had a lot of close calls. This place is a cakewalk," he said, redirecting his gaze to Luci. "As long as you can handle a little graffiti."

"I can only imagine," replied Mark.

"So, what do you do?"

"Me? You mean for a living? I'm an environmental cleanup consultant."

"Oh, okay. Like what?" pressed Charlie in a slightly less friendly tone.

"It's boring, mostly paperwork, and hard to explain." He leaned forward slightly before continuing. "But let's call it quality control."

Charlie smiled and shrugged his shoulders.

"Sounds good to me. God knows we need good people to do that stuff too."

A woman approached Charlie from behind and yanked the sunglasses from his head.

"I can see why you need these, Charlie. It's wicked dark in here," she said with a thick Massachusetts accent.

Charlie brought a hand to his head and spun around in his chair to face the woman. His neck and face started to turn red.

"Has he mentioned Queens yet?" she asked rhetorically in Luci and Mark's direction. Luci smiled while Mark watched, expressionless.

"Can I have my glasses please, Wendy?" Charlie asked through clenched teeth.

"Shooah. All you gotta do is leave these nice people alone. I'll be at the other side of the bah. If you want 'em, come and get 'em."

She winked at Luci, nodded at Mark, and walked to the other side of the Witch Hunt, wearing a proud grin from ear to ear.

Charlie shook his head back and forth, his mounting anger and embarrassment betrayed by a reddening face and neck. He stood up, pushed in his chair, and left without another word.

"My coworkers," said Luci.

"Yeah, I figured that out on my own. Is he the exception?"

"Exception to what?"

"The night I arrived, you said you liked just about everyone in the department. I'm guessing he's the exception."

Luci nodded vigorously and displayed an exaggerated look of surprise.

"I'm impressed. I guess you do listen. Point for Mark. And what do you make of him after this very brief encounter?"

Mark finished his beer and set the glass on the table.

"He's pretty much a douchebag."

She stared at him with disappointment.

"Minus two points. Do you try to be obnoxious or does it come naturally?"

Mark dropped his shoulders and head. "I'm sorry."

"For what?"

Here we go again. She's going to make me say it.

"Luci, I am sorry for being crude, classless, and dismissive of your question. May I take another whack at it? Please?"

"Yes, you may," she answered approvingly.

"Okay. He still hangs his hat on the few years he spent in a tougher environment before joining your department. He is probably the only cop here with that experience, but there are likely a few ex-military cops on the force who he thinks are somehow his peers. I also suspect that he's the guy you replaced as community liaison, because he's busting your chops about something that probably didn't start until after he left the position or he wouldn't be mentioning it … he seemed to enjoy pointing it out to you. Probably he was replaced because there were too many complaints that he was alienating people. He clearly has an issue with women, especially authority figures like the one who just snatched his glasses. My guess is that she outranks him because he didn't go after her in the same passive-aggressive style that he used with you. Maybe he has issues stemming from his relationship with his own mother … who knows. How am I doing so far?"

"I'm not sure about his relationship with his mother, but the rest of it is perfect. You get your points back. But you did leave out one thing."

"What's that?"

"That he's pretty much a douchebag," she said in a low whisper as she leaned across the table. "I have to go to the lady's room, and then I'm ready to leave whenever you are. Here comes your friend."

Mark watched as Luci stood up and disappeared into the crowd. He chuckled to himself as several other men casually glanced away from their dates to follow Luci with their eyes.

Does she even notice the gawking? Or is she just used to it?

"Mark Landry!" boomed a voice from behind as two large hands came down on his shoulders and shook them excitedly.

Mark stood and turned. Andy O'Rourke was looking down on him with his arms spread wide open.

"Give me a hug, little man!"

"Little man? You're not looking down because I'm little. You're looking down because you're part—"

Andy pulled him in tightly before he could finish.

"Part sasquatch," Mark said in a muffled voice, face pressed firmly against the big man's chest.

"Still in one piece, I see! Great to have you home. How long will you be around? Are you staying for good this time? Where'd Luci go? Are you two still an item—or an item again? What have you been doing with yourself? Can you talk about it or would you have to kill me? Say, can you come by and speak to my social studies classes sometime about your experiences? Probably not, right? Scratch that. Talk to me! Tell me something good, my friend!"

"Good to see you too, Andy. You look great. Teaching and coaching football, I hear?" Mark replied.

"Yup. Social studies chair, assistant varsity football coach, raconteur and bon vivant! Life is good, my friend. I do this every Thursday. I bring in the bodies and Lee pays my tab at the end of the night, as long as I don't buy too many drinks for others. He's a nice guy but he squeezes every nickel until the buffalo farts, if you know what I mean."

"Sounded like a great story, but I missed the beginning because we got here a little late and had to park way down the street. Was all of that true?"

"Most of it," he answered with a wink.

Luci reappeared at Andy's side and wrapped one of her arms around his thick waist, her lips bright red again with fresh lipstick.

"How's it going, Coach?"

"*Hola, Señora! Cómo está usted?*" replied Andy, unsuccessfully trying to mask his abundant gringo accent.

"I'm good. Nice job tonight. You have a gift, my friend."

"It's about time you came out to see me. I was starting to think you didn't like me. And I'm glad you dragged this guy with you. It's great to see the two of you together again."

Mark beamed with approval at the comment, but Luci glared back at Andy with her best poker face. He sensed the awkwardness.

"Well, some lucky guy better make an honest woman out of you soon. You should be a grandmother by now."

Luci exhaled deeply and shook her head while Mark looked away to scan the bar. Andy dropped his head and groaned out loud.

"You know, I'm an idiot. Please don't listen to me. I'm great up there," he said, pointing to the stone hearth with his chin, "but sometimes I really suck down here. I'm sorry, Luci. Please don't read into that comment too much. I missed yet another excellent opportunity to keep my big mouth shut."

She squeezed his waist one last time before letting go.

"Don't sweat it, Andy. You're a man. You can't help it."

"Touché, Madame."

"Mark, I have to talk to someone for a second. After that, let's get out of here. I have an early day tomorrow."

Both men watched as Luci walked across the room and leaned over the bar to speak with Lee Carter. Andy excitedly broke the silence.

"Hey, as part of the annual Independence Day festivities this Fourth of July, the town is having a special recognition ceremony for its veterans on Founders Field. It's going to be a big to-do, complete with marching band, cheerleaders, the whole football team, and yours truly as speaker. I know there's no way you'll sit as one of the honored," he said, pointing his beefy index finger at Mark. "But you should swing by and at least check it out. I've been pushing this idea for years. The town elders have finally given in."

"Yeah, if I'm around I'll definitely check it out."

Behind the bar, Lee Carter nodded and Luci shook his hand. Then she turned around, made eye contact with Mark, and motioned toward the door with her head.

"Looks like my bus is leaving. It's good to see you, man. Let's get together soon and catch up, okay?"

"You got it. And please apologize to Luci again for me. I didn't mean anything by that stupid comment."

"I will, but you shouldn't worry about it too much. Something tells me she's used to it."

Andy watched Mark weave his way through the crowd toward the door.

That's what I'm afraid of.

Thirty

"Do you really have an early day tomorrow? Or did you just want to get me alone?"

Luci ignored the question and searched for the window control with her soft fingers. Cool night air filled the car. She cautiously turned onto Main Street and checked the rear-view mirror before speaking.

"When it starts to get late, I go home. I'd rather not be around when people start getting louder and looser. Besides, I can only take being stared at for so long before it starts to get creepy."

"I wasn't sure if you noticed all that."

"Seriously? Do you think women are idiots, Mark?"

He held his hands up over his head in mock surrender.

This is not going well.

"Don't shoot. I give up!"

Luci laughed and kept one hand on the steering wheel while she ran the other through her straight, black hair. Mark watched and wondered if he would ever get another chance to hold a handful of it against his face and inhale slowly through his nose.

If angels exist, I bet they smell like her.

"Sorry, I've been a bit annoyed since the *Valley Insider*'s latest."

Mark furled his eyebrow.

"What's that?"

"I texted you about it earlier today. Print newspapers are dying. So three *journalists*," she said, momentarily taking her hands off the wheel to make air quotes, "got together and created the *Valley Insider*, an online local news site. It's a cross between a low-budget *Boston Globe* and an even lower-budget *National Enquirer*. They produce mostly pseudo-news and baseless gossip, but hey, it's a free country. Get my tablet from the glove box and check out their latest.
"

Mark removed the tablet and closed the compartment. He pulled up the browser, and the *Valley Insider* loaded automatically.

"You hate it so much you made it your homepage?" he asked.

"I never said I hated it. I just don't like reading about myself."

He scrolled to the latest post and read the headline aloud: "Growing Concern over Liaison Officer."

Under the headline was a picture of Luci with a smile on her face, one arm extended, with the palm of her hand resting flat on Latin King graffiti. The accompanying article was unnecessary; the picture said it all.

"Don't read it—at least, not to me. I already know it by heart. Complete B.S., anonymous sources, a pure hit piece. This is the fourth post about me in the last month, and the bitch has never even asked me for a comment. Not that I would give one, but you'd think she would at least want to give the impression she was a professional journalist."

Mark scrolled to locate the author.

"Lisa Lemon?" he asked.

"That's her."

"Two-hundred thirty-eight comments."

"Don't read those either. They boil my blood."

Mark flicked the screen with one finger and quickly scanned some of the comments.

"Jesus, some of these are pretty awful. Have you guys checked out any of these people?"

Luci rolled her eyes and laughed out loud.

"Sounds like a great idea—investigate anyone who says something on the Internet that we don't like."

"Not everyone—just the ones making the threats. Some of these are pretty explicit."

"Welcome to the twenty-first century, Mark. Control the things you can, try to ignore the things you can't. Know what pisses me off most? That picture looks like it could have come from my dash cam."

"Yeah, what about those body cams? Are those always on or what?"

"No. The department and the town are still trying to figure that out. For now, it's up to us to turn them on at our discretion. Which means some cops always have them on while others, like Charlie, never do. Next subject, please."

He returned the tablet to the compartment and seized the opportunity to redirect the conversation.

"So where are we headed? Are you going to show me your place?"

"You must be out of your mind, Landry. The only reason I drove you is because I believed you when you said you didn't have a license. Now I'm thinking I should have left you back there with Andy."

"Why didn't you?"

"Because you'd probably end up getting in a tussle and I'd prefer to just drive you home now rather than be woken up and have to get you at the station."

"A tussle? Hmmm … I don't think I've ever been in one of those. Or a fight, if that's what you're saying."

"You've never been in a fight?" she asked incredulously.

"Not one."

"I don't believe you. And you spent half your youth training in a basement with Father Peck. I suppose he was teaching you how to cook."

Mark opened his window and let his arm hang outside the car.

"Peck didn't teach me how to fight. He taught me how to survive."

"What's the difference?"

"Quite a bit. Nobody wins a fight. I have never willingly fought anyone in my entire life, and that's the truth. I avoid trouble like the plague, and the few times it has found me, I've walked away. I would never lie to you, Luci."

Neither spoke until she was about to turn onto Chestnut Lane.

"Just let me out at the top of the hill. I could use some air."

"You sure?"

"Yeah, it's nice out too."

"No problem," she said as she brought the car to a stop. "Did you mean what you just said?"

"About what—fighting? Yeah, Peck beat that one into me pretty good. Only idiots fight. How do you think I've maintained my good looks so well? By not getting punched in the face—that's my secret."

"I believe you about fighting. I meant about never lying to me."

Mark locked his eyes on hers and leaned forward.

"I have no reason to lie to you, Luci. I never have and I never will. Scout's honor," he said, holding up two fingers.

She leaned away and smirked.

"You were never a scout. Get out of my car. And please get a driver's license because I don't plan on being your taxi."

Luci winked. Mark felt lightheaded as his pulse quickened and all the blood rushed below his waist.

Don't do it, Mark. Don't blow it. Be patient and get the hell out of the car.

"Thanks for the lift. I guess I'll see you when I see you."

Thirty-one

Hector Gonzales was already running ten minutes late when Lourdes stopped the car in the alley next to the abandoned warehouse. He pulled down the passenger-side visor and examined his face closely in the small mirror. After wiping the inside of both nostrils with his index finger, he squeezed several drops of Visine into each eye and pulled two mints from his pocket. He was sweating profusely, but his mouth was bone dry.

"You want me to wait for you here, *mi amor*?" she asked.

"Fuck no. I got business so just get out of here fast."

"Can you give me a little bump for later then?"

He bent down, pulled up his pant leg, and fished around in his sock.

"Take this and get the fuck out of here. And don't talk to nobody, right?"

"Whatever you say, baby. Just don't forget about me."

"Just a little bit longer and I'll have enough for both of us to disappear forever, okay? Just trust me, Lourdes. I know what I'm doing."

He watched the car until it was safely out of sight. Then he turned and sprinted two blocks in the opposite direction to the real meeting site.

Never trust a puta.

Hector, known in the Almighty Latin King and Queen Nation as King Heavy, slipped into the building through a broken window and stopped to catch his breath. He glanced at the illuminated hands on his fake gold Rolex—he had pawned a real one for quick cash months earlier—and forced his skinny frame to start climbing the stairs toward the meeting room on the top floor.

Relax. Breathe. Nobody knows.

He paused on the fourth-floor landing and nodded to the two Kings who were standing in the shadows, handguns at their sides and index fingers carelessly on the triggers.

"*Amor de Rey, hermanos,*" he said before continuing the arduous climb.

"*Amor de Rey,*" replied both in unison.

When he reached the tenth floor his heart was pumping so hard that he did not hear the same greeting from the final two Kings guarding the door to the meeting. Instead of returning the salutation, he simply waved his hand, motioning for them to get out of the way.

The sentry on the left considered standing his ground until the other leaned in and whispered in his ear.

"*Recuerda, son primos.*" *Remember, they're cousins.*

"*Verdad. Perdóname.*" *Right. Sorry.*

The first sentry twisted the knob, pushed open the door, and stood off to the side.

"*Amor de Rey,*" the sentries said again in unison.

Hector wiped his forehead with both hands and used the sweat to slick back his hair before he walked nervously through the door without saying a word. The sentries closed the door behind him, shook their heads, and refocused their attention on looking out the large window to the street below.

Thirty-two

Agent Frank Tagala stumbled out his door and nearly fell down the front steps but grabbed the railing with both hands to catch himself. He swayed back and forth for several seconds on bent knees. Then he regained his balance, descended the stairs, and shuffled his way down the crumbling brick walkway toward the car—leaving the front door to his house wide open. Mark slowed his pace and watched as Frank crossed the cul-de-sac.

Not looking so good tonight, Mr. Tagala.

Mark wanted nothing more than a beer and an episode of *Magnum P.I.* before going off to bed, but when he climbed the steps to the side door he paused and turned back to watch his neighbor.

Frank stood next to his car and fumbled with a large metal ring full of keys. He cursed aloud, dropped the keys several times, and finally realized that he had the wrong keychain. Stumbling and mumbling, he started back toward the house but made it only a few steps before catching his foot on a loose brick and falling sideways onto the lawn. He lay on his back and flailed his arms and legs, eventually flipping over onto his stomach. From that position, after a few deep breaths, he pushed himself off the ground with both palms while slowly bringing his grass-stained knees up under his body, one at a time. Then he cautiously stood up and continued the journey.

Mark shook his head and exhaled forcefully through his mouth.

I guess Magnum will have to wait.

Frank had just let go of the handrail at the top of his front stairs and was taking baby steps through the open door as Mark approached.

"How's it going, Mr. Tagala?"

Startled by the voice, Frank fell face forward into the house with a loud thud. Mark jogged the last few paces and bounded up the stairs. When he reached the top, he froze in place and held his hands up in front of him. Frank lay flat on his back with one arm extended toward the open door—Glock 27 held firmly in his hand, trigger finger fully extended along the side of the gun frame.

"Hold your fire, Mr. Tagala. It's Mark from next door. Just relax. I was walking by when I heard you fall. It's your neighbor Mark—Agnes's kid. No need for the gun."

Frank lay still and did not move the gun, trained on Mark's upper chest.

"Please lower your weapon, Mr. Tagala. I'm here to help, or if you want I'll mind my own business and leave. Either way, you're going to have to lower that gun first. Why don't you do it right now. Look, I'm not armed—my hands are right here."

He waved his empty hands over his head playfully and managed a smile.

Come on, Buddy. Put the gun down. This is how accidents happen. If your finger moves just one millimeter toward that trigger, you won't be down for breakfast tomorrow. So just drop the gun and save us both the trouble.

Mark smiled even wider and slowly lowered his hands to his sides, bringing his shooting arm closer to the holster tucked behind his right hip.

"Do you need a ride somewhere? I can take you anywhere you want to go," he offered. "Where were you thinking of heading?"

Frank muffled a belch and tried to suppress his nausea. But the pressure mounting in his gut was slowly pushing a fireball up his esophagus and into his throat. He turned his head to the side and heaved a few ounces of bloody acid onto the hardwood floor before lowering the gun.

"Sorry, kid. Habit. I don't like anyone sneaking up on me," said Frank as he slowly pulled himself to his feet and clumsily reholstered his gun.

"Glock 27?" asked Mark.

"What? Yeah, it's a 27. Why?"

"Standard issue—so you must still be on the job, right? DEA or US Marshal? I can't even remember, it's been so long."

"ATF, son. ATF."

"Cool. So do you need a ride somewhere, Frank? May I call you Frank?"

"Frank's fine. I was heading for the liquor store but forgot my keys inside."

"Well, I hate to be the bearer of bad news, but it's almost 11:25. In the People's Republic of Massachusetts, that means you'll have to wait until tomorrow."

"Shit," muttered Frank as he wandered into the kitchen and sat down at the table, which looked as if it hadn't been cleaned in months.

Mark looked around the main entrance and family room. Dirty clothes and trash were littered about the house. He had been too distracted before by the gun in his face to notice the strong stench of urine in the air. The mess and smell got worse as he followed Frank into the kitchen.

"Kid, open the freezer and see if there's any more vodka," Frank said without taking his eyes off the empty glass on the table in front of him.

A dozen frosted glasses jingled on the door shelves as Mark opened the freezer. Half a bottle of vodka sat open on the top shelf.

Did you miss this one, Frank? Or did you know that it wouldn't be enough?

"Here we go, Frank. There's enough here for a nightcap."

Mark approached the table slowly with the bottle in his left hand, keeping his right hand free to draw his weapon if the booze in Frank's veins made him do something stupid. Guns and drunks don't mix, but Mark figured that trying to disarm an old-school agent would likely make things worse than simply managing the risk. The last drop had barely reached the glass before Frank snatched it from the table and guzzled its contents in one long gulp. He slammed the empty glass onto the table, almost smashing it.

"Again."

Mark nodded, refilled the glass, and watched Frank take a deep breath and drain it again, this time swishing the vodka between his teeth for several seconds like mouthwash before swallowing.

Holy shit, what a fucking train wreck.

"There's only a little bit left, Frank. Might as well just kill it, right?"

Frank finished the final glass and let out a long, guttural moan.

"You know, you may want to have your stomach looked at. Stressful jobs like yours can cause ulcers if you're not careful."

"The job's almost done, kid. Just a few more weeks and that little fucker will be nothing to me."

I'll just assume "that little fucker" refers to a boss of some kind. Raging drunks tend not to get along very well with authority.

"Retiring? That's great news. Any plans after that?" asked Mark, doing his best to sound interested.

Frank sat silently, examining the empty vodka bottle in his hand. Mark waited a few more seconds.

"Okay, unless you need something, I'm going to head home now."

No response.

"Good night, Frank."

You're not my problem anyway.

Mark locked the front door behind him, descended the front steps, and cut across the lawn. When the empty bottle shattered against Frank's kitchen floor, he simply glanced at his watch and kept walking.

Just in time for Magnum.

Hector walked quickly to the center of the large room to join the circle. He patted two Kings on their shoulders and waited as they reluctantly made room for him between them. Then he got down on one knee like the rest of the Supreme Council and tried to blend in. Tardiness for official meetings usually earned a group beating, but Hector was more slippery than most and knew how to leverage his relationship with Carlos. Unfortunately for him, a Latin King can play that card only so many times before karma catches up.

Standing erect in the center of the circle, listening intently with his hands clasped behind his back, was Carlos, known as King C., Supreme Inca of the Massachusetts Chapter of the Almighty Latin King and Queen Nation. Kneeling next to him and taking notes on a small tablet was Kelvin, his personal assistant. Kelvin took detailed minutes of the meeting while King C. focused his attention on his chief of intelligence, occasionally looking away to scan the rest of his advisors.

"Okay. That's enough. Thank you for your loyalty to the crown, King Juan. You're taking some major risks to get me the information I need to make good decisions, and I will never forget that. *Amor de Rey!*"

"*Amor de Rey!*" responded the council in unison.

"Let's make one thing clear to everyone right now. Once it's ours, we will never give up territory. Not to Bloods, not to Crips, not to anyone. We hold at all costs. Everyone know what I'm sayin'? *Amor de Rey?*"

"*Amor de Rey!*" responded the council members, their words echoing throughout the cavernous room.

"We gotta keep what we got, but we also gotta expand. You know what I'm sayin'? New territories, new members, new markets. Remember what I said last meeting? The future of any organization rests on its ability to attract new members and business opportunities. Let those other bitches waste their time trying to get what we already got while we keep that shit *and* get more. *Amor de Rey!*"

"*Amor de Rey!*"

King C. nodded his head and slowly scanned the circle clockwise before resting his sights on Hector.

"King Heavy. How are you doing tonight?"

Hector swallowed as sweat poured down his face and neck.

"Very good, King C.," his voice cracked.

The Supreme Inca raised his eyebrows in mock surprise. "You're not fooling anyone."

Hector surveyed the circle of burning eyes and forced an unconvincing smile to try and mask his paranoia.

"I serve the nation, King C."

Carlos paced slowly toward Hector as he spoke.

"I know you do, Heavy. But you're not looking so heavy these days. What's your secret? Diet? Exercise?"

Hector scanned the circle again, seeing the blank stares turned to smirks as everyone waited for his answer to the Supreme Inca's question. He removed a handkerchief from his back pocket and casually wiped his forehead.

"Just doing my part to battle obesity. You know how it is, Carlos."

Most of the council looked away at the sarcastic comment and familiar use of King C's real first name. Carlos stayed focused on Hector, his eyes burning with intensity.

"Yeah, I know how it is. Organizations are the same way— always looking for ways to trim the fat ... or remove tumors. Let's you and I talk in private after the meeting."

Carlos spun around slowly and addressed the nation's enforcer and chief disciplinarian directly.

"Let's hear from you, King Loc. Tell me something good. *Amor de Rey!*"

"*Amor de Rey!*" replied all but Hector, who was rattled from the group shaming and already worried about his meeting after the meeting.

Hector, you stupid fuck.

Thirty-four

Mark changed into shorts and a t-shirt, popped open a cold beer, and stretched out comfortably on the couch, his head propped up by an old, dusty pillow, only to realize that the remote control for the TV was sitting on top of the cable box.

Get up and get the remote, or just lie here until I die? Or at least until I need another beer?

He took a long sip from the bottle and thought about Frank Tagala next door.

What the hell happened to him? What happened to his wife and kid? And how the hell can you manage to work a job like his—or any job—when you're that fucked up? Agnes never mentioned anything about the neighbors over the years. Agnes. The box.

He took the last swig of beer and placed the bottle on the counter on his way to Agnes's den.

Thirty-five

Two Kings closed the double doors tightly, leaving Carlos and Hector alone on the balcony. Carlos rested his elbows on the railing and gazed out over the Boston skyline.

"You know, we've worked hard to get where we are today?"

"Yeah, we have. No doubt. This shit didn't build itself," answered Hector, glancing left and right to make sure they were alone while keeping his distance from the railing.

"There's more at stake now than ever. And that means we gotta be more careful than ever. Too much to lose, Hector. No weak links, you see what I'm sayin'?"

"Of course," he started, but Carlos quickly cut him off.

"Where's Pedro? I haven't heard from him today and he didn't show up tonight. That's not like him. Have you seen him?"

"No, man. I haven't seen him lately," answered Hector. Technically, this answer was true. He hadn't seen Pedro since the day before, when he strangled the nosy accountant and buried the body somewhere in western Massachusetts.

"Okay. Tell him I need to talk to him ASAP. He still owes me some answers, and I'm losing patience."

"No problem, C. Anything you need—you know that. I'm your guy—*Amor de Rey* for life, you know."

"For life. Ain't that the fuckin' truth," added Carlos matter-of-factly.

Members of the Latin Kings nation may disagree on many topics, but the oft-repeated maxim of "once a King, always a King" was universally acknowledged. The only way out of the nation was to die. Whether that came about through natural causes or someone else's plans was increasingly out of members' control, especially for the anointed few in leadership. When you join the nation, the death clock starts ticking. As you climb the ladder, the ticking accelerates. By the time one reaches the top, everyone knows he's on borrowed time. There are no retired Supreme Incas from Massachusetts. They are all either dead or serving lengthy prison sentences.

Carlos turned to face Hector, put a hand on his moist shoulder, and spoke softly.

"You know I love you, Hector. You're the son of my favorite *tía* and that means something. But one of the best parts of being a King is never having to choose between family and the nation ... because the nation *is* your family. I don't know what the fuck is up with you, but you need to figure shit out and fix it. You also owe apologies to the rest of the council for disrespecting them."

"You're right, Carlos. I was planning on doing just that as soon as we're finished here. I'll straighten shit out. Don't worry."

"It's my job to worry, Hector. You should worry sometimes too. That way you don't end up like King Shorty," he offered with a chuckle.

Hector swallowed uncomfortably and tried to block the image of a headless, armless torso out of his consciousness.

"We're done for now. Send in King Base on your way out," said Carlos over his shoulder as he returned his gaze to the skyline.

Thirty-six

Mark sat at Agnes's desk, pinching her vintage emerald ring between two fingers and admiring it in the light. Agnes had worn the ring on her right hand for most of her life, but he had never noticed the elegant, hand-carved designs that adorned the fourteen-carat gold setting until now. He rotated the ring slowly, and the modest stone flickered a brilliant green when the light struck it just right.

Placing the ring aside, he sat back and unfolded the letter, dated one week before Agnes's death. It was addressed to Mark with the words "Private and Confidential" at the very top of the page. Her handwriting was shaky but readable.

My dearest Mark,

As I prepare for whatever comes next, I wanted to share a few things with you.

I have but one regret in life, which I will explain momentarily, but my decision to adopt and to build my life around you was the single best decision I ever made. Thank you for accepting me, for allowing me to love you, and for loving me back. I could not be more proud of the man you've become.

Mark folded both hands over the letter, closed his eyes, and breathed deeply.

Of course, you already know that so I will not belabor the point. Nor will I offer trivial advice. People are different and they all need to choose their own paths, and opinions will vary as much as the weather in New England. But the one thing that all people can agree on at the end of their lives is this—it goes by so quickly, Mark. One second you are in the prime of your youth, the next thing you know you are in your forties. The journey from forties to late seventies passes even faster, and to this day I am wondering where all the time went! And then it hits me. I spent my time focused on the thing I loved the most in my life—you. There is no greater cause than giving your unconditional love to another human being, Mark. It is the only thing that matters at the end of the road. Did you love and allow yourself to be loved? If the answer to both of those questions is yes, you have lived life to its fullest.

Mark, you once asked me if I had ever known true love. The answer is yes, but for reasons that I do not fully understand, I kept it at a distance. The result is that I have a big, empty part of me that wonders how things could have been had I simply accepted the gift. By the time I realized my mistake, it was too late. It goes by so fast, Mark. Make the most of every second.

I'm not proud of this last part, but I hope you understand that I made promises and did not feel I had the right to break them. Mark, your birth mother did not abandon you and I did not adopt you through an orphanage. Nor is your birth mother's identity a mystery— I knew her.

Mark stood up stunned and continued reading.

I have always found comfort sitting and praying in an empty church, with none of the distractions or pretenses that come with corporate worship, just me and the Father. I have never doubted my faith, but I have often doubted the institution of the church and questioned the wisdom of giving men such power and influence over people's lives. The day I met your mother, I was feeling confused and directionless. I had dedicated my life to the service of God, but I felt like I was actually serving a thankless, aging clergy who were out of touch with the real world. I was asking God for strength when a beautiful young woman emerged from the confessional and broke my concentration. She wore a colorful sundress and tears were running down her face. Not the happy tears that sparkle and glow—these were tears of shame, the kind that cut and sting all the way down your neck. She was so graceful and radiant in the way she removed the handkerchief from her purse and dabbed the tears from her face.

I tried not to stare, but the clicking of her heels stopped when she reached the back of the church and a little voice told me to look. She waved toward the altar as if she was saying goodbye. Then she ran out the front doors.

I found her in the prayer garden next to the church. She sat on a stone bench with spring flowers in full bloom all around her. "I was hoping you would come," she said as I approached from behind. I sat next to her and held her until she ran out of tears, her smooth young hands never leaving her belly. She had sought advice, guidance, and love from the church. But all she got was guilt and shame for her sins against God. The details of your mother's life are not mine to share—only her identity.

I befriended your mother that day and, with the help of a trustworthy young priest and another sister with midwife experience, we helped her through the pregnancy and delivered you safely, right into my waiting arms. Seeing you come into the world was the most thrilling experience of my life, Mark. My only regret came later, when the priest offered to leave the church and marry me so that you would have a father and we could live as a family. I do not fully understand why I repeatedly declined, but he gave me the enclosed emerald ring and said the offer would remain open forever. When we moved to Massachusetts, he moved also so he could be close to us. That priest's name was Father Frederick Peck and he was the closest thing you ever had to a father.

During Father Peck's final days, he told story after story of the time he had spent with you and how thankful he was for having both of us in his life. I am thankful for him too, but there is a pain inside me that will never go away because I was too shortsighted and scared to fully accept his love. How difficult it must have been for him to always be on the outside looking in. I can't help but wonder how different things could have been for all of us had we lived as a family.

I am so sorry for burdening you with this when I'm not there for support. Sometimes events that don't make sense at the time end up being the best things that ever happen to you. The day I met your mother was the most important day of my life.

She insisted that she never wanted you to know her name, but she reached out a handful of times to check on you. She even visited once when you were a teenager, but she said meeting you and looking into your eyes was too much for her to bear. She left with a promise that she would never again make contact, not because she didn't care but because she felt it was unfair to you. I insisted that she take the only picture of you I had handy, a wonderful shot of you and Father Peck on the front steps of his parish. I have not heard from her since, but I can't bear the thought of leaving you without telling you the truth. What you do with the information is entirely up to you, Mark. Your mother's name is Lois Sumner. The last I knew, she was still living somewhere in New York, but that was decades ago. She never offered your father's name and I never asked.

You are a wonderful man with unlimited potential, Mark. Keep an open mind and be ready for life's little curveballs. Most of all, remember to seize opportunities while you can, because no door stays open forever.

With unconditional love,

Agnes

Mark folded the letter and placed it back inside the envelope, overcome by emotion—grief from the loss, shock from the news, and guilt for not being there. Then, for the first time in years, he bowed his head and cried uncontrollably.

Thirty-seven

Luci arrived at the station two hours before her shift. She fumbled through the dirty dishes in the break room sink and gave her favorite Red Sox mug a quick rinse.

Good enough.

She settled into her seat with a mug full of piping hot black coffee. Then she pulled up all the information on what the chief was now calling "the graffiti issue" and went to work looking for missed clues. Her cell phone vibrated and she reached down to punt the call to voicemail. But when she saw Mark's name on the screen, she changed her mind and answered the phone.

"Yes, Mr. Landry?"

"Yeah, my cat is stuck in a tree. Can you send someone to help me get him down?"

"Sir, I think you meant to call the fire department," Luci said, slightly more annoyed than amused.

"Oh, I see. Sorry. My mistake. How are you anyway, Luci? Haven't heard from you. Do you always take guys out, then not speak to them for a week?"

"I'm good. Busy. Working. And I didn't take you out—I gave you a ride. What have you been up to?"

"Nothing really. Just doing a laundry list of things to get the house ready to sell. Trying to relax a bit too. What about you?"

"Did you say you're selling the house? I guess that means you're not sticking around very long, then."

"How do you know? Maybe I'm thinking about buying a different place in town. Maybe something a little bigger and more modern with room to grow. Who knows?"

Luci shook her head and bit her bottom lip.

Don't take the bait, Luci.

"Sounds like you have a lot to think about, so I won't keep you," she said flatly.

"Graffiti?"

"What?"

"Graffiti. Are you working on the graffiti stuff?"

"Yes, as a matter of fact I am. But I can't seem to get any breaks no matter how many times I look at it."

"Then stop looking at it."

"Yeah, that's great advice, Mark. Seriously, can we talk later?"

"I am serious. Stop looking at it. Instead, look at the dates and times it happens and see what else was going on those days. Maybe those dates are significant in other ways. Anniversaries, full moon, whatever. What other calls or incidents happened on those shifts? Who was on duty? Who was off duty? Stop focusing on the graffiti so much and the rest of the picture may come into focus. Just a tip."

"That's actually not an awful idea."

"I'm full of 'not awful' ideas. If you hung out with me more, you'd know that."

No, no, no. Not the "poor me" approach, Mark. Don't go there.

Luci sipped her coffee and said nothing.

"You're busy. I'll let you go. Just wanted you to know I was thinking about you."

"Yeah, thanks. I'll give you a call when things slow down a little."

"Please do. Don't be a stranger."

Luci ended the call without saying goodbye and stared blankly at her monitors.

Okay, Mark. Let's try it your way.

Thirty-eight

Officer John McDonough was foot-patrolling the shops on Main Street, but his mind was still back at the house with Linda.

"Okay, right now! Right now! Feel that?" exclaimed Linda excitedly.

John lay next to her on the bed in full uniform, one hand flat against her womb.

"Nope. Nothing."

"You gotta be kidding! You're joking, right? You didn't feel that?"

He moved his hand around her belly, stopping every few inches and waiting patiently.

"Nothing. You sure it's not just gas?" he asked.

She poked him in the chest several times with a firm index finger, hard enough to hear her nails tap against his body armor.

"No, sir. That's our son. And it's getting pretty cramped in there. Just a few more weeks and he'll be in our arms. That means you'll be able to carry him around for a change. Are you excited to be a daddy?"

"Of course I am. Now don't say anything—just be quiet for a minute," said McDonough in a low voice, turning his head to rest his ear on Linda's belly button.

He closed his eyes and tried not to think about bills, healthcare, sleep interruptions, and all the future stress fatherhood would inevitably bring, stress he was not sure he could handle. They waited for more movement, but nothing happened.

Why doesn't he respond to me? Why does he seem to stop moving entirely whenever I'm around? Is it bad timing or is it me?

"Hi, John," said a shopkeeper, looking up from his broom.

"Hey, Mike. How's business?"

"No complaints. When's that baby coming?"

"Due date is July 4th, but we'll see. He may get out early for good behavior, and Linda's dying to get it over with so that would be fine with her."

"Great. And what about you—you ready?"

Yeah. I'm ready. Why does everyone ask me if I'm ready?

McDonough stopped strolling and froze for a few seconds.

Just keep walking, John. Just keep walking. It's not a big deal. He didn't mean anything by it.

Turning slowly, he stared at the shopkeeper out of the corner of his eye.

Let it go, John. You're making a big deal out of nothing. Just keep moving down the street and get some lunch.

With both hands resting on his duty belt, he took several small steps until his face was just inches from the other man's.

"Of course I'm ready, Mike. Don't I look ready? Is there something about me that makes you think I'm not ready?" he asked in a low, serious tone.

"Heck, no! Nobody's every truly ready for their first kid. Honestly, I think it took Wanda and me four kids before we knew what we were doing. You'll do just fine. Besides, I imagine you could handle pretty much anything. That's one of the many reasons we like having you around."

McDonough stared blankly into Mike's eyes. Finally he broke into a smile, trying to mask his confused rage.

"Yeah, well, the truth is I'm scared to death but don't tell anyone."

He winked, patted Mike on the shoulder, and continued on his way.

Calm down, John. Breathe and walk. Breathe and walk.

When he heard the gunshot he instinctively ducked into a doorway and knelt low, his body pressed firmly against the bricks of the building. Drawing his pistol, he coached himself to take deep breaths and scanned the area to determine the direction of fire.

He watched in amazement as the townspeople continued about their business without so much as looking up from their chores.

Didn't they hear that?

Ghassan stared sheepishly at McDonough from across the street, wiping his hands on his apron. He waved with one hand and called out, "Sorry! I forgot how much noise this metal door makes when it slams."

False alarm. Stand down. No fire. Get it together and keep moving up the street.

McDonough holstered his gun, waved back, and walked away briskly, hoping that no one had noticed his odd behavior.

Ghassan crossed the street and approached the shopkeeper. "Does he seem okay to you?"

"Who? John? Yeah, he's fine. First-time dads are always tense. He's used to being in full control. Little does he know it, but his life is about to change forever."

Ghassan watched McDonough disappear down a side street as he wiped his sweaty forehead with both hands and dried them on the front of his apron.

Yes, big changes are coming.

Thirty-nine

"What? Didn't I already hear from you today?" asked Luci, answering her phone on the second ring.

"How about dinner?"

"I'm off at six but usually too beat to go anywhere. Thanks anyway."

"No problem. How about I bring takeout to your place? We could have Thai or Indian. What are you in the mood for?"

Parked in her cruiser at the main gate of the high school's student parking lot, Luci glanced at her watch.

Two minutes to dismissal.

"I suppose that would be okay. I don't feel like cooking anyway."

"Great. Any requests? Or should I just surprise you?"

Students began trickling out the doors of the building.

"Surprise me but make it healthy—vegetarian. I'm beat and just want to eat and go to bed," she answered, watching students pile into their cars through her rear-view mirror.

"See you at seven?"

"Make it 7:30," she said, tossing her cell phone on the passenger seat and exiting the cruiser.

Within seconds after she opened the gates, the first line of cars was pouring out to the main road. Many students waved as they passed Luci, others simply nodded, and a few ignored her completely. When a red Honda Civic with heavily tinted windows arrived at the gate, she held up a hand and stepped in front of the car. After she knocked twice on the driver's window, it opened slowly and a male much too old to be a student smiled at her.

"What's up? It ain't my tints, right? They're legal and I got the papers to prove it."

"I'm sure you do. But your inspection sticker expired a week ago."

He squinted at his front windshield.

"Aw, shit. I didn't even notice. I'll go get that done right now."

"Please do. This is your verbal warning. Next time I have to ticket you," she said, scanning the rest of the car's occupants before continuing. "Are you a student here?"

"Nah, I'm just picking up my cousin and her friends. That's all."

"That's fine. In the future, remember that this lot is for students only. Pickups are supposed to use the circle at the main entrance, okay?"

"Whatever, *Mami*," he said somewhat dismissively as he turned up the radio.

"What did you just say to me?"

Luci banged her hand on the top of the Civic three times to get the driver's attention.

"Turn that shit down, now. Get out of the car and show me your license, registration, and proof of insurance."

"Come on, I was just leaving!"

"Not another word. Get out of the car and show me your documents. If I have to ask again, your day will get a lot worse. Do it now."

Luci scrutinized his papers while she redirected the current of cars going past. Curious passengers pressed their faces against windows as traffic squeezed to one lane before trickling out the exit.

"So that's how you act when an officer is trying to cut you some slack? 'Whatever, *Mami*?' How about I just give you the ticket or tow your car. Would you prefer that? How far would I have to dig to find some more shit?" She squinted at his license. "Mr. Ortiz? Any warrants? Any driving restrictions? See how much fun this game is? And all because you had to run your mouth instead of just shutting the hell up and taking a simple warning."

The driver's gaze oscillated between Luci and smirking looks back at his passengers.

"Hey, look at me. Look at me and take a break from trying to impress little girls. You want to disrespect me in front of everyone? Fine, I can embarrass you too. How about I search your entire car? Think I'd find anything interesting? And, no, I don't need a warrant. What about the ashtray in your car? I wonder if I'd find anything interesting in there. You're on school property too. That basically doubles penalties for anything and everything I find. All because you had to be a tough guy. Should I keep going or are you getting this now?"

He held up both hands with palms facing Luci.

"I get it. I get it. I didn't mean nothing by it—it was just a joke. All good."

"All good? No, *I'll* tell *you* when it's all good. And right now it ain't all good."

108

He took the rest of his chewing out with his head bowed and tail tucked firmly between his legs.

"Now you're going to get back into the car. Put on your seat belt. And apologize to me in front of everyone. Do it now. Don't say another word to me unless you want to continue this discussion from a jail cell."

The car grew quiet as he opened the door and buckled himself into the seat.

"Officer, I apologize for disrespecting you."

Luci stared at him and pointed toward the exit.

"Go."

Never underestimate the power of a little public shaming.

As the Civic turned the corner and accelerated, one of the back-seat passengers turned around and stared out the back window. Luci had not wanted to draw unwanted attention to her by acknowledging her during her interaction with the driver.

You won't go very far hanging out with assholes like that, Julia.

She closed the cruiser door and reached for her cell phone to text Mark.

MESSAGE: Nothing vegetarian. I want steak tips.

Forty

It took more than an hour and every ounce of patience Kenny Harrington could muster to get his father dressed and ready for his daily walk around the yard. The old man resisted, slapped his son repeatedly, and screamed out for help. His specific words were indecipherable but the message was clear: he was deathly afraid and confused, and he wanted to be left alone.

"I'll let you sit here for a few minutes before we go outside, Father. I'll be in the next room."

Kenny sat down, rested his head on his computer table, and burst into tears. When he raised his head, he stared at the framed newspaper clipping on top of the dresser—his favorite picture of Mrs. Harrington. She wore red, white, and blue ribbons in her hair and held a small American flag in her hand.

I don't know how much longer I can do this, Mother. I promised you I'd take care of him but sometimes it's too much. What happened? Where did he go? I look into his eyes and see nothing. He's dissolving. Doctors say this could go on for years, but how long can I go on?

Kenny ignored the flashing computer screens, folded his arms on the table, and rested his head on his forearms as three straight nights with little sleep finally caught up with him. He was awakened by the soft hum of the encrypted servers as they automatically rebooted and started their hourly diagnostics.

Kenny wiped the puddle of tears from the table and blew his nose. When he reentered the family room, Mr. Harrington was gone.

Forty-one

Kenny ran from room to room in a panic-fueled frenzy.

How long was I asleep? Is he still in the house? How far could he have gone? Call the police. No, I don't need them snooping around my house. Check outside first. Hurry!

"Father! Where are you, Father?"

He checked the basement and bathrooms, outside the front door, down the stairs, and around the house. Nothing.

Kenny stood lightheaded in the front yard and looked down at the cordless phone in his hands. He pressed the talk button and was starting to dial 911 when he noticed a police cruiser coasting down the hill. He ended the call and walked quickly to the end of the driveway, waving his arms.

Officer Charlie Worth pulled into the driveway and leaned his head out the cruiser window.

"I believe this belongs to you," he offered jovially.

Kenny looked at him confusedly.

"I found him at the top of the hill, standing in the middle of the road. He seemed confused as all hell and slapped me a few times so I had to restrain him, but he's still in one piece. Back seat."

Kenny scanned the cruiser and locked eyes with his father. Mr. Harrington was lying silently across the back seat with his hands cuffed behind his back, sheer terror in his eyes. Kenny immediately began pulling on the door handle.

"Let him out right now! Father, it's okay! I'm here."

"Okay, hold your horses. I'll help. Trust me, he's not going anywhere anyway."

Kenny's red face turned purple.

"Open the fucking door and take those handcuffs off him. He didn't hurt anyone! He's not a threat!"

Charlie paused and rested both hands on his hips.

"Seriously, is this the thanks I get for getting him out of the street and home safely? Relax, the cuffs are for his protection more than mine or anyone else's. He's fine. Nothing's hurt but his pride, and that's a hell of a lot less painful than getting hit by a car at forty miles per hour."

He opened the door, grabbed the old man by the arm, sat him up straight, and lifted him out of the back seat. Kenny wrapped both arms around his father and pressed the side of his face against his chest. When Charlie removed the handcuffs, Mr. Harrington's

111

petrified arms sprang forward and wrapped firmly around his son's shoulders. He whimpered as tears streamed down his cheeks.

"It's okay, Father. I'm here. I'm so sorry. I'll never leave you alone again. I promise. Don't cry, Dad. Let's go inside and forget about our walk for today."

Officer Worth stood erect with his hands on his hips as Kenny and Mr. Harrington slowly started toward the house.

"You're welcome," he said sarcastically.

"Go fuck yourself," muttered Kenny under his breath.

The officer's eyes popped wide as he moved toward the Harringtons.

"What did you say to me?"

Kenny ignored him and kept his father moving toward the safety of the house.

"I'm talking to you! Get back here, you ungrateful little punk."

Kenny froze and turned his head in Worth's direction.

"Little punk?" he asked.

"Did you tell me to go fuck myself?"

"No."

"You're lucky I found him when I did. If you don't like the way I brought him home, I really don't give a shit. You're his caretaker, right? If you were doing your job, I wouldn't even be here right now. So drop that fucking attitude and show me some respect or I'll lock your ass up for disorderly conduct and whatever else I feel like charging you with. Do you understand me?"

No response.

"Do you understand me?"

Kenny bowed his head.

"Yes, sir."

Worth nodded his head approvingly, then turned and walked back to his cruiser. As he backed out of the driveway, he leaned his head out the window and called to Kenny with a smile.

"The old man's not going to remember any of this anyway."

Kenny squeezed his father's hand and kept moving. Once inside, he took off the old man's shoes and helped him lie down on his bed. Mr. Harrington was asleep within minutes. Kenny immediately sat down in front of his computers in the next room and looked up at the picture of his mother.

Don't worry, Mother. I'll make him pay for that.

112

Mark pulled into Luci's driveway shortly before 7:30. Her small home sat about fifty yards off the main road, surrounded by trees. She had purchased the house a year ago, and it offered much more privacy than the busy apartment complex where she had lived when Mark was last home. He parked in front of the two-car detached garage and carried the food up the front walkway.

"It's open," Luci called from within when he rang the doorbell.

Of course it is. Why would a single woman living in the woods bother to lock her door?

He closed the door behind him, walked into the kitchen, and placed the food on the table.

"It's me. Where are you hiding?" he asked.

"I'm in here."

Mark followed the sound of Luci's voice and found her sitting on the sofa in the living room. Her hair was in a loose ponytail, and she wore black sweatpants and a white tank top. She pretended to be reading, but he could see smudged makeup around her eyes.

"What's wrong?"

"Nothing. Just reading something sad," she said unconvincingly.

He sat down on the sofa and placed a hand on one of her bare feet.

"Not buying it. What happened?"

"I don't want to talk about it. Where's the food? I'm starving."

Mark knew better than to push it.

"It's in the kitchen. Where do you want to eat?"

"Right here."

He set up dinner on the coffee table and she immediately dug in. He walked back to the kitchen, poured a glass of cabernet from an open bottle on the counter, and set it down next to her plate.

"You look like you need this."

"Thanks. What have you been up to?" she asked.

"Well, mostly just stuff around the house. It's in decent condition, but Agnes wasn't able to do much these past few years. A lot of painting and a few handyman projects—mostly inside jobs. Next up is getting the outside in order. Nothing too fancy."

"So you're selling it?"

"I don't know yet," he said, after chewing on a juicy steak tip and drinking some bottled water. "But it needs the work regardless."

Both were true statements. Mark had no idea whether or not he would retire and move on to the next phase of his life or head back to the Family. It was the only life he had known since high school, but part of him was telling him to let go, settle down, and smell the roses. The house could probably sell as is, but the upgrades would make it easier to market, and the work kept him occupied and gave him time to think.

After finishing their meals, they both sat back with full bellies. Luci spoke up after a few long minutes of silence.

"So I answered a call today for a three-car accident. First one on the scene."

"Yeah? I assume it was a bad scene."

"One of the worst," she added softly, draining the last sip of her wine.

Mark went to the kitchen and returned with the bottle of wine. He filled her glass and sat back down on the sofa, a little bit closer than before.

"Do you want to tell me about it? It's entirely up to you."

She took a long, slow sip before answering.

"Drunk driver. Middle of the day. Of course, he's fine, but one of the other drivers is in critical condition. And the third car—"

"You don't have to talk about this, Luci," he said after a few seconds of silence.

"The two passengers in the third car were a mother and her five-year-old daughter. Both dead on impact. It was a fucking mess, Mark. No matter how many times I see shit like that, I never get used to it. It never gets easier. As soon as the other cruisers showed up and the EMTs took over, I cried hysterically and threw up."

Mark put a hand on her leg and said nothing.

"They were driving home from the store. That's it. And now they're gone. Just like that." She locked eyes with him. "I cried and threw up in front of everyone. That's never happened before. Things are supposed to get easier, not worse. You're supposed to get used to it."

"Says who?" he asked.

"Says common sense, Mark. I'm a cop. This is my job and I cried like a little girl."

"You cried because you're human and just saw something most people only imagine in their worst nightmares. That's nothing to be embarrassed or self-conscious about."

"I was the only one who broke down."

"Bullshit. You were the only one who did it there. The rest may act stoic at the scene, but I bet a lot of them felt worse than you. Nobody gets used to that stuff. At least nobody normal."

"You're not a cop, Mark."

"No kidding. But I've seen some stuff, Luci."

"Are you trying to one-up me?"

He took his hand off her leg and leaned away.

"No, it's not a competition."

"I'm sorry. I'm just pretty wound up about this," she said, grabbing his hand and putting it back on her leg.

"Don't worry about it. Usually I deserve it—you just jumped the gun a little bit this time," he said with a smile. "And I can't tell you how happy I am to hear that you are not used to horrible things."

"You're just being nice," she said, squeezing his hand.

Mark stood up abruptly and clapped his hands once.

"Stand up, Officer Alvarez. When you feel like shit, you gotta move. Show me around your new castle."

The tour ended with both reclining on Luci's back deck. Stars came in and out of focus as invisible clouds drifted slowly across the night sky.

"It's supposed to rain tomorrow," Mark said to break the silence.

Luci turned her head sideways to face him.

"Can you tell me about any of the stuff you've seen?"

"Misery loves company, right?"

"Something like that," she said softly.

He thought hard to remember an experience that he could share without divulging classified information. What seemed like an eternity was really only a few seconds as he decided to reach back to the pre-Dunbar, pre-Family half of his career.

"Okay. Do you remember hearing about Jessica Lynch? She was a female soldier taken prisoner in Iraq during the early days of the war and eventually rescued."

"Vaguely."

"I was on that rescue mission. And—"

"*You* rescued her?" Luci interrupted.

"That's not what I said. There were a lot of people on that mission. I was just one of them. Anyway, about half a dozen other soldiers were taken prisoner as well when her convoy was ambushed. They were already dead by the time we determined where the shitbags were keeping them."

Luci shook her head back and forth silently.

"While the tier one guys were rescuing Lynch from the hospital building where they were holding her, I was across the street with my Ranger unit recovering the other bodies. They had been tortured, killed, bodies mutilated and buried in a shallow mass grave. We dug them out with small shovels and our bare hands. Piece by piece."

Mark stood up, walked to the edge of the deck, and leaned back against the railing.

"No matter what, I can never seem to shake the images and smells. It was one of the worst experiences of my life."

"One of the worst? What the hell could top that?" Luci asked rhetorically.

"The same thing you saw today. Kids. Mothers. Noncombatants and friends who zigged one day when they should have zagged. Sometimes it seems so random. You know what? That's the kick in the balls about life and combat. You can do everything right and prepare for every contingency and still lose through no fault of your own. You go left when you should have gone right. I try not to think about it. But lately, something's been telling me not to press my luck anymore."

Luci stood up and leaned against the railing facing the backyard. The moonlit grass swayed back and forth with the wind like waves on the ocean. Mark turned to face her.

"You know you should be proud of yourself. You got the job done first and worried about your own feelings later. You kept your shit together when you had to and that's the sign of a professional. Well done."

She bowed her head and dusted off the railing with her hands.

"Thanks. Can I ask you a question?"

"Anything," he answered cheerfully.

"What's combat like? What's it like to have to kill somebody? Police have to do it sometimes, but it's never happened

116

in this town and I've never talked with anyone who has gone through the experience. How do you deal with something like that?"

He folded his arms.

"Wow. That's a lot. You know … you've had a long, tough day. Maybe we should—"

"Please," she said softly. "I need to know at least a little bit about what you've been through too."

Mark sat back down in the chair and looked upward. The clouds were gone and the stars shined brightly.

"It's scary, but only beforehand. The anticipation is usually worse than the engagement. Once the action starts, your training kicks in and you don't have much time to think until it's over. Once it's over, it's hard to describe the feeling. Elation, maybe?"

"Elation?" she asked.

"Yeah. Whether it's one-on-one or a group thing, there's a moment of pure euphoria. You could have just been killed but you weren't. You were either better or lucky. Either way, you're the one still standing. Others feel survivor's guilt if they have lost comrades. Some get sick. Everyone's different."

"Have you ever been wounded?"

"Nah. Nothing big. Just some bumps and bruises. A few cuts," he said as he unconsciously rested his palms across his abdomen and felt for the scar.

"I'm glad you're home in one piece. And I'm glad for guys like you who are willing to do whatever it is that you do. I imagine you hear that from a lot people, but I want you to hear it from me too."

Luci was imagining throngs of people waiting on the tarmac for Mark whenever he returned from overseas. Her imagination was far from the truth, of course. He was almost always alone, often traveling under an assumed identity, and usually had to take a cab home from the airport.

Mark smiled and said nothing. Then he abruptly stood up and clapped his hands again.

"Enough of this. My guess is you have an early day tomorrow so I'm going to get out of here and let you rest."

She walked him slowly to the car in bare feet with folded arms.

"It's not my business, but did you ever read the note Agnes left you?"

Mark nodded for several seconds and looked down at the bricks on the front walkway before answering.

"Yeah. Just a quick 'I love you' and instructions on where to find everything. Nothing earth-shattering."

She wrapped her arms around him and squeezed.

"Thanks for dinner. And the talk. I needed both."

Then she cupped his face in her hands, kissed him softly on the lips, and returned to the house without another word.

Mark drove home with the radio off.

Euphoria.

Forty-three

Frank Tagala whistled as he walked into the Boston ATF office just after 11:00 a.m. with a cup of coffee in one hand and the *Boston Herald* in the other. He had awakened with a hangover that would send most people to the emergency room, but he had learned long ago how to self-medicate and get through the pain by keeping nips of vodka and a large bottle of extra-strength acetaminophen on his nightstand. That made the pain bearable as he answered each "Morning, Frank" with fuzzy eye contact and a slight raise of the chin.

On his way down the final corridor to his office, Frank paused at the glass door to the conference room. Ashton Brown and three others sat huddled at the far end of the long table. Brown noticed him immediately, glanced at his watch, and shook his head like a father disappointed that his child had broken curfew. Frank forced a wide, toothy grin and waved.

Whatever, asshole.

He continued down the hall and stopped in front of the office adjacent to his, where four members of the administrative support staff usually had barely enough room to breathe. When he popped his head in the door, he noticed that half the people and half the furniture were gone, but he thought nothing of it.

"Good morning, ladies. What's going on in the fishbowl?" he asked, cocking his head in the direction of the conference room.

Both women looked up from their desks at Frank, then at one another. The younger of the two immediately returned her attention to the task at hand; the older one paused for a second before answering in a low voice.

"Nobody knows. It's not on the schedule and the director said to keep it that way. Invite only."

"Oh well, not the first time I wasn't invited to a party," Frank replied wryly.

He sipped his coffee, walked next door to his office, and froze in the doorway, thinking he had made a mistake. His nameplate had been removed from the door. The formerly spacious though modest room was now packed with desks, filing cabinets, and other office furniture. Two nervous women stood when he entered. Again, the elder one took the lead.

"Frank, this was not our idea," she said with hands held high.

He looked around the room and nodded approvingly. "The more the merrier!"

"We were just going to lunch anyway, so you'll have the place to yourself for a while," she said. The younger woman took her cue, gathered her things, and left the room as if the fire alarm had just gone off.

Frank placed his coffee and newspaper on his desk, now tucked into the back corner. He rolled his head from side to side to relieve the tension and looked out the window. The older woman watched from the doorway and spoke again.

"We can always do our work somewhere else if it makes things easier."

Frank turned around and gave her a dismissive wave.

"Seriously, don't worry about it. It's only for a few more weeks, and I don't plan on spending much time in the office anyway. Not a big deal. Just pull the door shut and enjoy your lunch."

He booted up his computer to check his email. Nothing. Then he glanced at his in-box. Empty. After sitting quietly for several minutes, he removed the keys from his pocket and opened his bottom drawer. It was empty too.

No problem, Ashton. If you want to cut me out of the loop completely, just don't expect to see much of me. It's always happy hour somewhere.

Forty-four

"Slow down for a minute, Mark. While this may seem like nothing to a man in your chosen occupation, my more sedentary lifestyle is not as conducive to such endeavors," said Andy O'Rourke as he dropped his large frame onto the rock wall adjacent to the trail to catch his breath.

Mark stopped and made a quick 360-degree check of their location before sitting down on the wall a few feet from his friend. The trail to the summit of Holt Hill was just as he had remembered it: thick, colorful, serene. The trail was well beaten, but they had seen no other hikers during their walk.

"My friend, you haven't even broken a sweat," said Andy, taking a long chug of ice water from his plastic bottle and offering it to Mark.

"I'm good, thanks. It's all for you."

"You must be part camel. It's hot as hell today and I'm sweating buckets."

Mark smiled and kept an eye on their surroundings as they sat in silence for several minutes and Andy caught his breath.

"Oh, nice, perfect," Andy said as he retrieved a camera from his small backpack and snapped a picture off to their left.

Mark followed the direction of the lens and furled his eyebrow.

"Are you hallucinating? There's nothing over there."

"Perhaps not to the untrained eye. Look again, young Jedi," Andy answered professorially.

Mark scanned their left flank from side to side, up and down.

"Nope. Nothing."

Andy extended his arm and pointed a beefy finger toward a pair of large trees, each with its own pronounced V-shape.

"You see where those two Vs come together to make a W?"

"Yeah."

"Just to the right of that, the ground is flat for a few feet. Then it starts to slope upwards, making a natural amphitheater of sorts. It's perfect."

"Perfect for what?" asked Mark.

"A public execution."

Mark turned to face his friend.

"Dude, what's wrong with you?"

121

"Nothing at all, I assure you. It's for one of my lectures on early town history."

Andy stood, took a few steps from the rock wall, and turned to face his pupil.

"Imagine the accused standing under those trees on a raised platform, executioners at his sides, the hillside packed with eager townspeople waiting to hear his last words while vendors sold refreshments."

"Yeah, I've been there. It's called Saudi Arabia."

"That's true," said Andy, motioning with a hand to continue the short climb to the summit. "But this happy little tradition of being in someone's presence at the moment when they expire was, and is, the closest any living human can get to the afterlife. The condemned's final words represented their last chance to affect their own legacy, and those words were thought to contain nuggets of divine wisdom. Public spectacles kept people in line. Never underestimate the power of a good shaming, Mr. Landry."

"I can't argue with that. I saw a few of those spectacles in different parts of the sandbox earlier in my career."

"I assume the sandbox to which you refer is the Middle East?"

"Not necessarily. As long as the terrain's shitty and the majority of people are fucking crazy, it qualifies. Somalia, Libya, Iraq—they're all the same sandbox."

The trail weaved through the thick trees and eventually emptied into an open field at the top of the hill.

"Here we are. Take a look, Landry!" boomed O'Rourke, pointing his finger toward the Boston skyline some thirty miles to the south. "In April of 1775 the townspeople stood right here and witnessed the Battle of Bunker Hill. They say you could feel the heat from the flames when the Brits set fire to Charlestown."

Both men sat and relaxed for a few minutes, discussing how much the landscape must had changed over the course of more than two centuries. "Regardless, the flames must have been enormous to be seen from this distance," added Andy. He drank the rest of the water, and Mark pretended to listen as he launched into an impromptu lecture on the American Revolution.

"So roughly a third of the folks were in favor of revolution, about a third were loyalists to the crown, and the other third were apathetic and couldn't have given a shit either way. Not that different from today, really."

"I'm hungry," Mark replied.

The pair descended the trail until they reached the small, gravel parking lot where Andy had left his white, open-top jeep. A police cruiser was parked at the entrance, facing the sparsely traveled main road. Officer Charlie Worth sat inside with both hands gripped tightly around his radar gun, sunglasses propped up above his forehead. When the two friends emerged from the forest, Charlie turned his head and nodded in their direction.

"Morning, Charlie!" boomed Andy's voice from across the lot.

"How you doing, Coach?" he answered before returning his attention to the empty street.

Andy and Mark climbed into the jeep and buckled themselves in. Mark waited until they were half a mile down the road before speaking.

"How long have you known that guy?"

"Who? Charlie? Since he arrived on the force a few years ago. Why do you ask?"

"Just curious. Something about him rubs me the wrong way. Actually, everything about him rubs me the wrong way, but I can't place my finger on it."

"Allow me to help. He's a jackass. But he's a harmless jackass and he means well. He seems to rub a lot of people the wrong way. That's one of the many reasons why Luci replaced him as community policing liaison."

The jeep's tires hugged the sharp curves of the narrow road as both men swayed back and forth in their seats.

"What were the other reasons?"

Andy brought the jeep to a stop and looked both ways before turning left to exit the state forest and head toward downtown.

"Who knows? Like I said, he can be an ass. From what I hear, there were no official complaints but a lot of the young Latinos avoided him like the plague. The guys felt bullied, the girls found him creepy. Not a good combination for a liaison. Regardless, Luci was a no-brainer for that position. She has all the right skills and most people love her."

"Most people?"

"You're never going to please everyone, Mark. Some of the townies don't care for her, but that's nothing new. You could take half the stories I tell about the early days of the town, change the names and dates, and have a pretty decent snapshot of modern times. Don't get me wrong—we are much more enlightened these days. But some of the primal instincts and fears are identical. Where do you want to eat?"

"Wherever."

"Do you still suck at pool?" asked Andy with a raised eyebrow.

"Absolutely."

"Good. Then we'll hit the Witch Hunt and shoot a few games over lunch. Loser buys."

Forty-five

"Eight in the side."

"Clean?" asked Mark.

"Clean. The eight ball always has to go in clean. House rules," he replied without looking up.

Andy gently tapped the cue ball with a warped stick, sending it straight into the eight ball. The eight ball rolled slowly forward across the faded felt for several inches before unexpectedly rolling sharply to the left and dropping into the side pocket without touching the other balls. It was an impossible shot unless you knew the uneven intricacies of the beat-up table.

"Play here much?" asked Mark.

"Once or twice."

"I'll get two more beers."

Mark leaned his pool cue against the wall and approached the bar, where Lee Carter stood waiting with hands on his hips and a towel draped over his shoulder. Mark placed two empty mugs on the bar as Carter leaned forward and spoke in a low voice.

"FYI, the whole table rolls toward that side, but you gotta hit real soft to see it."

"Thanks. I'll remember that next time," answered Mark with a smile.

"Two more?" asked Carter, already walking backwards toward a freezer full of chilled mugs.

"Please."

Mark leaned back against the bar and casually scanned the room. A dozen or so regulars were drinking and eating, including a heavy-set man who sat with his back to the bar. Mark zeroed in on the bulge behind his right hip. As the man leaned forward to smother his cheese fries with salt and ketchup, his t-shirt rose up and exposed the butt of a Glock pistol. When he leaned back, he craned his thick neck to the side and glanced at Mark with his peripheral vision, a slightly haughty expression on his face. Mark was unimpressed.

Whatever, dude.

When Mark returned to the pool table with two fresh beers, Andy was fixated on the television mounted in the corner.

"Hey, Lee. Can you turn this up, please?" asked Andy in a raised voice.

Lee nodded and came out from behind the bar with a small stool.

"I can't find the remote, so we'll have to do this the old-fashioned way," he said as he slid his hand up and down the side of the television, feeling for the volume control.

"We have breaking news right now from Los Angeles, where earlier today two police officers and several bystanders were killed in an explosion. Warning: the footage you are about to see, taken from a nearby surveillance camera, is very disturbing."

The video clip opened with a wide shot of an inner-city street as several pedestrians went about their business. A police cruiser entered the scene in slow motion. When it neared the center of the screen a bright flash of light emanated from underneath the vehicle. A fraction of a second later, the entire scene was engulfed in a mixture of flames, smoke, and flying debris.

"Authorities have cordoned off the area and are trying to get a handle on the extent of the damage and casualties," the broadcaster continued. "Federal investigators and counterterror professionals are at the site, and the Governor has already elevated all law enforcement entities under his authority to the highest alert levels. Was this some sort of freak accident or a deliberate act of terrorism? Who is responsible? Are there more bombs? Are the streets of America no longer safe? Is this the new normal? In just a few moments, we will attempt to answer those questions and more with two very special guests who have very different perspectives, Senators Johnson and McDermott."

Andy took an enormous sip of his beer and turned to Mark.

"The new normal? I really hate that expression."

Mark drank from his mug as he watched the video play over and over on a continuous loop in the corner of the screen. "Looks like an IED," he said in a low voice.

"How can you tell?"

"I've seen a few before. I could be wrong."

"Think the cops had bad luck or something? Couldn't any car have tripped the bomb? How does this shit work?"

"Depends. It may not have been planted on the street. It could just have easily been attached to the vehicle."

Both redirected their attention to the television, where a female broadcaster sat in the midst of a bright red, white, and blue set. The words "Terror Alert" flashed boldly across the bottom of the screen.

"I'm joined now in the studio by Republican Senator Johnson of North Carolina, Chair of the Senate Committee on Intelligence, and remotely by Democratic freshman Senator McDermott of Connecticut, a member of the Senate Committee on Armed Services. Thank you both for joining us today. Senator Johnson, we'll go to you first. What do you make of this apparent attack in Los Angeles?"

"First, let me say that my thoughts and prayers go out to the victims," said the Senator, a distinguished looking man in his late sixties or early seventies. He wore an expensive-looking dark suit, a white shirt, a bright blue tie, and an oversized American flag lapel pin. His gray hair was neatly groomed and his demeanor was confident and smooth as if he had done this kind of thing hundreds of times.

"We are at war. I don't know what it's going to take to get folks on the other side of the aisle to recognize this very clear fact and get on board with winning it. There are people around the world and inside our own borders who are hell-bent on destroying the United States of America. And they are not stupid. They are well trained and they are patient. Is this the new normal? It doesn't have to be. But we need to have a united front in this war. It is simply not possible to locate and eliminate potential terrorists within the United States when the Democratic Party unwittingly runs interference for them by consistently sabotaging our efforts. The good men and women of our intelligence community and armed forces deserve better. Additionally, we need to ratchet up our efforts abroad so we can locate and kill terrorists before they enter our country. Ours is not an easy task, but it isn't rocket science either. Polls indicate that the American people support a much more aggressive approach to these issues, but too many people in Washington just don't seem to get it. Until they do, innocent people will continue to die. It is that simple."

"Amen," came a deep voice from behind Mark and Andy.

Both remained focused on the broadcast.

"Thank you, Senator Johnson. And what about you, Senator McDermott? What's your reaction to this attack as well as Senator Johnson's remarks?"

Senator McDermott cleared her throat and stared into the camera confidently. Her dark hair was short, cut just below the ear, and her modest outfit downplayed the fit body of a woman in her mid-fifties. A Mothers Against Gun Violence pin was proudly displayed on her lapel.

"This is yet another tragic incident, and there is absolutely no excuse for this type of violence on American soil, or anywhere else for that matter. But beating the drums of war is not the answer to this problem—it's simply the continuation of a disastrous, interventionist foreign policy that helped create the problem in the first place."

Senator Johnson started to interrupt, but she cut him off.

"Hold on, Senator Johnson. Hold on for a moment, please. You had your time. Now I'd like mine ... but allow me to preempt your tired old talking points about 'blaming America.' I am not blaming America for anything. The blame for senseless acts of violence sits squarely on the shoulders of the perpetrators. We can all agree on that. But to think our own actions have nothing to do with the threats we face is naïve. Every time we intervene in another country, we create more enemies. Every time a not-so-smart bomb or drone strike kills innocent people, we create more enemies. You have been a United States Senator for more than three decades and have voted for the use of force every chance you've had. It's not working, sir. It's time to start using our other available tools, not just our hammers. One more thing and then you can have your turn: I have no idea what polls you are referencing. My office is inundated with calls all day long from constituents who are vehemently opposed to military action unless it is absolutely necessary. I hear the same in my travels from coast to coast. Americans are tired of perpetual war and the blowback we never seem to learn from. It needs to stop now. No more."

"I wish some patriot would shoot this bitch in the head before she gets us all killed," said the same deep voice behind Mark and Andy.

This time they both recoiled and half-turned their heads to see who was talking. It was the portly man with the Glock. He was close enough that they could smell his thick, boozy breath.

"What? Just sayin'," he went on, looking back at Andy and Mark, before Lee Carter jumped in.

"William, you're free to think whatever you want, but don't say stupid shit like that in my pub. That woman's been through a lot, and even if she hadn't I don't want any talk like that around here. Got it?"

The man reluctantly nodded without taking his eyes off the television.

"Senator Johnson, would you like to respond?" asked the broadcaster.

"Yes, I would. Senator McDermott is a good person and no doubt an inspirational woman. We are all well aware of what she's been through, and I personally admire her strength and resilience. But those experiences do not give her any special insight into the intricacies of foreign policy, counterterrorism, intelligence gathering, and the way the real world works. And let me be very clear here. I do not like the way the real world works, but we need to see things the way they are, not the way we want them to be. Liberal idealism is a death sentence for the United States as the world's only superpower. And if we aren't fulfilling that role, someone else will step in to fill the vacuum, and it won't be Sweden or Canada. The result will be a much more unstable and dangerous world than the one we have now. There is nothing pretty or clean about war but—"

McDermott saw an opening and jumped in.

"How would you know, Senator? You went from law school straight into politics. It's the only job you've ever had. And this is part of the problem—lawmakers who are quick to start wars they know they won't have to fight themselves. You've got no skin in the game, sir."

Senator Johnson took a deep breath and exhaled slowly before replying.

"You're partially correct, Senator. A man of my advanced age has zero chance of finding himself on the battlefield. The closest I get to combat is D.C. traffic. However"—his eyes narrowed and he paused briefly before continuing—"let me remind you that I am the senior United States Senator from the great state of North Carolina, home of numerous military bases including Fort Bragg and Camp Lejeune. These good folks are not just my constituents; they are my brother and sister patriots, dedicated to preserving this republic for all of us. I do not take sending them into harm's way lightly. I also have a niece who lost a leg and a good chunk of one of her arms on the battlefield in Iraq. That was a war I voted to send her to, and a decision I have to live with every day. I have plenty of skin in the game, and tragedy does not discriminate, Madam. It strikes families on both sides of the aisle."

"I'm sorry I have to cut this conversation short," said the broadcaster, "but many thanks to Senators Johnson and McDermott for taking time out of their busy schedules to be with us today. Next up: the growing threat of cyberterrorism. Have terrorists already taken over your computers and smartphones? Be sure to stay right here with us—what you learn may save your life."

Forty-six

"And we are off the air," barked the producer.

The bright lights went dark and the crew immediately began adjusting their equipment for the next interview.

"Thank you for your time, Senator McDermott."

She nodded in his direction as she ripped the lapel microphone from her blouse and dropped it on top of the seat cushion. With her head held high, she strode out the door of the Capitol Building media room and headed down the long, marble corridor toward her office. She ignored the young assistant who was scurrying after her.

"Senator ... wait ... please. Senator, that was my fault. I should have prepped you."

No response.

After several turns, they arrived at an office. The plaque on the wall next to the door read, *Senator L. McDermott – Connecticut.* Someone had drawn a smiley face on a yellow sticky note and placed it next to the plaque. She pulled it off, crumpled it in her hand, and tossed it onto her secretary's desk as she entered the office.

"The minority leader's office is on the phone," announced the secretary.

"I'm not surprised," answered McDermott as she passed the desk and headed toward her private office.

Once inside, she stood with her arms folded staring out the window. When the door closed she turned to face her chief of staff.

"I'd say that didn't go very well. What do you think?" she asked sarcastically.

Thirty-year-old Meghan Sullivan bowed her head as she spoke.

"I'm sorry. That was my fault."

"You fed me the line about skin in the game but you didn't bother with some pretty basic fact checking."

"I know. And I'm sorry. I'll reach out to Johnson's staff and smooth things over."

"And what about the rest of the country? How do we smooth things over with the people who just watched me make a complete ass out of myself on national TV?" she asked rhetorically.

Meghan sat down on the only piece of furniture besides the Senator's desk and chair, a small loveseat tucked into the corner of the tiny office. She removed her bargain-basement pumps and rubbed her aching bare feet into the thick carpet for a few moments before answering.

"Mom, I said I was sorry. It won't happen again."

Senator McDermott shook her head and thought out loud as she sat back in the soft leather chair left behind by her predecessor.

"Sure, I'll run for office. The Senate? Why not? How hard can that be?"

Meghan groaned.

"You're doing fine, Mom. It's your assistant who needs work. I feel horrible, but I promise I'll do whatever damage control I can to keep a mistake from becoming a tragedy."

Tragedy. McDermott bristled at the word. For more than a decade, rarely had a day passed without her having to hear her name in the same sentence as that word.

"I know you will. And you can start by dealing with the minority leader's office. If they ask for me personally, tell them I've left the country."

"Will do. But please don't leave the country without me. You're all I have."

When Meghan closed the door behind her, the Senator kicked off her shoes under the desk and reached for the framed picture that sat next to her computer monitor. She and her husband Jack stood side by side, bookended by their beautiful twin girls.

You would have been so proud of her, Jack. She's been my rock.

And then the highlight reel started to play again in her head.

She is at home catching up on housework. The girls are at school. The phone rings. It's Jack. Lots of noise and commotion in the background. A poor connection, but she's able to make out the words "I love you" and "tell the girls." The phone goes dead.

She tries unsuccessfully to call him back. She paces until the phone rings again. A panicked friend asks, "Are you watching this?" She turns on the television to see images of the Twin Towers engulfed in flames. People are leaping to their deaths. Jack's remains are never identified.

Grief turns to frustration and anger. She walks for peace at countless antiwar rallies alongside her two girls, their fingers tightly entwined.

"This is the toughest thing you will ever have to deal with," her therapist says mistakenly. ...

"Are you watching this?" asks a different friend a few years later.

Images of an elementary school on lockdown. A gunman on a mass killing spree. Caroline, a first-year special-needs teacher, is killed while shielding her students. A mother stands over the bullet-riddled body of her daughter.

The only hand left to hold is Meghan's.

More protests and demonstrations. Antiwar. Gun control. Transparency. A silent activist becomes a nationwide keynote speaker. The speaker becomes a candidate with no chance. Another school shooting two days before the election. The underdog rides into office on a wave of public emotion.

Now what?

Staffing. Budgets. Arcane Senate procedures. D.C. power politics. Whispers behind her back.

"Do you really think someone with no experience or political capital can make a difference inside the beltway?" asks the Sunday morning broadcast journalist.

"Yes. If I can prevent one mother from losing her child in a school shooting—if I can prevent one foreign intervention that preserves American service members' lives and avoids the inevitable terrorist attacks on American soil that come in response to those interventions—then I will have made a difference. It's that simple."

She quickly establishes herself as one of the National Rifle Association's top public-relations threats. The spotlight intensifies. Jealous peers join in on the endless criticism. Hurtful lies. Sexism. Death threats.

Armies of private detectives and journalists digging for any hint of scandal or impropriety. Meghan's husband exposed as a philanderer. She is publicly humiliated. They quickly divorce. He leaves her with nothing but his last name.

More death threats. The Democratic Party's solution? Increased security. Surrounded by men with guns. Hypocrite.

From the other side, it's standing ovations and endless condolences. Speaking offers. Book deals. All blood money as far as she is concerned. No, thank you.

I don't want sympathy. I want to save lives.

The Senate Minority Leader rejects her letter of resignation and counters with a coveted seat on the Senate Committee on Armed Services. She accepts.

Jack always said to follow the money. She does, and she finds tens of millions of dollars funneled to classified units with funny names and phony addresses. Organizations with weaponry, operatives, and no oversight. Illegal entities run by criminals. Door after door gets slammed in her face. Stern warnings. Disconnected calls.

"For the love of God, I'm on the fucking Armed Services Committee! Don't tell me this is need-to-know! Hello? Hello?"

She contemplated reaching for the locked jewelry box in the bottom drawer of the desk and stealing a quick glance at the photo she had kept secret for decades. A knock at the door brought her back to the present. The secretary popped her head around the door.

"It's time for your security briefing, Senator. Whenever you're ready."

McDermott dusted off the frame and returned the picture to its place on the desk.

"Send them in."

Let's see who wants to kill me today.

Forty-seven

"Who was the nutjob standing behind us back there?" asked Mark.

Andy slowly maneuvered his jeep past a public works crew and briefly exchanged pleasantries with the two cops on detail.

"I'll have to introduce you to those two guys sometime. Great guys."

As he cleared the construction, he sped up and glanced at Mark.

"The idiot behind us at the Witch Hunt was William Lundgren."

"The village idiot?" asked Mark.

"One of them. People who know him say he's harmless – all talk. But he scares the shit out of me sometimes. Check out his video blog when you get a chance and you'll get to hear his unfiltered wisdom on everything from immigration to Islam."

"I think I'll pass."

Andy reached across Mark's chest and pointed his finger out the passenger's side window at the freshly mowed open field in the center of town.

"Founders Field. Remember, on July 4th my football players, other students, and I will be celebrating the town's veterans. I expect you to be there."

"You have my support, but please don't ask me to participate. It's nothing personal, Andy. I just can't do it."

"I figured you'd say something like that. What exactly is it that you do anyway?"

Mark took a moment to admire Founders Field. Groundskeepers were planting fresh flowers while others trimmed branches from the few scattered trees.

"I can't really talk about it much, Andy. But it's nothing exciting. A lot of paperwork. Meetings. Typical bullshit like any other job."

Andy laughed out loud and pounded two beefy hands on the steering wheel.

"My ass it is! You're good, man. You're very good at downplaying. I'll give you that."

Mark smiled and shook his head.

"You have no idea what you're talking about. Regardless, it may not matter for very much longer. I might be ready to retire and settle down back here."

"Interesting. And would Luci play a role in you settling down, Mr. Landry?"

"I hope so. But it's not easy. She's really making me work for it and I can't say I blame her."

Andy nodded slowly with an ear-to-ear grin.

"She's worth it, Mark. She's an extraordinary woman."

Mark squinted and looked at his friend sideways.

"Dude, it sounds like you might have a little crush on her yourself."

Andy turned onto Chestnut Lane and let the jeep coast down the hill toward Mark's house.

"Mark, every man who knows Luci has a crush on her. She's gorgeous, smart as hell, tough, and genuinely cares about people. Do the work. She's worth it and I'd love to see you two living happily ever after right here in town."

Mark unbuckled his seatbelt, hopped out of the jeep, and walked around to the driver's side.

"I'll be home watching the Sox game later on if you'd care to join me," Andy offered.

"Okay. I'll let you know. I'm not much of a sports fan but I appreciate the offer."

"So what the hell do you watch? News?"

"No. *Magnum*," answered Mark.

"You do know there's much better shows on these days than *Magnum P.I.* reruns, right?"

"Let me ask you something, Andy. That idiot back there got me thinking. I've seen some of the online comments and threats Luci gets over at the *Valley Insider*. She doesn't seem too worried about it, but they are definitely pretty extreme. You know the people in this town better than anyone. What do you make of it?"

"Yeah, it bothers me too, but I wouldn't put too much stock in anonymous comments. People can be idiots, especially when they feel threatened. The demographics of the town are changing; that's just the natural evolution of things. You can't stop it, but it will certainly change the local culture and that scares people. It's always been that way. Like I said before, none of it's really new."

Andy stuck his head out of the jeep and backed out of the driveway as Mark climbed the steps and entered the house through the side door.

Forty-eight

Frank Tagala held the full report of the Russian arms deal in his hands and resisted the urge to scream. Fifteen printed pages of typed content littered with marks from Ashton Brown's red pen. Fix this. Change that. Check your spelling. Be more specific.

You gotta be fucking kidding me.

He stuffed the report into his bag along with a laptop and headed for the elevator. Classified information was not supposed to leave the office, but if he made the corrections at home he could at least have a cocktail or two at the same time. But first he had to make a quick stop in the basement of the building where evidence is secured until trial.

Might as well add the serial numbers to the report and save Professor Brown some red fucking ink.

When the elevator door opened, he turned right and headed to the door at the end of the hall. He pushed the ringer and, a few seconds later, heard a voice from the small speaker mounted on the side of the door.

"Yes, may I help you?"

"Frank Tagala."

"Ah, yes. Agent Tagala. May I see your credentials, please?"

Frank held his middle finger up to the tiny surveillance camera embedded in the top of the speaker.

"Thank you very much. You may enter," said the voice.

The door jamb buzzed and Frank pushed his way into a small room with an additional security checkpoint. A heavy-set man sat at a desk on the other side of a reinforced chain-link fence.

"Good afternoon. May I help you, Agent Tagala?" he asked.

"Just open the fucking door. I'm not in the mood."

"All right. All right. Hold your water, Frank," he replied.

The cage door buzzed and Frank approached the desk.

"Bob, I need to see the hardware I brought in a few weeks ago."

"From Russia with love? No problem. Third aisle. About halfway down on the left."

"What are you doing, right now?" Frank asked.

"What does it look like I'm doing? I'm working my ass off here. Why? You need some help?"

"I'll be out of your hair quicker if you write down the serial numbers as I read them off. I'll owe you a beer. What do you say? Can you help an old friend on his way out of the agency?"

"Forget the beer. You getting out of my hair and the agency are reward enough."

Frank waited patiently as his longtime colleague slowly wobbled his way down the aisle.

"Here they are. Right where I said."

He unlocked the secured crates and stood ready with a notepad and pencil. Frank picked up the first AK-47, pulled the bolt to the rear to verify that it was unloaded, and read the serial number out loud.

"Slow down, Frank. These sausage fingers don't work so well these days."

Most of Frank's patience was used up before he got through the serial number from the final AK-47.

"Okay, that's it for the Kalashnikovs. Where are the Sigs?"

"I don't know."

"What do you mean, you don't know?" Frank asked.

"They're not here."

"What do you mean, they're not here? Where the fuck are they?"

"No idea. Not my job to keep track once they leave my facility."

"When did they leave your facility?" asked Frank in an increasingly annoyed tone.

"A few days ago."

"Are you going to tell me why and how, or are we going to play twenty fucking questions?"

The fat man sat down on top of an evidence crate and paused briefly before answering.

"I'm not supposed to say anything to anyone about it. But our fearless leader Ashton Brown and his right nut, Special Agent Stevenson, came in here a few days ago and took the Sigs. When I asked why, Stevenson started saying something about a sting operation. Mr. Ivy League cut him off and told me in no uncertain terms it was not my concern. Which is true. My job is to check shit in and out. So I checked them out and haven't thought about it since."

Frank rubbed his wrists and cracked his knuckles.

What the fuck do they need those for? What sting operation?

"Look, Frank. Seriously, don't let anyone know I told you that. You've got only a few weeks left, but some of us still have a few years until retirement."

Frank thought silently for a few moments. Then he leaned down and patted his colleague's large potbelly.

"Don't sweat it, Bob. It ain't my problem either. Thanks for the help. I'll let myself out."

Forty-nine

Amir drove south on I-89 with the cruise control set at seventy miles per hour. Events at the border crossing had been uneventful, and he had stopped in Burlington, Vermont, to fuel up and eat gas-station food while three young college girls in a black minivan took turns flirting in his direction.

The long drive had given Amir much time for thinking. He reflected on his faithless upbringing and typical childhood in Toronto. He reflected with disgust on the Sodom and Gomorrah of college life that he had inhaled with open mouth and nostrils—and for what? Emptiness. He smiled as he recalled with glee the moment he had first recited the Shahada, declaring that there is only one true God and that Muhammad is his prophet. In that very instant life began in earnest.

He glanced at the clock on the dusty dashboard of his rental car.

Just a few more hours.

Soon he would be introduced to his holy brothers—the chosen few with whom he would make history.

Fifty

Yasir turned off his bedroom light, opened the door a few inches, and quietly watched his uncle from the darkness.

Ghassan stood in front of the fireplace of his small cabin with a .357 revolver in one hand and a handful of rounds in the other. He released the cylinder and loaded five hollow-point bullets, one by one. When he had finished, he spun the cylinder with a chunky finger and returned it to the locked position with a lightning-fast flick of his thick wrist.

Yasir's eyes grew wide with surprise at the unexpected sight.

The aging Lebanese man then placed the gun behind the framed picture of his late wife that sat on the mantle. He paused for a few seconds to admire her beauty and to reflect quietly on the decades of joy they had shared together, and on the evil that had ripped them apart.

When the doctors had told him the end was near, he had refused to believe it. He doubled his prayers and demanded of Jesus Christ and his Father to prove their supremacy by saving the most caring, generous person he had ever known. But the harder he prayed, the faster she deteriorated.

The faithful husband whispered loving reminders to her throughout the night from his bedside perch before finally succumbing to the mental and physical exhaustion of wrestling with God. He awoke clutching her cold, lifeless hand.

Morning church bells had mocked him from outside the hospital window as a slovenly priest arrived too late for the sacrament of last rites. Desperate to save her soul, he found a local imam in the nondenominational chapel, dragged him to her room by his collar, and insisted that he perform the Salat al-Janazah.

"But this is not the way it is done," the imam pleaded.

"Do it now or yours will be next," threatened the furious widower.

The world was much less beautiful without her, and a little piece of his soul continued to die with each passing day.

We will soon be reunited in paradise, my love. My time is coming.

"Are you okay, Ammu?"

Ghassan spun around quickly to find Yasir standing directly behind him.

"I'm fine, Yasir!" he exclaimed with a hand over his heart. "And don't sneak up on me like that again or you may get hurt."

Yasir stared back with a curious expression on his face.

"Would you ever hurt me, Ammu?"

His uncle walked slowly to the kitchen and sipped from the glass of bourbon he had left on the counter. After catching his breath, he turned and spoke to the young man in a soft voice.

"Of course not, Yasir. You are my family and I would never hurt you. It's not you—it's me. I'm ready for my vacation."

"That's a good idea. You deserve a vacation, Ammu. When and where do you think you will go?" he asked with a warm smile.

Ghassan started to speak but stopped himself. Instead, he drank the remaining bourbon in his glass before answering.

"Yasir, I have already told you many times that I will be in New York City over the Fourth of July holiday and you will be in charge of the restaurant. Do you listen to anything I say? Can you be trusted, or do I need to cancel my vacation?"

"No, no, no. Do not cancel your vacation. I remember now and I can be trusted. I will make you proud when you are gone, Ammu."

"I do not want you to make me proud. I just want you to keep the restaurant open for my customers. It is not rocket science, Yasir."

"I do not understand. What do you mean by rocket—"

"Never mind. I'm going to sleep, Yasir. Good night," he said on the way to his bedroom.

Try not to screw things up too badly while I'm gone.

Yasir returned to his room, turned on his tablet, and scrolled through the only tangible remembrance he had left of his family: less than a dozen digital photos. He held back the tears until he got to the picture of his sisters that he had taken just before the fighting spilled over the Iraqi border into Syria. Tears streamed down his face and he kissed the screen repeatedly.

I am so sorry I was not there to protect you, my angels! Wherever you are and whatever they have done to you, do not lose hope! I am doing all I can to bring you home to me. With God's help I will see you both soon. I promise. Very soon.

Fifty-one

Luci parked her cruiser in front of Main Street Tailor and Fashion Accessories and retrieved her camera from the trunk. The graffiti itself was the same but smaller this time, and it was painted on the large bay window instead of on a wall. The owner waved from inside and motioned for her to come in.

"Good morning," Luci said with a warm smile. "I'm sorry you have to go through this today. But thanks for leaving it up until I could get a look at it. I promise you we're doing all we can to solve this issue."

"Maybe this will help," said the owner, holding up a small thumb drive.

"What's that?"

"Footage from the inside security camera at the back of the shop. There's no audio and it's a little fuzzy, so I don't know how much it'll help. But the time stamp is accurate—2:48 a.m."

Luci's smile widened as she extended her hand to receive the gift.

"May I take that with me?"

Twenty minutes later she sat excitedly in front of her monitors with a fresh cup of coffee.

Showtime!

Fifty-two

Mark was replacing shingles on the roof when his cell phone rang. He planned on ignoring it and letting it go to voicemail but reconsidered when he saw that it was Doc.

"Landry."

"How's it going, Mark?"

Mark straddled the peak of the roof and looked around at the other houses at the end of the cul-de-sac.

"On top of the world, Doc. What about you?"

"Wish I could say the same."

"Uh oh, what's up?"

Mark could hear Doc giving instructions to someone at the other end of the line and waited patiently for a response.

"Sorry about that. Listen, I have to be brief because I'm about to go into a meeting. But I wanted to make you aware of a major data breach."

"State Department again?"

"State, Defense, Treasury, Labor, you name it. We don't really know the full extent yet."

"Really? Any idea who? Or what they got?"

Doc took several moments to respond. Probably he was reading something, Mark thought.

"No. Like I said, we're still trying to assess things. But this is certainly the deepest breach ever."

"How deep?"

"Very deep. Maybe even Family deep."

"I thought that wasn't possible," said Mark as he did a quick 360-degree scan and started moving toward the ladder.

"Evidently it is. And this goes very deep, Mark. Personnel, budgets, even operations and history. We're moving forward under the assumption that everything might have been compromised."

"Everything? Even Berlin?"

He could hear Doc take a deep breath and exhale into the receiver.

"Yeah, possibly Berlin."

"Not good. Does the President know about this yet?"

"He's aware."

"What does Dunbar think?"

"Nothing yet. He's been busy preparing for a trip to D.C. to give his quarterly report and meet with some of the top brass off the record."

"Quarterly?" asked Mark. "I thought he gave semi-annuals."

"Mark, hold on a second again," said Doc.

Landry took advantage of the pause to mount the ladder and quickly descend. When his feet touched the grass, Doc continued.

"Yeah, reports used to be never. Then annual. Then semi-annual. Now it's quarterly. The political climate is changing and the leash is getting shorter and shorter around here. But you don't have to worry about any of that. Just watch your back like you always do, okay? And tell me, have you given any thought to your long-term plans?"

Mark climbed the stairs to the back deck and entered the house through the sliding glass door.

"Lot of thinking but no decisions. How about I take through the holiday and then let you know?"

"That'll work. I'll actually be up in Boston soon. I'm not sure for how long, but it could be a few weeks or so, depending on a few things. Let's make sure we get together."

"Boston, eh? Business or pleasure?" asked Mark, knowing full well that it was none of his business and Doc would likely tell him so.

"A bit of both. Talk soon."

The phone went dead and Mark poured himself a cold beer. *Berlin.*

Fifty-three

The thumb drive contained only one file and the shop owner had cut the video, so Luci didn't have to sift through hours of surveillance footage to see what she needed. It began at 2:46 a.m., and just as the embedded clock at the bottom of the screen rolled past the 2:48 a.m. mark, a dark figure quickly entered the shot from the right. Luci paused the video, squinted, and leaned forward until her nose was almost touching the monitor.

"Hello there," she whispered.

The fuzzy footage showed what appeared to be a male of average height, wearing baggy jeans and a dark hoodie that was several sizes too big. The drawstrings were pulled tight enough so that only a small portion of his face was exposed, and he was wearing gloves.

Luci clicked *play* and sat back in her squeaky seat.

After quickly glancing from side to side, the man held a stencil against the window with one hand and hastily sprayed paint over it with the other.

Stencils aren't very gangstah, amigo. But hey, it's your show.

He quickly painted the letters A.L.K.Q.N. underneath the stenciled crown and exited the shot the same way he entered. It was all done in under thirty seconds.

Luci watched the video a few more times until Sergeant Cromwell waved to her from the hallway.

"What's happening, Luci?"

"Hey, Sarge. Want to see my new favorite movie? It's only a few seconds long and kind of blurry, but I think you'll like it."

"Sure," he answered, turning toward Luci's desk. "That's about the length of my attention span these days. Whatcha got?"

"Not much. Just surveillance video of someone spray-painting Latin Kings graffiti on Main Street last night," she said with a hopeful smile.

Cromwell looked stunned and froze in place.

"Really? Can you make out who it is?"

"No. But it's more than we had yesterday."

"Good," he said as he pulled up a chair next to Luci's. "Let's see it."

After watching the video several times, she ejected the thumb drive and stood up.

"It's not great but it's better than nothing. I'm going to put it on the big screen in the conference room to see if I can make out any more details."

The station administrator, a civilian woman in her mid-fifties, entered the room carrying a thick pile of paperwork and a few file folders in her hands. She set the whole pile down on Luci's desk and rested her hand on top of the pile.

"Here's everything you asked for, Luci. Incident reports, call logs, and duty rosters from the dates you specified. It's all here. Let me know if you need anything else."

Luci thanked her, she left the room, and Cromwell scratched his bald head.

"What do you need all that for?" he asked.

"Just looking for patterns, Sarge. I've been focusing too much on the vandalism itself and not enough on the big picture. I'm going to catch this guy one way or the other—I can promise you that."

She picked up the pile of records and headed for the door. Cromwell stood up and followed her down the hall.

"Wait, Luci. Someone might catch him one day, but it probably won't be you. I'll take that stuff off your hands. I'm going to pass this off to the detectives. They can handle things from here."

He took the items from her grasp, and her smile gave way to an expression of pure shock and disbelief.

"What?" Luci asked. "I've been working on this for months, Sarge. Let me finish the job. I want to see this through."

"Not necessary. You've done a fantastic job, Luci. No doubt about that. But the detectives are much better suited to handle things from this point now that we have some hard evidence. It's also taking a lot of hours of your time, and I need you focused more on community policing and youth intervention. Those are your areas of expertise—not investigation. And we need you there big time right now."

You gotta be kidding me.

"Sarge, let's talk about this."

Without another word he continued down the hall, entered his office, and closed the door.

Luci contemplated what had just happened and weighed her options.

Screw it.

Cromwell had the phone to his ear when she burst into his office and shut the door behind her.

"I'll call you back in a minute."

"What's the real reason you're taking me off this?" she demanded. "It's not because I don't know how to investigate. I'm a damn good investigator. Why are you doing this to me, Sarge?"

Cromwell sat back and laced his fingers behind his head.

"I never said you weren't a good investigator, Luci. I said the detectives were better suited and have the time and resources for this. You don't. There's no hidden agenda here. It's a logical decision. Try not to get too emotional over it."

She wanted to speak but bit her tongue at his unintentionally sexist description.

Emotional? Why do women always get labeled emotional while men get to be passionate?

Cromwell held up a hand to encourage her silence and continued.

"Those are the only reasons I'm taking you off this thing. But as long as you're here, I gotta tell you, I'm starting to get a little concerned for your safety."

"Don't worry about me, Sarge. I'm a big girl," she replied with a hint of sarcasm.

"It's my job to worry, Luci. I worry about all my cops, but especially you."

"And what makes me so special?"

Cromwell stroked a few keys on his computer, focused on the screen, and began reading aloud.

" 'I hope she gets hit by a train.' 'I'd settle for a car accident.' 'She better hope she never finds herself in the middle of a crosswalk when I'm behind the wheel.' 'I wish that bitch would just kill herself. I'd even help.' And here's my personal favorite: 'Why don't they deport that spic and send her back to Puerto Rico?' I don't even know where to begin with that one."

"The *Valley Insider* is a digital rag, Sarge. Lisa Lemon is a joke. I've heard it all before and it doesn't bother or scare me."

"Bullshit. This would bother anyone, but that doesn't really matter. It bothers me and that's enough. There are other comments here that decorum precludes me from reading out loud. Listen, I'm not coddling you. I'm not treating you any differently because you're a woman – I never have. I'm simply assessing potential threats and I don't like what I see. Speaking of which, have you seen this picture yet?"

He turned the monitor toward Luci and she leaned forward.

"Or how about this other one?"

Bewildered, she leaned back and sank into the chair.

"Obviously you haven't. Let's talk about these, Luci. This first one was obviously taken at the gym. You're working up a pretty good sweat, by the way. I wish a few of the other guys would follow your example. But this second one, if I'm not mistaken, is you leaving your house."

When he had finished he sat back and waited for a response. It took her several moments to find the right words.

"Okay, I get it. I understand. I overreacted to losing the graffiti case and maybe I should pay more attention to some of this other stuff. I think it's all mostly noise … but I'll take it seriously and be careful."

"That's all I'm asking. This is a dangerous job to begin with, and we all knew that coming into it. But this other stuff is very different from the day-to-day risks. You always have to watch your back, but right now you need to watch it even closer. That is all."

Luci stood up and opened the door.

"One more thing, Luci. This is by any measure one of the best departments in the state, and you are without a doubt one of my most valuable players. And that is the only reason I didn't scoop you up and throw you out that window on your head when you burst into my office."

"Sarge, I—"

He cut her off with a wave of the hand.

"Don't sweat it. Everybody deserves a freebie. That was yours."

Fifty-four

Aside from occasional words of encouragement, Kenny fed Mr. Harrington his dinner in silence. The old man chewed, swallowed, and occasionally spit out his food with his eyes fixed out the window. He sometimes grunted, but he had not looked directly at his son in almost a week. Kenny felt helpless as he watched his father dissolve more and more each day. Kenny was starting to lose his mind too.

After a brief sponge bath and a sleeping pill mixed in with his other medicines, he put his father to bed and waited for him to drift off to sleep before applying the restraints. He hated tying his father to the bed, but he couldn't risk having him wander off again. It wasn't punishment, Kenny constantly reminded himself. It was safety.

Kenny locked all the doors and closed the drapes before sitting down at his computer and logging in. He pulled up an encrypted messaging program and clicked on the new message icon.

TO: OrcSlayer
FROM: Hobbit
MESSAGE: have job for you

His message traveled instantly through the maze of the dark web and popped up on the screen of someone he knew only by code name and quality of service. That person's true identity was as much a mystery as his own.

Kenny went to the kitchen and poured himself a small snifter of brandy. By the time he returned to his seat, he had a reply.

OrcSlayer: anything for you

Good.
He took a sip of brandy and waited a few minutes before replying, as appearing too eager could jack up the price.

Hobbit: dig for something embarrassing
OrcSlayer: no prob, subject?
Hobbit: charlie worth, former nypd, queens
OrcSlayer: priority?
Hobbit: no rush

Kenny closed the secure chat box, held the snifter to his nose, and was inhaling slowly and deeply as the doorbell rang. Startled, he logged out and tiptoed to the family room's bay window, through which he peeked at the front porch through a small hole in the blinds, the brandy snifter still in his hand.

Mark Landry waved at him from the landing with a smile on his face.

"Hi, Kenny, it's just me."

"Come on in," said Kenny, opening the door.

Landry hadn't been in the Harringtons' house for well over twenty years, but it was exactly how he had remembered it. And although outdated, each and every facet had been meticulously maintained, like a living museum of a past era.

"I'm sorry for coming over this late, but I saw the light on. Would you prefer I come back tomorrow? I would have called, but I couldn't find the number."

"You're already here, Mark. What's up?" replied Kenny as he leaned back against the foyer wall and took a slow, tiny sip of brandy.

This was a version of Kenny that Mark had not seen before—confident with a bit of a swagger. Landry figured it was either the booze or the home-court advantage. Maybe both.

"I'm doing a bunch of work on the house, but I draw the line at electrical work because I'm afraid I'll fry myself. Do you know a decent electrician in town who won't want my firstborn?"

"Yeah, sure. I think I have his card on my refrigerator. Follow me."

Mark remained in the foyer until Kenny noticed he wasn't coming and beckoned again.

"Come into the kitchen, Mark. Can I offer you a drink?"

"No, thanks. I can't stay long. I'm trying to get the house in order, and *Magnum*'s on in a few minutes."

"Suit yourself."

Kenny scanned the cards and notes on the refrigerator, then turned and rummaged through the drawer next to the kitchen sink.

"How's your father doing?"

Kenny made no response and continued his search.

"Here it is," Kenny said, holding up a faded business card with bent corners. "This guy is decent, but be sure to get an estimate up front or he might get creative on you."

He handed the card to his neighbor.

"Thanks. I appreciate it."

"Can I ask you a question, Mark?"

"Sure."

Kenny walked to the other end of the kitchen and topped off his drink.

"Are you still in the military?" he asked.

"Yeah, kind of. But that may be over soon. I'm thinking of retiring and settling down right here next door to you, bro."

Mark had yet to build a solid rapport with Kenny since his return, and the use of "bro" was probably a bit much. Kenny was awkward, but he certainly wasn't stupid or gullible.

"Are you a Delta operator?" Kenny asked out of the blue.

Landry was taken aback by the question but answered as matter-of-factly as he could.

"No. I'm not a Delta operator, Kenny."

"SEAL?"

"No."

"Special Forces?"

"Nope."

"Are you—"

Mark cut him off.

"Let me stop you before you go through every unit in JSOC, Kenny. The answer is no. My job is not nearly as exciting as you apparently imagine. But I appreciate the compliments."

His neighbor said nothing but gave him a sarcastic look that clearly said, "*I know you're lying.*"

Mark smiled and waved the electrician's business card in the air.

"Thanks for this. Before I go, can I ask you a question?"

"Shoot."

"What are you up to these days? I know taking care of your father is a full-time job, but what's your area of expertise? You were so friggin' smart growing up, I always imagined you'd end up a famous physicist or rocket scientist."

Kenny stiffened slightly at the backhanded compliment before answering.

"I'm a freelance technology consultant. Did a lot of work as a skip-tracer in the early days. Now I do mostly cybersecurity stuff. Nothing too exciting—just like you."

They wandered toward the front door and stepped out onto the front stoop.

"Sounds interesting," replied Mark. "What's a skip-tracer though? Educate me. I have no idea what that is."

"Skip-tracers find people. Missing persons, fugitives, deadbeats, criminals, former lovers, childhood friends, bail jumpers, whatever. In the early days of the Web it was pretty lucrative, but that's changed since so much information is now open-source and relatively easy to find. Regardless, if you know where and how to look, you can still dig up some interesting things these days. But that's more about connections and relationships."

Mark descended the front steps and started down the walkway toward home. But then he turned around before Kenny could go back inside the house.

"Hey, Kenny, listen. I don't want to bother you so feel free to say no. But if I gave you the name of someone I was interested in finding, could you help me?"

"Yeah, but don't you have the resources through your unexciting job to do something like that?"

Mark smiled at the sarcasm.

Not gonna let it go, are you, Kenny?

"It's not work-related. I plan on reaching out to some of Agnes's friends to let them know she's passed away. Unfortunately, she lost touch with a lot of people. As she got older, she wrote fewer letters and made fewer calls. Her closest friend told me that she got pretty reclusive over the last few years. No news, no TV. She just sat at home by herself and read. Anyway, there's a woman who she was once very close to when she lived in Watertown, New York. Always said she was like a daughter to her, but they lost touch like twenty years ago. I'd like to find her and let her know about Agnes. I started looking online, but it turns out there are a ton of Lois Sumners out there. Think you can help me out? Is there a standard fee for something like that? I'm not looking for a freebie."

Kenny swatted some mosquitoes from the porch light and finished his brandy.

"Typically, yes. But your money is no good here ... bro," he answered with a genuine smile. He beamed with pride and relished the fact that Mark Landry—some kind of super soldier—needed and apparently trusted him. "Call it a favor. Some day I may ask you for one. Just give me the name and as much detail as you can. I'll do it when I have time. No worries."

Fifty-five

Mark flipped through the channels and stopped at CNN. Fareed Zakaria was interviewing Senator McDermott.

You get around, Lady.

"You ran for office on some pretty specific issues that you are clearly passionate about, but now that you've been in office for six months, what has disturbed you the most about the way our government actually works and wages its wars?" Zakaria asked.

"That's an easy one, Fareed. Secrecy. There's a rampant lack of transparency and, in some cases, zero oversight. And that is all intentional. The system is rigged to be this way, the results are devastating, and too many of my colleagues have no desire to change it. It is disheartening when fellow senators avoid my calls and refuse to meet with me. I've sat in waiting rooms for hours while watching NRA and defense contractor lobbyists come and go as they please. And it's the American people and our service members who are paying the price. These policies and procedures are reckless and inevitably self-defeating. They make us all less safe."

"What would you change if you could?"

"I propose nothing short of full transparency and accountability for actions. Yes, I suppose there are occasionally things that might need to be classified and kept secret in the name of national security, but those cases should be exceptionally rare. We are conducting military operations in countless countries around the world. Countless, Fareed. And the last time I checked, the President only had authorization for a small handful."

"But aren't you being at least somewhat naïve about how to fight global networks of extremists? Are we to announce everything that we do in advance so they can adjust their strategies or simply wait in ambush for our forces to arrive?"

"Of course not, Fareed. But we are also trampling on our constitution. I can't get too specific, but we currently have organizations within our government with unaccountable leadership, highly trained operators, state-of-the-art weaponry, and carte blanche to conduct missions anywhere and anyhow they see fit. Their budgets dwarf those of very important education and healthcare initiatives. And the things they do—sometimes despicable acts— make them criminals by any definition."

"Strong words from a strong woman. Personally, I get the feeling that the country has never been more divided than we are today and that major changes are on the horizon—some of them drastic and perhaps too radical. Almost like the proverbial powder keg waiting for a spark. Do you get that same sense?"

"We've been divided before, Fareed. Remember, the Civil War cost almost a million lives. And—"

"But that was much more geographic than the divide we have today. North versus South was much more easily defined. Today the divisiveness is less geographic and more ideological, and it can be found in every city and neighborhood, on every street, and even within the same household."

"That's true and it is worrisome. But it also makes me want to dig deeper and work even harder because there's so much at stake."

"Thank you for joining me today, Senator."

Mark turned off the television and stared at the ceiling.

Whose side are you on, lady? It ain't the Boy Scouts we're up against.

His cell phone vibrated on the coffee table just as he was starting to drift off. It was Luci. She never called this late.

"Hey, what's up? Is everything okay?"

"Yeah, I was just thinking about you. Figured I'd call to say good night."

This is progress.

"I'm glad you did. Tell me about your day, gorgeous."

"You first."

He recounted the tasks he had completed around the house and his visit to the Harringtons next door, which reminded him that he needed to call the electrician.

"Your turn."

"Well, things were going great until I made a complete ass out of myself in front of my boss."

She shared her excitement about the video and how angry she was when Cromwell took her off the case. Mark laughed out loud when she recounted bursting into his office. But the levity dissipated quickly when the topic turned to her safety.

"Having a boss who cares about your safety isn't a bad thing, Luci."

"I know that. He was right about passing things off to the detectives and he was right to call it bullshit when I said the comments didn't bother me. But those pictures take things to an entirely different level and I'm not sure how best to handle it. Making a big deal out of something usually makes it worse."

"Well, you could start by doing something different with your hair," offered Mark.

"Huh?"

"And maybe touch up your makeup a little more before leaving the house."

"Wait, what the hell did you just say?" she asked, exasperated.

No response.

"Mark? Did you just say what I think you said?"

"Yes. But it's all just part of my plan to make you mad so I can take you out for dinner tomorrow night and make it up to you. I'm thinking some place nice and quiet. A decent bottle of wine. I'll pick you up so you don't have to drive. I'll listen and show you how much progress I've made on my road to domestication. What do you say?"

The phone was silent for several seconds before she answered.

"Actually, that does sound kind of nice. And you do have plenty to make up for."

"I'll pick you up at 7:30."

"Wait, do you have a driver's license yet?" she asked.

"Sweet dreams, Officer Alvarez."

He ended the call, closed his eyes, and breathed deeply.

Don't screw this up, Landry.

Fifty-six

"Open your eyes, Mark."

"Why? You said to do it blind."

"You will," answered Father Peck. *"But first give me the knife, have a seat, and just listen."*

Mark sat on the cool dungeon floor, caught his breath, and took a drink from his water bottle. The priest sent the knife spinning into the air. They both watched the shiny blade as it rotated and climbed within inches of the ceiling before losing momentum and dropping like a stone into Peck's waiting hand.

"Never forget that weapons—all weapons, even guns—are simply extensions of your body," he lectured as he gracefully flipped and spun the knife, passing it from hand to hand in a fluid dance. *"If you don't have control and awareness of your body, you can't possibly wield a weapon—or defend yourself against one. You understand that, right?"*

Mark chugged water and wiped his chin with his forearm.

"Yes. You've mentioned that since the beginning. I understand."

"Good. Now I want you to understand something else. You see all this flipping, spinning, and dancing I'm doing?"

"Yeah."

"It's nonsense," he declared as he closed his eyes and caught the blade behind his back with one hand. *"Nonsense that would certainly get you killed in a real battle. It's useless, Mark."*

"So how did you get so good at it?" asked the young apprentice.

"There's nothing inherently wrong with it, Mark. It's good to move your body in different ways and to know the weight of the weapon, how it flies, how it feels in your hands in different positions as you try to keep it moving like running water ... and how it can cut you if you're not too careful. Just don't ever equate that with real battle. I studied formal systems for years until I learned the reality of knife attacks the hard way."

"Where did you learn the hard way?"

"In prison," answered the priest matter-of-factly. *"Stand up and come here, Mark."*

Mark sat stunned and motionless, his eyes wide.

"Why were you in prison, Father?"

"I wasn't an inmate, Mark. I was a maximum-security chaplain. Now stand up and come here. I want to show you how it really happens."

Mark sprang to his feet and the priest positioned him in the middle of the floor.

"First things first. Prepare yourself mentally now, and if you ever find yourself in a real knife attack, expect to get cut. But the key is to try to protect

your vital areas and minimize the damage as much as possible as you counterattack with overwhelming force."

"Have you ever been cut?"

"A few times. A few scars," he answered, pointing to his elbow and thigh and finally lifting his shirt to expose a horizontal scar across his abdomen. "But each scar comes with a valuable lesson—a reason why you probably got cut."

Mark pointed at the priest's stomach.

"Why did you get cut there?"

Father Peck searched for the right words.

"Because I ignored my intuition and trusted someone I shouldn't have."

Fifty-seven

"When I was a rookie, my training officer said, 'Listen, Alvarez. If you remember only one thing, remember this: everybody lies. Everybody knows why they got pulled over. Nobody only had two beers. They know exactly where their buddy is. They knew what was in the trunk. And no matter what they say or how they look, assume everyone has a weapon.' "

"Sounds like good advice," replied Mark, grabbing the wine bottle and topping off her glass.

"It was," she answered.

The Mediterranean restaurant was packed. Mark had reserved the large, comfortable booth in the far corner of the dining room. It was normally reserved for parties of four to six, but a little extra cash made that rule temporarily go away. A sheer, white curtain separated the table from the rest of the diners and provided some privacy.

After the staff removed the empty plates and glasses from the table, Luci wedged herself into the corner, stretched her legs out on the booth's soft cushions, and admired her freshly pedicured feet and red toenails. Mark loosened his belt and removed his black loafers, leaving them beside her high-heeled shoes under the table.

"Actually, I take that back," she said after a few moments of reflection. "That all seems true a lot of the time, but I don't want to be one of those cynical cops."

"Like that Worth guy?"

"He's more creepy than cynical, but yeah," she answered.

"Not the first time I've heard that. What makes him so creepy?"

"I don't know. Nothing specific—mostly intuition. Anyway, there are plenty of good people out there; cops just don't get to interact with them very much. Unfortunately, if you're talking to me on the street there's usually a reason, but I can't let myself go down that road of automatically distrusting everyone. It'll just chip away at my soul and make me miserable. I got into the job because I wanted to help keep kids from screwing up their futures."

"How's that going?"

"Could be better, but I'm a realist. You can't save everyone, but if I can help just one kid make a better life, it's worth it. I know that sounds corny to a tough guy like you, but it's true."

"It's not corny and I'm not a tough guy, Luci. You care about people. And it's one of the things I love most about you."

She leaned forward with a mischievous smile, slightly tipsy from the wine.

"What else is on that list? I want to hear the whole thing."

"Nah, it's way too long."

"I've got time," she answered, but after glancing at her watch she corrected herself. "Actually, I don't. We need to wrap this up, Mark. I'm on the early shift tomorrow and I'm dead tired."

Mark flagged down the waiter and asked for the check.

"Did you hear about the knife attack on the Philly cop? Two attackers from opposite directions. He got one of them with a decent headshot but bled out before the EMTs could get there. The other asshole ran and slashed random people over a six-block area before a civilian woman emptied her .38 Special into him. Lone wolves inspired by the Islamic State."

"Saw it."

"I worry about you. I know you're a big girl and an experienced cop. But how often do you actually fire your weapon? How much have you trained for those kinds of ambush attacks? Are you ready if someone jumps you or goes for your gun?"

"We do some training, but thankfully stuff like that doesn't happen very much in town," she answered as she slipped her heels back onto her rested feet.

"That's good, but you never know when—"

"Mark," she said, cutting him off. "You've done well tonight. Don't blow it at the very end. Now take me home before I fall asleep on the table…"

* * *

"So, do you want me to come in?" he asked timidly as the car rolled to a stop in Luci's driveway.

"No need. I'm just going to brush my fangs and go to bed. And I can do that on my own," she answered drowsily as she stifled a yawn.

He turned off the ignition and removed the keys.

"Then I'll just walk you to the door."

"No need, Mark. But you can watch me from the car until I'm safely inside if it'll make you feel better."

"Fine."

She leaned over and gave him a long, soft kiss on the cheek.

161

"Thanks for dinner. Drive home safely and try not to get pulled over. If you do, don't call me."

With a shoe in each hand, she walked toward the house.

"Luci, do me a favor and start locking your door," he yelled from the car.

Seriously, that's just common sense. No training necessary.

"What makes you think it isn't locked?" she answered over her shoulder dismissively.

Mark put the key in the ignition and started the car. Luci climbed the front steps, twisted the knob and pushed the door open, without using a key. She tossed her shoes inside. Then she turned to face the car, stood at mock attention, and casually saluted with a brilliant smile on her face.

I love that woman.

Fifty-eight

"Don't even look at her, boys. If she says something, just keep walking," said Dunbar to the two intentionally unremarkable-looking operators who flanked him. The only thing he hated more than Washington, D.C. was the idiots who ran it.

Entitled, arrogant, greedy, clueless—every one of them. If you wanted to give the United States an enema, D.C. is where you'd stick the hose.

Senator McDermott stood alone in the long marble hallway, holding a large cup of coffee in each hand. The three men walked passed her unnoticed, slipped into the elevator, and entered a classified security code into the keypad on the interior wall. The doors closed immediately and the elevator soared toward S407, the Capitol's classified briefing room.

"Can I help you?" asked Senator Johnson.

McDermott turned and extended her arm with one of the coffees. "Good morning," she said.

Johnson smiled politely and accepted the offer. "Doctors told me to cut back, but what do they know?"

"Got a quick minute?" she asked.

"Those are the only kinds of minutes I have these days. What can I do for you?"

"I just wanted to personally apologize for what happened a few weeks ago. I would have done so sooner, but maybe your staff hasn't been giving you the messages. Regardless, I couldn't be more embarrassed and I wanted you to know that I would never intentionally say anything so insensitive. I know my assistant reached out—"

"Your daughter, right? Seems like a nice kid."

"Thank you. Anyway, is there any chance you could just forgive my boorishness? Or better yet—forget it altogether?" she asked sincerely.

"Already have. I've been around for a long time—as you were nice enough to point out—and it takes a lot more than that to ruffle my feathers. Don't worry about it, Senator. It's water under the bridge."

She breathed a sigh of relief. "I appreciate that. I'm still stumbling a bit while I try to get my footing."

"I know that, Senator. We've all been through it. Just keep at it and you'll settle in eventually. Now if you'll excuse me, I have a briefing."

"I hope you're right. There have been more than a few days when I don't even want to get out of bed, but that's my problem. Thanks again for your time."

Johnson looked at her quizzically as he sipped his coffee.

"You and I may not agree on much, but one thing I know for sure is that you're no quitter. Keep at it. But since we're talking, let me give you a tip. You're a good person and you obviously care about people. So consider shifting gears and focusing on less sensitive issues. Focus all that goodness and caring somewhere where those attributes might better serve the cause."

"You mean somewhere more appropriate for a woman?" she asked, with a tinge of sarcasm, but careful not to toss any matches on the bridge she had just built.

"No," he replied sternly. "If that's what I had meant, that's what I would have said. Strong women don't scare me, Senator. I just don't want to see you waste your time when you could be doing some real good. Take the tip for what's worth. I'm a D.C. dinosaur on the verge of extinction, but you've got a few more terms left in you if you play your cards right."

"Thanks for the tip. I know you have to go. What's your briefing about?"

"Nice try. Have a good day, Senator," he replied with a wink.

McDermott craned her neck and followed him with her eyes until he entered the elevator and punched in a few numbers on the keypad. The doors quickly shut.

Fifty-nine

Senator Johnson entered the room and sat across the table from Dunbar while the two operators stood off to the side. Nobody shook hands.

"I'll hold my questions and comments until the end and let you do your thing, Mr. Dunbar," Johnson announced.

"It's just Dunbar, Senator. That's fine. I know this isn't your first time at the circus, but I'm required to review some of the ground rules before we begin. Any information shared with you today is never to be repeated outside the company of duly vetted individuals with appropriate and current security clearances. You may not record any portion of this briefing, nor may you take notes. You may ask questions, but I may not be able to answer them. Do you have any questions before I begin, Sir?"

Senator Bradley Johnson of North Carolina was unaccustomed to the scarcity of courtesy and reverence in Dunbar's tone. Everything he had said was true, but he had added force to his words as if to taunt the Senator's ego. Johnson stared into the other man's eyes.

Got it. Enjoy your position of advantage while it lasts.

Johnson nodded his head and gave his best campaign season smile.

"I'll hold my questions until the end ... just Dunbar..."

* * *

"Does the total number of eliminations include domestic jobs? Or do we categorize those differently?" asked Johnson.

Although they were meeting for the first and hopefully the last time, Dunbar was fully aware of the Senator's support for covert programs and his willingness to look the other way when necessary. A close friend of the president's, Johnson had been instrumental in getting him to issue a classified Executive Order that essentially declared the entire globe a free-fire zone for Dunbar's operators. The order also put in place mechanisms to shield them from investigation and prosecution.

Dunbar answered the question.

"Domestic jobs are included in that number—it's all one battlefield. The targets were mostly foreign, but there's a few rogue citizens in there too."

Rogue citizens? Is that what we're calling them now?

Johnson had wholeheartedly backed a policy of targeted assassinations of American citizens who join America's enemies, and he had been an outspoken supporter of the administration when the press raised inconvenient questions about specific cases. But he silently worried about the dangerous precedent he had helped to set.

"Should it be this easy to kill one of our own citizens?" the president had asked Johnson over cocktails after viewing the footage of one such strike in Yemen. His lifelong friend and trusted confidant stared into his glass and jiggled the ice cubes as he searched for an answer.

"Hemingway wrote, 'Once we have a war there is only one thing to do. It must be won. For defeat brings worse things than can ever happen in war.' I don't have a crystal ball, Mr. President. But my gut tells me that if we can prevent a single major terrorist attack on American soil, it's worth it," said Johnson.

Dunbar sat silently waiting for the next question.

"And this list right here," said Johnson, pointing to a piece of paper but making sure not to touch it. "I understand these are their top potential assassination targets, but I would like to know more about the criteria for the list."

"Senator, this is a dynamic battlefield with lots of moving parts. The criteria change constantly. The entire list is much longer than this, though. The names you're looking at now are the people we consider our enemies' leading targets. Some of them are simply symbolic targets; others are on the list because of what they do and say."

"I'm still a little confused. It's not surprising to see my own name, given my political stature and proximity to the president. But there are a few folks here whose presence on the list boggles the mind, Dunbar. How would terrorist organizations benefit from eliminating people who crusade against foreign interventions, guns, secrecy, and all that good stuff? You'd think they would want more of them, not less."

Dunbar answered without hesitation while glancing at his watch.

"That all depends, Senator. If they whacked a dove and took credit for the hit, it might certainly work against them. Support for the cause could wane, donors could dry up. But attribution is everything. If they whacked that same dove but pinned it on someone else, they might benefit from the fallout."

Johnson sat back and breathed deeply.

"It sounds like you've thought about this, Dunbar. Keep going, please. Do you have any theories about who they would pin things on and why?" he asked.

Because I know you won't tell me unless I specifically ask.

"Our analysts have looked at this pretty closely and think it might represent an entirely new front in the war on terror. There is no force on earth that can go toe to toe with our military, so nobody's dumb enough to even try it. So they will continue to coax us into scenarios designed to bleed us dry, but that could take generations if it works at all. They're frustrated and not nearly as patient as people think. They know they cannot defeat America, so the plan may be a long-shot gamble to get America to defeat itself."

"What do you mean?" asked Johnson.

"The political climate in the United States these days is fragile. They want to take advantage of that and pit Americans against each other. Brutally kill enough cops, and law enforcement across the country will be wound so tight with paranoia that they'll assume everyone is a threat and treat them accordingly—sowing even more discontent than there is now. Targeted assassinations and attacks can also be pinned on domestic groups. For example, if the President of the NRA was killed and attribution was given to a far-left organization, or if a liberal icon was eliminated and the blame was placed on right-wing groups, it could stir the pot much worse than a few marches or some hasty legislation. Imagine five or six simultaneous attacks on abortion clinics where all evidence leads to mainstream anti-abortion conservatives. Or a string of Mosque, Synagogue, and Christian Church bombings."

"Civil war," whispered Johnson.

"Something like that, Senator. It's a long shot, but if it ever hits we're in for a world of shit."

Dunbar looked at his watch again and tapped his fingers on the table. Johnson took the hint and slowly stood up.

"Very well. Thank you for your time, gentlemen."

"Don't thank us, Senator. We were never here."

Sixty

Frank Tagala was in the operations center of the Boston Joint Terrorism Task Force office, but his mind was still back in his own office.

"What am I, a fucking delivery boy now?" he had said as another agent handed him a thick package, along with instructions from Ashton Brown to deliver it to the JTTF.

Whatever, Brown. Two more weeks. That's about all the time you have left to fuck with me. Enjoy it while it lasts.

Frank noted that he knew fewer people each time he visited the JTTF. His generation's presence was slowly fading away as younger, better-educated, and much easier-to-lead professionals moved in.

You're getting old, Frank. Deal with it.

After delivering the package and catching up with a buddy, he said goodbye and walked down the hall to wait for the elevator. When the door opened, a young woman in her late twenties and a much older gentleman abruptly ended their conversation and exited. Frank's head was down as he fumbled with the smartphone that the agency forced him to carry, so he did not notice that he was in the couple's path.

"Excuse us," said the older man.

"Oh, sorry," replied Frank as he looked up and stepped to the side.

The pair exited and walked down the hall toward the secure briefing room while Frank tried not to stare. The young woman was stunningly beautiful with a sculpted body and smooth skin. The older gentleman, tall and fit, carried himself with an air of quiet confidence. Frank's eyes were still fixed on the woman's body when she turned her head and glanced at him over her shoulder.

Busted. I need to retire before I get myself into trouble.

Sixty-one

Senator McDermott and Meghan waited quietly in the back of the armored car for several minutes before Meghan broke the silence.

"You know you don't have to do this," said Meghan. McDermott nodded her head.

"Yes, I do. It's a mistake to run from these people or act like they don't exist. If you don't engage with them, you can't influence the message. I have to do this."

"You don't have anything to prove to anyone, Mom."

"It's not about proving anything, Meghan. It's all for the cause. Softball interviews and appearances rarely sway opinion or compel change. I have to do this. Sway public opinion and Congress will have to answer. At least that's how it's supposed to work."

"Okay, I'm with you," she said, reaching over to squeeze her mother's hand.

Fox News, here we come ...

* * *

A very young, obscenely polite staffer who looked as if she had probably been born during the first term of the Bill Clinton administration greeted the women at the door.

"Think she's going prom dress shopping later?" joked Meghan as they followed her down the hall to hair and makeup.

Another staffer, a young man slightly older than the first, sat next to McDermott for preshow prep as an older woman touched up the Senator's makeup.

"And that's basically it, Senator. It's just a friendly conversation between you and him, and it'll air tonight at 8 p.m. Do you have any questions? Or can I get you anything to make you more comfortable?"

"I'm fine, thank you," answered McDermott with a smile.

"Great! You're up next, so just sit tight and we'll come and get you when it's time. And thanks again for coming, Senator. We really appreciate you accepting our invitation," he said cheerfully.

McDermott finished her hair and makeup and waited in the green room, the knot in her stomach getting bigger with each passing moment. She watched the monitor and listened as the host set up the next segment.

"Next up on *The Factor*, we'll welcome Senator McDermott of Connecticut, an outspoken critic of America and crusader for radical change. You won't want to miss this."

What the hell have I gotten myself into?

Sixty-two

"But certainly someone of your intelligence can see the hypocrisy of your positions. You want to change the Second Amendment of the United States Constitution and strip Americans of their right to defend themselves, yet you arrived in an armored car surrounded by armed men and women?" asked Bill O'Reilly.

"Let me clarify, Bill. If it were up to me, I'd change a lot more than just the Second Amendment, but I think that's where we need to start. Guns are simply too easy to get in this country, and we pay the price every day with our children's spilled blood. No more. Those lives may not matter much to the NRA, but they mean quite a bit to many of us, and we're not going to just sit back and tolerate it," she replied confidently.

"You didn't answer the question about your own security, and quite frankly, you've just served up more hypocrisy. You say it's all about children's lives, but you're an outspoken opponent of any restrictions on abortion whatsoever. How do you reconcile all these contradictions, Senator? And do you honestly think the NRA doesn't care about children?"

"Of course not, Bill. I think I was simply trying to make a point. But showing up within hours of a tragedy and screaming from the rooftops that the answer to our gun problem is more guns is pure insanity. If nothing else, the NRA leadership is tone deaf. And a lot of Americans agree with me."

"That's true, but there are an awful lot of Americans who, quite frankly, fear you. They fear your radical agenda and your vision of what America should be."

"That's their problem, Bill. I am unwaveringly committed to my causes and fully aware of the opposition. But they don't scare me."

"Something must scare you, Senator. There are armed guards and police officers following you everywhere. Which brings me to even more hypocrisy. You gave a speech last month in which you thundered away for more than an hour about America's police officers. You painted them as a 'militarized mob of unaccountable thugs,' and that's a direct quote. Why do you hate America's heroes so much? What have Officers Hale and McCracken done to deserve your vitriol?"

McDermott hesitated before speaking.

"Yes, I've used some pretty strong words, Bill. But every morning when the American people wake up, they wonder what it's going to be that day—another mass shooting or another viral video of police officers brutalizing the very citizens they've sworn to protect. Almost as scary as the brutality itself is the standard line from too many law enforcement officers who say that unless you've worn a badge and worked a shift, you can't be critical of them and your opinion doesn't matter. That mindset alone tells me that it's time for major police reform and that law enforcement officers across the country need to be reminded whom they work for. As for the names you just mentioned—I have no idea who you're talking about."

"I'm not surprised, Madame."

O'Reilly smirked and narrowed his eyes before continuing.

"Officers Hale and McCracken are two of the officers who have been escorting you around the city all day. They haven't left your side since 5:00 this morning. Right now they're waiting in the green room to escort you to safety once we're finished. Why do you have so much contempt for the people who keep you and the rest of America safe?"

Things went downhill from there, but when O'Reilly gave her the final word she rallied and finished as strongly as she could. Overall, the appearance was unlikely to sway people in either direction, but she had avoided disaster and could put this one in the tie column.

Meghan waited off camera with their personal items in hand and was ready to get the hell out of there as soon as the taping was complete. McDermott grabbed her bag from Meghan, and the two made a beeline for the elevators.

"I hate that man more than al-Qaeda," remarked McDermott.

The energetic young staffer who had talked with her in the prep room slipped into the elevator just as the doors began to close.

"Wow, that was close. Glad I didn't have to run down all those flights of stairs to catch you, Senator!"

"Thanks, but we can see ourselves out," said Meghan.

"Okey dokey. I can let you do that. But I'm afraid I can't let you leave with the microphone. Can I have it please, Senator?" he said, pointing to the tiny microphone still clipped to McDermott's lapel.

"Oh no, is it still on? How far is the range on this thing?" asked McDermott worriedly.

They knew by the expression on the perky young man's face that he had heard the comment about O'Reilly and al-Qaeda. As the Senator unclipped the microphone, Meghan noticed the smartphone in the staffer's hand. He was recording them.

"Turn that thing off right now," Meghan said, pointing to the phone. "Turn it off or I'm going to shove it down your throat."

Due to Meghan's distance from the microphone, her threat sounded a little muffled as it was replayed over the next few days on every media outlet imaginable, but there was no doubt to whom the voice belonged. By comparison, the audio of the Senator declaring her preference for al-Qaeda over Bill O'Reilly was crystal clear.

McDermott supporters applauded the Senator and Meghan gained a bit of street cred for her part. Opponents had a field day and O'Reilly basked in the controversy, milking it for everything it was worth.

"Unless you've been living under a rock, you are probably aware of Senator McDermott's recent appearance on *The Factor* and her subsequent slip of the tongue. Well, the Senator has personally apologized to me and I fully accept it. Honestly, it's not a big deal and I get called worse things on a daily basis. Sometimes much worse," he intoned with a smile on a subsequent program.

"Over the decades, I myself have occasionally let emotions take over and said a few things I later regretted. It happens. I do not think any less of the Senator or her daughter for simply being human. They are both good people and are welcome back any time. But I'd be remiss if I didn't say that many of those who share her radical vision for America probably do hate traditional Americans like me more than al-Qaeda. After all, whenever terrorists attack, we typically get to share the blame. And that's why their vision for America is so dangerous. If folks like Senator McDermott and her kind were in charge of the country, traditional Americans like me and the millions who faithfully watch this show would be an endangered species. Be vigilant, my friends. Electing radicals is a lot tougher to take back than a hateful comment. And that's the memo."

Sixty-three

Mark was on his ladder painting the house when Doc called. "I'm in Boston. How about lunch tomorrow, Mark?"

There was no set agenda, but Mark expected to be pushed about his plans. Would he stay with the Family in his current role, change roles, or retire and start a new life?

Doc was already seated at an outdoor table when Mark arrived at the restaurant. With his back to the building, he watched throngs of tourists file back and forth along the cobblestone streets around Faneuil Hall. A glass of ice water and two menus sat on the table in front of him. He stood when Mark arrived, and the two shook hands firmly.

"I'm glad you're here, because I'm starving," said Doc.

"Me too. I hate cooking, so I haven't been eating much. I already know what I want. A full rack of ribs and a Sam Adams."

"I'll have the same," replied Doc.

As the two men talked and caught up, both constantly scanned the environment from behind their sunglasses. When vigilant civilians scan the crowd in a public space, they try to see everything and often end up seeing nothing. They look for obvious anomalies like a guy wearing a heavy coat on a warm day or someone who is constantly adjusting his clothing to accommodate a concealed weapon. But when an operator scans the environment, he sees math. He sees probabilities and equations that need to be solved. He looks for ever-so-subtle anomalies—micro-expressions. The operator sees someone holding a coffee cup or steak knife just a little bit differently from everyone else. The operator intuitively assesses which person is likely to be the most dangerous and why, who will likely run at the first sign of trouble, how to get to the edge of any potential incident so he has only 180 degrees to deal with instead of 360, which way he would break if necessary. It's a difficult skill by itself, made even tougher by the need to do it naturally while simultaneously carrying out other tasks. Both men talked, ate, and continuously scanned without missing a beat.

"Well, you knew I was going to ask, so here it is: have you made any decisions?" asked Doc after the waitress removed the plates of bones from the table.

"Yeah, I think I have. I'm all done, Doc. I'm going to retire and settle down. I hope that doesn't adversely impact your plans."

Doc grinned widely. "Of course not, Mark. You're valuable, but we're all replaceable. And to tell you the truth, I think you're making the right decision. You're still young. Go start a family and enjoy yourself. You've earned it. Besides, things are changing so quickly, you might be returning to a completely different kind of unit if you decided to stay. Do you want kids?"

"I do. I want a family. I want to be a father. I never really had one, but I want to be one," Mark answered.

"I admire that. My kids have been grown for a long time. We're a close family, but I missed a lot and I can never get that time back. You're wise to avoid that if you can. Avoid the guilt."

"Guilt?" asked Mark. "What kind of guilt?"

"The guilt of not being there when they need you. When all the other dads were watching their kids score goals, I was nowhere to be found. When my wife was blindsided by another car and she and our two children were taken to the emergency room, they needed me to be there and I wasn't. The list goes on and on. What we do is important, Mark. We help to protect the country. But that job comes at a price—sometimes we're not there to protect the ones we love. I'm happy for you. It's not my business, but is there anyone else in the picture?"

"I'm working on that part, Doc."

Both laughed and finished their beers. Doc paid the tab. They exited the restaurant and walked along the Freedom Trail, the brick path that weaves its way in and out of Boston's most significant historic sites. Out-processing from the Family would be relatively painless but might take a day or two, Doc explained.

"And we can do that any time after the holiday, ok?" he added.

And that's when Mark saw her. Alone. Thirty to forty feet away. Big designer sunglasses. Shopping bags. He couldn't remember, maybe she was a brunette the last time he saw her, but the body was impossible to forget. And even though she had casually oscillated her gaze between the shop window and the two men walking near her like a seasoned professional, Mark had spotted her.

Sadie? Prague, was it?

Several years earlier, the Family had sent her, twenty-five years old and straight out of selection and training, to a field assignment with Mark. The two had playfully walked throughout the city, hand in hand, as they secretly followed a dangerous freelancer affiliated with several terrorist organizations. Mark was sure that their

175

cover was blown when the target abruptly turned around and looked directly into his eyes. Before he knew what was happening, Sadie had creatively pushed him against a building and started slapping and kicking him, screaming at the top of her lungs about his wandering eyes and prior infidelities.

The target had circled back and peeked at them from across the street before going on his way unsuspectingly, but she kept up her tirade until a shopkeeper shooed the couple away from his storefront. Mark remembered her as fearless, with the instincts of a much more experienced operator.

Doc waved a hand in front of Mark's face.

"Relax—she's with me, Mark. Security, believe it or not. I used to go everywhere unaccompanied, but Dunbar forbids it since the data breach. Everyone's on edge, and some have even moved their families. It's a good time to retire, Mark."

"Moving families, really?"

"Yes. The world is changing, Mark. The battlefield used to be a faraway place to which we deployed; now it's the ground under our feet."

Both men subconsciously looked down at the Freedom Trail bricks and noticed that they were at the corner of State and Congress Streets, the site of the 1768 Boston Massacre.

"Things have changed, all right. At least they were nice enough to wear bright red coats back then," said Mark.

Sixty-four

Frank Tagala was done for the day and on his way out of town when a minor accident in front of him halted traffic for a few minutes. Horns blared all around him, but Frank was transfixed on the two men talking on the other side of the intersection.

Is that Agnes's kid? And who's the other guy? He looks familiar. Where do I know him from?

Two Boston cops on foot patrol cleared the accident scene, and cars started moving again. One block down the street, Frank spotted the stunning young woman and instantly made the connection. He had seen her and the older gentleman getting off the elevator inside the Joint Terrorism Task Force headquarters a few days earlier. And now they just happened to be hanging out with his neighbor.

Interesting.

Sixty-five

"This kid is kicking up a storm in there, John. He's dying to get out and I'm dying to get it over with. Any day now," said Linda.

"I'm ready too, babe. You've done all the heavy lifting so far and my role has barely gotten started. I can't wait to get that boy out so I can put him to work around the house," joked Officer John McDonough into his cell phone.

"I hope he has my nose," she said.

"Why your nose? What's wrong with—"

McDonough was startled by the unexpected knock on his cruiser's trunk and froze momentarily.

"John? John?"

"I'll call you right back," he replied quickly.

He saw Ghassan waving in the rear-view mirror and exited the vehicle.

"Sorry if I scared you, my friend. I didn't mean to sneak up on you."

"No problem, Ghassan. I was just talking to my wife. The baby is due any day now, so we're both a little on edge."

"Great news! I am so happy for you and hope you will allow me to visit the boy when I return from vacation. I'm actually on my way out of town right now, but when I saw you parked here, it reminded me to ask a favor."

"What is it?" asked McDonough.

"I'll be gone for about a week, and Yasir will be in charge of Baba Ghassan's. He's supposed to keep the ship afloat through the holiday. I am sixty percent sure he can pull it off, but if you wouldn't mind keeping an eye on the place I would feel better. If that's not too much to ask."

"Not at all. I'll be working through the holiday anyway. Where are you headed? Anywhere exciting?"

"Not really. I'm going to visit my sister and her family in New York City. She's a pain in the ass and her family is worse. But I said I would go, and it would break my mother's heart—God rest her soul—if I didn't. You have a good week and best of luck with your son. I can't wait to meet the little prince!" boomed the old man.

"Thanks. Travel safely."

"God willing," answered Ghassan. "God willing."

Sixty-six

Luci arrived home from the gym to find that Mark had cleared out her garage and assembled protective mats on the floor. When she pulled up, he approached her unrolled window.

"Hello, beautiful. Your warrior training is about to begin."

"Seriously? Mark, I just did an hour and a half at the gym and I'm beat."

"Good. It'll be more realistic then. Bad guys typically don't wait for you to be well rested and standing like *this* before they attack," he said, raising one knee and holding bent wrists high above his head like the Karate Kid to illustrate his point.

"Very funny. Fine, just let me change my gym clothes. These are soaked."

"Good. You do that and I'll finish preparing the dungeon. Bring your duty belt with unloaded handgun and spare magazines—all empty. Body armor too."

* * *

Luci was taken by surprise when Mark lunged forward and slashed at her with the knife. When she hesitated, he pulled her in close with one arm and pushed the blade up and under her body armor with the other.

"Hey! You said on three, and you attacked me after one! Not fair, Landry," she exclaimed, huffing and puffing.

He let go and backed up so that she could catch her breath.

"Sorry, I've never been any good at counting. Besides, didn't your training officer teach you that everybody lies?" he asked with a sarcastic smile. "Take a quick break and drink some water. A few close-quarters pistol drills and we'll be done."

When Luci explained that she normally carried her pistol without a round in the chamber and with the safety on, Mark nodded.

"That doesn't make any sense. If you ever need your gun, you need to be able to draw with one hand and squeeze the trigger. You don't want to be messing around with a safety, and the chances that you'll have time to chamber a round are slim to none—less if you have to do it all one-handed while someone is attacking you."

"I know that, Mark."

"Then why would you carry like that?"

"If you must know, I had an accidental discharge once and it scared the hell out of me. Nobody was hurt, but just thinking about what could have happened freaks me out. I chamber a round when I do my annual qualification. Other than that, I prefer to err on the side of extreme caution. I'm constantly surrounded by kids."

"When did this happen?"

"In the academy. It almost cost me my slot."

"Luci, that was like fifteen years ago. It's all in your head. You need to get over it. It's dangerous to carry your weapon in any status other than ready to fire. Bad things happen quickly, and you may only have a split second to protect yourself and the kids you spend time with."

Luci nodded. "I know. You're right."

"First, show me how fast you can draw, disengage the safety, chamber a round, and fire your first shot. After that, I want to show you something."

She oriented herself toward a target taped to the far wall of the garage, breathed deeply, executed the drill, and reholstered.

"Not bad. Honestly, I was not expecting you to be that fast. Two things, though. First, don't get in the habit of immediately reholstering your weapon. If you do that in training, you'll do it in the field and it'll get you killed. Keep it out and scan the area for additional threats before you reholster. Second, come over here and stand against the wall, facing me."

When she was in place, he closed the distance between them so that they stood belly to belly.

"Now do it again, using me as your target."

"Sounds like a bad idea, Mark."

"We've both checked that weapon multiple times as well as each of the magazines. They are unloaded and there is no live ammunition in the dungeon at all. Do it."

As she inhaled and prepared for the drill, he unexpectedly pinned her against the wall, with one hand on her throat and the other on her left elbow. She was surprised but drew the handgun with her right hand, much more quickly than he had expected. Then came the lesson.

"What's wrong, Officer Alvarez? Someone is trying to kill you. Why aren't you shooting to protect yourself?"

She had the gun in her hand with the muzzle pressed up against his midsection, but with her left arm pinned she was unable to rack the slide of her Smith and Wesson M&P Shield 9mm and chamber a round.

"See how hard it would be to rack the slide off your belt or something with one hand to chamber a round when someone is attacking you? Looks like you were barely able to flip off the safety," he said as he released his grip and stepped back.

"Okay, I get it. The weapon needs to be ready to go at all times."

"Why?"

"There may not be time to undo the safety and chamber a round. And if I lose the use of my left arm, I'm screwed. I get it. You're right."

"Exactly. If it's not ready to go, it might as well be a paperweight. So, no safety—ever—and always have a round in the chamber. Also, don't ever press the gun up against anything or anybody like you did to me—you run the risk of knocking it out of battery, and then it's useless. Now let's do some retention and disarming drills with handguns and edged weapons. Are you having fun yet?" he asked.

"Actually, yes. I've been thinking about this stuff a lot lately and I appreciate the help."

For the grand finale, Mark took her handgun, magazines, and the training knives over to the sink. She followed and watched as he ran warm water over the equipment and added a few squeezes from a bottle of liquid soap to the mix.

"Germophobe?" she asked.

"Nope. Just making them warm, slippery, and a little bit sticky—just like blood."

He told her to face the wall so that she couldn't see. Then, after scattering the weapons at the far end of the mat, he turned out the lights and returned to her side.

"When I say *turn around*, do it, locate the nearest weapon, and kill me before I kill you. I know you have all kinds of rules of engagement in your job, but for our purposes, let's operate under the assumption that you're fighting for your life. So don't bother pulling out your pepper spray or threatening me with a citation. Understand?"

"Understood. Kill Landry. Got it," she answered.

He leaned in close and whispered softly in her ear.

"I'd better not get to a weapon before you do."

Sixty-seven

"You want a beer or something, Mark?"

"Not right this second. I want to finish cleaning your gun first," he replied.

Luci was cooking a Colombian dish and the smell was driving him wild.

"Man, what is that? That smells incredible."

"That's all me, Landry. Or did you mean the food?"

He stood up from the table and approached the stove.

"Mind if I try it?" he asked, gently grasping the large wooden spoon in her hand.

"Go for it."

Mark took a small bite and chewed it slowly, savoring the flavor.

"Not bad at all. Nicely done. On a side note, we should go to the range some time soon and do some live fire. I've seen cops at ranges before, and a lot of the time they make me cringe. You've got solid fundamentals and will be a great shooter with a little coaching."

He sat back down and finished assembling Luci's 9mm.

"Can I ask you a question? And I need a straight answer," said Luci as she finished her wine.

"Those are the only kinds of answers I give. What's the question?"

"Why are you doing all this, Mark?" she asked in a solemn voice that he had not heard since his return.

"Why am I doing what?"

"This. Everything. Why are you so concerned with my training? Why are you home? Why are you trying so hard to win me over? When are you leaving? All that stuff. I don't want to play any games. I just want to know what you're thinking."

Landry stood, grabbed a beer from the refrigerator, and looked out the glass door onto the deck.

"That was a lot of questions, Luci. Which one should I answer first?"

"Your call."

"Okay, I'm home because I had some leave time and needed to make a major decision whether or not to retire. I came here because this is the only home I've ever had. I'm training you because you need it. I'm never leaving. And you already know why I've been trying so hard to impress you."

"You need to elaborate on those last two, Landry."

Mark approached her from behind, wrapped his arms loosely around her waist, and watched her gently stir the food.

"I'm not leaving you, Luci. I'm retiring. Already told my boss."

Her pulse quickened as she turned her head and looked at him out of the corner of her eye.

"Is that right?" she asked.

"Yeah, that's right."

"Then why am I having such a hard time believing you?"

"You want some proof?" he asked.

Then he reached into his back pocket, pulled out his freshly minted Massachusetts driver's license, and placed it on the counter in front of her.

"I waited six hours at the registry to get that—and I was in the express lane," he whispered in her ear, kissing her neck gently. "How's that for commitment?"

"And why have you been working so hard to impress me?"

He pulled her closer than they had been in years.

"You already know why, Officer Alvarez—because I love you. I always have and I always will. I'm home now and I'm not leaving, Luci. And if you'll have me, I want to spend my life with you."

They stood silently for several moments. He maintained his embrace and she continued to stir. "You know, I'm not an expert at this, Luci," he said finally. "But I'm pretty sure you're supposed to talk next."

When she turned around to return the embrace, her mouth was smiling but her eyes were staid. He started to speak but she cut him off.

"Mark, you already know how I feel too. And I'm thrilled to hear you're here for good and want to be with me. And I can't believe you actually got a driver's license," she joked. "I love you too, but I have to tell you right now that there's a part of me that thinks I could wake up one day and you'll be gone. You have to promise me you'll never leave me again. I have to hear you say it."

He pulled her tighter and spoke softly into her ear.

"Luci, you're never getting rid of me. I promise you I will never leave you again."

"And I need you to promise me one more thing," she said in deep breaths as he kissed her neck and nibbled on her ear lobe.

"Anything," he whispered.

"No more secrets, Mark. I understand the past and I get that. But from this moment forward—no more secrets."

"Done. No more secrets. I promise," he murmured as he gently turned her around, lifted her shirt, and started kissing the small of her back working his way down.

Luci turned off the stove, arched her back, and breathed heavily.

"One more thing ... let's take this to the Jacuzzi."

Mark stopped and looked up.

"You have a Jacuzzi?" he asked.

"Yeah, it's upstairs," she said, pulling him up by his hair with both hands to whisper in his ear. "And I'd better not get there before you do."

Sixty-eight

Mr. Harrington had refused to eat all day and started crying hysterically just moments after Kenny strapped him to his bed for the night. There was no consoling him, so Kenny escaped to the family-room sofa and covered his head with pillows. He couldn't bear the sound of his father suffering and wanted to hide his own cries of pain from the world. The part-time caretaker was scheduled to start after the Fourth of July holiday, but that couldn't come soon enough.

When the old man finally drifted off to sleep, Kenny poured his nightly cognac and settled down in front of his computers. A secure message was waiting for him.

> TO: Hobbit
> FROM: OrcSlayer
> MESSAGE: got info on your target ... it's juicy

Kenny leaned back in his chair and sipped his drink.

> Hobbit: spill it
> OrcSlayer: had to go off-net for some of it

Going "off-net" indicated that he did not complete the task entirely digitally. OrcSlayer had investigated and collected some of the information the old-fashioned way—by physically interacting with other humans. Kenny knew that type of work required time, sharp investigative skills, and maybe even a payoff or two. OrcSlayer would not have done so without good reason and probably wouldn't be mentioning his effort unless he wanted to be compensated.

> Hobbit: better not be messing with me
> OrcSlayer: nobody messes with you
> Hobbit: money or favor?
> OrcSlayer: more money ... same as last time
> Hobbit: gimme the gist first
> OrcSlayer: major harassment issues in Queens ... almost kicked off force ... sealed records ... I have everything
> Hobbit: transferring money now ... want docs in my box within the hour ... good work
> OrcSlayer: anything for Hobbit

Transferring money anonymously had become very difficult in recent years, but Kenny had the funds delivered in just a few keystrokes.

He swirled his cognac and scrolled through a list of real-time freelance gigs available through an online clearinghouse buried deep in the Web—a place where anonymous customers paid top dollar for the cyber services of anonymous providers. These included some extreme jobs: advanced skip traces, cyber espionage, critical infrastructure attacks, bank crashing, disruptive operations, sabotage, identity wipe and destruction. The capabilities required to perform these jobs shrank the pool of potential contractors drastically. Conversely, the fees skyrocketed once one got beyond garden-variety tasks like causing denials of service (DOSs) and introducing simple viruses. There was big money to be made, but big money always came with substantial risk that most freelancers couldn't stomach, like walking into a sting operation. This made the pool even smaller and the fees even higher.

Who were the clients? Most of the time he had no idea. Other times he probably could have pieced it together if he cared; he just didn't. On at least one occasion Kenny suspected that he was doing a freelance gig for the Office of Tailored Access Operations (TAO), a clandestine group within the National Security Agency. Call it intuition.

Nothing interested him. Nothing got his blood pumping. Kenny had done it all and had plenty of money. Yet he stayed in the game, like a drug addict futilely chasing the first hit. He had done risky jobs that brought him small fortunes and notoriety in underground circles, but the inimitable rush he craved was elusive, like a blissful lightning that refused to strike twice.

He contemplated going to bed but looked at his watch and decided that he could put in an hour or two of work before turning in. More than enough time to cause trouble for a bank in Cyprus. Besides, he was curious to see what Officer Charlie Worth had been up to in Queens.

Sixty-nine

"Seriously, this is fantastic," said Mark, his mouth full of the Colombian dish Luci had made. "I'm impressed. You've always been a good cook, but this is a new level."

She smiled and leaned over to place her empty plate on the night table next to her bed and took a long sip of ice water.

"Thanks. I've been practicing and experimenting with different things for years. It distracts me from work and helps me relax. I'm glad you like it."

Mark finished his plate, leaned back against the headboard, and wrapped his arms around her. They lay there silently, their minds racing with excitement and curiosity about their future together. Both wanted to get married and have kids, but they had yet to talk about the timing or even where they would eventually live. Luci's house? New house? Those details would all be worked out eventually. The important thing was that they were finally together.

"I know you miss Agnes, Mark. And you've told me how much Father Peck meant to you. And I know you'd never change that for the world. But do you ever wonder about your real parents? Who they were? Why they gave you up for adoption?"

He thought for a moment while caressing her bare shoulder.

"No. Not really," he answered.

"It would bother me. I would have to know. What about Agnes? Did she ever bring it up or offer any information?"

"Nope. I guess she either never knew or had her own reasons for never bringing it up. I don't ever think about it, and at this point it doesn't matter anyway. I've got you and that's all that matters."

He leaned over, turned off the light, and rolled on top of her.

"Let me guess, you have an early morning tomorrow?" Mark asked.

She wrapped her arms and legs around him tightly and bit down firmly on his ear lobe. "Actually, I'm taking a personal day," she whispered through clenched teeth.

"No curfew?" he asked.

"No curfew," she said, gently tapping a soft hand on top of his head a few times before tenderly pushing downward. "So why don't you get back to work."

Seventy

McDermott and Meghan stood in the kitchen of the Senator's fifth-floor apartment and stared at the television in awe.

"What the hell happened? This is surreal," stated Meghan.

"Look at the fear in his eyes. He's petrified. And now I'm petrified," answered McDermott.

When screening her mother's mail a few days earlier, Meghan had opened an anonymous envelope with several typed pages inside. After she had picked her jaw up from the floor, she immediately interrupted McDermott's security briefing to share the new information.

Both agreed that the information must be shared with the public but were fearful of the fallout. So far, McDermott's attempted ventures into the black-ops world had been met with overt hostility. Leaking this information might go a bridge too far and make matters even worse for them. As they contemplated their options, a light bulb lit up over Meghan's head.

"Why don't we just give it to someone with more political clout—someone established and better at this, maybe even someone a bit narcissistic, up for reelection with eyes on the presidency one day?"

"The minority leader?" asked McDermott.

"Why not? He'll receive it the same way we did but will make a beeline for the cameras. The information gets out, but we don't have to look for plastic on the floor of every room we walk into for the rest of our lives. What do you say?"

"Are you sure we're not being cowardly? This is some of the stuff I've been digging for, and now that I might have something I immediately hand it off?"

"It's not cowardly. Remember what you said about the cause and having nothing to prove? As long as we stay true to the cause, we can sleep at night. Someone else can take the credit, right? It's not cowardly, Mom. It's altruistic. You can get the information to the American people without jeopardizing your position. And they have a right to know."

The minority leader invited a handful of journalists into his office within a few hours of receiving the information.

"Under my direction, my staff has just completed an exhaustive investigation into the unauthorized and perhaps illegal actions of the current administration. I cannot go into specifics just yet, but suffice it to say that the results of the investigation are beyond troubling. The American people and the world we lead deserve better."

He went on to broadly describe covert operations run by unaccountable organizations. "Such organizations are not only illegal, but costly to the taxpayers and irreparably damaging to the nation's credibility."

Then he dropped the bomb. For the first time since its inception, the Family was mentioned by name in public. At the end of his impromptu, invitation-only press conference, he took no questions. The journalists scurried to break the story and started sharing information before they had even left his office.

Six hours later, the minority leader stood at the podium a quivering mess. He had acted too soon. His announcement was premature. He was not really sure where the information came from and could not verify the claims. He may have been duped by a practical joke.

"In conclusion, I cannot verify any of the information I foolishly passed on and I apologize for creating a storm over nothing."

Meghan muted the television after he left the podium and pointed the remote control at her mother.

"You know what? This is profoundly embarrassing for a man obsessed with his own image and legacy. This could torpedo his entire political career. I can only assume that the alternative was much worse for a guy like him to completely fold and run away with his tail between his legs. And that scares the living shit out of me."

"Me too," said McDermott.

What the hell have I gotten us into?

189

Seventy-one

"I thought you already finished all the inside painting," Andy wondered.

"I did, but some spots needed a second coat and I've been putting it off. Now it's done," Mark answered, washing his hands in the kitchen sink.

"Putting it off? I hope your work ethic isn't slacking, Landry. I worry about you going to shit in your retirement years. Use it or lose it, right?"

Mark dried his hands with a dish towel and looked at his friend, who was lying on the couch and reading a magazine. "You're worried about my work ethic? Dude, it's the last day of school and you took a sick day. Use them or lose them, right? Maybe the guy who has sat on his ass all day and watched me bust mine should worry about his own slacking," Mark declared, startling Andy with a quick snap of the towel against the side of his head.

"Enough violence!" Andy protested.

Mark popped a muscle relaxer into his mouth, washed it down with a tall glass of cold water, and held up the prescription bottle. "My back and arms are killing me from all this painting. Agnes never took anything for pain or to help her sleep. But she never threw the stuff out either. You should see the stockpile I found in her bathroom closet."

"Throw it all out, brother. You don't want that stuff lying around the house. We've got a huge prescription drug problem in the state. I haven't taken so much as an aspirin in years. Don't be a wussy, pain is all mind over matter anyway," said Andy.

"What about beer? That doesn't count?" asked Mark.

Andy ignored the question and continued reading the local newspaper's profiles of the forty most interesting people in the Merrimack Valley of Massachusetts. "I can't believe some of the people on this list. Why am I not on this list?"

Mark heard a knock at the side door and assumed it was their pizza.

"Because people have to go to the Witch Hunt to hear your schtick. Maybe you need a bigger platform," he offered as he saw Kenny through the blinds and opened the door.

"Come on in, Kenny. You know the mayor, right?"

Kenny looked at Andy and smiled. "Yeah, hi, Andy."

Andy waved from the couch and continued reading.

"Mark, here's the information you asked about," he said, softly placing a thin folder on the kitchen counter. "You were right. There are a ton of women out there named Lois Sumner, but if you have some specific information and the right tools you can whittle the list down pretty quickly. The one you're looking for is very much alive and pretty well known, actually. I can't believe she was friends with Agnes. You know ..."

Mark raised a hand to cut him off and glanced at Andy on the couch, indicating that he wanted to keep the information private. "I appreciate that, Kenny. Thanks for doing this," he answered as he flipped open the folder to reveal its contents.

Kenny shrugged his shoulders and watched as Mark's curiosity turned to shock and disbelief within seconds. Mark looked up several times but said nothing as he rifled through the eight or ten pages of biographical data in the folder. When he had finished, he grabbed two cold beers from the refrigerator, popped them open on the side of the counter, and handed one to his neighbor.

"Kenny, are you messing with me? If you are, that's fine—good one, you got me. But I need to know now."

Kenny chugged half his beer and stifled a belch. "No, I'm not messing with you."

Mark ran his hands through his hair and paced the kitchen.

"I don't doubt you or your talents. But I was not expecting this," Mark said. Then he leaned in and spoke in a softer voice. "Is there any doubt in your mind about this? And remember, this needs to stay between us, okay?" he said, nodding his head in the direction of the couch.

"One hundred percent positive, Mark. So, how's Luci doing?" he asked.

"She's great, Kenny. Never been better," he answered as he continued to pace and shake his head in disbelief.

"Good. I'm glad. They say the kid is going to be all right too," he added.

"That's good," said Mark, staring out the window into the backyard. "Wait, what kid? What are you talking about?"

Kenny drained the rest of his beer and looked at Mark quizzically before answering.

"The kid she shot this morning."

Seventy-two

Luci had spent most of the morning making her rounds at the high school. Guidance counselors. Teachers. Coaches. Reaching out and building relationships in the community was not only her primary responsibility; it was her greatest strength. She always found ways to connect and offer help, and smiles lit up whenever she entered the room. When the final bell of the school year sounded, she left the special-needs department and bumped into Julia in the hallway.

"Julia! What are you doing here? You graduated, right? Back for more?" she asked cheerfully.

Julia beamed and squeezed Luci's hand.

"Yes, I did. I'm back to say thanks to a few people and beg for a letter of recommendation from one of my teachers."

"What for?" asked Luci.

"College," she answered. "*Abuela* thinks we can scrape together enough money for me to start taking classes this summer. Of course I had to get a job waiting tables at the diner to pay for most of it, but that's the plan."

Luci's brilliant smile filled the corridor as she opened her arms and beckoned Julia for a hug. "I am so proud of you! That's incredible, but I'm not surprised. I always knew you had it in you and would do the right things. Good for you, Julia. When do you start?"

"I start work today and hopefully classes by midsummer," she answered as she glanced over Luci's shoulder and her smile turned sour. "Creep alert. I gotta run anyway. I don't want to be late for my first day of work. Bye, Luci. I'll talk to you soon and thanks for everything," she added, subconsciously pinching the guardian angel charm around her neck with two fingers.

Julia disappeared into the current of liberated students as Sergeant Cromwell and Charlie Worth arrived at the same time and approached Luci from behind.

"Where are you headed right now, Luci?" asked the gruff sergeant.

"I was heading back to the station to do some paperwork and take a few reports. Why? What's up?"

"Negative. Charlie will do that. I need you to come to the office for an intervention with me," answered Cromwell.

Charlie rolled his eyes. "Seriously? That's what I was called for. Now you want Luci to handle this while I go take reports?"

192

Cromwell faced his patrolman. "Yes, and I need you to do that right now. Every time someone waits too long at the station, I get an earful from the chief. So disappear and thank you very much," he added, signaling the end of the discussion.

Charlie held up his hands in surrender. "You're the boss. I'll go talk with housewives about loud noises and suspicious neighbors. Good luck, Luci," he said sarcastically.

"Let's go to the office," barked Cromwell.

Handfuls of students waved and greeted Luci as the two walked down the hall side by side. Several hugged her warmly while others were deterred by Cromwell's presence.

"I see you've been here before," he remarked, his eyes looking straight forward. "You've got a connection with these kids that you can't put a price on. Good work, Luci."

She took the compliment in stride and, deep down inside, felt validated by the recognition. She did have a meaningful connection with these kids and it wasn't an accident. It was the result of hard work, a constant presence, and a genuine interest in their lives. Relationship building requires time and trust; Luci had put in the time and earned the trust.

"What's the intervention?" she asked.

"A fight in the cafeteria, not the first one for this kid. The other kid may have been seriously injured. We can arrest him or work it out some other way to save his record. Considering his pedigree, I doubt it'll matter, but he gets the same chance as every other kid."

Pedigree?

When they reached the door to the main office, Luci grabbed Cromwell by the elbow and took him aside. "Maybe you should let me handle this, Sarge. Two uniforms may be too much and I do pretty well on my own."

Cromwell pondered the idea for a moment and shook his head. "I'd feel better if we both went in, Luci. This kid's a troublemaker and way too big to pick up and spank over your knee if he gets out of line," he answered.

"I wasn't planning on doing any spanking today, but I do need the kid to talk to me. Which is much easier without your lovable presence. Besides, I can handle myself."

Cromwell ran a hand over his bald head. "Fine. It's all yours. But if you feel it's not going well, just put the cuffs on him and bring him into the station, okay? He gets one chance. One. I have to prepare for a planning meeting for the Fourth of July events anyway. Brief me later."

Seventy-three

"William Lundgren?" asked Luci.

"Junior. William Lundgren, Jr. The son," the principal explained.

"Ahh, right. Wonderful."

Great. The father is a complete jackass and the apple didn't fall far from the tree.

"I know. And I feel the same way. But it's important not to make kids pay for their parents' transgressions," offered the principal. "Transgression" was a euphemism for the outspoken racism and small-mindedness of William Lundgren, Sr. His worldview was obviously shared by others in town, considering the hits and comments that his vitriolic videos garnered online. But the older Lundgren stood out due to his brazen willingness to express his views to the world and put his name on them.

"Agreed. Where is he?" Luci asked.

"Follow me. He's in my office."

They walked past the staff and into the principal's spacious office. William was sitting alone at a table when they entered.

"William, I'm sure you know Officer Alvarez," the principal began.

He looked up at the adults and muttered something incomprehensible. Luci made mental notes. The kid was well over six feet tall and weighed at least two hundred pounds.

Bloodshot eyes. Enlarged pupils. Slurred speech. This kid's not all there.

"Hi, William. Can you tell me what happened?" she asked, sitting across the table from the young man.

He stared at the table and made no response.

"William, Officer Alvarez is here to help you but—" began the administrator.

Lundgren laughed out loud and shook his head. "That's what you think. Someone else might have helped, but she's going to lock me up as soon as she hears the other kid's name. Go ahead, tell her his name and see what happens. Go ahead."

"You're not being fair and this is a serious matter," the principal said as he turned to face Luci. "Witnesses say William threw the first punch without any provocation. The other student's parents are taking him for x-rays to make sure his nose isn't broken."

"What's the other student's name?" asked Luci.

"Jose!" answered William. "So you wanna put the cuffs on me now? Why even talk? You people always side with each other ... " His voice trailed off toward the end.

Luci breathed deeply and kept her cool in the face of William's racist comments. The kid had just been in a fight. She assumed he was upset and saying things he normally wouldn't say, but given his home life she was unsure. The principal jumped in before he could continue.

"William, whether you believe it or not, Officer Alvarez is here to help you. Insulting her isn't going to help your case at all."

A secretary popped her head into the office. "Sir, Jose's parents are on the phone from the hospital."

"William, get your act together. Officer, I'll be right back. Please continue."

Luci jotted down a few observations in her notebook and waited for the young man to speak. After several moments, she broke the silence.

"Can you tell me what happened, William? So far it sounds like a lot of people witnessed you assaulting another student. Do you want to explain your actions? Justify them? Apologize for them? It's entirely up to you how we handle this."

Nothing.

"I'll give you a few more minutes to think about it. But right now, you leave me with no choice but to arrest you for assault and battery. I don't know how the courts will process you. You're about to graduate. Believe me, you don't want a violent charge stapled to every job application you ever fill out. And I can't help you if you don't talk to me."

William glanced at the open door behind him and a smirk slowly appeared on his face. He chuckled and uttered something unintelligible under his breath.

"Is this funny, William? What did you just say? Would you care to let me in on the joke?" she asked.

He bowed his head, cleared his throat, and stared at her from the top of his eye sockets. "I said, punch a spic—talk to the chick."

She masked her reaction with a straight face and continued. "William, that's offensive and I won't tolerate it. If you keep it up, I'll have no choice but to arrest you and bring you to the station. I don't want that. You don't want that. Your parents don't want that. So let's try one more time. Do you want to tell me your side of the story?"

This time he yelled it. "Punch a spic—talk to the chick!"

Luci held up her hand at the two male teachers who appeared in the doorway, signaling to them that everything was under control. They nodded and went on their way. After another moment of silence, Luci concluded that William was either too angry or too high to be reasoned with. She stood up and pushed her chair back against the wall.

"Okay. You've had your chance. Now this is what's going to happen. I need you to slowly stand up, turn around, and put your hands on top of your head. You're under arrest, William." Luci pressed the transmit button on the radio attached to her shoulder. "Control, this is 307, I need immediate backup at the high school."

The boy began to laugh hysterically.

"This is not a joke, William. Do it now or you'll have disorderly conduct and resisting arrest added to your charges. Not another word. Just do it," she ordered.

"I'm gonna fucking kill you," he said staring directly into her dark eyes.

Before she could move out of the way, he leapt to his feet, flipped the table with both hands, and used it to ram the officer against the wall with all of his force. She crashed into the wall and fell to the floor with a loud thud. With the wind out of her, she struggled to get to her knees and draw the pepper spray from her duty belt. William had already slammed the door shut and wedged it with a chair. He ignored the men who had instantly appeared on the other side of the door's glass window and turned toward Luci.

She held out the pepper spray, but William slapped it out of her hand before she could depress the button. He effortlessly picked her up by the front of her uniform and pinned her against the wall with the full weight of his body. She struggled futilely to break free, both feet dangling several inches off the carpet.

"You're about to die, bitch!" he screamed.

She punched, slapped, and scratched at his face repeatedly with her left hand until he trapped it against his body. Then he wrapped his free hand around her throat and started to strangle her.

"Night, night! Go to sleep, Officer Alvarez. It'll be over in just a few seconds," he yelled loudly enough for the spectators, still trying desperately to open the door, to hear his intentions. He smiled at them maniacally before turning back to finish off his prey.

Blindsided by the events of the past twenty seconds, Luci realized that she was in a fight for her life against a young man who had the means and intent to kill her. She gasped for air and struggled with all she had as the lack of oxygen and adrenaline rush shook her central nervous system. She felt disassociated from her body, as if she had been standing off to the side and watching the events unfold.

She saw him smiling as he squeezed. She saw the faces in the door and wondered why they weren't rushing into the room. She saw the ceiling fan as it rotated above her in slow motion. She thought she could hear the clock on the wall ticking as if her ear were pressed against it. She saw the camera in the corner of the room and wondered if it was recording. As it all started to fade, she saw herself draw the pistol with her right hand and point the muzzle at William's heavy midsection. Then she saw her own eyes close as she pulled the trigger twice.

Seventy-four

Mark sat quietly in a chair on the other side of the room as the police union's chaplain visited with Luci at the house. The chaplain did most of the talking in a soft whisper, but she occasionally stopped to listen to Luci and to glance at the stranger in the room. Luci had indicated that Mark could be privy to the conversation, but she had not introduced him. When they had finished, the chaplain nodded politely to Mark before leaving.

William Lundgren, Jr., had lost a great amount of blood and needed several hours of surgery to close the two holes made by Luci's 9mm hollow-point bullets, but his vital organs were intact and doctors said he would recover fully, albeit slowly. The drug screen had revealed a cornucopia of prescription and illicit drugs in his system with levels indicative of regular abuse; quite possibly he might not even remember attacking the officer. Fortunately, the video and witnesses removed any doubt as to what had transpired. The young man had left Luci with no choice. Sadly, the video was not released until more than forty-eight hours after the incident, giving the *Valley Insider* and the national media plenty of time for baseless speculation.

"Of course we won't know for sure until the investigation is complete, but for all we know, this cop could have specifically gone after the kid because of his father's outspoken criticism of immigrants and police," said one news anchor.

"I just don't understand why police officers across the country are so trigger-happy. This was an unarmed child and she shot him twice in the gut. Of course we haven't seen the tape yet, but how is it that we can trap wild animals much bigger than adolescent boys without hurting them, but this child needed to be shot twice? Or have we adjusted physical standards so much that female officers who lack the necessary restraining power rely on their guns too much?" another expert opined.

The speculation came to a screeching halt once the video became public, but the damage was done. None of the talking heads bothered to go back and correct the record; they simply cashed their checks and moved on to the next story. Luci was beside herself with grief and post-traumatic depression.

"I shot a kid, Mark. I shot a child," she said.

"No, you didn't. He's not a baby. You protected yourself from a very troubled and violent young man who was going to kill you. He said so himself. People heard it. And the video is very clear that he gave you no choice. You did the only thing you could do. Nobody—I mean, nobody who matters—faults you for that. You did nothing wrong, Luci. I know it doesn't make things easier on you, but he's the one who made this happen, not you. You did the right thing."

"The right thing? Shooting a kid, the right thing? I don't know about that, Mark. Nothing feels right about this," she cried into his shirt as she had done for days. "The whole thing fucking sucks!"

William Lundgren, Sr., had arrived at the high school at the same time as the EMTs and firemen. He had to be restrained when he learned what had happened to his son. Officers discovered two handguns when they frisked him. High schools were gun-free zones in Massachusetts. Jail time was unlikely, but the violation would certainly cost him his license and therefore his gun collection. He had initially defended his son and publicly excoriated Luci and the entire department until the video was released. He had not been heard from since.

The investigation was still open, but the remaining steps were bureaucratic in nature. The facts were all in and Officer Alvarez's actions were deemed appropriate and justified. Even without the video, the ghastly purple and red damage to her throat and windpipe provided strong evidence of Lundgren's intentions. Regardless, in line with department policy, she was placed on thirty days' mandatory leave with pay and mandatory counseling. Psychological recovery would not be easy and taking away her life's work wasn't going to help.

Luci's union-appointed lawyer talked her through each step of the process and what to expect, giving her strict instructions to make no statements. He urged her to give the same advice to any living family members. She had not spoken with her mother for several years but placed a call to Colombia and spoke just long enough to pass along the instructions.

If I've done nothing wrong, why do I feel so guilty?

Thankfully, things had quieted down outside Luci's residence. Cromwell had ordered the whole street cordoned off to keep the fleet of media trucks and obnoxious reporters at bay. Most had left town and moved on to the next story as soon as the video was released.

Support had been overwhelming for the first few days as parades of fellow cops and well-wishers visited Luci at home. But eventually the visitors dwindled and she was left alone with her thoughts. Mark worried that things could get much worse before they got better …

He stood up and clapped his hands.

"Okay, Officer Alvarez. It's time to move. You have to move your body so you don't slip into a funk, okay? Why don't we go out for a drive and maybe a bite to eat? You could use the air," he said.

She shook her head. "My face has been plastered everywhere. I'm not like you, Mark. I'm not anonymous. When I do my job—right or wrong—everybody knows it. I don't want to see anybody and I sure as hell don't want to hear what anyone has to say—especially the congratulators. For God's sake, I could have killed that kid," she sobbed.

"Okay, okay. I have to go to the house to take care of a few things, but I promise I'll be right back, okay?"

"I'm not a child, Mark. I can stay at home by myself without a babysitter."

He wanted to speak but decided against it. He kissed her gently on the head and left her home alone.

Seventy-five

King Heavy's days as a Latin King had been over since the moment he decided to steal from the nation. The Supreme Inca, King C., was not stupid. If he hadn't figured it out by now, he would soon enough, and then he'd have no choice but to issue a T.O.S. order—find King Heavy and Terminate on Sight. If he didn't, the rest of the Supreme Council would smell weakness and he'd have a civil war on his hands. Hector was far beyond the point of no return.

He pulled up his pants and returned to the flimsy card table to finish counting the money while his girlfriend Lourdes cleaned up in the bathroom.

"Baby, I told you not to come inside me. I don't need no more babies. Why don't you ever listen to me?" asked Lourdes from the bathroom.

He ignored her and continued counting the large stacks of cash spread out in front of him.

Seventeen thousand. Eighteen thousand. Nineteen...

"Did you hear me? Hector, did you hear me? I asked you a question."

He tossed a small baggy of heroin in her direction without looking and continued counting but then lost his place. "Yeah, I fucking heard you but I'm busy right now. Can you just shut up until I'm finished? This is for us, baby. This is our future right here. I'm gonna double this shit. Add that to the rest of what we got and we'll be set for a long time. But you gotta let me work."

She was already snorting by the time he completed his sentence.

When he had finished counting the cash, he organized it into bundles and stacked them neatly in a red backpack. A loaded Glock 17 9mm with a round in the chamber occupied the front compartment.

Pulling the cheap curtains open just enough to peer out the second-story window onto the street below, he saw nothing to cause alarm. Two schoolchildren with backpacks and lunchboxes stepped over a junkie who had collapsed on the sidewalk. The occasional car passed by. Loud music could be heard from several directions.

I'll switch shitholes again tonight just in case.

"Let's go through this one more time so we're absolutely clear on what you need to do tonight," Hector said, turning to Lourdes who sat on the edge of the bed with her eyes closed.

He crossed the room, kneeled down in front of her, and slapped her firmly across the face. "Listen up, Lourdes! Pay attention. This is important, okay? Get your shit together."

"I'm listening, Hector. Stop hitting me!" she exclaimed, snapping out of her drug-induced funk. "Just stop hitting me. I'm here. I'm listening. What?"

"Let's go through it one more time. You'll be on the balcony with one of the gringos and I'll be with the car on the street below. Once they put the stuff in my trunk, I'll give you the sign so you know to give him the money. After that, I'll drive away and you get the hell out of there. Don't go straight home, though. Take your time and make sure there ain't nobody following you. When you get home, stay there until you hear from me. It'll be at least a few days, maybe even a week or two, but just sit tight and don't talk to nobody. When I can, I'll let you know where I am so you can bring me my shit, right?"

"I ain't stupid, Hector. I know what to do."

He raised his hand to slap her again but quickly pulled it back. He still needed her.

"Remember, there's three bags of money inside the wall in your bathroom, but all you gotta do is hit it with a hammer a little bit and that shitty drywall will come off easy. You bring those bags to me and we disappear together, baby. This is what we've always wanted and it's almost here—just a little bit of business left to do. But I need you to keep your shit together and focus. You want this, don't you?"

She nodded drowsily.

"Yeah, but I want some respect too, Hector. Why you always gotta be treating me like this? When you're not fucking me, you're hitting me. I've never met any of your friends or family. You've never taken me out anywhere, like you're ashamed of me or something. I love you, Heavy. But I gotta know things are gonna be different when all this is done. It's like you're using me. And what are they gonna be putting in your trunk anyway?"

"I ain't gonna tell you that, because I want to protect you, baby. You see what I'm saying? Everything I'm doing is for us, but you gotta trust me. And I promise things will be better when this is all done. Less stress, right? It's the stress that's making me do that shit to you—it ain't me, baby. If I didn't respect you, why would I trust you with some of my money?"

He reached for the baggy of cocaine in his pocket, used a matchstick to scoop out a line, and held it up to her nostril. She sniffed quick and hard. The same ritual was repeated with the other nostril. After a few moments, her eyes rolled back in her head and Hector's smile turned to a psychopathic scowl.

"You know I respect you, baby. Let me show you how much."

Hector rose to his feet and slowly reached for the button at the top of his pants.

Seventy-six

"I always knew the kid was a loser like his old man, but I never thought for a second he had that in him," remarked Andy as he threw another bag of fertilizer into his cart. "I'm so glad she's okay."

Mark walked down the hardware store aisle next to his friend and thought out loud.

"I'm worried about her. She can't compartmentalize things. She just keeps playing the highlight reel over and over in her head and second-guessing herself, and she won't leave the house. It's a recipe for disaster."

"I can only imagine. The kid gave her no choice, but that doesn't make it any easier to pull the trigger. What about you? How do you get past it after all these years? Can't you share some of that stuff with her so she has something to relate to?" asked Andy.

"Not really. In my line of work, we serve and protect a little differently. And she thinks I'm bulletproof anyway. So I just listen, but that makes me feel useless."

"So you're not bulletproof?"

"No. Definitely not."

Both men paid for their purchases and left the store.

"I don't know what to do. I guess wait it out, but it kills me to see her like this," Mark shared.

"I know it does. Just give her some time. I've told you before, Luci is an extraordinary woman. She'll figure it out. Here's the thing too—I don't know a whole lot about your career, but I'm guessing you've never had to stay around very long after pulling the trigger. That makes compartmentalizing a little easier, right?"

Mark was taken aback at the perceptive observation and nodded in agreement. "That's true. You're right. She just needs time."

"And if she's up for getting out of the house tomorrow, bring her to my Veterans Salute at Founders Field. I promise it'll be an event to remember," Andy offered as they parted.

Seventy-seven

Senator McDermott shook with anxiety. "Who do you think is sending me this stuff?" she asked.

"No idea," Meghan answered as she paused the video. "But whoever it is, they're risking their life."

This time the envelope contained a single thumb drive with undated video of an interrogation. The interrogator was masked and the lighting was poor, but the sheer brutality of the scene was painfully clear—vicious torture by any definition. The audio dropped in and out of the video. When it was audible, two men spoke mostly in English with occasional exchanges in German, all muffled and difficult to follow.

"This is over the top," declared Meghan. "I feel like I'm going to be sick. What are we going to do with this?"

The Senator paced the family room. "Do with what? No note. No explanation. We don't even know what this is. Who are these men? Where are they from? Where did this take place? We can't even tell what they're talking about. It looks real to me but …"

"It looks real? For God's sake, he's missing an ear and bleeding like mad! He's missing a fucking ear!" exclaimed Meghan.

"I can see that, Meghan, but we don't know anything about this. Someone could be setting us up. Let's say we share this—then what? How many questions would we be able to answer?"

"None," Meghan uttered. "I say we move and don't tell anyone where we live. Can't you get us into the witness protection program or something?"

Senator McDermott pulled the thumb drive from her laptop. "I'll tell you what I'm going to do—nothing."

"Nothing?"

"This is going into my safe and neither of us will mention it to anyone. We do nothing. If the person who sent it wants to come forward and explain things, fine. If not, we stay focused and just keep doing our work. Someone is either trying to do me a huge favor or sabotage me, and I'm not going to waste time trying to figure out which it is."

Seventy-eight

After Amir had ordered his warriors to bed and locked the door, he returned to the kitchen and closed his eyes in frustration. He breathed deeply and tried to separate himself from the worldly stress of the holy mission. Three warriors with known fates slept silently in the next room while their leader reviewed the details.

Twenty-four hours. It will all be over in twenty-four hours.

Would the truck be available? Would they have the nerve at the moment of truth? Would the weapons fire? Could they shift to knives if the guns malfunctioned? Would they execute the mission with sufficient brutality and viciousness, completely devoid of mercy and compassion for the infidels? Would they eviscerate the enemy when given the chance, or would they fold and run as many believers had done in the Levant? And what about the girl? Would she fulfill her role?

Too many unknowns with these amateurs. Too little time.

The warrior removed his shirt, socks, and shoes and made ablutions before approaching the makeshift prayer rug. With his forehead pressed vulnerably against the floor, he recalled Surah 3:151 of the Koran: "Soon shall we cast terror into the hearts of the unbelievers ..."

One more sunset. One more sunrise.

Seventy-nine

Mark toweled off after his shower, quietly put on his workout clothes, and laced up his running shoes.

"Why do you shower before you work out?" asked Luci.

"Sorry, did I wake you? I shower because it warms up my muscles. Getting old, I guess, and it's about three miles each way to Founders Field," he said as he kissed her on the forehead and sat next to her on the bed.

She smiled faintly and closed her eyes again. "Three and two-tenths. Enjoy your run; I'm going back to sleep for a few more hours."

Mark glanced at his watch; it said 10 a.m. "Understood, you got to bed pretty late and tossed and turned. But later today we need to get you up and moving—preferably outside. You can't stay inside for the rest of your life. You need to start going out and getting back to normal, okay? Okay, Luci?"

No response. He kissed her on the forehead again and headed outside. Luci opened her eyes and watched him leave the bedroom. She started to sob softly.

Back to normal? Mark. I'm dying inside.

Eighty

Mark jogged around the police barriers and slowed his run to a brisk walk with his hands on his hips. Hundreds of townspeople mingled in a sea of red, white, and blue in celebration of American independence. Flags waved in the gentle breeze, a five-piece band played patriotic songs, and children laughed and played in the grass. It was a peaceful and heartwarming sight, but Mark's mind was stuck on Luci.

Don't kid yourself—she's getting worse.

He weaved his way through the crowd and headed for the only permanent structure on Founders Field: a square brick building that resembled a highway rest area. The row of port-a-potties outside made the bathroom line inside the building short. Mark relieved himself, splashed cold water on his face, and headed back outside to locate Andy.

"Ladies and gentlemen, the Independence Day Veterans Salute will begin in fifteen minutes on the stage at the far end of the field. Please join us in recognizing our hometown heroes dating back to World War II," said a familiar voice over the loudspeaker.

Mark watched from behind the stage as Andy briefed a handful of volunteer football players and cheerleaders on the sequence of events. Approximately 125 veterans of various ages were participating. The cheerleaders would escort the older vets to their special seats on the stage, and the players would provide general crowd assistance, their athletic uniforms adding to the festive atmosphere. Andy finished briefing the kids as Mark approached.

"Not exactly dressed for the occasion, but I'm glad you're here," boomed Andy.

"I can't stay—I need to get back to Luci. Just wanted to say hello and wish you luck."

The two walked to the side of the stage and watched as the crowd started to gather and claim their spots on the grass.

"Wish you could stay, but I understand. It'll be broadcast on local access if you get curious. I invited a ton of media, but it looks like none of them showed up. This is all about the vets, but I was hoping we would get some coverage as well for putting this thing together."

"What's security look like these days for a town event like this? I haven't seen much," asked Mark.

"It's good. The roads around the field are blocked off to keep unwanted vehicles at bay, and there's a half-dozen or so cops on detail. We've never had any issues beyond the occasional drunk, firecrackers in the trash cans, and a few twisted ankles. There's an ambulance here somewhere. This event is pretty tame. Why, you worried?"

Mark scanned the crowd and shook his head. "No more than usual."

"So, listen. I'll keep my opening remarks short, but—"

Mark smiled and chuckled out loud. "Yeah, because you're not long-winded at all!"

"I beg your pardon, sir. I'm thorough, not long winded. Anyway, in the early days of the town, every male age sixteen and above had to gather on this field every year to recite an oath of loyalty to the British Crown. Their descendants faced that tyranny and fought for independence. Then I figured I'd mention those who answered the call and fought to preserve the republic in the Civil War, toss in a few quick statements about the Mexican War, Spanish-American War, the World Wars, Korea, Vietnam, all the way up through Iraq and Afghanistan. Just a bunch of quick hits—nothing too deep. What do you think?" asked Andy.

Mark nodded. "Sounds good. You know what you're doing, Andy. But I'd say definitely keep it brief—it's hot out here and you'll lose people quickly if you start rambling." He held up his hands. "Not that you ever would!"

"Mr. O'Rourke?" said one of Andy's football players nearby. "Just wanted to let you know we're all set. Everyone is lined up and ready to go."

"Okay, thanks, Matt. We'll get started in a few minutes once the crowd gets settled."

Andy turned to Mark. "See that kid? One of our captains. Fullback. Built like a brick shithouse and fast as a jackrabbit. Great kid too. I expect big things from him next year."

"Well, good luck. That's my cue to exit stage left and get back to Luci. I'll try to get her out later, but I don't see it happening. She's still pretty shaken up and I can't say I blame her. She got into the job to help kids, and even though she had no choice, she ended up shooting one. It's going to be tough for her to get past this."

"Send her my warmest regards," said Andy.

Mark started out again at a slow jog and ran around the perimeter of the field. When he reached the far side and started down the street back to Luci's house, he heard Andy's voice echoing from behind.

"Happy Fourth of July! And welcome to our special Veterans Salute. We will begin in five minutes—please take your places. You won't want to miss this!"

Eighty-one

As his body started to warm up again, thoughts of Luci and their future together raced through Mark's mind.

What can I do to help her? Does she need more intensive counseling? Medication? Does she just need more time? Will she go back to work, or did this end her career? If so, what's next? Too many questions. Come on, Luci. You can't let this beat you.

A quarter-mile from Founders Field, he slowed down and jogged in place while waiting for the traffic light. A few other pedestrians were scattered about. On the other side of the intersection, four men sat side by side in the cab of their public works department pickup truck. Mark heard Andy's voice through the public address system but could not make out the words. He tried going through a mental checklist of things to do around the house, but his mind always came back to Luci.

Some people can compartmentalize emotions and hold off the demons forever while others need to confront them directly before they can move on. Others obsessively second-guess their actions until it consumes them and ruins their lives.

He decided that if she didn't start showing improvement soon, he would push for daily counseling as a way to stop the spiral.

The light changed and he started to jog across the intersection. The public works truck grinded its gears and rolled in the opposite direction. Mark glanced at the vehicle and its passengers as he checked his watch and picked up the pace.

I'll be home in a few minutes, Luci.

Eighty-two

Mark decided to take a lazy shortcut through the graveyard on the way back to Luci's house. It was hot outside and he had completed the run to Founders Field much faster than he had expected; his body needed the break, but mostly he wanted to get back to Luci's side as quickly as possible.

He knew she needed to get up and moving. Being sedentary invites doom under normal circumstances; add the mental anguish of post-traumatic stress to the mix and you have a potentially deadly cocktail of emotions.

Doc always said that physical movement jump-starts the road to recovery, and he's right. Take control of your emotions—do not let them control you.

Mark slowed to a trot and let gravity carry him down the steep incline of almost a quarter-mile. The sun beat down from a cloudless sky, and his t-shirt was drenched with sweat. It would have felt good to take the shirt off, but the 9mm and small folding knife strapped tightly around his waist would attract unwanted attention. He glanced at his watch, estimated he'd be back at Luci's in roughly fifteen minutes, and set the goal of getting her out of the house for lunch.

Or at least she could come with me to pick up takeout. Breathe in the fresh air. Feel the warm sun on your face. Move your body, Luci. Fight it.

Mark unconsciously slowed his trot to a brisk walk as his mind started to race. He fought to stay focused on Luci, but the connection flickered like the reception on a vintage television set stuck between two channels. Taking deep breaths with his hands on his head, he tried to think of which restaurants she'd be most amenable to, but his thoughts were being hijacked by intuition. He tried to pick up the pace again, but an invisible force seemed to be holding him back and nudging him in the opposite direction. The little voice inside his head was screaming, but he could not hear the words.

"Listen to your intuition," both Father Peck and Doc had always said. "It's usually right."

I'm listening. What is it?

Then it hit him. The public works truck. The four men crammed side by side into a three-man cab. They had all appeared very young, even though most of the people who landed those positions kept them for years. They all had short hair and clean-shaven faces. Why get cleaned up for a messy day at work? And they were sitting attentively and silently with their eyes locked straight ahead. Nobody playing on his smartphone, no talking, no bitching that they had to work the holiday while everyone else celebrated, no apparent hangovers to nurse. The driver had grinded the gears badly. Was it his first time driving the vehicle, or was it simply in need of a new clutch or transmission? There were many reasons for suspicion, but it was the looks on their faces that Mark found most perplexing. Something was off.

Am I overthinking things? Has Luci's condition clouded my judgment? Has the recent string of attacks made me paranoid? Should I bring it down a notch and just jog home?

Mark turned around and started back up the hill at his quickest pace of the day.

No, something's not right.

Eighty-three

"Get out and move the barrier. Do it quickly but do not draw unnecessary attention," said Amir to the young man sitting closest to the passenger door. "And you two smile and move your lips a little like you're talking. Pray on the inside."

He drove through the gap in the barriers and waited for the other warrior to remount the truck. "Everyone, keep breathing deeply as we practiced and stay focused. Paradise awaits you," he coached as he turned the truck toward the distant, empty side of Founders Field. He considered his words and his blood began to boil.

Yes. Paradise awaits you—but not me. Not yet.

A little boy of three or four wandered carelessly into the vehicle's path as a frantic young babysitter scurried to catch up. Amir stopped, waved, and smiled warmly at the child standing in the middle of the cordoned street. The young girl took the boy by the hand and waved back. Amir winked at her and blew a kiss. She glanced side to side sheepishly before blowing one back with a coquettish grin on her face.

Whores—all of them.

Driving up and over the sidewalk, Amir slowly maneuvered the truck across the freshly mowed grass to the opposite side of the field from the stage and stopped.

"Get out. Unload the truck and wait here as you were instructed. Eat your food and talk to no one. Do not draw attention to yourselves. Stay focused. Do not open the bags and retrieve the weapons before the blast, and let the crowd come to you before opening fire. And brothers, do not hesitate when the time comes to act."

The three young men climbed out of the truck, opened the tailgate, and slid the long, heavy canvas bag onto the ground. They paid no attention to the crowd gathered in front of the stage at the other end of the field as they sat on the grass with their three brown lunches. Amir watched the three men and prayed that they could complete the mission.

A total of six brothers had been chosen, but Amir had taken it upon himself to whittle the group down to three. When all the would-be martyrs came together at the rally point in New Hampshire, he lined them up, ordered them to strip, and searched their belongings thoroughly. He instinctively began with the youngest man, who had a crazed and disconnected expression on his smooth face.

"Why did you bring so much with you? Were you not instructed to pack only the necessities?" asked Amir.

The recruit simply looked at him, nodded, and grunted unintelligibly. Amir dumped the contents of the large backpack onto the ground and moved things around with the toe of his boot. The bag contained half a dozen prescription bottles, including psychological drugs and one medication that Amir recognized as an HIV therapy. Given the possibility that he was homosexual, Amir made an immediate decision to drop him from the team.

"Okay, my brother. Take fifteen steps forward," Amir instructed.

The troubled young man obeyed the instruction and then looked back.

"I did not tell you to turn around!" Amir barked. "Now drop to your knees and do it quickly."

When he did, Amir drew the Ruger .45 from his holster, took aim, and fired three shots into the young man's head and back. Normally he preferred to execute up close and personal, looking into the victim's eyes whenever possible. But this sinner was especially unclean and Amir did not want to come into contact with his contaminated blood. He quickly spun around to address the remaining five recruits, their eyes wide with horror.

"This man was not worthy of your brotherly love and affection. He was not worthy of martyrdom. The rest of you have nothing to worry about as long as you listen and do exactly as I say. Leave your things here and follow me. Your training begins immediately."

Training. One day to train? One day to train for such a mission? These men are inexperienced and untested—not a warrior among them. And yet they are rewarded with martyrdom? These are the Islamic State's chosen warriors?

The other two eliminations were made within the first hour. One man proved unable to fire a weapon reliably and displayed a consistent inability to grasp basic warrior concepts. The other made the mistake of asking "Why?" in response to a command. Amir tied each to a tree under the guise of teaching escape techniques should they be captured. They screamed through gagged mouths as he asked for volunteers to execute them. All three of the remaining warriors raised their hands. Amir smiled approvingly and decided to honor all

216

of them as a bonding experience. He instructed them to put down their guns and work together, using their knives to hack and eventually behead the two.

The remaining recruits did not inspire confidence, but they were all he had. Instead of simply training them and sending them to their deaths, he had decided to adjust the plan out of necessity. Amir would play a limited role in the mission himself to ensure success before moving on to Washington as he had been instructed.

He tried to park the truck as close as possible to the back of the stage so that the first casualties would be the American war criminals being honored. The crowd would instinctively run in the opposite direction, toward the area where the three gunmen would be waiting to greet them. An ambulance was parked in Amir's intended spot so he attempted to park his vehicle next to it, but an auxiliary police officer waved him off and pointed an authoritarian finger toward a spot on the other side of the emergency vehicle. The location would place the ambulance between the blast and the intended target. He considered protesting or negotiating for a better position but quickly dismissed the idea. Why draw attention? Why risk having the bomb discovered?

"No problem," he replied with a smile.

After rolling up the windows and locking the doors, Amir slung a small backpack over one shoulder and headed toward the only building on the field.

"How's it goin'?" asked one of the EMTs as he passed by.

"Living the dream! How about you guys?" he answered jovially, making no attempt to conceal his face. Why bother? They would be dead soon anyway.

Once he was behind the building on the far side of the field, he casually glanced from side to side and shimmied up a drainage pipe. With all eyes and ears fixed on Andy's solemn salute to the town's veterans, nobody had noticed or cared about the young man standing on the rooftop.

From this vantage point, he had a clear view of the entire field. He counted only a few uniformed officers but had been briefed that even small towns like these were increasingly deploying undercover, plainclothes officers into crowds. No matter. Life in this town was about to change forever. He walked to the edge of the roof, lay in the prone position with a finger on the modified cell-phone detonator in his hand, and glanced at his watch.

Two minutes. Two minutes until three unworthy warriors get what I have worked years for—to strike at the heart of Satan and die as martyrs. Insha'Allah, the girl is in position and smarter than these idiots.

Eighty-four

Although there were many available seats, a heavily perfumed Dominican man with a pencil-thin mustache sat directly across from Fatima in the emergency room waiting area. He oscillated his gaze between the television—tuned to CNN en Español—and the beautiful young woman in front of him. She returned his initial salutation with a polite smile and nod. But when he started staring toward her and looking her up and down, she broke eye contact forever.

I feel like a whore.

"A pious woman like you will feel exposed and sinful without the hijab and modest dress, but you must not let that impact your behavior," the facilitator had said before she left Montreal. "You must embrace the look and appear comfortable. For you are not a Muslim when you do such things—you are doing Allah's will."

As a young woman, she had questioned the pressure to cover herself. Men are not animals, she thought. They do not lose control simply due to seeing a woman's uncovered hair and nape. But her experience since leaving her medical school dorm room at dawn—uncovered in public for the first time in years—had been illuminating. With her silky black hair bouncing around her shoulders, tight jeans, a belly shirt, and sandals, she could feel the burning eyes of men from head to toe. Young men and old, even men with girlfriends and wives at their sides all looked upon her lustfully. And it made her nauseous.

"Why Harvard?" the handsome immigration official had asked her at the Vermont border.

"Why Harvard? Because both my parents both went to Harvard. All my uncles went to Harvard. My cousins go to Harvard. I'm about to finish medical school at McGill, but I figure my parents will keep my name in their will if I at least get a master's degree from Harvard," she answered cheerfully and earnestly.

"Well, I guess that makes sense," he added as he stamped her passport, stroked a few keys on the computer terminal, and winked. "Not everyone can go to Boston College."

"Oh, you're a BC man? Well maybe I'll bump into you in Boston sometime and you can show me what I'm missing," she replied flirtatiously.

At the New Hampshire rest area, she did exactly as she had been told: park at the far end of the lot, leave the car unlocked, and go to the bathroom. When she returned, the backpack had been placed on the floor of the passenger side.

"You will let the first ambulance arrive unmolested. When the second arrives, you will simply reach down and detonate the device by pressing the single red button and holding it down. If nothing happens, let go and try again. If you are unsuccessful after three attempts, you will need to use the small plunger detonator that is attached as a backup. It's so easy even the Road Runner and Wile E. Coyote could do it! Pull the handle out of the box as far as you can and then plunge it back into place quickly like this. Now you try it," instructed the facilitator as he handed her the detonator mockup.

"Like this?" she asked.

"Just like that! Excellent. You are blessed to martyr yourself on this mission, Fatima," he continued. "I wish I could participate directly. Soon you will be in paradise. You certainly look the part dressed like that, but my concern is your demeanor. You must cast aside all religious modesty and blend in with the nonbelievers. You know, a woman who has had sexual relations carries herself much differently. Perhaps that is something I can help you with …"

So it's true. Not even devout Muslim men can control themselves in the presence of an uncovered woman.

She cut him off and ended the meeting without rejecting him outright. She would raise suspicion if she did not change out of the sinful clothing and return to the university quickly.

Later, at the hospital, Fatima mentally reviewed her instructions.

"If you think you will be compromised, detonate the bomb immediately. Do not be taken into custody. Otherwise, wait until the casualties start to arrive. Then detonate the bomb."

She began to sweat.

Eighty-five

Amir said a final prayer, closed his eyes, and pressed the button with his gloved thumb.

The heavy ambulance and fire truck parked next to the bomb helped to contain the blast, but the two EMTs who had been using the hood of the stolen public works truck as a lunch table disappeared in a cloud of pink vapor. Shrapnel-ridden victims tumbled through the air as the stage collapsed. Eardrums shattered and bled. The peculiar, almost peaceful blanket of silence that had spread across the field in the seconds following the explosion was soon pierced by bloodcurdling screams of human suffering.

Amir waited several seconds for the blast debris to disperse before slowly opening his eyes and raising his head to survey the damage. The stage area was draped in a thick black cloud of smoke and fire. Victims screamed in anguish and struggled to move away from the explosion any way they could—running, crawling, clawing their way across the warm, blood-soaked grass with their bare hands.

Some froze in place, their eyes wide, unsure of what had just happened, their brains scrambling for explanations. A handful of others came running out of the dark cloud, their final moments spent as red and orange balls of flame. Amir smiled and let out a muffled cry of *"Allahu Akbar!"* before directing his attention to his warriors.

They had been told to lie down on the ground behind their equipment fifteen seconds before detonation and to remain in place for ten seconds after the blast. They were then to retrieve their rifles, spread out, and kill as many people as possible before being killed or taking their own lives. There were two key goals: maximum casualties, and nobody is taken alive.

"Allah will be watching, and so will I," were Amir's final words to them.

By Amir's count, it was fifteen seconds since the blast and the three men continued to hug the ground next to the equipment. Twenty seconds. Twenty-five seconds. At thirty seconds he cursed them and spit, disgusted that three such men—losers with no futures—would squander the opportunity to martyr themselves and spend eternity in paradise. He reached back and gripped the Ruger .45 in his waistband.

Where did these unworthy pigs come from! Why? When there are so many truly worthy brothers! Why these fools! Why not me? Why not me—right now!

He hesitated to draw the weapon, resisting the urge with every ounce of his faith. He was not even supposed to be there. He was to simply train the men and send them on their way from the safe house while he continued onward to D.C. But after seeing the mental capacity and pitiable skills of the chosen martyrs, he had had no choice but to thin the ranks and alter the plan. Drawing attention to himself now could jeopardize the Washington mission and the only thing he truly cared about—martyrdom. As he slowly released the pistol from his grip, he saw one of the three warriors raise his head to peer over the equipment and became overjoyed.

Yes! Now do it! Do it!

Eighty-six

The three gunmen fired into the crowd and fanned out across the field as Amir watched from his perch.

Initially, the shooters sent bullets through the air in an undisciplined, adrenaline-fueled frenzy. All three were halfway through their second thirty-round magazines before they remembered their leader's instructions.

"First, take several long, deep breaths to calm the nerves. Then shoot at specific targets. Spray and pray only works in the movies, and you have limited rounds. Make them count!"

Amir praised God at the sight of the warriors and kept his eyes on the carnage as he began to crawl backwards from the edge of the roof to make his escape. But he froze when one of his soldiers stopped firing, held his rifle above his head with both hands, and disappeared into the smoke, sprinting toward the burning stage.

One of the remaining gunmen broke formation and headed for the edges of the field. He fired rapidly, choosing targets carefully and methodically as he walked slowly along the tree line with a psychotic smile pasted across his face.

Eighty-seven

Officer Charlie Worth had been chatting with a rookie cop on the far side of the field when the bomb exploded. Both immediately took cover in the tree line. When the gunmen opened fire, the rookie called on his radio for help and drew his pistol.

"Let's go!" he shouted.

Worth stood expressionless, frozen stiff as a board.

"Let's move, Charlie! It looks like the crowd near the stage took one of them out, but the other two are chasing people down. We gotta do something!"

No response from the veteran officer.

"What the fuck, Charlie! Let's go buddy. Time to get into the fight!" he pleaded, slapping his colleague firmly on the back to try and snap him out of his funk.

"Fuck it! I'll go alone."

The rookie moved out swiftly, using the trees for cover as he closed distance with the shooter. When the gunman paused to change magazines, the officer fired a single 9mm round into the middle of his back. When the terrorist simply paused, he fired three more rounds into the upper back and base of the skull. The gunman was dead before his body hit the ground. The officer sprinted to the other side of the field and disappeared into the smoke.

Eighty-eight

Mark reached Founders Field moments after the blast and paused in the tree line to assess the situation and catch his breath.

Helpless mothers and fathers shrieked. Bloody townspeople scurried in all directions. For a lucky few, t-shirts became bandages and belts became tourniquets while the majority of the wounded simply screamed and thrashed on the ground.

Landry scanned from left to right and checked his six o'clock position twice. He noted one active shooter in the center of the field and watched a police officer bounce from tree to tree on the other side before dropping one of the gunmen with several rounds to the back. Interpreting the data from the scene as quickly as he could, he formulated a plan and sprang into action.

Explosion. Likely a bomb. At least two gunmen. One still active in the center of the field, approximately ninety meters in front of my current position. I see no other threats. I see two cops giving first aid near the stage area. Gunman firing into the crowd has his back to me. I have a 9mm and can make that run in under ten seconds. Neutralize the threat. Go!

Amir redirected his attention from the stage area to the center of the field just in time to see a man sprint out of the tree line toward his only remaining warrior. With each stride, the runner dug his toes into the ground and pushed off with all his might. His eyes were locked decisively on his target and he pumped his arms madly as he closed the distance with remarkable speed and determination. A mesmerized Amir slowly rose to his feet with his eyes locked on the mysterious man.

Eighty-nine

Mark had briefly considered using his 9mm to neutralize the threat, but the distance was less than ideal, and too many civilians were passing through his line of sight. The only other option was to get up close and personal as quickly as possible. As he approached the threat, he leapt high into the air, extended his legs, and violently planted both feet squarely in the small of the unsuspecting warrior's lower back.

Landry felt the man's lower spine snap on impact as his body folded like a cheap card table. When both hit the ground, Mark immediately took control of the terrorist's rifle—a Sig Sauer M400—and rose to his feet.

The young terrorist was motionless, but his eyes showed signs of life and he was mumbling. Mark pulled the rifle into his shoulder, pointed the muzzle in the young man's face, and quickly fired two rounds. He felt the bolt lock to the rear and looked to confirm the magazine was empty. Then he dropped to his knees and started patting down the dead terrorist to find another magazine. He found one in the man's cargo pocket. The magazine contained only one round.

You gotta be kidding me.

Ninety

When he saw the mysterious man fire two high-powered rifle rounds into his warrior's head, Amir knew that the attack phase of the mission was over and it was time to get the hell out of there. He put the cell phone detonator into a cargo pocket and quickly looked around to make sure he hadn't dropped anything.

As Amir turned to leave, he heard the main door of the structure below him burst open, followed by the sound of a man screaming authoritatively. He peered down from the roof as a large man exited the building with a pistol in one hand, waving a badge in the other.

"Blue! Blue! Blue!" he screamed.

Amir's training and instincts told him he needed to leave the area immediately. Survivors would be taking pictures and recording video on their cell phones. Authorities would descend on the field rapidly, and escaping unnoticed would become more difficult with each passing moment. But his feet remained frozen on the roof as a small voice in his head chided him.

The bomb damage had been less than optimal. Had the last-minute appearance of the emergency vehicles suppressed the blast? Or were his bomb-making skills to blame? How many were dead? He had hoped for a record but that seemed unlikely; the gunmen had been silenced too quickly. Had they been poor choices for such a mission? Or had he failed to train them adequately and doomed the mission by cutting the number of shooters in half? Why not add one more dead American cop to the tally? Are you a warrior or a babysitter?

I am a warrior.

Amir rapidly drew the .45 from his waistband, aimed for the center of the plainclothes officer's back, and quickly squeezed off three rounds. The target continued for several steps before collapsing to his knees and slumping forward into a determined crawl. Grudgingly impressed with the undercover officer's determination, Amir raised the pistol again and aimed for the head. He breathed deeply, closed one eye, and tried to steady his front sight on the back of the man's head.

But his attention involuntarily refocused on the kneeling man with the rifle in the center of the field before he could pull the trigger.

Amir turned his head to the side to get a better look as the scene unfolded in slow motion. All sound was muted. Tunnel vision. As if someone had turned out the lights and shined a single spotlight on the center of the field.

With blinding speed the man jammed a magazine into the rifle and slapped the bolt release with the palm of his hand to chamber a round. Without pause he pointed the muzzle directly toward Amir and took aim. Amir dropped to his stomach, hugged the roof, and lay motionless for several seconds. When he lifted his head just enough to peer out over the field, he froze.

The man with the rifle was running straight toward him.

Ninety-one

Amir cursed himself for caving to his ego and getting involved unnecessarily. He should have detonated the bomb and then left during the initial moments of chaos. Now he was being pursued by what appeared to be a very capable and determined man. He considered trying to stop him with gunfire but hitting a moving target at such a distance was tough even under the best of circumstances. Better to let him get closer. He kept his head down and said a quick prayer.

Dear God ... forgive my selfishness ... and if you deem me worthy, give me the strength and wisdom to finish this day so that I may martyr myself for your glory in Washington. I will not fail you again. I beg for your mercy!

Amir took a deep breath and peered over the rooftop to check on the running man's progress. When he surveyed the scene, his anxious expression turned to a wide grin. God had answered his prayers.

Thank you. Allahu Akbar!

Ninety-two

Mark made a hard right turn as he neared the structure and took cover behind a tree. He quickly scanned the area and raised the rifle to cover the roof.

Come on, Buddy. Pop up just one more time for me. Do it. Take a peek. You know you want to.

Mark took several deep breaths to calm his nerves and prepare for the one shot he'd be able to take with the rifle before having to switch to the 9mm, which was still concealed in the small of his back.

Come on, asshole. Take a peek. Just one little ...

Ninety-three

The rifle dropped from Mark's hands as soon as the probes from Officer Charlie Worth's Taser hit him squarely between the shoulder blades. He screamed, dropped to his knees, and shook as 1,800 volts traveled through his body for a full five seconds.

"Don't move!" said Worth.

Still kneeling, Mark turned to face the officer. "Get that fucking thing off me!"

"I said, don't move!"

Another surge of electricity followed. Landry rolled onto his back and screamed. Worth removed the nightstick from his duty belt and fumbled for his radio. "I have one of the shooters! I have one of the shooters by the bathrooms. I need backup now!"

Mark lay flat on his back after the second shock and tried to catch his breath. He saw movement on the roof out of the corner of his eye and rolled onto his side to get a better look.

A young man gazed down at him from the edge of the roof with a faint grin on his face. Mark turned to Officer Worth, pointed at the roof, and screamed as best he could.

"Shooter! Shooter's right there! Look!"

Mustering all the strength he could, Mark rolled onto his stomach and tried to get up on all fours. When he looked up at the roof again, the shooter was gone.

"He's getting away! God dammit! He's getting away!"

Charlie Worth dropped the radio, stepped forward, and brought his nightstick down on Mark's head with everything he had.

Ninety-four

"Hi Bill. How's it going?" asked the young receptionist from inside her glass booth.

The thirty-seven-year-old security guard stuffed as much of his face as possible through the circular hole in the glass and whispered softly. "I'd be a lot better if I was on the other side of this glass with you."

"Not gonna happen," she answered without looking up from her computer terminal.

"That's okay. I get it. You're shy. Would you prefer I find us somewhere more private? Perhaps a nice little broom closet on the fourth floor?"

When she didn't respond, he blew a kiss and turned around to scan the emergency room's waiting area as he had done hundreds of times before, rotating his gaze back and forth with a neutral, somewhat disinterested expression on his face.

Approximately forty people sat, stood, or paced about in the waiting area. Kids with ear infections. Adults with nasty coughs. A bunch with cuts and scrapes, but nothing that couldn't wait while the more seriously injured or sick were seen first.

Bill was about to move on and check the pediatric wing when a young woman sitting in the corner with a backpack on her lap caught his attention. Visitors to the ER are somewhat predictable. They read, talk, watch TV, or keep themselves otherwise occupied. This young lady was different. She was just sitting there, holding the bag with both arms and avoiding eye contact with anyone who looked in her direction. The air conditioning was pumping but she was visibly sweating. Bill knocked twice on the receptionist's glass barrier.

"See the brunette by herself in the corner? How long has she been here?"

"Jesus, you sure got over me fast."

"No, seriously."

The receptionist glanced over at the young woman. "She got here like an hour ago but never checked in. I haven't had time to chase her down. She must be waiting for someone."

"She's been in this AC for an hour, wearing nothing but a little t-shirt, and she's still sweating like that. She looks nervous, doesn't she?"

"It's the ER, Bill. Everyone is nervous."

"Yeah, but not like that. I've seen that kind of nervous before."

"Oh yeah? Where?"

"Baghdad."

Bill walked across the waiting area to the drinking fountain, where he bent down and took a long drink of cold water. Then he casually walked toward the girl.

"It's a hot one today, hey?"

She didn't respond, so he moved closer, stood directly in front of her, and repeated himself.

"I said it's pretty hot today. Don't you think?"

Fatima looked up with a forced smile. "It's not so bad."

"Not so bad? Whew! I'm burning up in here. Looks like you are too," he said pointing to the sweat running down her forehead on her nose. "The water in the bubbler is cold if you want any."

"I'm fine," she answered, casually wiping her brow with one hand while keeping the other hand wrapped firmly around the backpack in her lap.

"Yeah, it's city water. Kinda rusty tasting. There's a cafeteria right down the hall if you'd prefer something else. Want me to show you where it is?"

"No, thanks. I'm fine," she answered abruptly.

"Suit yourself. I'm not bothering you, am I?"

"No. I just ... I just have a lot on my mind."

"Oh yeah? Sorry to hear that. You waiting for someone?"

Fatima shifted uncomfortably in her seat. "Yeah. Sort of. I'm waiting for something."

"Ma'am, everyone in the waiting room needs to check in with reception, and you've been here for over an hour without doing so. May I see your ID, please? Not a big deal. Just procedure."

Fatima appeared startled by the request. "My ID? Why? I haven't done anything wrong."

"I know that, ma'am. It's just standard procedure. Everyone in this area needs to show ID, and all bags are subject to search."

She unconsciously squeezed the backpack a little tighter but nodded in agreement. Sweat began to pour down her face and her voice cracked.

"My ID is in my bag. I'll get it for you."

She unzipped the top of her backpack and fished around inside with a sweaty hand as she recalled the instructions from her facilitator: *If you think you will be compromised, detonate the bomb immediately. Do not be taken into custody.*

"I know it's in here somewhere. Okay, here it is."

Fatima took one final deep breath, exhaled slowly, and bowed her head. Then she closed her eyes, smiled, and detonated the bomb.

Ninety-five

Mark was on the floor in the back seat of a police cruiser, his hands cuffed behind his back, when he regained consciousness. His head throbbed, his vision was blurry, and the nausea was overwhelming. He vomited what little he had eaten that morning. When the driver's side door slammed shut and the vehicle started moving, he struggled to his knees and eventually to a sitting position on the back seat.

Mark immediately recognized the female officer driving the cruiser. They had met at the Witch Hunt shortly after he returned to town. He recalled her thick Massachusetts accent.

"Hey … hey … your boy Charlie made a big mistake."

She ignored him and continued driving at high speed with the lights and siren blaring.

"Listen to me, Wendy. You know who I am. Look at me. I'm Mark Landry. I'm Luci's boyfriend."

She looked at him closely in the rear-view mirror for a moment before returning her attention to the road.

"You know I'm not a criminal. Your boy back there made a big mistake. He thought I was one of the shooters. I wasn't. And the sooner you help me get this worked out, the sooner we can get the guys who did this."

No response.

"Listen, I took out one of the shooters and was going after another when your guy decided to tase me. He screwed up. And I'm not faulting him for that. You guys don't know me. But listen, Wendy. I'm a counterterrorism operator for the U.S. government, okay? And I need your help."

She glanced at him again in the mirror but said nothing.

"You gotta believe me, Wendy. You think Luci would be with a terrorist? Listen, I'm going to give you a phone number. Just call it, say my name and location. That's it. Can you do that for me?"

No response.

"Wendy, I can promise you right now this will never come back to bite you. I'll personally make sure of that. But the sooner you call and I get this straightened out, the sooner we can find the assholes who just shot up our town and keep them from hurting more people. Look at me, Wendy. Look at me!"

The officer looked at him again in the mirror.

"I've been doing this a long time, and I promise you, if we don't move quickly they'll get away with this. The guy I was chasing is getting away as we speak. Fix Charlie's mistake, Wendy. I'm not asking you to let me go. All I'm asking you to do is call the number, say my name and location. Then text Luci so she doesn't worry and you're done."

Wendy looked at Mark long and hard through the mirror. Then she took a deep breath, nodded her head, and pulled a metallic pen from her uniform pocket.

"What's the numbah?"

Ninety-six

"Senator, our planners think this will be the biggest march in Washington history—well over one million strong. We know you have other people to meet with today, but do you have any questions that we can answer right now?"

Senator McDermott finished scribbling a note on the legal pad she had balanced on her lap and removed her glasses.

"No questions right now, but I might have some later. This is a lot to digest. Thank you for coming. I'll be in touch when I can."

Meghan ushered the visitors out of the apartment and returned with a bright smile on her face. "Well, what do you think? It's an amazing opportunity."

McDermott sat behind the antique secretary desk in the family room, quickly reviewing the agenda for her next appointment. "It's a little pie-in-the-sky, isn't it?"

Meghan frowned. "If successful, it would mean the complete abolition of guns in America. It's exactly what we want, Mom. We've dreamed about this, and for the first time there's a good chance enough Americans might actually support it. "

"Meg, they're asking me to propose a constitutional amendment. Do you have any idea how difficult it is to amend the constitution? We're not talking about naming a Post Office."

"Yeah, all you have to do is get two-thirds of the House and Senate to vote for the proposal. Then you get three-fourths of the states to go along."

"Much easier said than done. Let's choose our battles a bit more wisely."

Meghan sat on the sofa and turned on cable news with the volume down.

"Mom, you've been asked to be the featured speaker for the biggest public demonstration in D.C. history, at which you would get to make the big announcement about the single most important issue of your career. It's political gold."

McDermott looked up from her briefing papers with her reading glasses perched at the tip of her nose and stared at her daughter. "Political gold? It's a big crowd, Meghan. But the centerpiece of the movement is doomed. Listen, we have to prioritize and choose our battles. This one is unrealistic. Let's try to stick to things we can accomplish, okay? Enough of this for now."

Meghan walked across the office to the television and turned the screen toward her mother. "Enough of this? You don't get to make that decision, Senator. They do," she said, pointing to the breaking news headline: TERROR IN MASSACHUSETTS.

"Hold on, Meg."

McDermott finished jotting a note in the margin of the next meeting's agenda and then looked up. The past week had brought over a dozen incidents of domestic terrorism across the country. Each morning it was not a question of whether but where another shooting or bombing would take place. Her formerly sharp, emotional reactions to the events had become dull and detached. She bit her bottom lip, shook her head, and returned to the stacks of information on her desk.

"Where's this one?" she asked.

"Somewhere in Mass," Meghan replied as she reached for the remote and turned up the volume.

"Terror in Massachusetts," said the broadcaster. "Another day, another bloody attack on American soil—this time during a small town's veteran recognition ceremony. The story is still unfolding, but preliminary reports tell us there was some sort of explosion followed by several gunmen opening fire on the crowd. Warning: the images you are about to see may be disturbing."

Live footage from a news drone showed explicit images of the chaotic scene.

"Might be disturbing? Jesus Christ, lady. Look at the carnage. This one will end up being worse than Billings, Cleveland, and Miami put together."

Meghan stood up and approached Senator McDermott's desk.

"Listen, I know you care, but lately it's like you've become desensitized to all of this. Look at this, Mom. Then explain again why you're against leading the charge to stop this insanity!"

McDermott stood and removed her glasses.

"Give me a break, Meghan. You're not framing this fairly and you know it. I'm doing everything I can to fight the good fight and keep other mothers from ending up like me. But I can't waste time or resources chasing after unicorns. We need to be pragmatic and—"

The live drone footage now shared a split screen with stock photos and specific data on the targeted town. The images seemed vaguely familiar to McDermott.

238

"Where was this one, Meghan?" she asked.

"Massachusetts."

"I know that, but which town?"

Before Meghan could answer, the broadcast returned to a full-screen, live shot from the drone, with the town name spelled out in bright red letters at the bottom of the screen. McDermott's heart rate soared and her legs weakened.

"Mom, are you okay? You're white as a ghost."

McDermott reached for the glass of cold water on her desk and tried to shake it off.

"Yeah, I'm fine. Do me a favor, Meg. Hop on the phone and get all the information you can on this one, okay?"

"Okay. I think we're the only two people in D.C. working on the Fourth, but I'll try. Can I ask why this one is so important?"

"Just do it, please."

Ninety-seven

Luci got as close as she could to Founders Field and then ditched her car on the side of the road, threw the first-aid backpack on her back, and jogged the rest of the way.

The text from Wendy—"Mark is fine, don't worry about him" —hadn't made sense until she heard the breaking news. She had thrown on her uniform and was out the door within minutes.

Throngs of emergency vehicles were still converging on the site, including multiple police departments, ambulances and fire engines from surrounding towns, sheriff's deputies, and Massachusetts state troopers. Quick-reaction elements of the Boston JTTF were already on the ground as unmarked aircraft crisscrossed in the cloudless sky above the kill zone.

Authorities struggled to isolate the area so that they could cover the dead, treat the wounded, and begin the painstaking process of investigating. Their arduous task was made much more difficult by the hundreds of despondent, swarming townspeople seeking information on loved ones. Luci pushed her way through the growing crowd, entered the perimeter, and froze in horror at the smoldering scene.

Ninety-eight

"What the hell are you doing here, Luci?"

Sergeant Cromwell grabbed her by the elbow.

"You're on mandatory leave, but we could use the help if you're up for it. Can you handle this? If not, I need you to go home right now. Do you understand me?"

Cromwell tightened his grip and shook her arm firmly.

"Hey, are you listening to me?"

Luci shook off the initial shock of seeing such unfettered bloodshed and pulled her arm away.

"Yes, I'm fine, Sarge. Where do you need me?"

"There are a shitload of wounded on the other end of the field who need help. Work with the medics. Stop any bleeding you can. Comfort survivors. These people need us, Luci. Put aside the emotions and get the job done. We can grieve later. Do you understand me?"

"Got it."

Luci scanned from left to right as she jogged toward the far end of the field.

Keep it together. Breathe deeply. Focus.

Off to her right, firemen spread blankets over a row of bodies. To the left, paramedics worked furiously on a father and his ten-year-old son, both with gunshot wounds to the chest. As she neared the blast area, the grass turned slippery. The smells intensified. She glanced down at her bloodstained boots and tried not to vomit.

"You shouldn't be here, Luci!" screamed Charlie Worth as he grabbed her from behind.

"Not now, Charlie. And get your hands off me!"

Worth grabbed both of her biceps and pulled her in tight.

"You shouldn't be here. You're on leave and way too close to this!"

Luci pulled her arms back, then pushed Worth in the chest with both hands.

"Back off, Charlie!"

He stumbled backwards, stunned. Quickly recovering himself, he sprang forward, grabbing Luci by the front of her white uniform with his gloved bloody hands.

"Your boyfriend was part of this! He killed an unarmed man in the middle of the field and went after another before I stopped him."

"What? Are you crazy, Charlie? Mark's not a terrorist—he hunts them! Now get your fucking hands off me!"

Luci struggled to free herself from Worth's grip, but he pulled her in closer and squeezed.

"Charlie, let go of me right now."

"No. We don't need you, Luci. Nobody wants you here."

She kicked him in his shin as hard as she could with the sole of her right tactical boot. When he let go she reached far back with her right arm and struck him in the temple with the palm of her hand. Worth's knees buckled and he staggered backwards.

"Stay the fuck out of my way, Charlie! I don't have time for your bullshit!"

As Charlie shook off the blow, his eyes widened. His face turned purple and the engorged veins in his neck and forehead pulsated with each beat of his racing heart. He snarled like a rabid dog and lunged forward with outstretched hands.

Sergeant Cromwell's muscular arms enveloped Officer Worth around the waist from behind and dragged him backwards.

"At ease, Charlie! What the hell is wrong with you? Get a hold of yourself," he said as he dragged his officer from the scene.

"She shouldn't be here, Sarge!"

Cromwell released his bear hug, spun Charlie around, and pulled him close.

"I don't want to hear any more from you, Charlie. We've got the worst disaster in town history on our hands and I need every one of you to do your fucking job."

Worth began to protest, but Cromwell tightened his grip and cut him off.

"No! No, Charlie! Don't say a word. Not a fucking word. Listen to me. There was an explosion at the hospital. Did you hear me? Someone may have bombed the hospital, Charlie. I need you to get your cruiser and escort Engine Two to the hospital right now. Go!"

Cromwell pointed Worth in the direction of his cruiser and pushed him on the back. "Go! Now!" When he turned back to face Luci, she was already comforting two blood-spattered cheerleaders.

Ninety-nine

"How fast can you get us there?" Doc asked.

"About twenty minutes," replied the Family pilot.

"I'll get you a week of vacation for every minute you shave off."

The former U.S. Army Task Force 160th aviator nodded his head calmly and turned around to verify that the other passengers were strapping in. Once the DOJ attorney and three plainclothes operators had fastened their harnesses and given him a thumbs-up, he spoke into the intercom.

"Hold on tight, Gentlemen."

The modified Bell 407 helicopter sprung into the city skyline, banked hard left over Boston Harbor, and headed north at full speed.

One hundred

James Woodbridge was overwhelmed when he entered the police station. A lifelong resident and former deputy mayor, he had happily accepted the title of acting chief of police. The sixty-five-year-old retired accountant had been assured that the search committee would quickly vet suitable candidates and recommend three finalists for consideration, and that a permanent chief would be in place in fewer than thirty days. The lieutenants and sergeants would run the day-to-day operations. He would simply be a figurehead with little to worry about.

All of that changed the moment terrorists attacked the town.

"Slow down and explain it to me again, Lieutenant? What's NEMLEC?"

The department's ranking lieutenant put his arm on Woodbridge's shoulder, ushered him into the chief's barren office, and motioned for him to sit behind the empty desk.

"It's the Northeastern Massachusetts Law Enforcement Council. They have SWAT assets on site, along with a whole host of other organizations. From this point forward, things will likely become even more confusing than they already are."

The lieutenant opened the small refrigerator on the floor next to the desk, opened a bottle of cold water, and put it on the desk in front of Woodbridge.

"All these organizations know what they're doing, but they are going to need time to sort things out. The Governor's Office has already called and offered to help in any way they can. All we have to do is ask. Up at Founders Field, people are being questioned and scrutinized. One man is currently in custody, but it's still unclear whether he was one of the shooters or a civilian who got involved. He is being questioned right now. I have already recommended that from this point forward any detainees be handed over to the county. They have more appropriate facilities and more manpower than us."

"What about casualties? What do we know?" asked Woodbridge.

"It's bad. We're still not entirely clear, but we're looking at a minimum of thirty dead and over a hundred injured. That doesn't include the attack at the emergency room, which was apparently a less powerful charge. There we have another three or four dead and several more wounded. Surrounding area hospitals are picking up the slack and have raised their security postures. The most critical patients are being airlifted to Boston Medical Center and Mass General Hospital. They'll get the best trauma care in the world if we can just get them there quickly enough. The biggest challenge with that is ..."

Another officer abruptly entered the office and interrupted. "Sir, the Governor is on line three for you."

"Can you give us a minute, Smitty? I'm almost done here and I've already spoken to the Governor's Office, okay?" answered the lieutenant.

"It's not the Governor's Office. It's the Governor himself. Said he needed to speak to Mr. Woodbridge ASAP. Told me to interrupt him no matter what. Sorry, Lieutenant."

The lieutenant nodded his head and pointed at the phone on the desk. All the lines were lit.

"Press the third button from the left and pick up the receiver. I'll stay right here in case you need me."

Woodbridge depressed the button for line three, wiped the perspiration from his forehead, and lifted the receiver to the ear.

"Yes? This is James Woodbridge."

The lieutenant checked the time on his tactical watch and scrolled through the messages on his department smartphone.

"Yes, that's correct. One man. I don't know the name offhand, but I can find out ... uh huh ... yes ... okay then, Governor ... I'll take care of it. Yes, thank you for your support. I'll speak to you later, sir."

"That was quick. What did he say?" asked the lieutenant without averting his eyes from the list of urgent messages on his phone.

"He offered his support. And he expressed how important it was for us to cooperate with the men who are about to land on our department's helicopter pad."

The lieutenant put the phone back into his pocket and focused his attention on his trembling boss. "Mr. Woodbridge, we don't have a helicopter pad."

"I already told you, the four guys in the public works truck just didn't look right. By the time I got back to Founders Field, the attack had already begun. I arrived right after the blast. I'm ninety percent sure the shooter I engaged was one of the men in the truck," said Mark.

"Yeah, we got that part, but why did you kill him?" replied the detective.

"He was standing in the middle of the field shooting into the crowd. What was I supposed to do? I had to stop him. Regardless, he's not a problem anymore, and I already told you there was another shooter on top of the building and he's getting away as we speak."

"Can you give me a description of the other shooter?"

"Not really. He was young. Maybe in his mid-twenties. He was wearing a ball cap and sunglasses so I didn't get a good look at his face. But he definitely had blond hair."

"How tall?" the detective pressed.

"I don't know. Like I said, I was lying on my back with a Taser up my ass thanks to one of your colleagues. I couldn't tell how tall he was. But he had an athletic build and moved like he knew how to handle himself."

A young uniformed officer sitting next to the detective chimed in. "What does that mean? How does somebody move when they know how to handle themselves? How would you know?"

The detective shot his colleague a quick look that said "I got this" and motioned to Mark to continue speaking.

"Call it intuition based on experience. He was fast. Knew to take cover immediately when I got my sights on him. Like he had done it before. And he was patient. He could have fired on me but had the discipline not to draw any more attention to his position. Trust me, I just know. This guy is dangerous."

"Right. We believe you. But what did you say your name was again?"

"I haven't given you my name, Detective."

"Why were you carrying a handgun? Do you have a license to carry that handgun?"

Mark ignored the question and leaned back against the wall on the far side of the sterile cell. He alternated his gaze between his two inquisitors, who were sitting on stools outside the cell bars. Then he shifted his focus to the ceiling.

"Let's leave him here for a little while. Take a few minutes to see how things are developing up on the field. See if he loosens up. What do you say?" whispered the young uniformed officer.

"Not yet. Let's just sit here for a few minutes. My guess is he changes his story a few more times before we get to the whole truth. Go grab us a couple of waters and get one for him too."

The senior detective was scrolling through the urgent messages on his phone when a faint humming noise broke the silence of the holding area. With each second, the noise level increased until it felt like the building was throbbing.

"What the hell is that?" he asked out loud.

Mark Landry dropped his gaze from the ceiling and looked at the senior detective.

"Probably my ride," he said.

One hundred two

Three sets of civilian hiking boots hit the pavement within seconds after the helicopter touched down on the far edge of the police department's parking lot. With M4 carbines slung at the low ready position and badges hanging from their necks, the three operators scanned the perimeter.

Once Doc and the DOJ attorney had exited the aircraft, all five walked briskly toward the rear door of the station.

"You stay here with me," Doc said to the nearest operator. "And you two go retrieve our package. Get him in the helicopter as quickly as possible and wait for me there."

* * *

The DOJ attorney had already furnished his credentials and was formally presenting John Woodbridge and his lieutenant with a series of orders that he had retrieved from his briefcase. Both men listened silently and nodded whenever the lawyer paused to ask if they understood.

The other two operators followed the detective down the hall, through the large security door, and into the holding area. When they arrived in front of Landry's cell, he was standing with his handcuffed wrists stretched out in front of him. "Would somebody please get these things off me?"

"Do me a favor, brother. Unlock the cell and give us a minute," said one of the operators to the detective in a friendly but firm tone.

"No problem. Here are the keys for the cuffs."

When the detective had left the holding area, the operators entered the cell.

"So there I was," began the lead man with the handcuff keys, "sitting at home in Oklahoma and enjoying my time off when Doc called and invited me to join him in Boston for a few days. I thought, 'Why the hell not? I've always liked Boston, and maybe there's a chance I'll get to have a beer with my soon-to-be-retired partner while I'm there.' Little did I know I'd end up having to save your sorry ass instead."

"Billy, if you want to hug it out, you're going to have to shut your mouth and unlock these cuffs first," said Mark. The last time he had seen Billy, they had been on a ship somewhere in the Mediterranean after completing a covert mission in Ukraine.

"This here is Max, the newest member of the Family," Billy said, pointing to the other operator. "I'm not saying he's a better partner than you, but he has managed to keep himself out of jail so far."

Both men exchanged nods. Billy dropped Mark's handcuffs on the floor and gave him a hug before backing off so he could stretch his arms. Then he glanced behind him to make sure they were alone.

"Here's the deal. Doc's here along with some DOJ egghead. They're laying down the law with the local guys down the hall and will grab any shit they took from you when they brought you in. They've already shut down the cameras and all that stuff. So our only task right now is to simply walk outside and get on the chopper. We'll move on your cue, but I suggest we do so as quickly as possible."

"Let's go," replied Mark.

"Okay, then. Max, let's make a Mark Landry sandwich. You lead the way out and I'll bring up the rear."

The three men exited the cell and walked briskly through the open security door and down the hall toward the station's rear exit.

One hundred three

Doc waited until he saw the three men exit the building before nodding to signal the remaining operator at his side that it was time to go. He interrupted the DOJ attorney in mid-sentence.

"Pardon me for one second please," he said softly. "Gentlemen, several others will be here shortly to help you comply with these orders, as well as with the National Security Letter. I urge you to listen to them very closely. Violating any aspect of an NSL—even unintentionally—is a very serious crime and gets treated accordingly. We're all on the same side here. Let's keep it that way. Thank you for your cooperation and professionalism."

Doc shook each of their hands and looked both men in the eye for several seconds until each nodded to indicate their understanding. The attorney picked up where he had left off and Doc headed for the helicopter, followed closely by his third operator.

Mark was already buckled in tight and wedged between Billy and Max in the rear when the last two men boarded the aircraft. Doc turned around to get a look at Mark and winked.

"You okay?"

"I'm good, Doc. Thanks for coming to get me."

"You're family, Mark," he answered before nodding to the pilot. He didn't speak again until the helicopter was racing back to Boston at top speed.

"Listen, Mark, I need to go to JTTF, but we're going to drop you three off someplace else on the way so you can cool off and get cleaned up. In the meantime, tell me everything you know about what happened today."

Amir had acquired the first getaway vehicle from an elderly gentleman less than a mile from Founders Field. After snapping the old man's neck, he quickly dumped the body in a nearby trash can and hoped nobody would notice until he was far away. Running out of gas a short time later, he had praised God when a young woman pulled over almost immediately to help. He strangled her, left the body in a deep ditch on the side of the road, and headed north.

At the New Hampshire welcome center, he parked at the far end of the lot to avoid surveillance cameras, feigned car trouble, and flashed three hundred dollars in front of a young man who looked like he needed the money. The two were immediately on their way in a brown Chevrolet pickup truck with New Hampshire plates.

"Do you smell something? Seriously, I feel nauseous," Amir said once they had turned onto a dirt road just a few miles from the safe house.

"No. How much farther did you say it was to your aunt's house?"

"We're almost there. It's just up the road, but can you pull over? I seriously think I'm going to throw up and don't want to mess up your truck."

The vehicle came to a stop and Amir stepped out. The driver checked the time on his wristwatch and exhaled impatiently. Before he could raise his head, Amir had opened the driver's side door, pulled him to the ground violently by the neck of his t-shirt, and fired two bullets into his head. He disposed of the body deep in the woods.

Amir prayed silently as he drove and reflected on the successes of the day. The bomb, gunmen, and girl at the hospital had not been as deadly as he had wanted. But according to radio reports, they had still shaken the infidel world, and of that he should be proud.

He turned off the main road and followed the winding dirt driveway uphill to the cabin, where he would rest and alter his appearance before heading south to Washington where his true glory awaited. But first he had to return to the safe house to retrieve the weapons and explosives that he had been forced to leave behind when he amended the original plan. Just as important, he needed to kill the only person who could positively identify him.

When he reached the cabin, he drove far beyond the end of the driveway and parked the truck well past the tree line. The sight of the truck and the subsequent sound of Amir's boots against the wooden steps of the cabin sent chills through the structure's only occupant. Amir knocked and waited. A trembling voice answered from within.

"What do you want? Why have you returned?"

"Open the door, Yasir. I will not ask you twice."

"Billy, let me use your phone," said Mark.

"No problem. And *mi casa es su casa*. The shower is down the hall and you can have any of the clothes in the closet."

Mark dialed Luci's number and walked down the hall toward the bathroom. No answer. Voicemail.

"Hey babe, it's me. Just calling to see how you're doing. I hope you got the message that I'm fine. Don't worry about me. I've just got a few things to take care of before I can head back to town. I'll call you again later. Be safe … and don't ever forget how much I love you. Talk soon."

Mark felt somewhat better when he emerged from the bedroom, freshly showered, but his head continued to throb. Max sat in a chair near the window on the other side of the safe house, located in Boston's Back Bay neighborhood.

"These are for you," Billy said as he handed Mark his handgun and an ice pack. "Listen, all kidding aside—how are you doing? You okay?"

"Besides my head, I'm good," he answered.

Billy turned Mark around to look at the back of his head.

"Damn, that's the size of a golf ball. Lucky he didn't catch you with the edge of his stick or you'd have quite a gash on your noggin," said Billy.

"I've had worse. I just wish I could have gotten that other bastard before he got away. I have a sick feeling he's long gone by now and they'll never find him."

"At least you got one of them. If you hadn't been there, he could have done a lot more damage. Still, I know how tough it is. I'll never forget the day McVeigh blew a hole in Oklahoma City. I knew people who got killed that day. Hell, everyone in OKC knew someone who got killed or hurt." Billy cracked a smile, pointed across the room, and raised his voice. "Hey, look at Max for a second and tell me if he looks familiar."

Max looked up and rolled his eyes. "I was just doing my job. Are you ever gonna let it go?"

"No, seriously," Billy insisted. "Stand up, tie a bandana over your face, and see if Mark recognizes you. I swear, this is the last time I'm gonna do this."

"Screw you, Billy."

"Calm down. It doesn't matter anymore anyway. Actually, I think you totally redeemed yourself today when you helped rescue the great Mark Landry from captivity. Unfortunately, nobody will ever hear about or see this one," Billy said.

Billy threw an arm around Mark, pulled him in close, and whispered the explanation. "I'm just busting his chops. Some Army guy deserted his unit and ended up getting his ass captured by the Taliban. Max drew the short straw at his last job and got stuck having to go pick the guy up in some bullshit prisoner exchange. The ragheads filmed it and the video has like four billion hits on YouTube. It pisses him off to no end."

"Good to see you haven't changed," Mark said as he pulled Billy toward the kitchen. "Tell me you have something to eat in this place and fill me in on what's happened since I've been out of the loop."

"Chow is limited, bro. But budget cuts are the least of my worries."

Mark browsed the contents of the refrigerator and decided on a bottle of water and a tightly wrapped takeout sandwich from a nearby deli.

"Go on."

"Things are changing quickly. Politically and culturally. The heat is on, big time. Doc summed it up the other day—it's no longer just about terrorists and hostile governments. He and Dunbar are spending just as much time playing defense against our own politicians and media who think we're the bad guys. I've never seen him this pessimistic."

"Yeah, he mentioned some of that to me the last time we spoke. Something about a major hack too. Lots of information might have been compromised. Anything new on that?" asked Mark.

"Might have been compromised? Oh no, my friend. We're operating under the assumption that everything has been compromised, Family business included. Which raises a whole bunch of other issues we never thought we'd have to deal with. Personnel records, mission debriefs, you name it. Every morning I wake up wondering how long it'll be before we're all competing with Max for top spot on YouTube."

"Any idea who's behind it? Are we doing anything to control the potential fallout?"

"Who did it is anybody's guess these days. A pimply faced high-school kid in his parent's basement or North Korea's Bureau

121. And what the hell can you do about it after the fact, man? Once it's out there, it's out there. We'd get a pass on most of it, but you and I both know there are some missions the American people would lose their shit over."

"Like Berlin," said Mark.

"Among others. But that particular one does come to mind."

"Yet another time when you saved my ass, right? I still owe you for that one," Landry added.

"I ain't keeping score, Mark. Besides, you went on to save a hell of a lot more people than we can even imagine. I know you, brother. And I know you probably still think about what you had to do to get the job done. But you didn't have any choice. You did the right thing, and a shitload of people are still alive because of you."

Mark didn't respond. He finished his water, grabbed another one from the refrigerator, and changed the subject.

"What brings you guys to Boston anyway?" asked Mark.

Billy glanced over his shoulder at Max and took a moment to choose the right words. "We aren't one hundred percent certain, but the local JTTF may have an issue that needs to be addressed."

"Yeah, like what?" pressed Mark.

"Like maybe some kind of information leak. Could be digital. Could be human. Delta raided an ISIS site in Syria last week and found some thumb drives full of stuff from the Boston JTTF. So we're watching a couple of folks. It's probably a digital hack instead of a mole. Doc doesn't seem too worried about it, so my guess is it's more of a precaution. But Doc likes to keep his cards pretty close to his vest, so who the hell knows."

Mark and Billy rejoined Max, who had been flipping through the news channels.

"What are they saying, Max?" Asked Mark.

"Very few facts but plenty of speculation. Theories vary depending on the channel. Islamic terrorists. Lone wolves. Right-wing extremists. One of the local outlets said something about gang activity in the town—Latin Kings. But then they quoted a Kings spokesperson who denounced the attack and denied they even had any members there. The only thing everyone knows for sure is a bomb went off and three gunmen with shotguns and hunting rifles started shooting."

"Not exactly," replied Mark. "They used Sig Sauer M400s. I didn't see any shotguns or hunting rifles, but I guess that doesn't really matter."

Billy's cell phone vibrated in his pocket. "Yeah, he's right here. It's Doc," he said as he handed the phone to Mark.

"How are you doing, Mark?" Doc asked.

"I'm good. Have you heard anything new?"

"The Islamic State is taking credit, but we haven't corroborated their claim, and it wouldn't be the first time they tried to piggyback off an attack they had nothing to do with. JTTF says a bomb went off followed by at least three gunmen with AK-47s, but they haven't ruled out the possibility that more people were involved. Thanks to your lead about the men in the truck, they checked out the public works area and found one of their drivers in a dumpster, strangled."

"They weren't AKs, Doc. But I imagine some of the people giving the briefings don't know the difference anyway. What else?"

"All three gunmen have supposedly been preliminarily identified, but their identities won't be released until the forensic and biometric evidence has been verified and investigators seize any assets and property. Identification was quick because all three already had prints or DNA in the national database. Two of the three had violent criminal records, and the other had managed to serve in the Air Force for about two weeks before being chaptered out for mental illness. What's interesting is they're all from different places: one from Massachusetts, one from New Hampshire, and one from Connecticut. It's unclear whether they knew each other beforehand and planned this together or if they are just three lone wolves put together by a facilitator. ATF has the weapons and is trying to trace them. FBI has the surveillance tapes from the hospital bombing, but I heard something about the blast coming from a blind spot in the corner of the ER. The rest is still unfolding. Me, Max, and Billy need to get to Washington ASAP. Our analysts say there's been lots of chatter about targeted assassinations, and Dunbar wants us around just in case we get actionable intelligence."

"Sounds like business as usual."

"Not exactly. Our top analyst says the typical chatter recently turned into a full-throated scream. Regardless, I need you to stay put for a while, okay?"

"Got it."

"Mark, things are changing pretty rapidly in our world and it wasn't as easy to extract you from this situation as it would have been in the past. There are a lot more moving parts these days. At one point I was doubtful we'd be able to do it at all."

"I understand that, Doc. And I appreciate the risk you took by coming to get me personally. How can I repay the favor?" he asked.

"All I want you to do right now is sit tight where you are until I'm convinced you're out of the woods. Once you are, I'll send Sadie over to give you a lift home. If you want to return the favor, there is something you can do for me once you get home."

"What's that?" he asked.

There was a brief pause on the line as Doc cleared his throat before speaking. "Start planning the next phase of your life, Mark. I already told you I think you're making the right choice by getting out now. The Family's days are numbered, and I don't want you to get caught in the crossfire if things get as ugly as I think they might. Get out and start the family you said you wanted. Then be there for them."

Mark had never heard Doc sound so despondent and was briefly taken aback by his remarks.

"I will," he answered.

"Good. We'll meet up in D.C. in a week or two to formalize your retirement. Until then, stay safe and keep a low profile."

"Give me your phone," Amir demanded.

"Why do you want to see my phone? I told you I haven't had any contact with anybody since you left the cabin."

"Do not question me!" screamed Amir as he stepped forward and struck Yasir on the side of his face with an open hand. The young man's knees buckled and he fell to the hardwood floor with a thud. Amir pulled the cell phone from Yasir's back pocket and scrolled through the call and text history. Satisfied, he tossed the phone onto the kitchen counter. "Get up."

Yasir scrambled to his knees and held his hands up in front of him. "Please, I am telling you the truth!" he pleaded.

Amir grabbed a bottle of cold water from the refrigerator, entered the main room of Ghassan's cabin, and sat in the big leather chair facing the television.

"Get in here," he commanded.

Yasir struggled to his feet and scurried to a seat on the sofa against the far wall.

"I did not tell you to sit down! Stand in front of the fireplace and face me!"

The blond terrorist took a long, slow sip of water and cleared his throat.

"Have you left the cabin today?"

"No. Not since returning from the rest area this morning. When the girl left the car and entered the building, I put the backpack on the floor in front of the passenger seat, just as you instructed."

"Has anybody else been here since you returned? Neighbors? Friends? Deliveries? Anything?"

"No, I swear it! I have had no contact with anybody. I have followed your directions to the word. I have kept up my end of the deal, but I have not received any confirmation that my sisters have been freed. You must have contact with your brothers in Syria. Can you please find out for me?"

"No," Amir answered abruptly.

Yasir breathed deeply and chose his words carefully. He did not want to be beaten again—or worse.

"Please. I have done everything the Caliphate has asked of me, and more. I have fulfilled my part of the deal. Now I beg of you. Please confirm my sisters have been freed."

"Ah, yes. I do remember something about a deal, but I can't seem to remember the details. Can you refresh my memory, Yasir?" asked Amir with a smile.

Yasir felt an impending sense of doom. The knot in his stomach started to grow. He began to sweat profusely and struggled to speak.

"Sir, as you are aware, both of my younger sisters were imprisoned by the Caliphate. In exchange for their freedom, I agreed to provide temporary safe haven for a group of holy warriors while my uncle was away. I have provided that service. I also delivered the backpack as you instructed. I swear to you on my sisters' souls that I will never speak a word of this to anybody—including them." He paused to breathe deeply. "Would you please find out if they have been freed?"

"No."

"Sir, I beg of you to find out!"

"There is no need. I already know the answer. Yasir, you are so stupid I almost feel bad for you," Amir said with a sarcastic grin.

"No. No. Please do not say that. We had a deal! We had a deal and I fulfilled my obligations!" Yasir cried out as the tears began to stream down his face. To hide the shame, he turned away and rested his head on the mantle next to the framed picture of Ghassan's wife. "Where are my sisters? What have you done with my innocent little sisters?" he sobbed.

Amir spat a mouthful of water onto the floor in disgust and rose to his feet.

"Look at yourself! What a pathetic excuse for a man," he scolded. "There was never any deal, Yasir. I have no idea where your sisters are, but I can promise you will never see them again. More than likely they were sold as slaves long ago. Or perhaps they have already outlived their usefulness and have been executed. In which case, may their souls rot in hell."

Yasir screamed out in anguish and held his hands over his ears. "No! No! That was not what you promised! I helped you! I helped you kill innocent people in exchange for my sisters' lives! You will not get away with this!"

Yasir flung the framed photo of Ghassan's deceased wife out of the way and grabbed the loaded .357 revolver his uncle kept hidden behind it. He gripped it tightly with his trembling hands and spun around to face his target. Instead, he found himself staring into the barrel of a gun, mere inches from his face.

Amir quickly squeezed the trigger. The .45 caliber hollow-point bullet pierced the bridge of Yasir's nose, tore through his brain, and exited through the back of his skull. Blood gushed from the exit wound and his lifeless body fell to the hardwood floor.

"Doc says he's going to have the intel guys send you some watch list pictures to look at. Maybe the fourth gunman was on the list," said Sadie as she backed into the driveway just before sunrise.

"Good idea. Okay, I'm just going to run in and grab a few things. Then you can drop me at Luci's. You can wait here, or you're more than welcome to come in. It's up to you."

"I've been stuck inside the JTTF a little too long. I'll wait out here and get some air. But take this before I forget. Doc asked me to give it to you," she said.

"What is it?"

"Federal law enforcement credentials of some sort. I'm not really sure," she answered as she exited the vehicle. "I was there when he was working his magic trying to erase you from everyone's radar. The fact that you lacked a gun permit seemed to bother some folks more than anything else that happened. That's when he got madder than I've ever seen. Heads rolled and he had someone from Justice take care of it."

"Ok. Thanks. I'll be right out."

Twenty minutes later, Sadie backed the car into Luci's driveway. When Mark entered the house, he found Luci sleeping on the sofa in full uniform. She had managed only to kick off her tactical boots before crashing from exhaustion. He had to shake her gently several times before she awoke.

"Luci? Luci? I'm here. Are you okay? Luci?"

When she opened her eyes, she wrapped her arms around Mark's neck and squeezed tightly. "Mark! I'm so happy you're okay. They wouldn't tell me a word at the station. Like they had never heard your name. What happened? Where have you been? I want to hear everything you can tell me."

"I will. But first, tell me how you're doing. I'm not surprised you went up there to help. Are you okay?" he asked, gently stroking the side of her face.

"Yeah, I'm okay. I'm tired as hell but okay."

"Get out of that uniform and take a shower while I cook. I imagine you haven't eaten all day, right?"

"Not a bite."

"We can talk more over breakfast."

Mark's mind was racing as he did his best to prepare a quick meal.

Who was the man on the roof? Where is he now? Is anyone even looking for him?

Mark Landry had debriefed enough missions to know how important it was for participants to talk afterwards, so he mostly listened as Luci spoke about the horrors she had seen on the field. He nodded his head and placed his hand on hers as she recounted several races against the clock to stop the bleeding. She had won the race more than she lost, but she seemed to remember the losses in much greater detail.

"You're extraordinary. You know that, right? I'm so proud of you, Luci. You showed up. You did your job under the worst of circumstances and you saved a lot of people."

"Thankfully, a lot of people really stepped up and helped each other out, especially Andy."

Mark put down his fork and straightened up. "Oh my God, Andy. I've been so preoccupied thinking about the fourth gunman, I haven't even stopped to think about him. Tell me what happened. Is he okay?"

"He will be. Witnesses say he and his star fullback ran through the gunfire and charged one of the shooters. A round caught him somewhere on the edge of his arm, but he just wrapped a t-shirt around it and started helping people. He was still going when I got there. You should have seen him, Mark."

"I can only imagine. Thank God for the two of you. Very few people have what it takes to do what you guys did."

She wiped the tears from her eyes and forced a smile. "I know, but there's a part of me that feels a little … guilty. I can't explain it. Maybe it's part survivor's guilt, but there's something else too."

"That's a very common reaction, Luci. Try not to think too much into it. You've seen the absolute worst thing possible today. Our minds don't know what to do with all that."

"When you first got home, we talked a little bit about your experiences. I asked you about combat and you mentioned the same thing, Mark. You said you sometimes felt elation and that it scared you. Well, that didn't make any sense to me until today, because I felt it too. It was the most horrendous thing I have ever been a part of, and I would have preferred that it had never happened, but I felt a jolt of something I never knew I had in me. I came alive. I felt needed, useful. But that makes me feel awful, because people had to suffer for me to feel it. Is this making any sense?"

Mark finished the last sip of his coffee, grasped both of Luci's hands, and leaned forward. "You just said what I've been feeling for twenty years but haven't been able to explain. I understand you perfectly, Luci. And now I finally understand myself. Thank you."

Luci's phone vibrated and he kissed her on the forehead as she read a text message. "Wendy is getting off in an hour or so and is going to crash here for a few hours before we both go back on duty tonight," she said.

"Good, I don't want you to be alone. I slept a few hours at the safe house, so I'm good for now. But I need to go back to the house and grab a bunch of things so I don't have to keep going back and forth. I also need to do a little bit of work while I'm there. Listen, Wendy definitely did the right thing by making the call for me, but don't tell her anything else, okay? It's for her own good."

"Got it. Please be safe, Mark. We still don't know if this whole thing is over yet. There could be more to come when we least expect it."

Frank Tagala held the blinds of the window open with one hand and held a tall glass of straight vodka with the other. After watching Mark exit the car and enter the house, he chugged the rest of his drink, marched confidently across both lawns, and knocked twice on the side door.

"Mark, it's Frank from next door," he announced.

"Hi Frank. What's up?" asked Mark after opening the door.

"Can I come in? I'd like to talk to you?"

"I'm pretty busy but, yeah, I have a few minutes. Come on in."

Both men walked to the center of the kitchen and looked at each other awkwardly.

"Listen, I'm sorry to just come by like this, but I was just wondering if you had anything new about yesterday that you could share with me."

Mark stuffed his hands in his front pockets and frowned curiously. "Uh, no. Not really. You probably know more than me."

Frank scanned the kitchen from left to right and cleared his throat. "Okay, listen. The young broad who dropped you off this morning—I've seen her before."

"You mean my cousin?"

"Yeah, your cousin, whatever. Listen, I've seen her at the JTTF a lot lately, including yesterday. She's always with an older guy about my age. The same guy I saw you talking to in Boston a few weeks ago. My guess is you work in the same business. Normally, out of professional courtesy, I wouldn't ask. But seeing that there was just a terrorist attack a stone's throw from my house, I'm dispensing with all that bullshit. What can you tell me?"

Mark slowly paced to the refrigerator. He grabbed two bottles of water, placed one on the counter in front of Frank, and took a long, slow sip from his own. Besides the occasional neighborly wave, the only other interaction he had had with Frank Tagala included a gun. And he could smell the booze from across the kitchen.

"I don't know what you're talking about, Frank. I probably know about as much as you do. Honestly, I don't think anybody knows very much right now, judging by the news."

Frank knew the deal. Landry was rightfully playing it safe. "Were you there when it happened? Were you at the scene?" he asked.

Mark thought for a moment. "I happened to be running by at the tail end of the attack after the explosion, yes."

"And did you see three gunmen open fire on our town with AK47s?"

"Just like a lot of other people, I saw the gunmen, but they weren't using AK47s. And that's all I know about the whole thing. Listen, I hate to be rude, but I have a bunch of work I need to get done. Can we talk some other time?"

"Yeah, sure. I'll get out of your hair. So, how do you know they weren't using Kalashnikovs?" he asked as both men moved toward the door.

"Because I saw them. And I know the difference between Kalashnikovs and Sig Sauer rifles."

Frank froze in his steps and turned around with a stunned expression.

"Did you say Sig Sauer?" asked Frank.

"Yeah."

"Everyone else keeps saying AKs and shotguns and all kinds of other shit. This is the first time I'm hearing Sig. How sure are you? Any chance you're confused?"

Mark opened the side door and looked directly into Frank's eyes. "I am one hundred percent sure. And there is zero chance I'm mistaken. I know what they look like. And I know what they feel like. I had one in my hands, Frank. It was a Sig Sauer M400."

Frank halted in the door and started thinking out loud. "That's interesting. AK47s and shotguns are a dime a dozen on the black market. But Sig Sauer rifles are very rare. They're also next to impossible to sterilize of serial numbers, so we should have tracing information by now. That can be done in just a few hours. I wonder …" Frank turned to face Mark but couldn't finish his sentence. His face became ashen and he ran his fingers through his thick gray hair.

"You okay, Frank? You look like you need to sit down."

"No, I'm good. Listen, I just realized something. I brought in a bunch of Sig Sauer M400s in a sting just a few weeks ago. But they disappeared from the evidence lockup and I never thought twice about it. Something stinks here, Mark. I'm going to the office and I'm not coming back until I know exactly where they went. And if those guns somehow fell into the wrong hands and ended up being used for this, I'm going to crack some fucking skulls."

Mark followed Frank down the steps. "Listen, Frank. I don't know much about all this stuff, but—"

Frank waved his hand and cut Mark off in mid-sentence. "Cut the bullshit, kid. Now you're just insulting my intelligence."

"Fine," said Mark. "Here's a bit of advice. If you do find anything out, you may want to be very careful who you share that information with at JTTF."

"Why?"

"There's a possibility that particular organization has challenges controlling sensitive information," Mark answered cryptically.

"You saying they have a leak or someone's been compromised?" asked Frank.

"Perhaps. Nothing definitive, but I'd play it safe if I were you. In fact, if you do get new information, just let me know and I can make sure it gets to the right people."

"Yeah, I'll do that. But first let me see what I can find out," answered Frank, who then strutted back across the lawn and disappeared into his house.

Mark had just booted up his laptop to surf through photos of people on the terrorist watch list when he heard two nervous knocks at the side door.

That was quick, Frank.

"It's open," Mark called out.

The door opened, followed by soft footsteps on the kitchen floor. Mark looked up to find Kenny standing in front of him with an extended index finger held tightly to his lips. He started to speak, but Kenny waved his arms and said nothing, indicating that Mark should remain silent. "Trust me," Kenny whispered.

As Mark sat back in his chair and watched, Kenny grabbed Mark's cell phone from the kitchen counter, opened the freezer, and placed the phone inside. The little man held his finger to his lips again as he approached the kitchen table, where he closed Mark's laptop and removed the battery.

"Now we can talk," Kenny declared.

"Good, let's start with you telling me what the hell you're doing."

"Just making sure this conversation stays between you and me, Mark."

"By putting my phone in the freezer and shutting down my computer? Listen, I don't have time for games right now, Kenny. I have work to do."

"So do I!" said Kenny, raising his voice. "But I need your help, so let's talk."

"What do you need from me?" Mark asked impatiently.

"I want to know who is responsible for yesterday's attack."

"And you're asking me?" Mark asked, rising to his feet. "Watch the news, Kenny. I can't help you."

"You and I both know that's not true, Landry. I need to know. Tell me who's behind this and I'll be on my way."

"I don't know what you're talking about, and why the hell did you put my phone in the freezer? Have you lost your mind?" asked Mark.

"Because I can't be sure they're not listening," replied Kenny with a sober stare.

"You can't be sure who isn't listening?"

"The Family."

Mark took a deep breath, moved toward the door, and opened it wide. "I have no idea what you're talking about, and quite frankly, I don't have time for this right now, Kenny. Can we talk some other time, please?" he asked.

"No, we're going to talk right now. I'm not playing around here either, Mark. I want to know who is responsible for these attacks. If it's a country, I'll crash every bank and electricity provider they depend on. If it's an organization, I'll steal every penny they have stashed away and fry every machine they own. If it's an individual, I'll make him so fucking miserable he'll kill himself. But in order to do any of that, I need to know what you know. So please start talking, Mark. Tell me what you know. Tell me what the Family knows."

Mark was spellbound during Kenny's rant until the end, at which point he forcefully rolled his eyes. "Jesus, what family are you talking about? Agnes was my only family and she's gone. Listen, the whole town is devastated by yesterday, Kenny. And we all want revenge. But you've come to the wrong place if you're looking for information beyond what you can get from CNN."

"Bullshit," Kenny replied, walking across the kitchen and pointing to Mark's laptop. "I hooked a rootkit into your kernel."

"Come again?" asked Mark.

"You've been connected to my Wi-Fi since you got home, Mark. I hooked a rootkit into your kernel. That means I infiltrated your machine, and from there I just followed the crumbs into your servers once you connected. But I swear I backed out once I realized whose yard I was playing in. Regardless, I know whom you work for. And I know what you do. So please don't tell me you can't help."

Mark shut the door. He breathed deeply, bowed his head, and shook it back and forth as he spoke very slowly. "If what you just said is true, you have no idea how much trouble you could be in. The penalty for something like this could be worse than anything you have ever imagined and entirely under the radar. Do you understand me, Kenny? This is bad."

Kenny reached into his back pocket and flopped his father's ball cap onto the kitchen counter. The Vietnam veteran embroidery and 82nd Airborne patch were stained with freshly dried blood. "Worse than having my own father bleed to death in my arms on Founders Field, Mark?"

268

"Mom, can I interrupt your reading for two minutes? I have some information you asked for. If not, just tell me when to come back."

McDermott looked up from the large oak desk in her Senate office and smiled. "Now is good, Meg. And I could use the breather. Honestly, I haven't had this much to read since, well, never."

"You know you have people who read all this stuff and then brief you on it, right?" asked Meghan, pulling up a chair next to her mother.

"I know that. But I still like to read as much as I can on my own. What have you got?"

"Before I give you what you asked for, let me share something interesting. As you are painfully aware, the majority of your peers don't speak to you very much and their staffs speak with me even less. Actually, in my case, only one other staffer speaks with me at all, Muriel. She works for her uncle, Vermont Senator—"

"Samson. Yes, I know," said McDermott.

"I saw her in the food court and she looked white as a ghost. Remember the anonymously leaked information on covert operations we were getting? The documents? The gruesome video of an interrogation labeled Berlin? The guy with one ear ripped off? The one that looked like a clip from some low-budget slasher movie?"

"Tough to forget, Meg. Get to the point," answered the Senator.

"Well, whoever sent it to us apparently got impatient when we didn't do anything public with it. So they moved on to Samson's office, but Muriel and her uncle don't want anything to do with it either. Just wanted to let you know."

McDermott removed her glasses and rubbed the bridge of her nose. "Okay, thanks. What else have you got?"

"I have the most current casualty list from the Massachusetts terrorist attack. There are a few names with asterisks, because the next of kin have yet to be informed, and there are still several people in critical condition. But this is as up to date as of one hour ago." Meghan folded her arms across her chest and held onto the file. "Mom, can I ask you a question?"

"Obviously," answered McDermott.

"Why are you so interested in this attack? In this town? I could see something different in your face when you heard the news. You don't have to tell me. But I'd really like it if you'd share with me. What is it? Do you know people who live there or something?"

The Senator took a deep breath, sat back in her chair, and exhaled slowly. "I did once. But I honestly don't know any more, Meg. I appreciate your concern, but it's nothing you need to worry about, okay? And I have a lot on my mind, so try not to read into things too much."

McDermott waited for Meghan to leave the office before opening the file. She held her breath as she slid her index finger down the list of casualties. When she reached the end, she exhaled and reached for the glass of water on her desk. Glancing at her watch to confirm that she had enough time before the next appointment, she reached for the jewelry box in the bottom drawer of the desk. The past came roaring back as she gazed into the photo of an older gentleman beaming with pride, his arm wrapped proudly around a vibrant-looking young man with a peculiar smile.

"Senator, your security coordinator is here and ready when you are," said the secretary's voice over the intercom.

McDermott quickly snapped back to the present. She returned the photo to its secret place, took a deep breath, and depressed the intercom button. "Go ahead and send him in, please. I'm ready."

Special Agent Stevenson knew what the rest of the Boston ATF office called him behind his back: Ashton Brown's Right Nut. But it didn't bother him. While the rest of the agents and administrative staff had tried to swim against the tide of Brown's management style, the five-year veteran agent simply lifted anchor and went with the current. As a result of his cooperation and no shortage of brown-nosing, he was in good stead with the boss but sorely disconnected from the rest of the team.

Frank Tagala had arrived in Boston to confront Ashton Brown about the missing rifles but instead found an empty office. Brown was out of the office, probably at the JTTF or somewhere in between, he had been told. When Stevenson saw Frank storming in and out of offices with a determined look on his face, he quickly fled the building. Unfortunately for him, Frank Tagala was not so easily avoided.

Stevenson scurried east for several blocks before deciding to turn south toward his regular haunt, a hole-in-the-wall pub with cheap drinks. Once a week for the past eight months, his wife had sat at home with the kids, believing that her husband was out bonding with the guys. In reality, Stevenson had sat and drank alone. He had no friends to bond with, and he didn't seem to care.

Frank's already substantial distaste for the Right Nut grew with each step as he tailed him through Boston's narrow streets. He had seen the expression on Stevenson's face and his panicked body language as he rushed out of the building. Stevenson knew something. And whatever that something was, it had made his bones shiver when he saw Frank Tagala.

The bartender delivered a shot and disappeared without saying a word. Stevenson tilted his head back, poured the whiskey down his throat, and quietly put the empty shot glass on the bar in front of him. The pub was more than half full and the music was louder than usual. He scanned left to right and slid the empty glass toward the far edge of the bar to indicate that he wanted another. He checked the time on his phone—and nearly fell off his stool as Frank's palm came down hard on the back of his shoulders.

"Stevenson! How the hell are you? Mind if I join you for a drink?"

The startled agent took several shallow breaths and composed himself as best he could. "Oh, hey Frank ... actually, I was just on my way out."

"Bullshit!" said Frank with a smile as he wrapped an arm around Stevenson's shoulders. "You just got here. So what do you say we have a drink together and catch up?" Frank pointed at the empty shot glass in front of them and bellowed to the bartender. "Sir, two more of these, please."

Stevenson waved a hand toward the empty seat next to him. "Yeah, sure, Frank. Have a seat. I'll have one more and then I have to get home. The wife's been busting my balls lately about never being there for dinner, and I'm already cutting it close."

"You bet, buddy. No worries. Just relax. You'll be home for dinner. I promise." Frank said cheerfully. "I have just one question that needs to be answered and then you'll be on your way."

"What's that, Frank?"

The bartender dropped two shots of whiskey in front of them and disappeared again.

"Let's do these first, eh? Let's do these two shots first and then we'll get to business. Sound good?"

"Sure."

"Good. What should we drink to? Never mind, I know. Raise your glass, Stevenson."

The junior agent raised his glass, bowed his head, and braced himself. Frank leaned in close to Stevenson's ear and spoke softly.

"I say we drink to the dozens of victims of yesterday's terrorist attack on my hometown. What do you think, eh? Should we drink to them? Or should we drink to what I'm gonna do to the bastards that did it? Because you know I'm gonna make them fucking suffer. Which do you think, Stevenson? To the victims? Or to what I'm gonna do to the assholes who did it?"

Stevenson took a moment to collect himself before answering. "How about both?"

"Good idea," Frank replied, raising his glass high above his head. "First and foremost, to the innocent victims and their suffering families. And to the future suffering of those responsible. I'm gonna find them and make them pay. They picked the wrong town. Salud!"

Both men drained their glasses. Frank stared into Stevenson's eyes until the younger man couldn't take it anymore and turned away. "Frank, I gotta hit the head, okay? I'll be right back.

Then maybe we can have one more, but I really do have to get home."

"No problem. You can leave as soon as you tell me what you and Brown did with the Sig Sauer M400s I brought in from the Russian sting."

Stevenson leapt to his feet. "Frank! Come on, man. I don't know what you're talking about. Listen, I'll be right back. Order two more for us if you want."

Frank held up two fingers to the bartender and tried to keep his cool.

Don't tell me you don't know what I'm talking about. I know you were there with Brown when he withdrew the rifles from evidence and mentioned something about a sting. So don't waste my fucking time.

The next round appeared in front of him and he exchanged polite nods with the bartender.

Fuck it.

Frank poured both shots down his throat as if they were warm water and headed toward the bathroom.

* * *

Stevenson splashed cold water on his face and looked at himself in the mirror of the tiny bathroom.

I haven't done anything wrong. I just did my job. I did what I was told. This is not my fault. We didn't sell guns to any terrorists. It was a sting. Stings can go bad and I can't control where the hardware ends up. How the hell do I get away from Tagala? He's a crazy man.

He patted his pockets, cursed himself for leaving his cell phone on the bar, and took three deep breaths to compose himself before unlocking the bathroom door.

The instant Stevenson turned the knob, the door burst open and crashed into the side of his head. He reeled backwards. Frank slipped into the bathroom, locked the door, and pinned him against the wall by his throat with remarkable speed. Stevenson struggled to speak as Frank tightened the grip on his throat.

"No, no," whispered Frank. "You've already wasted enough of my time with your bullshit. Look into my eyes. Look! Do I look like a man who gives a shit about anything anymore? Do I?" Stevenson shook his head in horror. "Good. I'm glad you understand that. Now understand this—the next thing out of your mouth will be the answer to my question or I'm going to break your nose. No second chances. No do-overs. Answer my question or the nose gets broken. What did you do with the Sigs?" Frank released his grip on Stevenson's throat so he could speak and took a step backwards. "Tell me right now."

Stevenson bent over, coughed forcefully, and held his throat with both hands as he struggled to catch his breath. After several moments of silence, he stood as tall as he could and held up both of his hands in professed innocence. "I don't know anything about any Sigs, Frank. I don't know what you're talking about."

Before he could complete the last syllable, the calloused knuckles of Frank's tightly balled fist came crashing down on Stevenson's nose with whirlwind speed and an audible crunch. Blood sprayed from his nostrils and he would have collapsed to the floor if Frank hadn't advanced, snatched him up by the front of his shirt with both hands, and thrown him head first into the far wall. Stevenson's body crumpled to the bathroom floor. He tried to scream, but Frank was immediately on top of him, one hand wrapped tightly around his throat and a knee buried deep into his chest.

"When I remove my hand from your throat, you will answer my question. If you don't, I will break every bone in your right arm. I'll start with the fingers and work my way from your wrist all the way to your collarbone. No second chances. No do-overs. Do you understand?"

Stevenson sobbed and gasped for air. Frank casually looked at the stainless steel watch on his free hand and shook his head disapprovingly. "I'm trying not to get too nasty with you, but this is taking too long, Right Nut. I already know that you and Brown took the rifles from evidence, okay? I already know that. I was about ninety percent sure those same rifles were used in the attack, but judging by the way you ran from me and the look in your eyes right now, it's more like ninety-nine percent. So answer my fucking question and I'll be on my way. When I let go, you have three seconds to answer my question or I will break both of your arms. I know I just said I was only gonna break the right one, but it's getting late so I'm trying to save time. As we speak, the terrorists who shot up my town are celebrating. And you have no idea how much that pisses me off." Frank released his grip, rose to his feet, and stared deep into the younger agent's tear-filled eyes. "Three, two, one."

Stevenson covered his head with both hands and moaned desperately as he rolled back and forth on the filthy bathroom floor. Blood ran down his face in all directions. He pulled his knees tightly into his chest. "Okay, okay! I was just doing my job … doing what I was told … it was all Brown's idea … all of it!"

"What was all Brown's idea? Get to the fucking point. What did you do with the rifles?" Frank demanded.

"We set up a sting and sold them. We took them out of evidence and sold them. I told him it was a bad idea. I told him it was crazy, but he wouldn't listen."

Frank turned on the bathroom faucet, washed his hands, and ran his fingers through his hair as he spoke. "Who did you sell them to? And why? Tell me right now."

"Some gangbanger. A Latin King who is related to the Supreme Inca of the whole thing."

Frank turned and looked down on his bloody colleague. "Why would the Latin Kings set off a bomb and shoot up a town? That doesn't make any sense. They're criminals, but they've never been terrorists," he asked.

"They didn't. At least I don't think so. We sold him the guns and were planning to track him. Brown said he'd lead us right to the pot of gold at the end of the rainbow. We'd get a huge bust, press coverage, promotions. I told him he was crazy to try it with just the two of us, but he didn't want to hear any of it."

Frank ripped open the broken paper towel dispenser mounted on the wall, tore off a dozen sheets from the roll, and handed them to Stevenson. "Keep talking. Tell me exactly who you sold them to and how you fucked it up."

Stevenson's nose was swelling quickly as he struggled to speak. "Brown set the whole thing up. We did it on some side street. We put the hardware in his car and attached a tracking device to the vehicle. He drove away and that was it. I told Brown it was a bad plan. I told him the guy would just …"

"He drove away and immediately switched vehicles," interjected Frank.

"Yeah. We tracked him. When we found the vehicle, we staked it out for four hours before I could convince Brown it was empty. By then he was long gone. I swear I never wanted to do it, Frank. When it went south, I said we had to tell someone but he wouldn't listen. You gotta believe me. It wasn't my fault!"

"Bullshit! You didn't have to do it. You could have told someone. Hell, you could have told me and I would have stopped it. Now tell me exactly who you sold them to and don't fuck around. If you fuck around, I'm gonna start breaking shit again. Tell me right now."

Stevenson raised his aching body and leaned back against the discolored bathroom wall. "His name was Hector. Hector Gonzales."

"What's his King name?" asked Frank.

"King Heavy."

"Why don't you think the Latin Kings were behind the attack? Do you think this Hector guy fenced the hardware?"

"Yeah. Supposedly he'd been stealing money from the nation for a long time, which is unforgivable in their eyes. My guess is that he used their money to buy the guns, then sold them to the highest bidder and disappeared. Every Latin King in New England is looking for him as we speak. Which means he's probably already dead or will soon wish he was." Stevenson winced as he inhaled through his nose and spat out a mouthful of blood onto the grimy floor.

"So you do know for a fact that the guns used yesterday were the same ones you and Brown sold to this Hector asshole?" asked Frank.

Stevenson bowed his head, unable to look Frank in the eye any longer. "One hundred percent, but Brown is moving heaven and earth to cover the whole thing up. He has erased every record of those guns at the office, running interference with all the other agencies, and spreading enough misinformation to spin everybody's heads. I protested, but he threatened to pin it all on me as well as a whole bunch of other shit I never even did. He's a fucking lunatic, Frank."

Frank was trying to absorb all of the information and formulate a plan at the same time. "Hector Gonzales. Latin King. Anything else? If you know anything else, I want to hear it right now."

"That's it. That's everything I know. I'm sorry, Frank."

"Don't apologize to me, asshole. There are a lot of other people you owe an apology to, people whose lives have been ruined. I promise you'll eventually pay the piper for what you've done. But for now, clean up and go home. Don't say a fucking word to anyone, and call in sick for the foreseeable future. If you don't, I swear to God I'll find you and pick up where I left off."

Frank checked his look in the mirror one last time before exiting the bathroom. He walked briskly past the two empty shot glasses still sitting on the bar and shouted above the music to the bartender on his way out the door, "My buddy's gonna take care of the tab."

John McDonough parked his cruiser in the empty lot of Baba Ghassan's restaurant and exited the vehicle with his cell phone pressed to his ear.

"I'm telling you, John. I think today's the day. It feels like there's a cage match going on in my belly!" said Linda.

John removed the flashlight from his duty belt with his free hand and shined it through the glass door of the dark restaurant. "I'm not surprised. The little guy even woke me up a few times last night. I thought I felt a tremor."

"Has it been quiet today?" she asked.

"Thankfully, yes. And I hope it stays that way through the night and into tomorrow, because that's how long I'll be on duty. It's a long one, but after that I'm all yours for two weeks. Just the three of us—you, me, and our little man."

"The three of us. I love the sound of that. And I'm telling you, this kid wants out!"

"I know he does. And the doc says he's been in there long enough anyway, so he's welcome any time. Listen, babe, let me call you back later, okay? I need to go make a quick welfare check," said John as he walked back to the cruiser.

"Okay. Be careful, baby. We love you."

"I love you guys too," he answered with a smile.

Officer John McDonough pulled out of the parking lot, turned onto the main road, and headed toward Ghassan's cabin to check on Yasir as he had promised.

"I have some work to do, so I'll have to talk to you later, Kenny. If I hear anything I'll let you know," Mark said as he walked his neighbor to the door.

"Please do that, Mark. Don't just say it. I want to know who did this. And if I can help in any way, I will. You have my word on that. Anything."

"I believe you. But my advice is to leave things to the professionals. Don't get involved where you don't need to get involved, Kenny. You've already put me in a difficult position by accessing information you had no business accessing. What do you expect me to say when someone finds out and asks me about it? 'Oh, yeah, no problem. That was just my neighbor Kenny the hacker.' Is that what you expect me to say? Or should I deny it? Maybe they'll put us in adjacent cells so we can be neighbors forever."

"I never intended to put you in any danger, Mark. And like I already told you, once I realized whose backyard I had wandered into, I got out quick and covered my tracks. Nobody is ever going to ask you anything."

"I wouldn't be too sure of that. You're betting on yourself against some of the best cyber security experts on the planet," said Mark.

"The best in the world?" asked Kenny, looking as if he had just bitten into a lemon. "Please, I've seen toy companies with better security. And if they're so good, how come they haven't found out who hacked them last month?"

"I don't know what you're talking about."

"Yes, you do," Kenny said on his way out the door. "Don't forget what I said, Mark. I'll do anything to help catch the bastards who did this. And I bring a lot more to the table than you can imagine."

* * *

Mark sipped his coffee and scrolled through the pictures a third time, although he knew it was an exercise in futility. The catalog of photos sent to him primarily contained headshots, and Mark had never gotten a good look at the fourth shooter's face. The young man's build and how he moved his body were seared into his memory, but the combination of hat, sunglasses, and Mark's angle of view made facial recognition impossible. None of this came as a surprise to him. In contrast, the earlier visit from Kenny had been extraordinarily surprising.

If what Kenny had said was true—and Mark had no reason to doubt him—he had breached security and accessed classified information about one of the U.S. government's most secretive organizations. The Family consisted of less than one hundred people, and its existence was known by perhaps two dozen more.

How and why did he do it? And what else is there that he's not telling me?

Kenny had shared enough information and dropped enough buzzwords to convince Mark that he was telling the truth. He had also mentioned that some of his freelance work over the years had been less than above board, and occasionally in collaboration with some pretty unsavory characters.

"Not so different from your own career," Kenny had added. *He had a point.*

But the raw pain he had seen in Kenny's eyes as he recounted his father's last moments and Kenny's fierce commitment to avenge that loss had compelled Mark to share some limited information. He never confirmed or denied outright the existence of the Family or his alleged affiliation, but he did share his experience with the fourth gunman and Frank Tagala's suspicions about the weapons used.

Mark checked the time and started to pack up his things so that he could head back over to Luci's house. He intended to catch a few hours of sleep and have breakfast ready and waiting for her when she got off duty in the morning.

The home phone rang just after he had walked out the door and pulled it shut behind him. He considered ignoring it at first but ended up dropping his bags on the porch, fumbling for the right key, and quickly reentering the house.

"Hello?"

"Mark? Is this Mark?" asked the female caller.

"Yes, who's calling?"

"Mark, it's Wendy. Luci's friend. Her coworker. Remember me?"

"Of course. What's going on?"

"Do you know where Memorial Hospital is?"

"Yeah, why?" he answered. Memorial was about fifteen miles away and had been handling all emergency overflows since the attack on the local hospital.

"Can you come here right away? It's Luci," she said. "I found her in her car … she was parked in her garage with the engine running …"

Before Wendy could finish her sentence, Mark hung up the phone and raced out the door.

One hundred fourteen

Frank Tagala stood inside the unlit doorway of an out-of-business pawn shop across the street from Lourdes's apartment. He scanned the area to become familiar with the poor neighborhood's sights and sounds. Loud music came from a second-floor apartment above Frank's position. Traffic was light. Most of the drivers kept their doors locked, windows shut, and their eyes straight ahead as they rolled through the sleazy neighborhood. Few passers-by noticed the tall man standing in the shadows with the black eye and swollen knuckles. Those who did paid scant attention. Frank reached for the fifth of cheap vodka in his back pocket and took a long pull from the bottle. He winced at the taste, but it was the best he could find at the dive that passed for a liquor store just a few blocks away.

The previous hours had been a whirlwind of hunting, identifying, and interrogating scumbag after scumbag. He had taken one good punch to the head from a guy in Quincy and barely escaped getting stabbed by another guy an hour later in Dorchester. But the damage he sustained paled in comparison to the fury he had unleashed across the city. He had spent two decades on the streets without ever getting too emotional about the job; this time it was one hundred percent personal. Frank Tagala was unhinged and there was no turning back.

Hector Gonzales was a psychopath, but he wasn't entirely stupid. He had kept his girlfriend out of sight and mentioned her only once or twice in front of other Latin Kings. Frank had been extremely lucky that the King he had interrogated an hour earlier in Lynn just happened to be one of them. He held his Glock to the young man's head as he called a girl who knew a girl who knew a girl. Now Frank was across the street watching Lourdes's third-story apartment and wondering if he should wait outside or just kick in the door.

He finished the vodka and threw the empty bottle on a pile of trash on the sidewalk next to a rusty fire hydrant. When he peered back up at the third-story window, the lights had been turned off. Two minutes later, a Latina woman in her mid-twenties exited the building with a bag over her shoulder and two more clutched in her hands.

Lourdes turned left and walked slowly for half a block. She stopped to look in both directions before approaching the vehicle Hector had instructed her to use. She opened the trunk of the beat-up Honda Civic with stolen plates and dropped the bags inside. When she opened the driver's side door and slid behind the steering wheel, the passenger door flew open and Frank Tagala had his Glock pointed at her ribs before she knew what was happening. He held up his badge with his free hand.

"Just relax, Lourdes. I'm not going to hurt you. I just want to talk to you."

"Who the fuck are you? Get out of my car, man!"

Frank grabbed her by the bicep and squeezed tightly. "Do exactly what I say and everything will be fine. But fuck with me and I promise you'll regret it. Understand me? All I want to do is talk to you. Now drive straight, take the first right, and turn into the first parking lot on the left. Do it now." He squeezed harder and pulled her closer. "I don't want to hurt you, Lourdes. But I will if it becomes necessary."

Lourdes nodded and started the car. The two rode in silence to the dark lot Frank had staked out. "Park over there," he said, pointing to the far corner behind an empty guard shack. When they arrived, Frank reached down, put the car in park, and removed the keys from the ignition.

"What do you want from me?" she asked.

"Shut up and listen. We don't have a lot of time and I'm not in the mood to screw around," Frank began. "Look at me. I could see to it that you spend the rest of your life behind bars, okay? That's what you're looking at here if you don't cooperate with me. Do you understand that?"

Lourdes looked at Frank with glazed eyes and spoke in slow, slurred speech. "I'm on probation. My probation officer says one more time and I'm going to prison. So you know I'll do anything," she said, reaching over to put her hand on Frank's thigh. "You want a blow job or something?"

"No. That's not what I'm here for," he replied, brushing her hand away. "I want information. But first I'm gonna put my gun away so you know I'm not here to hurt you, okay? But don't get stupid on me, Lourdes. So far, you're doing good. Let's see if we can keep that going."

Frank returned his badge to his back pocket and his Glock to the holster behind his right hip. He unrolled the window to let in some air and shifted in the seat so that his whole body was oriented toward Lourdes.

"I'm going to ask you one question. It's the only question I need answered. If you answer it, we're not gonna have any problems. Here it is. Where's Hector Gonzales?"

"Who's that?" she asked as she struggled to keep her heavy eyelids from falling over her glassy eyes. "I don't know who that is."

"Yes, you do, Lourdes. He's your boyfriend. I already know that, so don't bullshit me. I need to know where he is right now. Where is he?"

"You talking about Heavy? He left me a long time ago. Haven't heard from him in I don't know how long. For real," she answered.

Frank removed a rolled-up newspaper from his back pocket and held up the front page. "Have you heard about this, Lourdes? The terrorist attack just north of here? Did you know Hector played a role in this?"

She squinted at the headline and gruesome photos. "Listen, I don't know where Hector is and he wouldn't do nothing like that anyway. He may be an asshole, but he ain't no terrorist. Now you're just lying to me and it ain't gonna work."

"Do you know anything about guns he might have sold lately? Did you ever hear him talk about it? Because the guns your boyfriend sold are the same guns that were used to kill these innocent people. Here, look at the pictures. Men, women, kids." Frank held the collage of victim photos up to her face. "Look at these people, Lourdes. They're all dead because of Hector. And if I don't find him soon, more people may die. So tell me where he is."

She reached for the door handle, but Frank grabbed her by the arm and squeezed as tight as he could. Lourdes shrieked and he loosened his grip. "Stay put! I told you I wouldn't hurt you, but you're not going anywhere. If you try that again you'll regret it."

Lourdes put both hands on the steering wheel and rested her head on top. "That's the kind of shit Hector says—'I don't want to hit you but you make me do it.' " Her eyes became teary. "But that was a long time ago. I don't know where he is these days."

Frank looked down and flipped through the pages of the paper. "Do you have kids, Lourdes?"

She nodded slowly. "Three girls. My mother takes care of them, and Hector always said he was gonna help them out too."

"Forget about Hector. You and I both know he's a liar. He's never going to lift a finger for those girls. Do you care about them?" asked Frank.

"Yeah, they're my angels."

"Do you ever want to see them again?"

"Man, don't start that shit! Hell yeah, I wanna see my babies again."

"Then you're gonna have to tell me where he is. But first, look at this picture right here," he said, tapping his index finger against the newspaper. "Her name was Julia. She was eighteen years old and had just graduated from high school. Tough life. Raised by her grandmother. No money. But she dreamed of a better life. With a little guidance and some hard work, she had just gotten her first job and was about to start her first college course. She was on her way out of the projects and had a whole new life to look forward to. Then some asshole shot her three times with an assault rifle he got from Hector."

Frank reached up and turned on the car's interior light. He slowly stretched out his arm, touched Lourdes gently on the chin, and turned her head in his direction. He examined her eyes and glanced at each side of her face. "Your bruises and scars read like chapters in a sad book, Lourdes. And believe me, I know how it ends. Hector's a fucking nightmare. As soon as he's done using you for what he needs, you'll be dead too. And deep down you know I'm right."

Bloody mucus burst from her nose and tears gushed down her cheeks. "I got nowhere to go! I got nothing. Shit! He was the only one who did anything for me."

Frank handed Lourdes his handkerchief and touched her tenderly on the shoulder. "Listen to me. It's not too late for you, but there's not much time, so you have to make up your mind quickly. I can help. Lourdes, I can help you and I will."

She blew her nose into the handkerchief and sobbed. "You don't even know me, so stop playing me! Why would you help me?"

Frank took a deep breath and quickly scanned the area. "Because I had a family once. I had a wife and a beautiful daughter. But I was never there for them. I lost them and I can never get them back. It's too late for me, but it's not too late for you. I'm not playing you, Lourdes. Look at me. If you help me, I will help you. But make no mistake—I am a serious man with a serious mission and limited time. So right now I'm gonna make you an offer and give you the opportunity to fix your life. But I'm only gonna make it once, okay? Look at me, Lourdes. Look at me."

Lourdes turned toward Frank and held the handkerchief over her face to muffle her sobbing. Frank held her free hand between his palms and looked directly into her eyes.

"You said you love your babies. Your angels, right? And you don't want them to end up like you, right? You want them to have good lives? You want them to have it better than you did, right?" She nodded and Frank continued. "Then tell me where Hector is. If you tell me where he is, I won't bring you in. I'll call a very good friend of mine and she'll take care of you. You want treatment? You want to beat this drug bullshit? She can help you, Lourdes. I promise you she can and will help you. And then you can be there for your daughters. Kids need their mothers, Lourdes. You owe it to them to be around. It's not too late to make things right, but you have to tell me where Hector is right now."

Lourdes squeezed Frank's hand and gasped. "I will. But please don't be lying to me."

Frank hesitated for a moment and then reached out with his long arms and pulled her closer in his best attempt at a fatherly embrace. "I'm not lying to you, Lourdes. Tell me where he is. I'll call my friend right now and she'll help you get clean. Just promise me you'll do whatever it takes to be there for your girls. Can you do that?"

"I promise. Just please help me," she whimpered.

"I will. And I'm also gonna let you keep the bags you put in the trunk. Hector's not gonna need them."

Wendy was texting in the hallway when Mark burst through the doors at the end of the corridor. As he approached, she slipped the phone into her cargo pocket and started to speak, but Mark cut her off.

"Where is she?"

Wendy put a hand on his shoulder. "Listen to me first, Mark."

"Tell me where she is," he demanded.

"Mark, you hung up before I could fill you in. She's conscious. Groggy as hell and being monitored closely, but she's conscious."

"Okay. Now where is she?" asked Mark.

"She's in there," Wendy answered, pointing with her thumb to the door behind her. "They kicked me out so they could do some more tests. As soon as they're done, we can go in."

"No, I'm going in now," he insisted.

"Mark," she said, placing her palm on his chest. "Give the professionals a few minutes to do their jobs. I told you, she's conscious and knows where she is. Maybe they can make her better, but they can't do it with you in the way. Just give them a couple of minutes and I'll fill you in on everything I know. Okay?"

Mark stepped back and nodded his head silently.

"I spent the whole day at the house with her. We talked about everything that's been going on in town. We ate. We slept. She was fine. She was better than fine. I hadn't seen her that positive since the incident with the Lundgren kid. We were both scheduled to work eight to eight. I left first. She never showed up for her shift. No answer at the house or on her cell phone. I got worried and went to the house to check on her."

Wendy took a deep breath and looked up and down the hallway. "Her car wasn't in the driveway, but I figured that maybe you had it or something. So I went inside to check the house but couldn't find her anywhere. Walking back to my cruiser, I heard the hum of a car engine coming from inside the garage. I pulled the door up and found her out cold in the driver's seat, in full uniform."

Mark winced and placed both hands on his head. "How long was she there?"

"There's no way to tell for sure, but we don't think it was very long. When I reached her, she was still conscious but couldn't really move or respond to me. I pulled her outside into the fresh air as fast as I could. She threw up, so I put her in the front seat of the cruiser and brought her here myself. They're pumping her full of fluids and have her on oxygen and she's been improving. I would have called you sooner, but once she grabbed my hand she wouldn't let go, and I didn't want to leave her alone until I knew for sure she was going to be okay."

Mark walked across the hall and sat down on a metal folding chair outside Luci's room. "Oh, my God. I don't understand. She's been through a lot, but this morning she seemed rejuvenated. Why would she try to do this to herself? It doesn't make any sense to me."

Wendy sat down next to him and waited for two nurses to pass by. Then she leaned in close and lowered her voice. "Maybe she didn't, Mark."

"What do you mean?"

"She's been drifting in and out of sleep. But the last time she woke up, she spoke to me. You know what the first thing she said to me was?"

Mark shook his head. "What?"

"She asked, 'Did you get him?' The docs asked me to step out before I could any more out of her."

Mark's eyes widened with surprise. "You think it's possible that someone tried to kill her?"

"I don't know. It's possible. She's got her fair share of haters in town. But it's also possible that she did it to herself and is now trying to cover it up. Or maybe what she said to me was just plain gibberish. I don't know what to think. But I do know she was fine all day when I was there. I was the one freaking out over things. She was the calming voice of reason. None of this makes sense to me."

Wendy reached into her pocket and handed Mark a silver necklace with a guardian angel charm dangling from it. "Have you ever seen this before?"

"No. Where did it come from?"

"She had it in her hand when I found her in the car."

The door to Luci's room slowly opened and two women exited. The one wearing blue scrubs smiled and made her way toward the nurse's station while the other woman, wearing a long white lab coat and with a stethoscope hanging from her neck, finished scribbling notes on a chart. Mark leapt to his feet and startled her.

"How is she?" he asked.

The physician clutched the chart to her chest and took a step backwards. "Who are you? And what is your relationship to the patient?" she asked.

Wendy stepped in before Mark could answer. "This is Luci's fiancé, Mark. I just briefed him on what I know. Can you bring us both up to speed, please, Doc?"

"Of course. Mark, I'm Doctor Marcy Chang," she said, extending her hand.

Mark shook it gently and glanced at Wendy. Being referred to as a fiancé was technically accurate but sounded odd. He and Luci had discussed their desire to marry, but had yet to make anything official. Either Wendy and Luci had discussed it earlier in the day, or Wendy was simply ensuring that the doctor would share information with him.

"No major changes. She's improving, but much more slowly than I'd prefer. Exhaustion from recent events doesn't help and makes it difficult to accurately assess the damage, if any, from the carbon monoxide. Luci is conscious but drifting in and out of sleep. She's been through a lot, and her body needs time to rest. She's very lucky Wendy found her when she did. That's all I know. I'll advise you immediately if anything changes."

"Can I go in now?" asked Mark.

Doctor Chang nodded and retrieved the vibrating pager from her belt. "I have to see another patient."

"I'll wait out here," said Wendy.

Kenny watched from the front window as Frank Tagala's car swerved into his driveway and screeched to a halt. After wrestling with his seatbelt for several moments, he opened the car door, fell to the pavement, and coughed up a mouthful of blood. Kenny checked the time. It was almost midnight.

Frank stumbled up his front walk, falling hard every few steps before deciding to crawl the rest of the way on his hands and knees. He had paused to catch his breath before attempting to climb the stairs to the front door when a voice came from behind.

"You want a hand, Frank?" asked Kenny, kneeling next to his neighbor.

"Yeah, just help me get to the kitchen and I'll be all set," he answered. "I think I got a punctured ear drum and my balance is fucked up."

Kenny looked closer at Frank's right ear and saw a trail of dried blood that extended all the way down his neck. He helped Frank to his feet and steadied him as they walked up the stairs together, just as Kenny had done countless times with his own father. When they reached the kitchen, he guided Frank to a chair, grabbed a towel from the sink, and wiped the blood and grime from the front of his own shirt. He glanced around. The house looked like a disaster and smelled like a dumpster.

"What happened?" asked Kenny.

"Huh? Oh, nothing you need to worry about," answered Frank. "Grab me an ice pack and a glass from the freezer. And hand me the vodka bottle next to the refrigerator while you're at it."

Kenny obeyed and watched as Frank filled his glass and chugged the entire contents while holding the ice pack on his swollen, bloody right hand. "That feels better already. Thanks, kid."

"Listen, Frank. Mark filled me in on your theory about the guns that were used at Founders Field," Kenny said matter-of-factly.

"Oh yeah? That was nice of him to bring another person in on my failures. Here's to Mark," he replied, raising his glass and pouring half of it down his throat.

"What did you find out? Anything that might help the authorities find the guys who did this to us—the guys who killed my father?"

Frank put the glass down on the table and looked at Kenny through bloodshot eyes. "I didn't know he was one of them. I'm sorry, kid. Your pop was a hero. Yeah, I found out what happened. The guns used in the attack definitely came from the bureau. Someone there actually arranged for those rifles to fall into the hands of a psychopath, some rogue Latin King member."

"Latin King? Is that the gang that's been spray-painting around town? Why would they jump from vandalism to mass murder just like that?" Kenny asked.

"They didn't. Terrorism isn't their thing. They're all about the money. So he turned around and sold the guns, and they somehow ended up in the hands of the gunmen who shot up our town and killed your father. And it's my fault."

"How is it your fault, Frank?"

"Because I didn't track the guns like I should have when I brought them in. I should have kept a closer eye on them so this couldn't have happened. But I didn't."

"What about the guy who got the guns? Is there any way to find out who he sold them to? Does anybody know where he is? Is anybody trying to find him?" asked Kenny.

"I found him," answered Frank as he finished his drink and poured another. "He put up a pretty good fight for a scrawny bastard. He's the one who punctured my ear with a pen or some shit."

"Well, did you get a chance to question him? What did he say? Did he tell you anything? Come on, Frank. I want to know!" begged Kenny, raising his voice to get Frank's attention and instill some sense of urgency.

"He wouldn't tell me anything at first. So I broke his nose and both of his arms. After that, things got out of hand."

You mean breaking someone's nose and both of their arms isn't considered out of hand already?

"Frank, what happened? What did you do?"

"I had him tied to a chair and was working him over. I told him he was either gonna die or tell me what I needed to know. Eventually he begged me to stop and said he'd tell me. But what he said didn't make any sense. All he did was talk fucking gibberish. So I got upset and went to work on him again even harder. Face. Throat. Neck. I guess I went a little too far."

"Is he dead, Frank?" asked Kenny in astonishment.

Frank took a long sip of his drink and nodded his head. "Yeah, and you're looking at another dead man right in front of you."

"You? Why? I don't understand, Frank."

Frank struggled to get to his feet but quickly collapsed back into the chair. "You're looking at a dead man because it's just a matter of time until someone finds his body. And when they do, my DNA is all over the scene, as well as half a dozen other scenes across the city. It's over. My life is over."

Kenny stood silently with his mouth agape and his fingers laced tightly behind his head. He had known for years that Frank was a loose cannon. Everyone on the street knew that. But he never thought Agent Tagala was capable of brutally murdering someone with his bare hands. His instincts told him to get the hell out of the house and tell nobody what he had just heard.

"I can see you have a lot to think about, Frank. So I'm going to go home unless you need something. And as far as I'm concerned, this conversation never happened. Try to get some sleep."

"I got nothing to think about. I'm done thinking. But suit yourself, kid. Do whatever you want."

Kenny left the kitchen and was heading for the door when he stopped dead in his tracks. "Hey, Frank," he called back, "what was the gibberish?"

"Huh?"

"What was the gibberish? You said he started to talk but it didn't make any sense to you. What did he say?" asked Kenny.

"He was slumped in the chair and I could barely hear him. He kept saying the same shit over and over," answered Frank.

"Do you remember what it was?"

"Yeah. He kept mentioning New Hampshire. Then some bullshit that sounded like 'bubba gussin.' But by that point he would have said anything to get me to stop. And I'm not even sure I could have. You should have seen how this guy abused women. The guy beat the shit out of the mother of three little girls. He deserved to die. Good fuckin' riddance, Hector."

"Bubba gussin, New Hampshire?" Kenny confirmed.

"That's it. Pure gibberish."

Mark had seen many people in many hospitals over the previous twenty years. Some of those visits had been pleasant enough, even cheerful. Others had been gut-wrenching. But seeing Luci with an oxygen mask strapped tightly to her face and IVs running into both arms rattled him in an entirely different way. He felt helpless, as if a piece of his soul was dying and there was nothing he could do about it.

She had woken up several times so far. The first time was shortly after Mark's arrival. She had squeezed his hand and tried to speak but succumbed to exhaustion and drifted back to sleep. The second time, she simply looked over at him in the chair next to the bed for a few seconds before fading.

When Luci opened her eyes an hour later, he spoke softly into her ear, told her he loved her, and asked if she was okay. "Yes, tired," she said after he pulled off the oxygen mask so that he could hear her whisper. He kissed her on the lips before replacing the mask gently over her nose and mouth. She smiled and fell asleep again. She had not been awake since.

Mark was exhausted too. He had slept for a few hours in the safe house, but the toll of the past two days on his mind and body had been significant. He leaned back in the chair, folded his arms across his chest, and closed his eyes.

The phone on the night table next to Luci's hospital bed rang, startling Mark and causing him to leap to his feet. Luci was fast asleep, so he quickly lifted the handset from the receiver to avoid the possibility of waking her with a second ring. Grabbing the base of the phone, he walked as far away from the bed as the cord would allow.

"Hello? Yes?"

"Is this Mark?" asked a familiar voice at the other end.

"Who's calling, please?" asked Mark.

"It's Kenny. We have to talk."

Mark checked the time on his wristwatch. "How did you know I was here, Kenny?"

"That's not important. But what we have to talk about certainly is. First, is Luci okay? Can you come over, or do you need to stay there with her?" pressed Kenny.

"No, it is important. Tell me right now how you knew I was here."

"Fine. I pinged your phone, but for obvious reasons there's no way I'd ever talk to you on that device. Once I saw you were at the hospital, I scrolled through their recent admissions until I saw L. Alvarez on the list. Then I called and asked for her room. I figured you'd be there and I was right. Not that hard. Not a big deal."

Mark's blood pressure rose and his pulse quickened. "Yeah, it is a big deal. You can't simply scroll through hospital admissions and private medical records, Kenny. So you hacked into the hospital? That quickly?"

"I didn't look at anybody's medical records, Mark. Those are none of my business. I just looked at the names. People like me do have some ethics, you know. Anyway, I hope she's okay," Kenny offered earnestly.

"She is. She fainted at home in the kitchen, so we came here so she could get checked out. It was just exhaustion and a little dehydration. She needs rest. That's all."

"Good. So I need to talk to you and show you a few things. How soon can you get here?"

"It's late. I don't know what you think is so important that you needed to do this, but can it wait until the morning, Kenny?"

"I don't know, Mark. Maybe, maybe not. He may not be there in the morning."

Landry took a long, deep breath and tried to keep his cool. "Who the hell are you talking about, Kenny?"

"I'm talking about the fourth shooter. I think I might have found him."

Mark turned onto Chestnut Lane just after 1:00 a.m. But instead of taking his foot off the gas and letting gravity deliver him to the bottom of the hill as usual, he pushed the dark blue Ford Explorer as quickly as he could until he had reached Kenny's driveway.

He knocked twice on the front door with his knuckles and reached for the knob. Before he could twist it, the door flew open. "Follow me," Kenny said, turning around and heading to his office in the spare bedroom, where he dropped himself into the chair and started typing furiously. Mark stood behind him and scanned his setup. It did not seem very impressive.

"So this is your command center?" Mark asked.

"If you must know, this is connected to a hell of a lot more firepower in a climate-controlled room in the attic," he replied, sensing the hint of sarcasm in his neighbor's voice. "Give me another minute and then we can look behind the curtain."

Mark pulled his smartphone from his pocket and checked for new messages. On the way out of Luci's hospital room, he had given the number to the uniformed officer who was assigned to her as a security precaution. It was the same young officer who had briefly questioned Mark at the police station before Doc liberated him.

"Call me or text me if anything changes. If she asks about me, tell her I got called away by work but will be back as soon as I can, okay?" Mark had requested.

"No problem, sir. And here's my number in case you need me for anything. Don't hesitate."

Kenny stopped typing for several moments and focused on a blizzard of numbers, letters, and symbols that decorated his monitor. He scribbled several notes on a small pad of paper and pointed to the wall opposite his workstation. "Mark, turn around and pull the curtain to the side, please. This will be easier for both of us if we use the big screen."

Mark slowly opened the large black curtain, exposing a six-by-four-foot HD monitor.

"Hit the switch on the right side, please," Kenny added.
"Done."

"Then give me your attention over here for a minute." Kenny spun around in his chair and started the briefing. "Okay.

Here's where we are. Earlier I helped Frank get from his front yard to his kitchen where we talked. To put it bluntly, he's fucked."

"How so?" Mark asked.

"Let me back up. First, he said he was able to verify beyond any doubt that the guns used in the attack came from his bust last month. No question. Someone inside the bureau actually sold the guns to a criminal, who then slipped away in some kind of sting gone wrong. So Frank spent the day trying to find the guy they sold them to, which apparently included assaulting God knows how many people. Regardless, he was actually able to find the guy to whom the idiot at the bureau had sold the guns originally."

"Seriously? And did he find out who that guy flipped them to?"

"Not exactly. By his own admission, Frank said things got pretty rough during the questioning. The guy repeated some gibberish a few times but Frank couldn't make any sense of it. That's when he lost his cool and unloaded on the guy until he was dead."

"Get the fuck out of here, Kenny. Did Frank actually tell you that? Did he use those exact words?" Mark asked. "Are you assuming he killed the guy or did he come right out and tell you he killed him?"

Kenny grabbed two bottles of water from the refrigerator next to his desk and handed one to Mark. "He came right out and said it. He told me I was looking at a dead man because his DNA is all over the place so it's just a matter of time before they come for him, and that his life was over. Those may not have been his exact words, but I believe I've captured the spirit of what he said pretty damn well. He was drunk as hell, beat up, and seemed to have his mind made up that it was all over. It wouldn't surprise me if he just drinks himself to death."

Mark took a swig of water and screwed the cap back onto the plastic bottle. "Okay. So how did you get from that to locating the fourth shooter?"

"Baba Ghassan's in New Hampshire," Kenny said. "That was the so-called gibberish Frank couldn't make any sense of. But it's not gibberish. It's a location—a restaurant, actually. Baba Ghassan's, which I imagine is supposed to be a takeoff on the Middle Eastern dish baba ghanoush, is less than an hour north of here in New Hampshire. A Lebanese immigrant named Ghassan Massoud owns it. Massoud moved to the U.S. from Beirut in the mid-eighties to get away from the civil war there. He became a citizen and has been here ever since. A couple of months ago, a relative of his, twenty-two-year-old Yasir Qureshi, arrived from Syria on a refugee visa and moved in with him. Here is what they both look like."

Kenny pulled up U.S. Customs and Immigration photos of both men on his desktop computer.

"Hold on. I'm almost afraid to ask, but where are you getting your information from, Kenny?"

"Reliable sources, Mark. What does it matter?" he quipped.

"It matters. And if you're accessing government information that you're not authorized to access, it really matters. How can you be so casual about this, Kenny? You're doing things that could get you put away for the rest of your life. Do you realize that?"

Kenny sat back, crossed his legs, and shook his head in disbelief. "I haven't gotten to the best part yet, Mark. But let's pause for a second, since you brought up this very important topic. You are so arrogant. You know that, Mark? You people run around the globe, shooting your way in and out of countries without giving a flying fuck about international law or sovereignty. You treat the world like it's your own little playground where you get to make all the rules. Then you have the balls to stand there and lecture me and not even see the irony?"

Mark finished his water and threw it in the wastebasket in the corner of the room. "That's different. I work a very specific mission and you don't know what you're talking about, Kenny."

"Yeah, I know your mission. Find terrorists and kill them, right? The only problem with that is how we sometimes define terrorists and the lengths that you people are willing to go to kill them once they're labeled as such! I'm not naïve, Mark. I know what kind of things you've done for God and country. But now I've found a terrorist who helped to shoot up our hometown and murder my father, and you're looking down on me from your high horse lecturing me about ethics. I bet if we were in Berlin things might be different. Anything goes, right?"

Kenny's breathing accelerated and his hands shook as he reached for his water. That last part about Berlin had been over the top and he knew it. He tried to hide his fear as both men stared into each other's eyes. Landry nodded and his steely glare gave way to a peculiar smile. "Okay, then. Go on. Impress me."

"Turn around, Mark."

Landry pivoted to face the opposite wall behind him and was astonished at the glowing image on the big screen. He stepped forward to study it more closely and marveled at what Kenny had pieced together, all based on a few words that an experienced (albeit inebriated) field agent had mistaken for meaningless gibberish.

"This is a live aerial view of Ghassan Massoud's home, taken from an unarmed MQ-1 Predator. We've had eyes on the objective for almost an hour, operating between twelve thousand and fifteen thousand feet."

"Are you in direct control of the aircraft, Kenny? Or is someone else flying it and sending you the images?"

"I'm receiving the images, but I'm in contact with the person in direct control of the drone."

"And whose drone is it?"

Kenny hesitated. "Honestly, I'm not one hundred percent sure. There were a number of choices, but I think this one belongs to the Air National Guard or maybe DEA. I called in some favors. This is actually my first drone jack. But I was told that whoever owns it will be looking at a continuous decoy feed and altered location until we give it back."

"Drone jack? Is that what it's called?" Mark asked. "So tell me why you think the fourth shooter is in that house."

Kenny returned to his workstation and typed as he talked. "Thermal imaging suggests there's only one person in the house. Right before I called you, we saw him exit the building and walk to the truck parked in the tree line. There's something else next to the truck; judging by the size and shape, it's another vehicle, but it's covered with a tarp or something, so we aren't sure. After that he went deep into the woods. When he returned, it looked like he was carrying an armful of firewood. But when we tightened up the shot, he had what appeared to be assault-style rifles. He put them inside the house, made a second trip to the woods, and returned with more similar-looking items. It's definitely not Ghassan Massoud or the kid. I've been recording the video feed. The images aren't perfect, but it's probably good enough for you to make a positive ID or scratch him off the list. I'll interrupt the live feed and play back the video whenever you're ready."

"I'm ready. Let's see it."

A blank screen replaced the live transmission for several seconds before the video playback began. The clip opened with a wide view of Ghassan's cabin and zoomed in tighter as a man emerged from the front door, descended the steps, and paused. He scanned the area for several seconds, then purposefully marched across the open driveway.

"Freeze it," said Mark. "That's him."

Kenny looked up at Mark from his keyboard. "There's more, you know."

"I know. And I want to see it. But I already know it's him. Look at the image. Lean. Athletic. See how he moves? Calculated and confident. Somewhere between a swagger and a strut. It's him. I'm ninety-nine percent sure, but when we factor in the assault rifles hidden in the woods and that this lead came directly from the last guy we know was in control of the weapons, it becomes one hundred. That's the fourth shooter. Good work, Kenny."

"I wish I could take all the credit, but I've had help. I had to pull a lot of strings and call in a bunch of favors. I would have preferred more time to take a few more security precautions on my end, but this was short notice so I pulled the trigger."

Mark turned to look at his neighbor. "What about the Lebanese guy and the Syrian kid? What else do we know about them? Any idea where they are?"

"Neither appears on any watch lists. No criminal records. Not even parking tickets. As for their current locations, I was just waiting for that to come up when you arrived. Let me check." Kenny sat down and entered a few keystrokes on his machine. "My guy is telling me that Ghassan Massoud used his credit card this afternoon at a gas station in Queens. Later on in the evening, he used the same card at a restaurant in Manhattan. That was just a few hours ago. He has a cell phone, but it hasn't been turned on and connected to the grid in three days. A car registered to the kid, Yasir, is parked at the cabin but we haven't seen him. No digital trail to follow on him. No bank accounts. I guess it's possible that he's in the house, but we haven't gotten any thermal images from the house that suggest anything other than one occupant."

"Yeah, but those are easy to trick," offered Mark. "There could be half a dozen armed men in there, but if they have half a clue on how the technology works, they could easily mask their presence. Then again, from what I've personally seen and heard about the guys who hit Founders Field, they weren't exactly sophisticated professionals, so there's a good chance number four is the only one in the house."

"Why do you suppose he was bringing the guns inside?" Kenny asked.

"Maybe he was worried about someone finding his stash. Or depending on how they've been stored, he may just want to wipe them down and lubricate them so they're ready to go and less likely to malfunction when needed. Maybe he's preparing for another attack. Any number of reasons. Does the cabin have a phone line or Internet connection you can tap? What about local police traffic? What else is going on up there right now?"

"There's phone and Internet, but nobody's using either. I'll know the moment that changes. I have someone monitoring the local first responders up through the New Hampshire State Police and any elements of the federal government that may be active in the area. It's quiet up there. No chatter whatsoever. He could be lying low for a little while or about to squeal rubber out of town. There's no way to tell. What does your gut tell you, Mark?"

Mark buried his hands in his front pockets and paced to the window overlooking Kenny's backyard. He pulled back the curtain, gazed at the full moon, and stood silently as Kenny waited patiently.

"The answer is obvious," Mark began. "He's preparing for another mission. That's why he's gathering the weapons. And maybe that's why he ran from the Founders Field attack when the others stayed and died. Maybe he had another battle to get to. Whether the next attack is something complex that requires orchestration and collaboration or something as simple as driving into town and opening fire is anyone's guess. One thing's for sure—more people are going to die unless he's stopped."

Kenny stood up and joined Mark at the window. "Then who should we tell so they can go bring him in?"

"The attack on Founders Field started with a bomb. If he has more explosives, there's a chance he's rigged the cabin so he can blow it up if he feels threatened. If he's smart, he's scanning police frequencies for early notice. There's a good chance he wouldn't let himself be taken alive, which would deny us any intelligence we could have extracted during an interrogation. Cops and SWAT take time to assemble and have a huge footprint. He'd smell them coming. JTTF has better capabilities, but I'm reluctant to pass information to them right now for reasons I can't go into. I don't think we should pass this off to anybody."

"So what do you want to do?" asked Kenny.

"I want to pay him a visit, see what information I can get out of him, and then pass him off after I'm long gone. But that is much easier said than ..."

Kenny jumped in before Mark could finish his sentence. "Okay, I'm in. How can I help?"

"I'm not surprised at your willingness, Kenny. But you may want to slow down and think things through a bit more. A lot of what you said to me before was true, so I'm not going to lecture you. But you could already be in a world of shit for some of the things you've done. And that was before you jacked a drone." Mark closed the curtains and turned to face his neighbor.

"I know all that, Mark. But stopping this guy before he kills someone else's children is a lot more important. I can live with the things I've done, but I couldn't live with myself if this guy strikes again when I might have been able to help stop him and didn't even try. So I'm in. When do we leave?"

"Really?" asked Mark. "What are you going to do, Kenny? Drive up there and bust into the cabin with a knife clenched in your teeth? Then what? This guy is a professional. You'd just get yourself killed."

"Don't mock me because I have different skills from yours, Landry," he said, pointing his finger in Mark's face and then at the images on the big screen. "And let's not forget who found the bastard in the first place. Whether you'll admit to it or not, you need me. So drop the sarcasm and tell me how I can help."

One hundred nineteen

Amir finished reassembling the last of the rifles and laid it on the floor next to the others. The stuffy air inside the cabin was laced heavily with the odor of gun cleaner and lubricant. Satisfied that he had not been followed and encouraged by news reports indicating only three shooters, he opened several windows to let in the cool evening breeze.

Somewhere near Washington, D.C., an Islamic State facilitator was wondering why Amir had not shown up for their meeting. He had arrived at the coffee shop near Georgetown University precisely at 11:00 a.m. At noon he left. In accordance with protocol, he would return to the meeting place 48 hours later for one final attempt before aborting the entire mission. Amir, meanwhile, was committed to doing whatever it would take to be there.

He had realized after the explosion on Founders Field that he had not packed enough military grade C4 explosive material into the bomb, and he had put even less inside the backpack bomb. The girl had successfully detonated the device, but the damage was far less extensive than he had expected. Looking down at the remaining C4, he promised himself that he would not make the same mistake again.

After quickly showering and changing his clothes, Amir sat in the soft leather armchair and turned up the volume on the television. Aside from the occasional update, the news media had already moved on from his debut attack on U.S. soil. Instead, they covered breaking news on the other shootings and targeted attacks that were peppering the national landscape almost daily.

Amir had risked much by altering the plan, and so far the reaction to the attack had been less than he had anticipated. He seethed at the short burst of attention and closed his eyes to rest.

Be patient. In Washington you will make history.

Mark went next door to change his clothes and pack his gear. Minutes later he exited the side door and jogged to his vehicle, which was still parked in Kenny's driveway. He placed his backpack on the passenger's seat and accelerated quickly up the hill. Kenny had given him an encrypted phone to enable them to communicate with each other, suggesting that Mark leave his own phone behind so that it couldn't be used to track him. Prior to leaving the house, Mark made one last call to the officer on duty at Luci's hospital room.

"Anything new? How is she?" he asked.

"She's been sleeping, sir. But she did wake up about half an hour ago. She's still pretty weak but managed to sit up and eat something, which made the nurses happy. She asked about you. I said you got called away for work but that I could call you if she wanted. She said no and went back to sleep."

"Okay. Listen, I'm going to give you a different number to call if you need me. Ask for Kenny. He can get messages to me."

Mark accelerated up the on-ramp and sped north on I-93. There would be few cars on the road at 2:00 a.m., so he could make good time. If he were pulled over the federal law enforcement credentials Doc had acquired for him would keep anyone from snooping into the backpack. The phone in his pocket vibrated. It was Kenny.

"I'm on my way," Mark reported. "Barring any unforeseen circumstances, I should be there in less than an hour. Do you still have eyes on the objective?"

"Yes," Kenny answered. "For now at least. I have no reason to think we've been compromised, but that can't go on forever. Eventually, either the true owners of the drone will discover they've lost control of it or it'll run out of gas. I'd prefer to give it back before either of those things happens."

"That makes two of us. As soon as I get close to the cabin, you can send it home. Have you seen anything new?"

"Not really. There's some light spilling out of a few of the windows that wasn't there before, but I don't know if that tells us much." Kenny stated.

Mark drifted from the center of the three-lane highway to the far left to pass the only car within sight of him. "It might. If he thought he might have been followed or was being watched, he would keep the place buttoned up tight. If he just opened the windows, that might mean he's less worried so he's getting comfortable. If that's the case, let's hope it continues. In this game, the line between comfortable and sloppy is very thin. And you only have to be sloppy once to get killed. Keep watching and take a quick look at the surrounding area if you can. I'd prefer not to bump into anybody during my approach."

"Will do."

Mark took a deep breath and continued. "Listen, I appreciate everything you've done so far, Kenny. I'm impressed. You're a pro. But even if we do everything right, there's always a chance that this thing goes south and we both end up with a lot to answer for. My boss has already had to save my ass once this week. I'm not so sure even he could do it a second time."

"It's a little late for either of us to back out, Mark. Are you saying you're screwed if we get caught? Join the crowd! My only friends are virtual and anonymous. And I doubt the authorities would be nice enough to provide me with an encrypted Internet connection to contact them for help anyway. I don't have any real friends. I'm just doing this because if we don't stop this guy, innocent people will die. What's his next target? A school? A mall? A day care center? No way can we let that happen. Essentially we're both doing the wrong things for the right reasons, if that makes any sense."

"It does. And it pretty accurately describes much of my career the last few years," answered Mark. "Listen closely for a minute, okay? If things do go to shit and you end up in somebody's custody, I have one piece of advice: don't say anything. Not a word, okay?"

"Go on," said Kenny.

"Don't tell them anything. Don't answer any questions. I won't let you hang out to dry, but you have to trust me to take care of it. They'll try to trick you. They'll lie to you. They'll rough you up just enough to scare the shit out of you and maybe more. They'll make horrifying threats and offer bullshit deals to get you to talk. Don't do it. Just keep your mouth shut and stay strong. I will not abandon you. Understand?"

"Yeah, I understand." Kenny answered. "But how the hell are you going to help me when you just said you don't think you can count on your boss to save you? That doesn't make any sense, Mark."

"Because there's someone else I might be able to count on. Let's just call it a higher power. It's not necessarily a 'get out of jail free' card, but it could be. Regardless, it's the only play I have left if things get hot. Let me worry about that if the time comes, okay?"

"Sure," Kenny answered.

"One more question on an unrelated topic. You mentioned something yesterday about a big-time government data breach. If you wanted to, do you think you could determine who was behind it?" Mark asked.

"It depends. With the tools I have, it would be tough but not impossible. But if I had access to the right tools—yeah, I don't see why not."

"Good. That's good to know. Keep an eye out and call me if anything changes."

The plan was simple. Ghassan Massoud's cabin was located on a wooded hilltop on the outskirts of his sparsely populated New Hampshire town. A serpentine gravel driveway stretched nearly a quarter-mile from the main road to the front porch. The rest of the property was heavily wooded with no visible trails. Mark would park near a public camping and fishing area half a mile north of the cabin and make his final approach from there on foot. Dressed in civilian hiking gear with an innocuous-looking backpack, he would easily blend in and not attract attention from anyone he might encounter along the way.

Mark pulled into the campground entrance and followed the dirt road to the very end. Vehicles and tents dotted the scenery along the way. While most people slept, a dedicated few guzzled beers and passed bottles of whiskey around the orange glow of their campfires. At the end of the main road, he turned left and parked.

Mark rolled down the window and took several minutes to acclimate to the sights and sounds of the area. Satisfied that there were no nosey campers nearby, he locked the car, tightened the backpack around his shoulders, and walked due south into the woods. One hundred meters into his walk, his cargo pocket vibrated. It was Kenny.

"Mark, nothing has changed, but I don't know how much longer I can hold onto this drone. My guy is freaking out. So far I've been able to threaten and coax him into keeping it in the air, but I don't know how much longer I can do that for you. I see where you are, but how long do you think it'll take to get into position so I can cut this thing loose?"

"Not long. Just a few more minutes once I gear up. If things get too hot, send the drone home. Just be sure to continue monitoring local authorities and any other chatter you think is important. Do you see anything in the woods between me and the objective? If I know it's clear, I can move a lot faster."

"A couple of dogs or coyotes when you get closer to the cabin, but other than that I don't see anything."

"Okay, then. I'll get there as fast as I can."

Mark ended the call and slipped the phone back into his cargo pocket. He pulled the backpack from his shoulders and knelt on the forest floor. After securing the four-eyed panoramic night-vision goggles to his head, he reached into the bag for the Colt

M4A1 carbine and quickly twisted the suppressor onto the muzzle. Once the holographic sights were switched on and glowing, he loaded a thirty-round magazine, strapped the backpack on, and sprinted due south.

One hundred twenty-two

The imminent loss of his eye in the sky driving his sense of urgency, Mark traveled through the forest with extraordinary speed. The terrain had been just as he expected—flat for the first half of the journey and then a slow, steady incline. He traveled straight ahead, cutting through several open areas that he would normally have skirted around to avoid exposing himself if there was more time. Ghassan's home sat atop one of only two hills in the area, so he didn't have to constantly check his compass heading. As a result, he closed the distance between his car and the cabin remarkably fast.

Mark paused and took a knee approximately one hundred yards from the objective to make final preparations. Sweat poured down his head and back. He pulled a bottle of water from a cargo pocket and guzzled it. The phone in his pocket vibrated. A text from Kenny.

MESSAGE: DRONE IS GONE.

It doesn't matter. I have my own.
Mark made a final check of his equipment and headed toward the cabin at a deliberate pace.

Two vehicles: a Toyota sedan in the middle of the driveway and a Chevy truck pushed approximately twenty feet into the tree line. Likely a third vehicle under a tarp next to the truck. Mark approached the Chevy and glanced inside: empty. Crouching low, he moved around to the other side and slowly lifted the tarp, finding a police cruiser with the dashboard electronics ripped out. He scanned the area and quietly approached the Toyota in the middle of the driveway. Empty. Keys in the ignition.

Mark retreated behind the two vehicles in the tree line and pulled a small black plastic box from his backpack. He opened it and removed a tiny gray pouch and a handheld device slightly larger than an iPhone. Once the device had booted up and indicated a ready status, he grabbed the gray pouch and dumped the black, four-propeller mini-drone into the palm of his hand. Seconds later it silently lifted off and hovered above his position. Live thermal images appeared on the control screen as Landry sent the drone high above the cabin.

Let's get the bird's eye view first.

After scanning the perimeter for movement from above, Mark had the drone hover about fifty feet from one of the open windows—far enough away that no one inside the cabin would see or hear it. From there he inched it closer until he had a good view of the building's interior.

Besides a small light above the kitchen sink, the only other light in the home came from the television, tuned to Fox News. Mark maneuvered the drone from side to side to observe as much of the interior as possible. On the floor at the far side of the room were a half-dozen or more rifles and an assortment of magazines, ammunition, and several tactical bags. On the table were several knives, a sharpening stone, and a case of military-style MREs.

Mark flew the drone to the next window for a better look at the television area. The quality of the lighting depended on the ever-changing banners and other graphics coming from the broadcast, but he could clearly make out the figure of a man sleeping in a large armchair. Landry nudged the drone slightly closer to the window to improve the camera angle as a commercial brightened the room.

There you are.

The fourth shooter was asleep in the armchair. A pistol sat atop a small table within arm's reach, and a rifle rested against the armchair between his legs, the muzzle pointed at the ceiling. He was fully dressed and still had unlaced work boots on his feet.

Landry flew the drone up and over the house to peer through a window on the opposite side next to the front door. A trail of blood led from the fireplace to what looked to be the door to a basement. He scanned the interior of the cabin and committed the floor plan to memory. Satisfied that he knew what to expect once inside, he brought the drone back to his position.

Crouched low with his carbine at the ready, Mark tiptoed up the front steps of the cabin and quietly sidestepped down the farmer's porch until he was in front of the screenless window he had chosen. After quickly peeking to ensure that the target was still in the chair, he retrieved the flash-bang device from his cargo pocket. He took a deep breath, pulled the pin, and lofted the device through the window toward the television.

Landry bolted for the front door and paused momentarily. The device landed on the hardwood floor with a thump. A fraction of a second later a blinding flash of light burst through the windows, followed by a nearly two-hundred-decibel bang that shook the cabin. Landry lunged forward and kicked with everything he had. The door flew open and he rushed into the building with his carbine held high.

Landry could hear his interrogation instructor's voice in his head as he prepared to question his prisoner.

Interrogation is more art than science. Once a man studies the different approaches, like a sculptor learning to wield his chisel, a personal style begins to form. Some men are soft-spoken, with an almost soothing presence meant to build rapport and attract the detainee like a moth to a lantern. Others are horrifyingly brutal, with the goal of compelling the detainee into cooperation through fear and pain.

Mark Landry's approach was a hybrid of the two.

Landry unscrewed the cap from the bottle of cold water and held it upside down over Amir's head until it was empty. "Wake up." Amir was securely fastened to a wooden chair with his hands bound behind his back. Mark placed another chair approximately five feet in front of his prisoner and sat down with his rifle cradled in his lap. "I said, wake up!" he yelled.

Amir bobbed his head from side to side and spat up a mouthful of saliva mixed with blood. The flash bang had taken him from a state of deep sleep to complete disorientation long enough for Mark to enter the room, strike him in the head with the butt of his rifle, and bind his hands and feet with zip ties.

From there, Landry went to work clearing the rest of the cabin. Crouched low, he bolted room to room, quickly checking under beds, behind doors, and inside closets on the main floor before turning his attention to the basement door in the kitchen. He turned off the light over the sink, flung the door open quickly, and stood to the side for several seconds, then peered down the stairs and activated the tactical light mounted on the barrel of his rifle.

Green light spilled down the stairs and illuminated a small, unfinished cellar. At the bottom step was the body of a young, Middle Eastern–looking man with a bullet hole where the bridge of his nose used to be. Mark descended several stairs and swept his muzzle from left to right. He saw stacks of napkins, cups, and paper plates overflowing from three boxes labeled "restaurant supplies," but nothing else. He focused the light on the dead man's face and recognized Yasir from the photos. Satisfied that the cabin was clear, Landry sprinted back up the stairs to prepare his prisoner for questioning and look more closely at the equipment spread out on the floor. He counted nine Sig Sauer M400 rifles and discovered a pound of factory-sealed C4 plastic explosive material inside a backpack.

Amir slowly opened his eyes and tried to regain his bearings. He struggled violently for several moments to free his arms and legs before noticing the shadowy figure sitting in front of him. He blinked furiously to adjust his vision to the darkness. The only light in the cabin came from a burning candle somewhere behind the masked man.

"What's your name?" Mark asked.

The prisoner struggled again to break free. "Please! Quick! You have to help me! He's going to kill me! Get me out of here, please!"

"Who is going to kill you?"

"I don't know what his name is. Yasir, I think. He and his uncle are terrorists. Please help me!" Amir begged as tears rolled down his panic-stricken face. "I don't want to die! I swear I haven't done anything wrong! Just get me out of here and I'll tell you anything you want!"

Landry stared at Amir through the wide, oval opening of the black ski mask that enveloped his eyes. He showed no reaction to the prisoner's words. He simply waited patiently and watched the show in silence until Amir had finished pleading.

"You shouldn't lie to me. I can't help you if you lie to me. Now tell me your name."

Amir gasped for air and contorted his face like a three-year-old who just had all his toys taken away. "No! Please! I swear I'm telling the truth. I'm in danger. I've been held here against my will. Why don't you believe me?" he sobbed.

Mark held up his hand, indicating that he had had enough. "I don't believe you because Yasir is in the basement with a bullet in his head. And I'm guessing the bullet came from the .45 you had with you when I caught you napping. Listen, if you lie to me again, I'm going to hurt you. Do you understand that? Do I look like I'm fucking around? Look at me."

An effective interrogator knows the importance of setting precedent from the very beginning. If he threatens violent punishment for non-compliance but doesn't follow through, he effectively transfers power to the prisoner. Furthermore, when the interrogator does follow through, the violence must be sufficiently shocking to the prisoner. Insufficient force that is easily tolerated may actually empower and motivate the prisoner to continue his resistance.

Mark did not plan on making either of those mistakes. He was fully committed to setting the precedent early, and more than ready to get violent if he had to—especially with a man he already knew to be a cold-blooded murderer.

Landry leaned his rifle against the table, reached a hand up under his long-sleeve hiking shirt, and pulled out the karambit-style, curved blade from the sheath that hung around his neck. "I'm going to count to three. If you lie to me, if you say anything other than your name and why you shot up those innocent people two days ago, you will regret it. One ..."

Amir's jaw dropped and his eyes widened.

"Two ..."

He shook his head furiously.

"Three."

"Wait! Wait! Wait! I swear I had nothing to do with it!" he screamed out.

"Wrong answer." Mark leapt from his seat, grabbed Amir's right ear with his left hand, and held it tightly. With his right hand he slid the razor sharp karambit's blade down the side of Amir's face and separated the ear from his head in one clean motion.

A thin stream of blood spurted from the wound as the prisoner screamed out in anguish. He gasped for air and struggled to free himself. Mark returned to his seat, tossed the ear onto the floor between the two chairs, and waited patiently for the screaming to die down.

"You bastard! You pig! You better kill me now ... if I ever get the chance I will cut off your head!"

Amir's fake tears and false claims of innocence had changed to pure rage. With one single knife motion, Mark had peeled back the mask of the innocent young man and exposed the terrorist. The next few minutes would be crucial. As the interrogator, Mark had established precedent with his swift and shockingly violent follow-through. But now he needed to evaluate the likelihood of gleaning any valuable information from the prisoner. In his past experience he had seen plenty of men, true believers in their cause, endure ruthless violence without uttering a word. And he had seen others soften up quickly and spill their guts when threatened with much less. Mark had a feeling that this one would end up in the former category, but he needed time to make an educated assessment.

"I saw you on the roof. I saw you shooting. Tell me about the attack. Who chose the target and why?" he asked calmly.

"Go to hell!"

"Were you acting on your own? Or do you belong to a larger organization? At least tell me what your beef is. That wouldn't be betraying any secrets. Hell, you should be proud, right? So why did you do it? Did you have a reason or do you just get off on hurting people?"

"You might as well take the other ear because I'm not telling you anything."

Mark leaned to the glance at the ear. "One's enough for now, but let's see if we can slow down the bleeding. I don't want you passing out on me." He retrieved a stack of napkins from the kitchen and pressed them hard onto the side of Amir's head from behind with his gloved hand. Amir screamed.

"Let me bleed! Let me bleed!"

The glow from an electronic device lit up a corner of the room behind Mark and caught his attention. He released his grip and walked out of Amir's sight to the corner to retrieve the phone. The control screen indicated dozens of missed calls and almost fifty unread text messages. Mark scrolled to the most recent one, from someone named Linda.

MESSAGE: JOHN! WHERE ARE YOU! ARE YOU OK? I'M AT THE HOSPITAL! THE BABY IS COMING! PLEASE CALL ME! I DON'T WANT TO DO THIS ALONE!

He scrolled down. All the messages were similar. All the missed calls were from the same person. He pocketed the phone and returned to his chair in front of Amir.

"What's your name? Where are you from? Is your name John?" Mark asked.

"John?" Amir chuckled. "No, I am definitely not John. Did you just find his phone? I threw it at the wall when that stupid woman wouldn't stop calling and texting. Call her back and tell her that her baby will be fatherless, just as many babies across the Muslim world are fatherless thanks to men like her husband."

"Where is he? What did you do to him?"

"I'm not telling you anything, so you might as well keep cutting and save us both the time," Amir said, looking directly into Mark's eyes.

314

If a prisoner makes a violence-provoking statement at the beginning of an interrogation, he is often bluffing and may still be motivated through violence to share information. However, if he has already been subjected to substantial violence when he makes the statement, it is possible that the interrogator is dealing with an extremist who is unlikely to crack. In those cases, any further escalation of the violence runs the risk of becoming a distracting battle of egos rather than a deliberate attempt to extract valuable information. Do not take the bait. Instead, change to a nonviolent approach and keep control of the interrogation.

"I guess I could do that, but what's the use? If you're not going to talk, you're not going to talk and there's no need to get myself any dirtier. I'll just turn you over to the authorities and they can deal with you." Mark kept eye contact with his prisoner for a few moments. Then he removed Kenny's encrypted phone from his pocket and slung his rifle onto his back. He walked to the far end of the kitchen to escape the glow of the candle and texted Kenny.

MESSAGE: CHATTING WITH #4

The response came within seconds.

MESSAGE: AND?

Mark looked up to check on Amir before tapping his reply. His head hung low. The shock of being taken prisoner coupled with restricted blood flow was taking its toll.

MESSAGE: WORKING ON IT. HEAR FROM FRANK?

Again, Kenny's response came almost instantly.

MESSAGE: NOTHING. LIGHTS OUT.

Landry put the phone away and quietly returned to his seat opposite the prisoner.

"Just kill me now. Or don't you have the courage?" Amir goaded him.

Mark rubbed his face through the mask. "Courage? It doesn't take much courage to kill a man who's tied to a chair. And it didn't take any courage at all to do what you did on that field two days ago. You blew up, then shot up a bunch of unarmed people, including women and children. Then I watched you run like a pussy

315

when the other three guys stood and fought like men. So don't lecture me about courage."

"Burn in hell!" Amir screamed, causing a stream of blood to shoot from the side of his head. "You are the cowards who drop bombs on innocent Muslim families from thirty thousand feet! You fly drones from soft leather chairs thousands of miles from the battlefield because you lack the courage to fight God's true warriors face to face."

Mark exhaled and leaned forward in his chair. "Listen, I don't want to get into a pissing contest with you. But I've fought plenty of so-called jihadists up close and—no offense—I wasn't very impressed with what you guys can do. Seriously, unless you're slaying unarmed women and children, you're pretty much fish out of water. That's just a fact."

"You're lying. If you had ever faced the fury of God's holy warriors, you wouldn't have lived to tell about it," Amir declared.

"Okay. Whatever. You don't have to believe me. But unless you've actually been in battle—like, real battle—your opinion doesn't mean shit, ok? And from what I saw of you, I'm guessing this attack was your first rodeo."

Amir smirked at the insult and responded slowly. "Fallujah, Tikrit, Mosul."

Mark nodded his head. "Okay. So you've seen some shit. But listen. I hate to burst your bubble, but the spiritual leaders in the Islamic State fill the heads of the common, low-level nobodies like you with a lot of bullshit."

Amir bowed his head. "I am not a low-level nobody. You're the one who doesn't know what he's talking about. Common soldiers are not sent on important holy missions."

"What? Shooting up civilians at a picnic? Yeah, I'm sure only the pick of the litter get to go on those missions. Tell yourself whatever you want, buddy. But you're not worth my time, so I'm done with you. I'm going to hand you off to the feds. You're going to jail for the rest of your life, and the security on you will be so tight you won't be able to take a dump or jerk off without somebody watching. And all because you were so awesome that the Islamic State sent you to shoot up a picnic."

Amir started to speak, but Mark laughed out loud and walked into the kitchen.

"What's your claim to fame? You're just an ass in a mask. Why do you hide behind that mask anyway? What have you got to hide? If you were really there on the field, you saw all of our faces because that is how real men fight. You weren't even there, were you?"

"Whatever you say, Top Gun!" Mark yelled from the darkness. "You could have at least martyred yourself but you didn't have the balls. Or let me guess—Allah had a different plan for you, right?"

Amir wrestled with his restraints and screamed. "I am not a coward! I am not afraid to die! My martyrdom awaits me in Washington and I promise you I will make it there. Do you hear me? I will fulfill my destiny and there's nothing you can do to stop it."

Landry walked slowly back into the candlelight. "Odds of you making it to Washington are looking pretty slim right now, wouldn't you say? But just for shits and giggles, what were you planning on doing once you got there?"

"I'm done talking to you. Kill me. Hand me over to the authorities. I don't care. But I won't entertain your stupidity anymore."

"Suit yourself," answered Mark.

Both men averted each other's gazes and sat in silence for several minutes. As Landry started to speak, a long, agonizing moan drifted up the basement stairs and eerily pierced the silence. He leapt to his feet with his carbine at the ready and pressed his ear to the basement door in time to hear a second faint groaning sound.

"Go ahead," said Amir. "Look downstairs so you can see what a low-level foot soldier was able to do to one of your finest."

Landry closed the distance between him and his prisoner in three determined strides and delivered an uppercut to the chin with the butt of his rifle, knocking Amir unconscious.

One hundred twenty-five

Officer John McDonough was in grave condition. Mark had found him in a puddle of blood behind the boxes in the basement and cursed himself for having missed the wounded officer when he had hastily cleared the cabin. Either the shooter had left him for dead or was letting him suffer and keeping him around for more torture. He was shirtless, shoeless, and bound at the hands and feet. Several of his fingers and toes had been cut off, his face and torso were beaten to a pulp, and the USMC tattoo on his left bicep was covered with burn marks. Landry put an ear to his mouth. The officer's breathing was shallow and barely audible.

"Can you hear me? Can you hear me? Are you John? Is your name John?" Mark yelled.

McDonough grunted and opened his mouth. "Yeah," he answered in a low whisper that took every ounce of his remaining strength.

Mark looked closer at the officer and former Marine's wounds and considered his options.

This guy isn't going to make it unless he gets help right now. He may have only minutes. The nearest hospital is fifteen miles away. If I call for EMTs, I lose control of the site and he could die waiting for them. His best chances are for me to stop the bleeding and get him to the ER, and I may not even be able to get him there in time. Shit!

Landry retrieved the tourniquet and pressure dressing from one of his cargo pockets and put them on his patient where he thought they would stop the most blood. They weren't nearly enough. He quickly scanned the basement and grabbed several bags of napkins from the restaurant supplies.

"Listen, John. I'm going to get you out of here, okay? But I need to stop your bleeding as best I can before I move you. You've been through a lot, my friend. And it's going to hurt some more if we're going to make it to a hospital. Okay? Can you hear me, buddy?"

McDonough grunted. Mark started packing piles of napkins onto his wounds and securing them in place with a roll of duct tape he had found at the bottom of one of the boxes. "All you have to do is stay with me, John. I'll get you there, but you gotta fight, brother. And judging from that tattoo I think you know what I mean. Who's Linda?"

Mark struggled to plug the holes in McDonough's body, glanced down at his left hand, and saw a wedding band wrapped around what was left of his ring finger. "Is she your wife, John? Is Linda your wife?"

McDonough grunted and tried to speak. "Yes ..."

"Okay, save your energy, brother. I'm going to move you now and it's going to hurt. But you have to push through the pain for me, Marine! You have a lot to live for, John. Linda says your baby is on the way. Keep thinking about her and that baby and don't give up. I'll do my part but you have to do yours and stay in the fight. We're out of here right now."

Mark took one last deep breath and strained every muscle in his body to pull McDonough up from the basement floor. He carefully stepped over Yasir's body and slowly ascended the basement stairs with the wounded officer hoisted on his shoulder.

Kenny nervously paced back and forth in his office, his fingers laced behind his neck.

This can't be happening. This can't be happening. He's probably wrong. We covered our tracks.

He stopped and looked down at the message on his screen to make sure he hadn't misread it.

MESSAGE: DRONE JACK COMPROMISED. WIPING MY DRIVES AND BUGGING OUT. SUGGEST YOU DO SAME.

No. No. No. This isn't happening. What the hell should I do? Should I bail? Should I stick it out and see what happens? Call Mark.

"I was just about to call you, Kenny," Mark said when he answered.

"I'm freaking out over here, Mark. My guy is telling me the drone jack was compromised. But he doesn't know whether it was compromised from the very beginning or not. He's bugging out and I don't know what the hell I should do. My connection to him was encrypted and rerouted through at least half a dozen different jurisdictions, but nothing is impossible to trace."

"You're the only one who can make that call, Kenny. So do what you have to do. But for what it's worth, I can tell you from experience that nobody gets away forever."

"I know that. Are you finished with the shooter? I can see you're nowhere near the cabin. What did he tell you?" Kenny asked.

"I was just starting to get some information out of him when I had to alter the plan. I found a wounded cop in the basement. He's alive but won't be for long if he doesn't get to a hospital. The nearest ER is about fifteen miles away and I'm en route."

"Where's the shooter, Mark? Did you just leave him there?"

"Yeah, I didn't have much of a choice. This guy is bleeding out quickly."

"I understand and I'm not questioning you, but if he gets away a lot of people could die."

"The cop's wife is giving birth as we speak. I never had a father. You lost yours. Think I could live with myself if I let some kid's dad die? The shooter is tied up tight and I'll get back as fast as I can."

"Okay. Let me know if you need anything from me," said Kenny.

"I need you to remember what I told you before I left. If they come for you, try not to say anything. I won't leave you, Kenny. I promise I'll help, but it could take time."

"Let's hope it doesn't come to that, Mark."

"One more thing. If they do come for you, depending on whose drone you jacked, they may not show up flashing their badges with the sirens blaring. Be careful, Kenny."

"I'm going outside to have a cigarette," the young uniformed security guard said to the emergency room receptionist through his walkie-talkie.

"You're off duty in like ten minutes. You can't wait?" she replied.

"I suppose I could. But then it would be on my time and I only smoke when I'm on the clock. Besides, I like to see the sunrise."

"You're unbelievable!"

The security guard stepped through the automatic doors, clenched a cigarette between his teeth, and removed the lighter from his front pocket. He bowed his head, lit the cigarette, and took two deep drags. When he looked up, a Toyota sedan was speeding across the parking lot toward the emergency room entrance. "Slow down, man!" he said out loud.

The Toyota screeched to a halt in front of the automatic doors and a masked Mark Landry jumped out of the driver's seat, holding his credentials high. "Federal agent! I have a wounded police officer who needs urgent care. You clear the way. I'll carry him in."

The security guard stood stunned.

"Put out your friggin' cigarette and clear the way for me. He's going to die if he doesn't get help right now!"

Seconds later, Mark passed through the doors with the bloody John McDonough over his shoulder. "Stay with me, John. We made it, brother! We made it to the hospital. They're going to take good care of you now. Keep fighting, John! Remember, you have a wife and kid to live for."

Landry lowered McDonough onto an open bed in the ER, the medical crew sprang into action, and he bolted for the door. On the way out, he grabbed a nurse by the arm and pulled her close. Her eyes were wide with horror. Mark pulled down and stretched the mask's opening under his chin to expose his face. "Calm down. Look at me. It's okay—we're both good guys, okay?"

She nodded nervously.

"Listen, his name is John McDonough. He's a cop and a veteran. His wife Linda is somewhere in this hospital and about to have a baby. You guys can take it from here. I have to go."

Kenny downed a glass of cognac, placed it on the kitchen counter, and continued nervously pacing the house.

I could wipe my drives right now just to be safe. But if they don't come, I did it for nothing. If they do come, I just destroyed evidence and I'm even more screwed. I could wipe it all and bug out, but they'd eventually find me. What the hell do I do? Another drink.

He returned to the kitchen, refilled his glass, and stared out the front window.

What the hell is Mark going to do? Like nobody is going to see him drop off a wounded cop at the ER? Like he can just sail in and out? And what if the shooter isn't there when he returns? What then? We are screwed. We are both screwed.

Kenny's worst nightmare soon came true as several dark sedans and State Police cruisers appeared at the top of the street. His heart sank as they silently descended the hill toward the cul-de-sac.

Mark was right. No lights, no sirens.

He drained the rest of the cognac from the glass and set it down on an end table.

Here I am. Come and get me. I'm not going to run.

When the cars reached the bottom of the hill, they turned right into Frank Tagala's driveway. Uniformed officers and agents exited their vehicles and rushed to surround the agent's home. After several unanswered knocks, the three men at the front door entered Frank's house.

"Well, I'll be damned," said Kenny out loud. "Maybe it's my lucky day."

As he reached up to close the blinds, a gloved hand covered his mouth from behind and pulled him violently away from the window.

One hundred twenty-nine

Ghassan Massoud had driven the entire way from New York City with the radio off, preferring instead to review in his mind the litany of reasons why he would never visit his sister and her family again.

It wasn't the hints that she needed money that pushed him over the edge—she'd been cashing a yearly check from him since they were teens. And it wasn't the nagging comments about his weight or how much wine he consumed. Those things he could get over. What caused Ghassan to blow his stack was her husband, a Somali engineer, and their three unbearable children.

On previous occasions, when Ghassan had reached his boiling point he would simply slip out the door. Later he would call with an excuse, and his sister would eventually get over it. But this year things had unfolded differently, and he could not resist the urge to share a piece of his mind on the way out.

With a full belly of Lebanese food and wine from his beloved Bekaa Valley, he stood at the table with his glass raised. "I'm afraid I must leave this evening, but before I go I wanted to say a few words. First, thank you to my wonderful sister Sara for your hospitality. But I would also like to say a few words to the three of you," he said, turning to Sara's children.

"I bounced each of you on my knee when you were babies and still can't believe you are now in your twenties," he began, filling his glass to the brim with more wine. "I can't believe it, not just because you are so much bigger, but because you still act like children. You are all very smart. But you are also incredibly spoiled and disrespectful."

The room full of relatives gasped and started to interrupt Ghassan until he slammed a beefy palm of the table. "I am not finished! Seriously, if you spent half as much time being grateful for what you have instead of bitching and complaining about the injustices you endure, you would be much happier and more successful. Try it, please. Especially, you," he said pointing to his niece, who was in her third year at an Ivy League university on a full scholarship. "Either toughen up or be sure to spend the rest of your life on campus, because the real world doesn't give a shit about your feelings."

"Ghassan!" gasped Sara. "Please!"

He dismissed her with a wave, guzzled his entire glass of wine, and directed his attention to her husband, seated at the head of the table. "And you, Farooq. This country has been good to you. You have been able to work and make a living. You met your wife here and were able to raise your family in peace. But I have never heard a good word about the United States pass from your Qat-stained lips. If you had stayed in Somalia, you would be either dead or making a living as a low-rent pirate. Keep that in mind the next time you want to complain about having to take your shoes off at the airport or show ID to the police. If it was up to me, I would send your skinny ass back to Mogadishu the way you arrived—with nothing but the clothes on your back."

Ghassan smiled for the first hour of the drive home. But now, as he pulled the dark green Range Rover into his driveway, all he wanted to do was sleep. Yasir's car was not in the driveway.

Good, maybe he is at the restaurant actually doing what I asked of him.

He left his bags in the car and was slowly climbing the stairs to the cabin when he noticed that the door had been broken in.

Ghassan entered the house and froze. The air was thick with a foul odor, the furniture was in disarray, and there were pools of blood everywhere. "Yasir!" he yelled. "Yasir, are you okay?"

Hearing no answer, he ran for the fireplace mantle to retrieve his revolver. He gasped at the bloodstained floor along the way and panicked when he saw that the revolver was gone. He began to sweat and the room started to spin. As his panic grew stronger, his instincts screamed for him to run.

"Help! Please help me!" he heard from across the room.

Ghassan shook off his tunnel vision and saw a young man tied to a chair on the other side of the room. He approached slowly, mouth wide in horror at the sight of the boy's swollen, bloody face and missing ear.

"Please help me!" he repeated.

"Who are you?" asked Ghassan, his voice quivering with fear.

"Don't let him kill me! Untie me before he gets back! He's crazy! He's already killed a bunch of people. I tried to stop him but he tortured me!"

"Who are you talking about? Who has killed people and tortured you?" asked Ghassan.

"Yasir! He's a terrorist! He helped hurt those people in Massachusetts two days ago. Please, I'll tell you everything, but untie me before he gets back!"

Ghassan's heart raced and he started to lose feeling in his arms and legs. He steadied himself with one hand against the wall, bent over, and gasped to catch his breath.

How can this be? My God, what have you done, Yasir!

"Please! I'm begging you! Untie me before he gets back or he'll kill both of us!"

The big man breathed deeply and tried to calm his nerves. Then he examined the prisoner's restraints and screamed over his shoulder as he scurried to the kitchen. "I'll get a knife and cut you loose."

One hundred thirty

The first thing Mark noticed when he returned to the cabin—besides the missing prisoner—was the missing weapons. From there, things got worse.

Ghassan's body lay face down in front of the fireplace in the same area where Yasir had taken his last breath. But instead of putting a bullet in his head, Amir had cut Ghassan's throat from ear to ear. Mark recoiled at the quantity of blood that had flowed from the big man and immediately set out to clear the cabin again and look for any more surprises.

Finding the rest of the cabin the same way he had left it, Mark returned to the main floor to get a closer look at the body. He recognized Ghassan Massoud from his picture and tried several times to call Kenny. No answer. He assumed that Amir had probably used Ghassan's car to escape, but he probably would not keep it for very long.

Mark slammed the rifle onto the table. "Dammit!" He had known it was risky to leave the prisoner, that there was a remote possibility of him slipping out of the chair or someone else showing up. But he had decided to roll the dice and try to save the wounded cop's life. And now he had to live with the consequences of that decision.

The fourth shooter was on the run, there was no reasonable way to give chase, and another dead body had been added to the tally. There was only one thing left to do: call the emergency number. After that, he would wait for the helicopters and hope the ensuing manhunt was successful.

Regardless, Mark knew he was potentially in deep trouble and hoped to God that the only card he had left to play would be strong enough to get him out of this.

One hundred thirty-one

A federal agent removed the darkened goggles that had served as Kenny's blindfold for the first time since his arrest. He squinted at the bright lights and quickly looked around to try to get his bearings. So far he had not uttered a single word and neither had his captors.

"When the cell door closes, stand with your back to the door and I'll remove your handcuffs," said the agent before exiting.

Kenny was sitting on the steel plank that would serve as his bed, wearing a baggy orange jumpsuit. No pillow or sheets. The only other fixtures in the sterile cell were a metal toilet and a metal sink with a metal mirror. The cell door slammed shut and echoed throughout the cellblock.

"Where am I?" Kenny asked.

"Come over here and stand with your back to the door," replied an older gentleman in a gray pinstriped suit, standing outside the cell with his arms folded across his chest. "Unless, of course, you'd rather keep the cuffs."

Kenny did as he was told. The man in the suit continued speaking as the agent removed his cuffs. "Welcome to FMC Devens, Mr. Harrington. You're now in custody of the Federal Bureau of Prisons. But I wouldn't get too comfortable because I honestly have no idea how long you'll be here. Maybe some of that is up to you, but at this point I doubt it."

Kenny rubbed his wrists, stretched his arms, and retreated to the far wall of the cell in silence.

"We have some questions for you and will give you the opportunity to make a statement. Are you willing to cooperate? I don't usually give advice to criminals, but I'm aware of the charges against you and would highly encourage you to cooperate if you ever want to see the sun again."

Kenny splashed rusty, lukewarm water from the metal faucet onto his face and rubbed his eyes. "What charges?" he asked.

"More than enough to put you away for life. Maybe even a couple of lifetimes. But that's only if you're lucky. You facilitated the hijacking of a drone belonging to U.S. government intelligence assets. Depending on your motive, that could get you charged with treason—a capital offense. We've got you on dozens of illegal hacking offenses that could earn you five to ten each, and we're still just scratching the surface of your computer system. Those are all

328

the official charges we're writing up right now, but the day is young and some of your associates are singing like canaries. Do you go by any other names you want to tell me about, Mr. Harrington? Huh? Like Hobbit? Does that sound familiar? Because there's easily a half-dozen countries interested in extraditing someone who goes by that name. Do you want to answer some questions and make this a lot easier on yourself?"

Kenny remained silent and turned away.

"Suit yourself. If you change your mind, just wave to the camera and let someone know. Otherwise you might as well get comfortable." The man started to walk away but stopped and returned. "By the way, that washed-up drunk of an agent who lived across the street from you is dead. Yeah, the State Police found him soaking in a tub of his own blood. Both wrists slit. I'm not sure how close you two were, but I look forward to finding out."

Once he left, Kenny gasped and splashed more cold water on his face.

Oh my God! Frank!

"Sorry to interrupt. Just one more thing," said the man returning for a second time. "Just a little trivia for you. Dzhokhar Tsarnaev spent his time here in the same cell. You remember him, right? The Boston Marathon bomber? Now you guys have two things in common. You're both terrorists and you slept in the same cell."

One hundred thirty-two

Mark was removed from his cell and escorted down the hall in silence by three armed men, one on each side and one trailing behind with a shotgun at the ready. He wore an orange jumpsuit, his eyes were blocked by darkened goggles, his hands were cuffed in front of him, and heavy iron shackles connected his ankles, making it impossible to walk at more than a slow shuffle.

Once he was seated behind the table in the small interview room, the goggles were removed. As the three men exited, a tall, athletic man in his early sixties entered and sat on the other side of the table. His gray hair was cropped close to his head in a crew cut, and he wore a navy blue suit with a pressed white shirt and red tie.

Mark had spoken with the gentleman before, during a legal briefing for Family members in northern Virginia. He was a retired Marine Corps JAG officer and lawyer who handled legal crises for covert operators, but Mark could not remember his name.

"Remember me, Mark?" he asked.

"I do."

"Then you remember the last thing I told you in our briefing, right?"

"Yeah, that you were the guy we should hope we never see again."

"That's right. But here I am, so let's get down to business. I don't know what they're planning on doing with you, but it doesn't look good. Doc is doing his thing and I'm here to do as much as I can, but as of right now they are treating your case the same way as they would a domestic terrorism case."

Mark started to speak, but the distinguished attorney held up his hand to silence him. "I know. I know that's not accurate, and it offends me too. But in their eyes, you were part of a hacking venture that took control of a CIA drone. Then you withheld valuable national security information and went on a manhunt. The alleged terrorist escaped. People are dead and the only person left standing around happens to be you. It doesn't help that this is the second time some of these people have seen you this week, Mark. Remember, you killed a man in the middle of that field just a few days ago. But we won't get anywhere by telling them how stupid they are, right? In fact, we're not going to tell them anything for now. No questions. No statements. Do you agree?"

"Yes, sir. I wasn't planning on answering any questions. Listen, Doc told me he spent what little capital the Family had to get me out after the attack. But I need to talk to Doc or Dunbar ASAP. I know they're probably doing all they can for me right now. But I want to make sure they're considering another way we may be able to get some help on this. Help from someone very important," Mark emphasized.

"Are you referring to the letter in your file, Mark?" asked the attorney.

"Yes, are you familiar with it?"

"I am familiar with the existence of a letter in your file. And although I do not know definitively whom it is from, I believe I could make an accurate guess if pressed. Unfortunately, Doc already thought of that option and as of an hour ago it didn't look good. Dunbar said he thought the letter wasn't worth the paper it's printed on. Listen, let's not give up hope, Mark. But, as your counsel, I'm advising you to at least consider the worst-case scenario of federal charges."

Mark sat expressionless as the dark reality of the situation started to sink in. "Twenty years. For twenty years I've done everything that was ever asked of me. I'm supposed to retire. Luci and I are supposed to get married and start a family. I have a mother I haven't met yet. My friend Kenny is counting on me. Sir, I may have done some wrong things, but I did them all for the right reasons. My record should count for something. This can't possibly be the way it ends for me."

"Don't lose hope yet," the attorney repeated, removing a cell phone from his breast pocket. "Doc said he wanted to speak with you. I'll get him for you and step outside. He asked me to arrange for you to call your fiancé. I'll take care of that when I can. I understand she's doing much better."

Mark took several deep breaths, then held the phone to his ear with both handcuffed hands. "Doc?" There was a long pause before he heard Doc's voice.

"I hear you've had a busy week, Mark."

"I did the right thing."

"Maybe you did, Mark. But that's doesn't seem to matter as much as it used to. The political and cultural climate in this country has changed drastically. And some of the people in power these days don't see the gray areas that we have to operate in. It's all black and white to them, and guys like us are paying the price."

"So I've noticed. I also heard the letter in my file isn't worth the paper it's printed on. How can that possibly be true when I essentially saved his ass?" asked Mark, raising his voice to Doc for the first time. Doc paused before answering.

"That remains to be seen, actually. Dunbar is working on it right now. But you're right, so far he can't even get an audience with or a message to the President."

Mark stood up to stretch his legs and looked down at the iron shackles fastened around his ankles. "That's crazy. I've read the letter. I remember what it says. Do I need to recite it? 'Mark, I owe you a personal debt of gratitude I can never repay. If you ever need my help I will be there for you. Any time, any place, anything.' Sound familiar, Doc?"

"You're upset. And I share your frustration, but let's have a little faith in Dunbar. He cares about you a lot, Mark. People can say what they want about Dunbar, but he goes to hell and back for his people. And that's what he's doing for you as we speak. So just sit tight, okay? I have to go, but I'll get a message to Luci telling her that you're okay so she doesn't worry too much. With a little luck you'll be back at her side soon."

"Doc, wait. There's one more thing, and at this point it might sound crazy, but just hear me out. My neighbor, a guy named Kenny Harrington—was he brought in too?"

"Yes, and I know where you're going with this. But trust me, it's going to be hard enough to do anything for you. The chances we can do anything for him are pretty much none. I'm sorry, Mark."

"Just hear me out for a second, okay? Kenny may be more valuable to you than me."

Doc replied that he had only one more minute, so Mark explained about Kenny as quickly as he could. After the conversation, the darkened goggles were again placed over Mark's eyes and he was led back down the hall toward his cell. After the handcuffs and shackles were removed and the guards had left, he sat on the cold metal bench. Mark thought of his impending retirement, of Luci lying in her hospital bed alone, of Kenny, and of the mother he had yet to meet. Then he bowed his head and cried.

One hundred thirty-three

Dunbar stood silently in the entryway of one of the Watergate South's most exclusive condominiums for several minutes before being ushered into the study and asked to wait. He checked the time on his watch and prepared for the impending battle.

The White House chief of staff did not like to be bothered at home during the evening hours. But he especially disliked visits from people who had strict instructions never to contact him directly. When he entered the study, Dunbar was standing off to the side of his desk, gazing at some of the books stacked on the hand-carved mahogany shelves that adorned the walls.

"What the hell are you doing, Dunbar?"

"Checking out your books, Mr. Edwards," he answered, pointing to the shelves.

"I meant what the hell are you doing here?"

"You didn't answer my calls. I got worried and figured I'd swing by to see if you were okay," Dunbar remarked.

The chief of staff walked around his antique desk, opened the large bottom drawer, and retrieved a bottle of scotch and one glass.

"Are you going to drink alone?" asked Dunbar.

Edwards reached into the drawer, grabbed a second glass, and handed it to Dunbar. "Only because my wife could walk in and she hates it when I drink alone. Now what the hell do you want?"

"As you have already been made aware, one of my operators is in a jam and I need to get him out. Unfortunately, he's in pretty deep so I need the President to step in. That's pretty much it," said Dunbar, taking a sip of his scotch. "This is excellent. What is this?"

Edwards raised his eyebrows and shook his head. "No, that's not pretty much it. Your guy helped jack a drone from the agency and went after a terrorist who might have been responsible for a major attack in Massachusetts when he should have passed it off to agencies with domestic jurisdiction. Then he let him get away, and there are multiple deaths involved. Don't expect the president to get his hands dirty by helping someone with that kind of record."

Dunbar brought the glass slowly to his lips. He poured the scotch over his tongue and down his throat. Then he slammed the glass down onto the antique desk.

"What the hell are you doing? Are you out of your mind? Keep it up and you'll be in the cell with him," Edwards snorted.

"Don't expect the president to get his hands dirty by helping someone with that kind of record? Do you have any idea what you're talking about? Mark Landry is one of the best operators I have ever had the honor to serve with. And he just happened to save your boss's ass—and probably yours along with it—just a few years ago. Let me refresh your memory."

Dunbar pulled a folder from his bag and threw it on the Chief of Staff's desk. Edwards reached for his bifocals and quickly read the letter. "Berlin?" he asked.

"Yeah, Berlin. How many lives do you think he saved? A thousand? More? And unless you've forgotten, he did it almost entirely on his own and never asked for a thing in return. He just went right back to work. But the things he's done since then probably wouldn't interest you because they didn't involve saving your ass."

Edwards leapt to his feet and stuck a finger in Dunbar's face. "At ease!" he yelled. Then he removed his glasses and rubbed the bridge of his nose. "I've allowed you into my home and I'm listening to you, but don't get too carried away. I'm a patient man, Dunbar. But you're starting to piss me off. I'll talk to the President. I'll see what we can do for your guy."

"He's your guy too, Mr. Edwards. I'm going to get out of your hair now. But let me leave you this," Dunbar said, handing him a plain manila folder. "There's a copy of the President's letter inside along with everything else you'll need to get the other guy out too."

"What other guy? You're insane. I'll go to bat for Landry but for nobody else."

Dunbar snatched the folder from the chief of staff's hands, pulled out an eight-by-ten photo, and held it up. Edwards squinted his eyes to examine the photo and gasped. "You wouldn't dare!"

Dunbar smiled widely. "And to think you were worried about her seeing you drinking alone. Imagine if she saw that on the front page of every paper in the United States! Do the right thing, Mr. Edwards. You do the right thing and so will I."

"I have the detailed results from your latest toxicology report," shared Dr. Chang. "And they show trace amounts of chloroform."

Luci smiled and nodded her head. "Good, that's good."

"Why is that good, Luci? It means someone tried to … harm you," said Chang.

"Yeah, I know that. But it also validates what I've been saying. I did not try to kill myself. I would never do anything like that. The last thing I remember is getting into my car to go to work when someone covered my face with a rag, which we now know was soaked in chloroform. I tried to get away but he was a lot stronger than me. I passed out and woke up here, and everybody's been acting like I tried to kill myself. That ends now."

"I understand. It's difficult when people don't believe you. But you have been through a lot lately. Just be happy so many people care about you, Luci. You're obviously a very special person, because the parade of people calling my office or trying to see you has been impressive."

Luci yawned and stretched her neck from side to side. "Well, unfortunately that must also mean a lot of people heard about what happened. Listen, I want to get up and go to the bathroom. Give me a hand, will you?"

"Sure, and there's something else we need to talk about," answered Dr. Chang.

As Luci sat up in her seat, the phone next to her bed rang. She reached over and picked up the receiver. "Hello?"

"Hi, baby. You sound good. How are you feeling?"

"Mark? Yeah, I'm bouncing back. What about you? Where are you? You sound so different!"

Dr. Chang whispered, "I'll step out so you can have some privacy and will send in one of the nurses to help. We can talk later."

"Listen, I have only a minute," said Mark. "I'm sorry I'm not there. It wasn't my choice. I got pulled away for something related to the attack that I really can't talk about. And all I want to do is just come home and be with you."

"Where are you? Baby, are you crying?" she asked.

"Me? Never. Listen, I'll be there as soon as I can. And I promise you I'll never leave you again. Ever. For anything, Okay?"

"Okay."

"The thought of you being there alone is killing me," said Mark.

"Don't worry about me, Mark. Actually, I'd kill for a few hours alone. I hope you don't think I did this to myself. I didn't. I have too much to look forward to. I was attacked. And the doctor just told me they found chloroform in my system. I'm not suicidal or crazy, Mark. And I have no idea how that necklace ended up in my hand."

"I would have believed you no matter what the tests said. And hopefully we can find whoever did this to you. I'm so sorry, but right now I have to go," Mark whispered.

"Okay, I love you."

"I love you more than you'll ever know, Luci. Bye."

One hundred thirty-five

Kenny splashed water on his face and looked at his reflection in the small metal mirror welded to the wall above the sink. The lack of a clock and the constant glow from the fluorescent lights in the cellblock made estimating the time nearly impossible. His best guess was that two or three days had passed, but the man he saw in the mirror looked as if he had been there much longer.

Where are you, Mark?

"Mr. Harrington, come here and stand with your back to the door so I can put these on you," said an official with handcuffs.

The prisoner dried his face on the front of his jumpsuit and took one last look in the mirror.

Be strong. No questions. No statements. No deals. Trust Mark.

When the cell door opened, Kenny turned around and found himself facing two men dressed in casual civilian clothes whom he had never seen before. The bigger of the two, wearing an Oklahoma Sooners ball cap, stepped forward and grabbed the prisoner's arm. "Listen very closely and don't say a word. I'm going to put your blinders on you and then we're going to go for a walk. Just relax and do what we tell you to do and everything will be fine. Understand?" Kenny nodded nervously. "Good," said the man, slapping him firmly on the shoulder.

The goggles went on, each man grabbed an arm, and the three walked briskly down the hall. After a short elevator ride and several more hallways, they exited the building. Kenny felt the fresh air and drank it in with both nostrils. He heard a vehicle approach. The brakes squeaked as it came to a stop in front of him, and Kenny soon found himself sitting in the back seat between the two men.

"You're doing good. Just keep doing what you're told and I'll take the goggles off as soon as I can. Don't speak until I tell you it's okay. Nod your head if you understand." Kenny nodded. Another slap on the shoulder followed.

After a short ride, the car came to a stop and Kenny was lifted out by both arms. The deafening noise combined with the smell of jet fuel caused him to panic and struggle momentarily. "Calm down, little man. Nobody's going to hurt you," the big man said into his ear, screaming to be heard over the aircraft. "We're just going on a little plane ride to get you as far away from this place as we can, okay? Hang tight. You've done good so far, okay?" Kenny

337

stopped struggling and offered another nervous but submissive nod. "Good. We'll talk once we get up in the air."

When the small jet reached cruising altitude, the goggles came off. Kenny opened and shut his eyes rapidly several times to adjust his vision. The man with the ball cap sat facing him. The other man was sitting off to Kenny's left. There were no other people in the ten-seat cabin of the private aircraft.

"Max, go ahead and take his cuffs off," said the big man, leaning toward Kenny. "I'm Billy. That's Max. Nobody is going to hurt you while we're around, so you can sit back and relax. I'll grab you a meal in a minute. Listen, I can't tell you much just yet. But it looks like the worst is behind you if cooperate and play ball. Do you understand? You can speak now."

"Yes," said Kenny. "I understand."

"Good, we'll be back on the ground in less than two hours."

Kenny devoured his meal and had closed his eyes for what he thought was just a few minutes when Max nudged him awake. "We can dispense with the handcuffs, but I need to put these back on you for now," he said, holding up the goggles. The three men emerged from the aircraft, descended the stairs, and were quickly whisked away by a waiting car.

Another elevator. The three men's footsteps echoed as they walked down a series of corridors. A door opened, and Kenny was ushered into a carpeted room and to a comfortable chair. The goggles came off. "Just wait here and don't touch anything. He hates that," said Billy.

Kenny found himself sitting alone in a spacious office in front of a large wooden desk. The room was modestly decorated. His intuition told him it belonged to someone important. He breathed deeply and tried to calm his nerves.

Where am I? Whose office is this? Stay calm. Keep your cool.

The door opened and a voice came from behind. "Sorry to keep you waiting, Mr. Harrington. But there were a few things I had to take care of before we could chat," said an older, distinguished-looking gentleman as he crossed the room and stood behind the desk.

"Who are you?" Kenny asked.

The gentleman smiled, grabbed a bottle of warm water from a table against the wall, and handed it to his guest. Then he folded his arms across his chest and leaned back against the desk. "Everyone calls me Doc. I'm your new boss."

Mark splashed water on his face and looked at himself in the mirror. The few hours of sleep had helped, but the events of the past week had taken an enormous cumulative toll on him. He thought about the fourth shooter still on the loose and felt nauseous.

Where the hell is he? Why hasn't he been caught yet? What is his final target? Doc says it's not my concern, and ordered me to stay out of the way. But I can't get the bastard out of my mind.

Then he thought of his future with Luci and smiled. He reached for the soft towel, dried his face and hands, and exited the small bathroom attached to Luci's hospital room.

She was back in her signature look—jeans with high heels—and smiling proudly as two nurses admired Agnes's vintage emerald ring on her left ring finger. "Congratulations!" both said cheerfully. Mark entered the room and admired his fiancée as she joked and laughed. In spite of all she had been through, she was glowing with love and optimism.

What an extraordinary woman.

"Are you ready to get out of here?" he asked.

"Oh, yeah. I want to go home, eat, soak in the tub, and sleep. Then get up tomorrow and do the same thing. After that, I think I'll be good. I feel better with every hour that passes, and I've never had so much to be happy about thanks to you." Luci wrapped her arms around Mark's neck and kissed him on the lips. He squeezed her tight and lifted her off the ground in a bear hug. "Let's get the hell out of here," he said.

When they pulled out of the parking garage, one of Luci's nurses waved them down from the sidewalk. Mark pulled over and the nurse approached Luci's unrolled window. "Listen, it's not much, but we just wanted to give you something to wish you guys the best of luck. All three of you!" she said with a smile, passing a small stuffed teddy bear and a copy of *What to Expect When You're Expecting* to Luci through the window.

Luci covered the title and laughed. "Okay, thanks. Let's go, Mark. I'm hungry."

"What book is that?" Mark asked. "Let me see that."

The nurse backed away from the window with both hands over her mouth. "Oh, my God! I'm so sorry. You haven't told him yet? Oh, no! I'm so sorry, Luci."

Luci turned to Mark, flashed her thousand-watt smile, and held up the book with one hand. "It's still early. But Dr. Chang assures me there's a healthy baby growing in here," she said, tapping her stomach with her free hand. "You're going to be a father, Mark."

Luci was asleep within seconds of her head hitting the pillow. Mark's head was still spinning from the news. Two days earlier he was sitting in a cell, wondering if he would ever see daylight again. Now he had everything he had ever dreamed of.

Landry needed to unwind and get back to some sense of normalcy. He cracked open a beer, plopped down on the couch, and turned on the television.

Five minutes to Magnum P.I.

He took a long pull from his beer and savored the taste in his mouth before swallowing. As he was finally beginning to relax, his phone rang. It was Doc. He paused the television.

"Hi, Doc."

"How are you, Mark? How is Luci?" he asked.

"I'm fine. Luci is better than anyone could have imagined. She's one of the most resilient people I've ever seen. Anyway, we are officially engaged and she also happens to be pregnant."

"Really? Wow. You didn't waste any time, did you, Mark? Congratulations to both of you. That's great news and a perfect way to start the next chapter of your life."

"Thank you. I was caught off guard a little bit, but I'm excited. We both are. What about you? Anything new? Anything on the fourth shooter?" asked Mark, jumping right into business.

"Yes, that's why I was calling. Whoever he is, he's dead. At least we think it's him. A few hours ago, the Virginia State Police found the body of a young man on the side of the highway just outside Washington, shot twice in the back of the head. He was also missing an ear. We have plenty of DNA from the cabin to match, but those tests are in progress. In the interests of time, I was hoping you could take a look and verify the identity. Check your phone."

Mark scrolled through the controls on his phone and pulled up the photo. In it, the fourth shooter was lying on his side, his hands and feet bound with duct tape. His mouth was open and blood covered much of his face. "Yeah, that's him. You know, he swore to me he would make it to Washington and I almost laughed at him. Turns out he was right. But I imagine whoever he met once he got there wasn't too happy with his excuse for being late. Probably saw him as a liability."

"Whatever the reason, the decision was made hastily. We found fingerprints on the shell casings that matched a Belgian citizen who had entered the U.S. six months ago as a tourist. He tripped several facial recognition systems in Alexandria. Agents followed him back to an apartment where he ended up dying in an exchange of gunfire."

"What about the weapons?"

"Hidden in one of the bedrooms were nine Sig Sauer M400s and a pound of factory-sealed C4."

Mark exhaled. "Thank God. Anything else?"

"So far we have absolutely nothing connecting the three dead shooters, which is more than a little perplexing. If the Islamic State is telling the truth when they say they were behind it, it's even more puzzling, because two of them were not known to be religious at all. The third was a Muslim convert but not considered devout by anyone who knew him. Analysts are still digging into everything. But whoever put them together and planned the attack was very good at covering their tracks. Similar story with the girl who bombed the ER. Her parents, both well-respected physicians, have been all over the Canadian news. She was known to be religious, but her family and friends say she never said or did anything extreme."

"Yeah, until she blew herself up. Any pictures or video I should be worried about?"

"Thankfully, no—at least not yet. There are a small handful of pictures and a few short clips from the attack, all taken by townspeople, but the overall quality is bad. Of course, someone might still be negotiating a deal with the *National Enquirer,* but at this point I think you got lucky. By the way, Ashton Brown is in custody and facing a number of charges, including obstruction of justice and evidence tampering. That should keep him locked up for quite some time. I am also happy to say the Boston JTTF is no longer under the microscope," Doc offered.

"What happened? Was there a mole?" asked Mark.

"No, their servers had been breached by some pretty sophisticated hackers out of Yemen. Our new guy fixed the vulnerability and introduced a virus that fried all their systems—all on his first day of work, believe it or not. Sound like anyone you know?"

"Kenny? I told you he was good, Doc. Is he working on the DOD breach?"

"That and a number of other things. Listen, I have another picture I'd like you to see if you have a minute," Doc continued.

342

"Send it," answered Mark as he finished his beer. When the new photo arrived, he sat back and breathed a sigh of both relief and accomplishment. The picture showed John and Linda McDonough side by side in a hospital bed, holding their beautiful newborn baby boy between them. John's wounds and swollen face were no match for the elated smile of a proud new father.

"You made that photo possible, Mark. You made a judgment call a lot of people would argue against. But when I look at that picture, I can't help but think you did the right thing. I'm proud of you. And I'm also thinking of following your lead and retiring," said Doc.

"Really? I can't imagine the Family without its Doc."

"The Family's days are numbered. It's just a matter of time before we're forced to close up shop, and I'm too old to help set up the next one. I've done that too many times and I don't think I have the energy for it any more. So I'm going to go home and spend time with my wife, and try and reconnect with my kids and their families. Would you believe I have one granddaughter who is almost two and I've never met her? Don't ever let anything like that happen to you, Mark."

"Sounds like a plan. Keep in touch, Doc."

"I will."

"And thanks again to you and Dunbar for always being there for me."

"You're family, Mark. You'll always be family. But unless you have a letter in your file from God that I'm unaware of, I'd advise staying out of trouble. Take care. Talk soon."

Landry pressed *play* on the TV and headed to the kitchen for another beer as the theme from *Magnum P.I.* played in the background. As soon as he sank back into his spot on the couch, the phone rang again.

"What did you forget, Doc?" he asked.

"It's not Doc, Mark. It's Kenny."

"Mr. Harrington! Let me guess, you're calling to brag about your first major accomplishment, right? Well, I already heard about your work on the JTTF and I'm happy for you. A few more jobs like that and you'll be in the running for employee of the month," Mark joked, taking a sip of his beer.

"Very funny. And no, that's not why I'm calling. I'm calling about Luci," Kenny replied.

"What about her?"

"I heard about what happened to her. But when she was admitted to the hospital, you told me it was for exhaustion or dehydration or something," Kenny said.

"Yes, I did. And it was nothing personal, Kenny. I was just trying to give her a modicum of privacy," Mark replied.

"I understand, but I really wish you had just told me the truth from the beginning. It would have saved a lot of time."

"How's that?" Mark asked.

"Because I think I might know who tried to kill her."

Landry paused the television and rose to his feet. "Keep talking."

"Charlie Worth. You know him, right?"

"Yeah, I know who he is," answered Mark.

"I'm not saying he definitely did it, but based on what I know about him, he's the first person I'd be looking at," said Kenny.

"Why? Tell me how you got there."

"I'm going to have to be quick, so here it is. The guy is a jerk—a lot of people know that. But a while back he went too far and pissed me off. It happened when my father wandered out of the house. Long story short, it was a nightmare and Charlie made it worse. In the process he belittled me and showed zero respect toward my father. I decided I wanted to teach him a lesson, so I hacked into his stuff and found a few things."

"Like what?" Mark asked.

"Like an anonymous email account he used to send things to Lisa Lemon at the *Valley Insider*. Things like police department gossip and dashcam pictures. I didn't think much of it at the time, but he sent a lot of things that pertained to Luci. Annoying things with no real evidence, such as claiming that gangs had moved in as soon as she replaced him as point person for the projects. Photos too—mostly just annoying stuff. Definitely a jerk move, but not the kind of stuff I was looking for."

"What were you looking for?" Mark asked.

"If I had wanted to drain his bank accounts or something, I could have. But that wasn't what I was after. I wanted him publicly shamed and humiliated and I wasn't in a rush. So I called in a favor and had one of my associates do a deep background check on him. But then the attack on Founders Field happened and I forgot about it all—until I heard about what happened to Luci."

Mark paced into the kitchen and leaned back against the sink. "What's the connection, Kenny? The guy is a raging asshole.

Everyone knows that. He tased me when I was seconds away from neutralizing the fourth shooter. But that doesn't make him a murderer."

"Well, he talks a lot of garbage about his time in the NYPD in Queens, but I've actually seen his official records and they tell a much different story. It turns out he had a female partner for a while—a Latina, by the way—who ended up filing a ton of complaints against him for harassment. On two different occasions she even tried to get a restraining order against him for stalking, but the police union's lawyers and department officials ran interference because they were scared shitless of the bad press it could bring."

"Really?" Mark asked.

"Yeah, and instead of dealing with him, they just shuffled her around to different partners and eventually an entirely different precinct. But it didn't help. He kept at it and she ended up leaving the force entirely."

"Okay, so he's a bigger asshole than we thought. But that still doesn't make him a murderer, Kenny."

"Mark, just a few weeks after his ex-partner left the force, she committed suicide. Would you care to hear how she did it? Carbon monoxide poisoning. They found her in the front seat of her car."

One hundred thirty-eight

Mark crept through the house wearing a set of dark overalls and a black mask. Thick neoprene gloves covered his hands, and surgical booties were wrapped tightly around his running sneakers. He could hear Dunbar's voice in his head as he searched each room.

Skilled operators like you have a responsibility to keep people safe, Mark. If we can do that and play by the rules—great, everyone's happy. But there may be times when you're tempted to act as judge, jury, and executioner, and there won't be a federal prosecutor looking over your shoulder. Trust your instincts, but never do anything that can't be undone unless you're one hundred percent sure you'll be able to live with it.

As the search unfolded and the damning evidence continued to mount, any doubt in Landry's mind quickly dissipated. Charlie Worth had tried to kill Luci. The only thing left to do was wait for the target.

Lee Carter pulled into the driveway and started to get out of the car.

"I don't need you to walk me inside like a chick, Lee. I can get there myself. Thanks for the ride. I'll come get my car in the morning," said Charlie, slurring his words as he sloppily exited the vehicle.

"Fine by me, Charlie. Just don't leave it there too long. I share that lot with other shop owners and don't want them getting mad at me," said Carter.

Worth pulled the badge from his back pocket and held it up. "Don't worry about it, Lee. I can take care of the shop owners," he said before stumbling off to his front door.

Lee grimaced, shook his head in disgust, and sped away without looking back.

After several moments of fumbling with his keys, he unlocked the door, twisted the knob, and stumbled into the house. Worth never saw the masked man who snatched him from behind in a rear chokehold that squeezed the carotid arteries in his neck and restricted the blood flow to his brain. Seconds later he was unconscious, and his limp body was being carried up the stairs to his bedroom.

Charlie Worth wanted to scream, but the thick gag tied tightly around his mouth muffled his cries. He struggled furiously to free his hands and feet, but the restraints that tethered his wrists and ankles to the four bedposts were too strong. Helpless, he laid spread-eagle on his bed, staring up at the skylight and out into the darkness. Someone was typing on his computer in the far corner. "I'll be right with you," said a voice.

Worth's mouth was bone dry, his stomach was aching, and he had what felt like a few small pebbles stuck in his throat. He strained to swallow and closed his eyes. When he reopened them, he recoiled in horror at the sight of a masked man hovering over his bed. Charlie struggled furiously and gasped for air through his nose. The masked intruder waited for him to tire and stop squirming before he sat down on the bed. He grabbed Charlie by the gag and poured a glass of water over his mouth. Most of it spilled down his chin, but just enough got through for him to swallow. The pebbles slid down his throat and into his aching stomach with the others. The intruder placed the glass on the nightstand next to the unlabeled pill bottles and started to speak.

"They say that once you've already decided to kill someone you should just do it, that the target should never know what hit them. What's the use of talking if you've already decided they need to die, right? That's what I've always done. But I'm going to make an exception this one time because I want you to know it was me who got you."

The intruder removed his mask. Worth tried futilely to speak and shook his head rapidly from side to side until the intruder grabbed him by the chin and steadied his head. "No. No, Charlie. You don't get to speak. You will never speak again," said Mark.

Worth continued his efforts to escape until he was exhausted. Reluctantly accepting the hopelessness of his situation, his furious struggling gave way to desperate sobbing. Tears streamed down his face.

"I couldn't let you go thinking you got away with everything. I'm sure I could get a lot more out of you if I had time, but I already know enough about you that I won't lose any sleep over this. You harassed your partner in Queens until she couldn't take it anymore and quit her job. Then you killed her and made it look like a suicide, didn't you? I wonder how many of her family members and friends blame themselves to this day for not being there for her. Then you ended up here and it wasn't long before you were stirring things up again. You harassed people in the projects just because you could, and you hated it when they replaced you with Luci. So you tried to sabotage her from the very beginning. You played off people's fears and tried to make it look like everything in town was going to hell in a handbasket. You know what I found in your basement, Charlie? Cans of black and gold spray paint and a stack of different-sized stencils for Latin Kings symbols, plus the outfit you were wearing in the shopkeeper's video. You painted that graffiti all over town to scare people. Then you stoked the flames by feeding bullshit about Luci to some tabloid website."

Worth exhaled and his eyes started to roll back in his head until he was nudged in the ribs. "Are the pills starting to kick in, Charlie? Are you tired? That's what two months' worth of sleeping pills will do to you. Wake up. I'm not done with you yet. Open your eyes and look at me. You know what else I found down there? A bottle of chloroform and a rag sealed in a zip-lock bag. You tried to kill, Luci. Didn't you?"

Worth closed his eyes, nodded, and squealed.

"You tried to kill the best thing that's ever happened to me and make it look like a suicide. You pulled a necklace from a dead little girl's body and put it in Luci's hands, hoping people would think she was depressed and couldn't take the pressure. You're a psycho, Charlie. You're a dangerous man. And I cannot let you live."

Worth's eyelids fluttered and his breathing became shallow. "I hope you can still hear me, Charlie. When the police come and find you dead, they'll search the house and find all the evidence they need to corroborate the confessions in your suicide note. So rest assured that after you're gone, everyone in the world—including your family and whatever friends you had—will know the truth about you. And most of them will be happy you're dead."

Landry checked the time on his watch. Satisfied that Worth was gone, he removed the gag and untied the dead man's wrists and ankles. He took a quick look around to make sure he left nothing behind. Then he went to the computer, clicked SEND, and donned his mask again before disappearing.

* * *

On the other side of town, Lisa Lemon was up late writing an article for the *Valley Insider* when a new message arrived from

Officer Charlie Worth. She skimmed the email, leapt to her feet, and paced the floor.

Five minutes later she published a breaking news blog post.

EXCLUSIVE: Confessed Killer Cop Commits Suicide!

Then she called 911 to report the email and verify the story.

Once the authorities had blocked Main Street from traffic, a silent crowd of candle-bearing mourners spilled into the area for the memorial service. Its ranks swelled until the road and sidewalks were filled with thousands of townspeople, their attention oriented toward the powerful public address system on the roof of the Witch Hunt. With the exception of the governor, every person inside the capacity-filled pub was a town resident, and all media were restricted to covering the event from the streets. The politicians and authorities had said their collective piece over the preceding weeks. The featured speaker tonight was teacher, coach, and historian Andy O'Rourke. The man whose actions on Founders Field had earned him the additional title of hero was about to emerge as de facto leader of the town.

With tired eyes and his arm in a sling, Andy stood on the center of the raised hearth in front of the microphone. The crowd had been listening in hopeful silence, desperate for leadership from its own ranks and confident that he could alleviate some of their pain, begin the healing process, and help point the way forward. The blank stares and empty eyes were unlike any he had seen in his previous appearances as featured speaker at the Witch Hunt. Today he saw eyes drained of energy and purpose, anxious for some source of replenishment.

Andy spoke slowly at first, pausing frequently to let his words travel through the loudspeakers to the multitude gathered outside. Without notes he had recited the names of each victim and told heroic stories of others who had fought back, some sacrificing their lives so that others could live. Now, as he worked toward the end of his remarks, he began to gradually quicken his pace and intensity.

"I have always taken pride in the fact that so many of the most important events in our nation's history started right here in the Bay State, and that the courageous elders of our town played such significant roles in shaping the country. It all started right here on the sacred ground under this hearth, and from here it spread across the continent. The founders of this town and of our great country were prepared to spill their own blood for what they believed in. Deep down they knew they were blazing a new trail for humanity and that eventually the entire world would come to know their names and what they stood for. Now, almost two hundred and fifty years later, the world consistently looks to their creation—America—for leadership."

Andy paused and winced as he reached for the glass of ice water sitting on a small table next to the microphone. His eyes surveyed the hungry crowd as he adjusted his sling and breathed deeply between sips. So far they had hung on his every word. They had been moved, but they had yet to be reborn. They needed a leader, and anyone within earshot knew Andy could be that leader. There was a resonant, magnetic quality to his words, but the people still needed one final nudge. The outpouring of thoughts and prayers from across the country were not enough. They needed direction and purpose. They needed a local source of strength to rally around. Andy returned the glass to the table with a loud thud and decided to depart from his scripted concluding remarks. He cleared his throat.

"Our town is no stranger to tragedy. Since our earliest days we've faced countless threats and challenges. We've been battered and beaten by enemies, Mother Nature, and, from time to time, even ourselves. But all these challenges had one major thing in common: none of them could defeat us. None were able to make us quit and give up. My friends, we've been knocked down before, but each and every time we got right back up and kept marching forward."

Andy pointed toward the front door of the Witch Hunt and unleashed the signature boom in his voice to which the town was now accustomed. "There have been a handful of mass shootings, ambushes on police, and bombings in small towns across the country since the cowardly attacks on our Independence Day celebration," he intoned. The crowd, jolted by the change in the tone and volume of his voice, leaned forward attentively. Andy removed the cordless microphone from the stand and paced to the edge of the hearth. "But I part ways with the conventional wisdom that this is simply the new normal. I'm sorry, but I just can't accept that defeatist line of reasoning—not after being born and raised in this town."

"That's right!" yelled a woman standing in the back of the room, followed by a wave of nodding heads in the crowd.

"Wanton violence, terrorism, and the fear they sow are not things I'm prepared to simply live with. Nor can we bury our heads in the sand and pretend they don't exist. They do. And you can bet they will return to our town in some way, shape, or form." Andy walked to the other side of the hearth and directed his words toward several of the decorated police officers and firemen, wearing full dress uniforms and white gloves. "We are blessed to have some of the finest first responders in the Bay State," he declared. "But they can't do it all. And they can't do it alone. They need our help."

O'Rourke stepped off the hearth, descended the portable wooden stairs, and paced slowly down the center aisle toward the front door, his microphone held firm in his good hand. "So let's each pledge to become more self-reliant, more resilient, and capable of responding when evil decides to rear its ugly head again. This town is no stranger to adversity. And we have never been beaten. We always get back up stronger than before. That strength doesn't come from the size or makeup of our population or the physical barriers we build. No, sir. We draw our strength from the values and ideals set forth by the founders of our town and this great country—men and women who valued freedom enough to spill their blood in its defense and who refused to live in fear."

Andy O'Rourke stood in the doorway of the Witch Hunt, looking out over a sea of vulnerable, candle-bearing townspeople. "My friends, evil will be back. It will return. We can't control that. But we do have a choice. We can be ready or we can simply be afraid. I vote for the former. Who's with me?"

Epilogue

Senator McDermott exited the SUV and answered one quick question from a reporter waiting in front of her building. "No, I have not committed to speaking at that event. That's just a rumor. Now if you'll excuse me, I have a lot of reading to do tonight." She entered the building and rode the elevator up to her fifth-floor apartment.

"In for the night, Senator?" asked the evening security supervisor as he opened the apartment door.

"Yes, no visitors. No calls. No nothing."

Once inside, she dropped her things, turned to face the young man, and gave him a tired smile. "What's your name?" she asked.

"It's Jonathan, ma'am. Is something wrong?"

"No. But you've been here every night for over a week and I've never actually spoken with you. You must think I'm a real jerk," she said.

"No, ma'am. Not at all. My job is to—"

She waved her hand and cut him off. "Your job is to protect me. I know that, Jonathan. And I know it may not seem like it, but I appreciate what you do. Are you married? Kids?"

"Yes, ma'am. Both. We have a six-month-old baby girl."

"What's her name?"

"Katie, ma'am," he answered proudly.

"Katie. Cute name. Do you get to spend much time with her?"

"All day, ma'am. So my wife can catch up on sleep. Katie came out screaming and hasn't stopped since. She's feisty."

"So if you're here all night and with the baby all day, when do you get to sleep?" she asked.

"I catch catnaps here and there."

"It'll get better, Jonathan. All my babies were feisty too."

"Yes, ma'am."

She secured the deadbolt, leaned back against the door, and took several deep breaths.

All my babies.

McDermott glanced at the stack of mail and briefing papers on the kitchen counter, shook her head, and spoke out loud in the empty apartment. "You can wait. Shower time."

McDermott emerged from the bedroom twenty minutes later wearing white cargo shorts and a black t-shirt. She poured a glass of red wine and flipped through the stacks of paperwork that covered most of the kitchen counter space. Connecticut economic reports. Board of Education test results. Speaking invitations and pleas for support from various nonprofit organizations. An official-looking envelope exclaiming, "Open immediately! Lois Sumner McDermott, you don't want to miss this opportunity!" found its way into the trash.

Nice try, guys, but I dropped the Sumner a long time ago.

She settled on the most recent statistics on gun violence and headed for her evening reading spot on the couch near the balcony. A flexible reading lamp hovered overhead like the boom microphones that seemed to follow her everywhere. The sliding glass door was open and an unseasonably cool breeze gently blew the drapes. Two pages into the report, she was startled by a voice from outside.

"Good evening, Senator."

Surprised, she rose to her feet and dropped the papers on the coffee table.

"Jesus! You scared the heck out of me. I thought I had made myself clear to your boss, Jonathan. No security inside the apartment once I'm in for the night."

"It's not Jonathan, Senator," the man answered after several seconds of heavy silence.

McDermott shielded her eyes from her bright reading lamp and focused on the silhouette in the doorway. "Well, he should have passed those instructions along to the entire security detail. So thanks for your help, but I can take it from here. Now please show yourself out. I have a lot of work to do this evening," she said in a firm tone before taking a quick sip of wine.

"I'm not part of your detail, Senator."

Senator McDermott froze. There was no sound other than those of her own breath and the plastic tips of the balcony curtain drawstrings gently tapping against the glass in the breeze. Her pulse quickened and she turned the lamp away from her eyes to get a better look at the stranger.

"Who are you?" she demanded.

He took several relaxed steps inside the apartment and stopped. The presence of an uninvited man in her apartment at night should have been cause for panic, but this man's tone and physical

355

demeanor, as he stood casually with his hands in his pockets, felt strangely disarming, eerie yet inexplicably familiar.

Why am I not screaming and running for the door?

"You know who I am," he answered.

"I'm going to ask you one more time. Tell me who you are, right now."

"I already told you, Senator. You already know who I am," he said, slowly drifting to the far side of the room and flipping the overhead light switch to fully illuminate himself. "Look closely."

The stranger took several gentle steps across the soft white carpet to the edge of the coffee table. McDermott looked deep into the man's eyes and squinted. She curiously tilted her head to the side and focused her tunnel vision on the man's face. Her heart raced and her arms and legs went numb, but she did not yet understand why. Then he flashed a warm, peculiar smile, and memories from the past came roaring back like a freight train.

"Oh my God … is that … it can't be … is that really you?" she whispered.

The wine glass slipped from her grasp and she brought both hands to her mouth.

"Mark?"

Thank you for reading my book!

If you liked it — please tell someone about it.

The next Mark Landry novel will be available in 2016. Subscribe to my mailing list at www.RandallHMiller.com to receive news, updates, special offers, and a behind-the-scenes look at my projects.

Randall H. Miller

About the Author

(Photo by Michael McLain, Stockholm, Sweden)

Graduate of Norwich University, the nation's oldest private military college (B.A. in Criminal Justice; M.A. in Diplomacy with a concentration in international terrorism). U.S. Army Officer in a prior life (2nd Infantry Division, S. Korea; 82nd Airborne Division, Ft. Bragg). Stints in pharmaceuticals and high tech. Currently live in Massachusetts where I teach college, write, and worry about what the future has in store for my three-year-old son.

Ways to connect with me:

rhm@randallhmiller.com

www.RandallHMiller.com

Facebook.com/randallhmiller

Twitter.com/randallhmiller

Instagram.com/randallhmiller

LinkedIn.com/in/randallhmiller